AND A GOLDEN PEAR

Recent Titles by Jean Chapman

AND A GOLDEN PEAR

Jean Chapman

This first world edition published in Great Britain 2002 by
SEVERN HOUSE PUBLISHERS LTD of
9–15 High Street, Sutton, Surrey SM1 1DF.
This first world edition published in the USA 2003 by
SEVERN HOUSE PUBLISHERS INC of
595 Madison Avenue, New York, N.Y. 10022.

British Library Cataloguing in Publication Data

Chapman, Jean, 1929-
    And a golden pear
    1.   Farm life - England - Fiction
    2.   England - Social life and customs - 1945 - Fiction
    3.   Love stories
    I.   Title
    823.9'14 [F]

    ISBN 0-7278-5863-7

Typeset by Hewer Text Ltd.,
Edinburgh, Scotland.
Printed and bound in Great Britain by
MPG Books Ltd., Bodmin, Cornwall.

One

It's a bit like walking on thinly iced puddles, feeling the support, then the let-down. The corn stubble's just the same, bearing my weight, then crumpling beneath my sandals. I tread, balancing for a second, experiencing the wobbliness, then the buckling either one way or the other.

Ahead, my parents reach a gate. I run, calling, hurling myself on to one of the bars for a ride.

'No wonder my gates go to rack and ruin,' my father says.

Was I too heavy? Should I jump down? By my side, my mother puts a hand over mine on the top bar. 'He's only teasing,' she reassures me.

He makes a disapproving sound. 'At ten she should be able to stand a little teasing.'

'I don't think Bess will ever be able to stand *your* teasing,' my mother murmurs as if to herself, then, patting my hand, adds more forcefully, 'And *you* mustn't take your father so seriously.' Her lips part as if she would say more, but she stops, smiles, and I know I am not old enough, or wise enough, for what she wants to say. I think how beautiful she is, her hair so black, as mine is, but mine has a springy, undisciplined nature like my father's, while hers has calm gentle waves taken softly back into a wide, loose knot which just rests on the nape of her neck.

I climb down from the gate and follow towards the last one of our fields to be harvested. The end of a harvest is always time for celebration, and in a few weeks there will be a supper in our big barn. Families from the neighbouring smaller farms will be there as well as our own men, plus the casual workers. This year there are men just released from the forces, or from enemy prison camps.

This day, this last Saturday morning in August 1946, will see the farmhands and the casuals all paid their dues and invited to our Harvest Home. My father always pays as soon as ever the work is finished, going to the fields to do so, with pound notes in his inside pocket, ten shilling notes in his left jacket pocket, a quantity of half-crowns in the other, and a list in his head of exactly how many hours each man has worked. His fair and prompt payment means he is never short of workers for seasonal labour.

This pay-day has a special feel, though I always feel special when I'm with my pa, but it's more than that. My father seems to know and stops to wait for us, not speaking, so we all walk together into the field where the men are working. I'm careful to keep our line straight, so I am neither in front nor behind. When I look up, there's a boy, perhaps eleven years to my ten, coming towards us. I view him with the air of a princess who sees a strange knight approaching unassailed family ramparts. My only surprise is that a strange boy should be in our fields. Who is he? Where has he come from?

I drop slightly behind my parents so when he comes up to us he can speak to my father more directly, but as I move, he too slightly alters his course. It seems to be *me* he is heading for as he circuits my father. The fortress walls seem to have disappeared.

'What have we here?' Pa asks in a quiet voice.

He's a bigger boy than I realized, but as he comes to within a hand's reach of me, I stand my ground as any self-respecting Bennett should do, as I had learned to do by my father's side when farm animals forget they are domesticated. From behind his back the boy brings out a large ripe pear, one side of which the sun has blushed to pink. 'It's for you,' he says.

'What do you say?' mother prompts as I neither speak nor move.

2

'Thank you very much,' I say automatically, but hold out both hands for the large fruit.

He beams, and, turning, struts away like a boy who has achieved much.

I look from the fruit to my father, then to my mother, who is smiling, happy, almost laughing aloud as I hold the pear by its stalk so they might admire it the better. I keep my other hand close underneath, so if the stalk parts from the ripe fruit, it will not fall to the ground.

'Seems to me,' my mother says, 'you have an admirer.'

My father makes a noise in his throat, and I'm not sure whether it sounds like a laugh, disbelief, or disapproval. 'We'll wait over in the shade for the men to finish,' he tells us, and strides ahead.

I slip the pear into my handkerchief pocket, a gathered, pouch-like addition my mother always has sewn to the front of the dresses she has made for me. The weight of the fruit pulls the red gingham down, making a tight line of the stiff rickrack binding across the back of my neck. She takes and swings my hand as we follow, and I feel we are celebrating something quite secret behind my father's back. I'm not sure what, and I'm not sure I like my father excluded.

The midday sun is hot and, from the shade we watch as if in a dream. The golden colours, and the film of dust from the corn, haze over the reality as the men take apart the last few stooks of corn, separating the sheaves on to their pitchforks. Each man has to push their weighted fork to full length, arms full stretch, to reach the top of what will be the last cartload. I hold my breath as Noel Wright, our diminutive waggoner, receives each sheaf and places it neatly, corn ears to the middle, as precisely as he will later help the men in the stackyard build and thatch the ricks.

The men then begin to come over to the shade, first rounding, then stretching their shoulders to ease aching muscles, throwing their pitchforks to stand upright in the less solid ground beneath the hedge. They receive their money with a *Thanks, gaffer*, then go to find and finish bottles of tea or Tizer kept under their jackets. This is when my mother confirms the invitation to the Harvest Home supper. 'And your wives and families, of course,' she adds, accepting in turn the offers of their wives' help with the preparations.

There is now only Noel, who was paid on Friday with all our own men, and one other casual hand. This man is with the boy who gave me the pear. I scoop it out of my pocket. A tall woman in a floaty blue floral dress walks into the field from the lane and goes to this man, but her scrutiny covers everyone.

'Think the Air Force chappie has had enough,' one of the men says from behind the neck of his bottle as he is about to drink.

'Aye, in more ways than one.'

'Poor bug—' The word is cut off as my father glances from him to me.

'I'll go over,' Pa says. 'He won't know the routine.'

I sit at the edge of the shade, watching my father, as everyone else is watching, as he goes towards the man and woman with the boy. Why is he a poor bugger? I see Pa reach up to pat Captain's neck, lift the shire horse's mane to let the air in; can imagine him saying, *Last load, old chap.*

The tall man shakes his head as he is spoken to, spreads his hands wide, and there seems to be a problem. My father stands with the money in his hand, he turns to the woman, who immediately steps very close and takes what my father offers; but there is an awkwardness about the small scene, and someone makes a long deep 'Hmmm,' as if he understands.

I hold up the pear so that it blots out my father's figure at the far side of the field. I lower it a little to see if things are alright, and see he has begun to walk back towards us. Noel is now sitting on the shafts, ready to take the last load to the rickyard. The boy waits by the gate as if to close it. Noel lifts a hand to stop him. The gate will be left open now for the gleaners, the villagers who will feed up their Christmas cockerels with the broken ears of grain they gather.

I hold the pear up again, so it obliterates my father, and I wonder how near he will be before I can see him. I keep it quite still, and I can soon see his head above it and his legs below.

As he comes closer, the pear is in front of his waistcoat, then on his watchchain, like a huge teardrop. I lift it towards his face, and to my surprise he reaches down and takes it.

'A bite for me, is it?'

I nod, though I had not thought of it, had not really thought of the pear being eaten at all. I watch closely as my father turns the pear, bites into the green side, a big bite, so its heavy, dropping roundness, its perfection, is gone. 'Mmm, good!' He hands it back down to me, and as he does so I see the boy still in the gateway. He lifts a hand. The woman too turns and looks our way, but the man keeps his face averted in a strange unnatural way, as if he is searching the earth at the far side of his feet for something.

I feel obliged to nibble at the edge of father's bite, rolling the faintly gritty but sweet flesh around my mouth, but the novelty of the gift is spoilt for me, and I don't want to eat it.

My father and mother are moving away, talking to the other men.

'Don't know how he lives with that,' one of the men comments quietly.

I go to the bole of the tree, pretending to just lean there, then, in a little drama of my own, feel my way over the black segmented bark, and edge along until I come to where a short piece of fencing reinforces the hedge next to the oak. I lean over and drop the pear into the ditch the other side. It disappears swiftly, without a sound, between the high old stalks of cow parsley. I sense I will always remember just where I discarded that tear-shaped bomb of a fruit.

It is the second week of the new school term when I see the boy again. We are all lining up in our classes in the playground as

Miss White, in her habitual green pinafore dress – *Poured into it, and belted up ugly*, Noel says – blows the first whistle. The boy is standing apart, alone, unattached to any line or any other boy, any friend. I watch him steadfastly. He doesn't fidget, doesn't look awkward, doesn't droop as tall boys usually do. He is fair too, *fair-haired and fair of face*. I read that description in *Heroes, Real and Mythological*, one of Pa's Sunday school prizes.

I glance around, suddenly self-conscious, afraid others may read my thoughts. I can often read theirs from their faces. But most are also watching the new boy, and quite a few have their hands before their mouths, whispering, not taking their eyes off him.

He stands watching as we push and shoulder ourselves into our class lines. Miss White whirls her arms like a city policeman directing traffic, and has her whistle clamped between her teeth. Another long single blast, then comes a rhythmic continual tooting, and the babies begin to march in, lifting their knees in time, then the second year, while we wait our turn.

There is only one line, the top class, after mine. It is obvious the new boy will be in the top year. I wonder why he did not come last Monday? I turn to have a final look at him as I follow my classmates, then feel my face flame as he looks straight at me and smiles.

I miss a stride and my best friend, Colleen Rawlins, treads on my heel and pulls off my sandal. Those in line behind all collide with deliberate delight as I hop and shuffle. The tooting stops, Miss White snatches the whistle from her mouth and shouts, 'Wait for me outside the classroom, Bess Bennett.'

'But, Miss . . .' I begin displaying the sandal.

'Outside . . . my . . . room,' she reiterates – and someone adds, 'Toot–toot,' and we all dissolve into giggles, which get worse, out of control, spluttering through hands clasped tight over mouths. That culprit escapes, though Miss White's neck and face grow red, with white streaks down each side of her nose.

I don't in fact feel guilty of very much. 'It was an accident, Miss White.' I have my defence ready, though I am not unused to being in the corridor. Last Friday's sewing lesson had found me standing in this same spot, guilty of finishing a pincushion with just two enormous tacking stitches. I had also unwisely stood on my chair and displayed it like a pendulum on the end of my needle and cotton when I thought Miss White's back was turned.

I stare stonily ahead as the last class files in. The new boy makes a rueful mouth as he is ushered by. I look at and through him as Miss White takes him into the headmaster's class, then returns to her own, and shuts me outside with dramatic pursed-lipped finality.

It is always amazingly quiet in the corridor. I can hear a bee. It is high, near the ceiling, in the pointed pane at the top of the old Gothic window, bumping and buzzing crossly to get outside. The classrooms have a low buzz too, registers being called. 'Here, Miss White.' Milk and dinner money being collected.

Then comes the sound of a door opening. Mr Collins, the headmaster, comes striding along the echoing quarry-tiled corridor. 'It is not good girls who are sent to stand outside,' he says in passing, or he and I think he's passing, but at that moment Miss White comes out of her door and confronts both of us.

'Mr Collins,' she says in her sternest voice. 'I would like you to have a word with this girl, who thinks other people's misfortunes are a laughing matter.'

'Oh!' He looks down.

I feel smaller than the bee, which I see fall to the floor and begin an ungainly walk towards the door.

'I think,' she says with an expression of controlled but severe fury, 'you will understand, headmaster, when I tell you it seems to be the Sinclairs who are the cause of this child's amusement.' She pauses to screw her mouth tight, so there are lines like a web all round it, and adds, 'The butt of this girl's humour.'

'The Sinclairs? Ian Sinclair, our new boy?' he queries. 'Ooh!'

7

His exclamation is long, low and grave – and the bee falls upside down as it tries to scale the doormat.

I remember the pear, I remember Mr Sinclair's averted face as he left our harvest field. Surely he could not have seen me throw the pear away? Wasting food after all I've been told – the war, ships going down, sailors drowning; children always starving in Africa.

'You had better go and wait outside *my* room, young lady.'

So I go to stand where the really wicked are sent: a boy who threw an atlas at his teacher; a girl who bit a piece out of another's arm . . . awful things.

I can hear Mr Collins back in his classroom and I know everything that is happening. I hear desk lids close, a thump of books, a rustle of pages. They are being given something to do while I am dealt with. I draw in a shuddering breath. I am a thing set apart, in limbo, not belonging anywhere. Then the door reopens and again the headmaster comes towards me. He looks taller this time.

He opens his office door and gives a small jerk of his head, indicating I should enter. I know precisely where to stand, the small mat in front of his desk has a worn patch in the middle.

'Bess –' he says my name in a slow sad way '– Your father sets an example to all in this part of the world . . .'

My heart begins to thump. I had not expected my father to be brought into this.

'He is known to be a kind, fair-minded man, a thoughtful man. He would not be pleased to know you are here, would he?'

I swallow, only managing to say, 'No, sir,' when he repeats his last two words.

'Or, more importantly, why you are here.' He sits behind the desk and looks at me gravely. 'To laugh at other people's misfortunes is certainly not what we expect from you.' He again pauses and shakes his head as if there is no hope for me. 'Particularly when this involves a new pupil in our school. What a way to welcome a stranger, whose father fought so bravely, made such a sacrifice for his country.'

I remember how Mr Sinclair averted his face as he left our field. I wonder if he has died.

There is silence, except for the ticking of the clock.

'What have you to say for yourself?'

In my head the clock is deafening, like the auctioneer's hammer in the cattle market.

'Laughter, *giggling*, is an insult to such a man, such a family, to his son, a newcomer, a near neighbour.'

'I never laughed, sir, not at—'

'Not what your teacher says.'

'I only laughed because the others were laughing, and—'

'Sheep brain, then,' he says. 'Didn't think that of you either, Bess.' There is a long pause and my heart drowns out the clock. He is saying something else, but I can't hear until he asks, 'Do you know what that means?'

I shake my head.

'It means that it is rude to stare at, or whisper about, people because they are unfortunate.'

'I thought—' I begin, but the thought will not be put into words. We both wait to see if it will come, but, as Mr Collins sits in his chair, making a tent of his fingers and looking at me through them, to say that I think Ian Sinclair is beautiful is impossible.

'Do you know the story of the Good Samaritan?'

I nod.

'You will please write it out for me in your own words and bring it to me on Wednesday morning. Try to be more as the Good Samaritan, Bess, helping, not giggling or passing by. Go to your class and be sure to apologize to Miss White. You obviously upset her very much.'

I feel it is with a sense of relief he goes to *his* classroom.

Later, at home, I display the six squares of material and the strands of green silk. Miss White has told me to make three extra pincushions for the Church bazaar. So much for saying sorry.

'Is everyone making extra ones at home?' mother asks.

'No, just the children Miss White hates,' I tell her.

'Bess, I'm sure that's not true.'

'And I've got to write out the Good Samaritan for Mr Collins by Wednesday. I'll never do it all.'

'So, what have you done to deserve all this special treatment?' father asks, coming back from the kitchen doorway.

'What's the matter with that Ian, that new boy?' I burst out.

'There's nothing the matter with *him*,' my father says, coming back to sit at the table, but his tone infers there is certainly something very wrong with someone.

I am aware of the evening sounds outside, just an odd bird or two still singing very high in the top crown of the nearest elm; the creaks and cracks as things cooled down after the heat of the day; and Patch, our black collie with one white eye, his claws on the doorstep as he comes to see where my father is.

They listen as I tell about my sandal and what Mr Collins said.

'So, Miss White thought you were laughing at Ian Sinclair, is that it?' Mother asks.

'But what she feared was that our daughter was laughing at Ian Sinclair's father,' Pa adds very quietly. My mother gasps.

The sound makes me impale all six squares of material on my needle and into the white-wood table.

'I'm going to do my rounds,' he adds, and I think it's an invitation, but I find he's just looking hard at my mother, who's nodding back at him, and I'm outside *again*, excluded.

'Coming, then?' he asks. This time Patch and I both know he does mean us, we scramble to our feet, running into the yard, Patch nipping at my heels, catching my sock in his teeth, nearly tripping me over. 'Why does he do that?' I complain.

'He's hurrying you along like he does the other things on the farm.'

I look at Patch with new respect. At least I understand the dog.

The sheep are in the field called Home Close, so this saves a lot of walking. Patch is told to stay by the gate while we climb over. We've only gone a little way, looking and checking, when Pa points to the far hedgerow.

I see a sheep standing sideways by the hedge, close in, not feeding. It's my job to run over, and I can soon see it has pushed into the hedge to feed, then come out with a thick old briar twisted and tangled between its legs and over its back. It begins to pull again as I get near. My father's advice for such times is: *If you can't do anything yourself, get help.* I step carefully away from the distressed animal and beckon.

'It's alright,' I tell the sheep. 'Pa's coming.'

'Stupid old gel,' he says, taking out the huge shut-knife he is never without. Then, kneeling by the ewe, he grabs a handful of her fleece behind her head. 'Now . . .' He pauses and looks steadily at me. 'What should we do first?'

I know this is a test. I study the sturdy briar wrapped so closely under the animal's belly, up between her back legs, even tangled into her stumpy tail.

'Well, what shouldn't we do?'

That he has to ask twice makes me feel a failure. I frown, concentrate.

'If you cut the briar at the hedge, she could get away still all tangled up.'

'Good girl,' he says. 'What we'll do is cut the briar into sections and take a piece off at a time.'

My heart grows large and warm at this approval, and as he cuts the briar, I disentangle each piece from the wool.

'You can pull a bit harder than that,' he tells me. 'You'll not hurt her.'

I work as quickly as I can. When we come to the final thicker piece near the hedge, the sheep suddenly gives a tremendous jerk, kicks out. The solid bulk of its body catches me as it leaps for freedom, and I feel the harsh scrape of its wiry fleece across my cheek . . .

I am being lifted up before I feel I've properly landed and had time to hurt.

'Alright? I should have been ready for something like that.'
He brushes my dress, examines my face.

'Why didn't she wait?' I ask, wanting to throw my arms
around his neck, he is so close and dear to me, but this is a
work situation. He might think I am just a stupid girl, or really
hurt, if I did such a thing, so instead I exclaim, 'Look at all her
wool!'

'Enough to fill a pincushion, you reckon?' He sits back on his
heels and his voice is laughing, now he knows I'm alright.

I look at him solemnly, then begin to pull the wool from the
briar. Soon I have a handful. He holds out his hand, and as I
gather, he cleans, pulling out the thorns and leaves, patting the
stiff, oily wool back into a springy ball.

I can imagine making three splendid pincushions, ready
stuffed, a neat loop at one end for hanging up – and I can
imagine the praise from Miss White. I wonder why I want
praise from Miss White? I am imagining the whole class
pretending to faint when such a thing happens, so I am startled
when Pa suddenly says, 'You're ten, Bess.'

My heart plummets.

'When you were about four years old, in 1940, at the
beginning of the war, we had what's called the Battle of
Britain.'

Usually, when someone mentions your age it is to tell you to
act it or *grow up*. This taking me back in time, in my own
lifetime, is something quite new to me. I watch his face very
carefully as he goes on.

'It was when our Royal Air Force stopped England being
invaded. Many men, many pilots, like Ian Sinclair's father,
were shot down. Many aircraft were shot down in flames.'

I have seen planes coming down in flames on the newsreels at
the cinema. Since my tenth birthday on February 18th – when
I'd been given a new bike, with blocks on the pedals so I can
reach the seat – mother and I sometimes go to the pictures, first
house, cycling the three miles and back. The treat has become a
regular occurrence, because Ma and I love it, and I've seen films

where pilots crash in flames, but everything always comes right in the end.

'Do you understand what I'm telling you?'

I look up, guilty of having let my mind wander when he is talking to me. 'That Mr Sinclair's plane was shot down, and he was—'

'Badly burned. His face was very badly burned. He has had twenty-eight operations.'

I gasp. Noel calls it being *put to the knife* and says he'll never go into the town infirmary for such a thing.

'God help him!' I say. This was what Noel says about anyone who has to go into hospital *to be cut*.

My father looks surprised, but kind of soldiers on with what he is saying.

I squeeze the great ball of wiry oily wool in my hands and soon dread ever meeting Ian Sinclair's father.

Two

'So, who are you hiding from?' Noel asks as he moves the empty beer crate around the stable.

I don't answer, just breathe in the warm smell of straw and dung. Noel draws in *his* breath each time he lifts the brush from Captain's coat, expels it with more hiss and effort as he runs the brush hard down the horse's withers; he can only just reach, standing on the crate.

I *am* hiding, from remarks like, *There are lots of little jobs I could do*, if *I wanted*, and, *Fifty-three this year, including children, if the Sinclairs come.* The whole house is in an uncomfortable bustle because of the harvest supper tomorrow.

'Can I help you?' I ask Noel.

'Expect your ma could find you something to do in the kitchen.' He doesn't stop grooming.

'There'll be masses of people here in a bit.'

'Yes.' The single word does not excuse me, but he adds, 'You can fill the water buckets.'

'Wish I was a boy.'

'What can't be cured must be endured.'

I understand why my father gets tired of his sayings. Then we hear footsteps coming across the yard. Noel raises his eyebrows, queries what I'm going to do. I go into the next stall and crouch down.

'Seen Bess?' Pa's voice is loud as he leans in over the stable door. There's a pause, then he adds, '*I've* got a job for her.'

I emerge. Noel continues sucking in, hissing out.

'Come on, we've got visitors. Your mother wants you.'

14

'*You* said *you* had a job for me.'

'Pleased you were in hearing distance,' he says.

From the kitchen pours today's smell, pastry. All week it's been meat. Our hams have been boiled in coppers, cooled, then hauled out through a great layer of soft rich fat used in the pastry for pork pies and game pies; tongues have been boiled, skinned, curled round into metal presses that have screws, ratchets and cogs like instruments of torture.

What I hadn't expected to hear as we returned was laughter. I run ahead and swing in on the latch handle, then try to swing back out, still holding the latch. The visitors are Mrs Sinclair and Ian.

'Hello. It's Bessie, isn't it?' Mrs Sinclair asks. She has on a floaty red spotted dress today, slim over her hips then flared out.

'Well, Bess,' my mother corrects, giving me a cursory look which invites me to let go of the latch, stop swinging on everything, come in properly – and grow up – which, with Ian Sinclair watching, I wish I had done some minutes before.

'Good Queen Bess. Lovely . . .'

'More *Porgy and Bess*, if I'm honest.' Ma laughs self-consciously.

'Ooh!' Mrs Sinclair's voice has lost all its round vowels. 'Do you like the shows? I go to lots in London.'

I go to Ma's side, she does like shows, and the pictures, and stories in books and magazines, and so do I. She puts her arm around my shoulders.

No one answers Mrs Sinclair's question, and her gaze wavers over us and Ian, then rests on the small skip of apples. 'Perhaps I could peel those. I've come to help.'

I think she's come too dressed up to help.

She looks at my father, who stands proprietarily in front of the range, and asks, blinking her eyes, 'Do you do all this every year?'

'We do,' Ma answers for him. 'It all goes back into the mists of time.'

'Well, not quite.' Pa beckons Mrs Sinclair through from kitchen to front hall, where there are family portraits. We can hear him pointing out his Great-Grandpa Bennett – high wing collar and cravat. 'We always have our harvest supper as close to the seventeenth of September as possible. That was the old boy's birthday.' He sounds indulgent, as if he is giving her a present. His voice is deeper, with rich falling tones, like a fat ripe pear. She is laughing – too much – as he explains. I've always been told about the Bennetts very seriously, as if they have a say in what I am and what I must do when I grow up, because there's only me to carry on the line. I've never wanted to laugh.

'Oh, do call me Isabella!' Mrs Sinclair exclaims – the round vowels back – and I look at Ian. He goes to the door as if he would like to leave, steps just outside to where Patch is chained up. He lifts the dog's chain, and stands weighing it in his hand.

Now we are all still and listening, as if we hear false echoes, as if what comes to us is not what is really being said.

'They're really nice,' Mrs Sinclair is saying as they come back to the kitchen. 'The ones painted outside, and the house – it is this house, isn't it?'

'In some,' Pa answers, 'what's left of the original house is now our machine store.'

And before that there was a crook cottage and its beams were used in the roof of that first farmhouse. I complete the story silently.

I watch as he goes on telling her about the Bennetts, and she stands smiling at him. She is pretty, like a doll. She has fair hair, and really blue eyes, but when her smile goes, her brightness goes too. My mother is beautiful all the time, when she's tired, or cross, or asleep.

'All this cooking. All this work,' she simpers at Ma.

'I do have help. Lots really,' Ma says and, as if to make the point, hands her a peeler, then begins to fill a huge bowl with water and throws in salt. 'For when you've peeled them,' she adds.

'You ladies enjoy all the fuss,' Pa says, standing with his arms crossed, leaning on the dresser. 'It gives you a sense of power.'

Ma laughs briefly, ironically, Mrs Sinclair pouts prettily and, I think, does not really understand that remark any more than I do. Power over what – pastries and apples? I can't imagine ever enjoying that.

'And if Isabella doesn't want to peel apples—' Pa begins, but is stopped by, 'But I do,' from Mrs Sinclair, and a cross look from my mother.

Pa just stands beaming at them both. Then I see Ian is looking at me and, out of the blue, I wish my name was Isabella. Isabella Sinclair. Why can't my name be something elegant, something that flies off the tongue, not *Bess*. Bess Bennett! It was like hammering a peg into a hole, *a round peg into a square hole*. I would never have gone wrong if they had called me Isabella. Isabella Bennett.

'There are plates on the top shelf of the pantry to be lifted down,' Ma says.

'Hmm.' Pa levers himself upright. 'But I've wasted enough time indoors today. I'm going to chisel-plough the top field.'

'You could wait until *after* harvest supper.'

'The soil's just right now,' he says, lifting the plates down in two huge piles. 'You'll excuse me, Isabella . . .' He half bows. 'We shall look forward to seeing you all tomorrow evening.'

I see Ian look expectantly from his mother to my father. I go to the door, where Patch drags his chain across Pa's path, but is stepped over. We all want to escape to the ploughing.

'My husband doesn't like children around when he's using the tractor,' Ma explains. 'Bess, why don't you take Ian down to the brook, show him around a bit.'

'If he wants,' I say with a shrug. 'But . . .' I look around the table, laden with everything for tomorrow. Lunch had been an early, skimpy affair.

'Look.' Ma pushes her hair back into its knot, swoops to the far corner of the table and, in several swift movements, takes a

17

scorched plate tart, cuts it into four, wraps it in a piece of greaseproof paper. 'Share that between you.'

'And don't come back for at least a couple of hours,' his mother adds.

'Where is the brook?' he asks as we walk past the cows, which he doesn't seem to mind. Colleen hates them.

'Do you want to see our tractor first?' I ask.

'But your mother said—'

'She won't know. No one will.' I feel justified in taking him along behind the hedgerows until we can view my father on the Ford tractor. This was allocated to us during the war, when we had to plough up more land to grow more food. Noel called it *the rape of the virgin pasture.*

Ian and I lie close together, peering through the hedge, silently watching as the tractor goes to and fro across the field. Pa looks back often, as the short blades of the chisel-plough break the hard surface, uproot the stubble, ready for proper deep ploughing later. I unwrap the tart, which has also become fairly broken up, and we share the treat, scrupulously, down to the last wipe of the jam left on the paper.

'Come on, we can wash our hands in the brook,' I tell him.

'You're lucky to live on a farm, and I guess your father didn't have to go to the war.'

'He tried to join the Royal Flying Corps in the last lot.' I am word perfect on family stories. 'But Grandmama found out and Grandpa and Noel fetched him back, because he was only fifteen.' I am about to launch into the story of Noel going and fighting in the First World War, then I think about his father and what happened to him flying. 'This way to the brook,' I shout instead, and run ahead, then leap up in the air before sliding down the dry clay and pebble bank, which in the dry weather has crumbled into hard scree.

I hear him call out alarmed, then he's above me on the bank laughing. 'I thought this was just a hedge. I thought you'd fallen into a hole.' He slides down to the water's edge. I'm already on the stepping stones over to the far side, but as I begin to throw off my sandals and socks I stop to watch Ian. He is looking all around him and suddenly I see how this place really is. I see the sun dappling the water through the hawthorn bushes, how their close-packed leaves are turning to red, but still vault over the water, making it enclosed, private, a bower. He looks all about as if it is enchanted. I notice that the sun dapples his blond hair, white in the sun, gold in the shade.

'Is this your den?'

I shrug. Colleen and I make it into whatever we fancy.

He is pulling off his shoes and socks, and is soon in the water. He begins to walk slowly along, though he winces and wobbles as he stands on pebbles. I laugh.

'How far can we go?' he asks, peering along the tunnel of bushes.

'Come on. Two brooks join.' I go ahead, eager to show him. I stand in the middle. 'If you follow that one,' I point to the greater flow of the two streams. 'That is the Swift, which joins the Sense, then the Soar, which goes through Leicester, then on and on to the Wash and the North Sea.'

He looks impressed.

'Pa says.' I authenticate the information.

'And that one?'

'Goes back along the fields and you can follow it to the spring, where it rises in Red Pool Spinney. That's why –' I quote my father again '– Red Pool Spinney is called that. The spring begins in a red pool. It's the minerals.'

'Can we go and see?'

'Now?'

'Is it too far?'

I consider. 'I don't suppose so.' It was a long time since I'd been there, and then only to the edge to see a vixen and her cubs playing.

'We'd hear the church clock,' he cajoles. 'They won't worry until five or half past.'

I don't tell him that I've never been to the very middle of the spinney, never actually seen the red pool. I couldn't tell him that

19

on windy nights, when the rain drives at the windowpanes, my mind makes up stories about this spinney. On such nights, I imagine the awful things that lurk there venturing out, coming to my bedroom.

'Shall we go?' he asks, turning, already paddling back. 'It would be an adventure, our adventure.'

I look at him and think about the pear I threw away, I think about his father, and I want to share something special with him. 'We'd better take our shoes,' I tell him. 'And we'd better not be late back.'

I throw my socks down on the bank and he throws his on top. He has plimsolls, and can tie the laces together and hang them around his neck. I buckle my sandals together, but they won't hang round my neck.

'I'll carry them for you. He takes my sandals and stands smiling, waiting for me to show the way.

I am very conscious that he is behind me. I am very aware that this offer to carry my shoes is some kind of service I have not had before. He is not related to me; he's not trying to teach me anything; he's not even a friend, not like Colleen. He's just carrying my shoes.

We go back upstream, into the sunlight, all the way to where the watercress grows around and under the footbridge. We stoop under the wooden planks and paddle on until, just beyond the next bend, I step out on a shelf of soil below a steep bank.

'That's Red Pool Spinney.' I point to the heads of the trees we can just see. Before I have to ask, he is unbuckling the straps, separating my sandals. He smiles as he puts them into my hands. I feel special, chosen, but wary. I push my wet gritty feet into the sandals and buckle them tight. I have a feeling we should hurry, get this adventure over.

The spinney is part of the boundary of my father's land, but Mr Paget, the lay preacher, owns the spinney. Pa says Daniel Paget deliberately neglects it to deter walkers, that there should be a public footpath through the wood. 'He don't want to share what he's got hidden away in there,' Noel reckons. But no one ever says what it is, they just shrug. It makes the subjects of my nightmares. I rush on almost as if we're already being chased.

'Is something wrong?' Ian asks, out of breath. 'Are you afraid of being late back?'

I don't answer, because that's the least of my worries.

'I don't want to upset my mum either. She doesn't have many good days like today.'

I slow down, wondering why peeling apples made for a good day.

'She's forgotten herself for a bit,' he says, as if answering. 'Like going to see this red pool makes me forget.'

This baffles me. For a moment I thought we might find a reason for not going, instead of which, it now seems inevitable.

When we reach the spinney, our boundary is well fenced and the shrubby undergrowth the other side makes it impossible to go in that way. Without speaking, I beckon him along a hedge and through a gap on to Mr Paget's land. I keep low and gesture Ian to do the same as we run along the hedgerow back towards the spinney. I am very cautious. I know very little moves across our land – man or beast – that either my father or Noel doesn't know about. Mr Paget is said to be even more watchful.

We circle the trees and have almost reached halfway round without finding any trace of a footpath or any possible way in. No one comes walking here. Everything is so overgrown, neglected – trees have been broken down or uprooted by gales, some are half held up by other trees, many have taken other trees down with them. Every way looks blocked and it is dark in there.

We come to a part of the spinney which falls back, and, as we follow the curve of trees, the ground beneath our feet is quite wet. A little further in, we come upon a wide shallow pool, a small lake really, with trees right down to the water's edge on three sides. The water is alive with every kind of wild duck and goose, more than I have ever seen before, a mass of waterbirds.

By my side, Ian gasps and we creep steadily forward. 'There's swans,' I hear him say, and feel him stand up straight. Immediately there is panic – ducks set up a chorus of quacking, dozens of pairs of feet slap the water as the bigger birds rise. Once airborne, the geese set up a tremendous honking, and all – geese, ducks, swans – fly in a kind of wondrous flock. They circle the wood – once, twice, and again – then fly off towards Mr Paget's farm.

'Wow!' Ian sounds awed. 'My father would have liked that. He loves anything that can fly.'

Suddenly why Dan Paget does not want walkers on his land or in the spinney is much clearer. He has a larder of Sunday dinners here just for the taking.

'So, is this the way to the pool?' Ian asks. He is at the innermost edge of the secret lake. 'The water does come from this way.'

Intrigued, I go to see. The earth smells wet, boggy, dank. There is no clear stream, just an all-over seeping, which comes together and forms the lake. 'It must be,' I say.

'Don't you know?' he asks.

I hesitate between the truth and outright lie. My father's system of rewarding a right answer with great approval, but punishing a wrong answer with silent censure makes me cautious. 'I've never been this way,' I compromise.

'The spring must fill the lake, then, somewhere, it runs out into your stream,' he reasons. 'Where's that, I wonder? But come on, let's find the red pool first.'

It has become his expedition. I'm just following, trying to keep up. The more the trees crowd in, the more fallen ones there are to climb over, or creep under, the wetter the ground gets, and the faster he seems to go. I think of Pa's *Heroes, Real & Mythological*. The book illustrations suggest this is what heroes do, fight harder when things get tough.

I glance back – not what heroes do – and see behind us the way the water seeps into and covers our footprints. There's a strange smell, like Mrs Noel's brimstone and treacle remedy she makes to clean the system and cool the blood, a teaspoonful to be taken the first nine days in March.

I can't let Ian go on his own. He's a visitor. I feel too shy of his possible scorn to be able to shout that we shouldn't go any further, that I've been forbidden to go into the spinney; that Dan Paget is *a mean bigot*, that no one goes mushrooming, blue-legging or even sticking on his farm. He's been known to go round to a cottage to collect money for wood picked up from his land.

The fallen trees we're having to climb over are green with moss or black and slimy wet. My foot goes right under, and as I lever it out, the ground makes a noise like it's trying to suck me and my sandal down into boggy depths. All the bad thoughts I have at nights about this place are becoming real. If we turn back, I think we could wash our shoes in the brook and no one would know. I think of my father's anger – worse, his scorn, and at last I open my mouth to shout Ian back – but he calls first.

'I can see it! I can see it! The Red Pool. It *is* red, sort of . . .'

Then there is a splash, and floundering, exactly like a sheep being thrown into the dip. He shouts out. Just a cry, I don't hear words, but I see a picture of sheep in the dip pit, their heads being held under the water by the shepherd's crook. They all come up panicking.

There's silence ahead, and it is me who is shouting. 'Ian! Where are you? I'm coming.'

I stumble on, too fast for my feet, panting with panic, falling, my hands and up to my elbows disappearing in the black mire. At this level, I suddenly see his hair, the top of his head in the gloomy bowels of this place. He has fallen forward. He looks as if he is trying to swim. His bestreaked face comes up out of the mire, gasping for air.

I wade in. It is well over my thighs. It is like walking in cold, thick nightmare porridge. As I get near, he sees me and reaches out, then his face goes under again. He comes up gasping, desperate. Then he submerges again. I see one of his feet is caught between branch and trunk of a fallen tree. I push my legs and body through the mire towards it. I am going deeper and deeper. An icy cold clamps my waist, takes my breath.

His foot is wedged, heel and toe, sideways, his floundering weight holding it tight. I try to pull him nearer to the forked trunk to ease the foot out, but I know I can't. *If there's nothing you can do, fetch help.* I make an instant reckoning of what this would mean and reject my father's advice. I decide all I can do is try to get his plimsoll off. He doesn't seem to be struggling so much, but he's tied a double bow.

I hear someone – me – making little sobbing cries as I struggle. His free foot catches me in the back. If I fall face down, we will die. I've seen sheep that have drowned in swollen winter streams, their life dragged away by the weight of their own wool.

At last the lace is undone. Immediately, his foot slips free and he disappears altogether, everything – head, hair, as if he'd never ever been there. I think I scream, I certainly lunge down to try to catch his leg, then fall. The thick filth is in my mouth, but just before my eyes close as I go under, I see a figure like Uncle Remus's Tar Baby rising from the bog. Then I am grabbed and pulled upwards and we both stand, he to his waist, me halfway to my chest in the bog.

I keep shuddering as we spit and try to wipe the filth from our faces, and he becomes the rescuer. He points back towards the tree trunk. 'We'll be alright as long as we don't fall.'

Now I know what it is like to sink, moving is terrifying. Though it is not more than ten long strides, it is an infinite distance of energy-sapping inches. I push my legs forward twice, then suddenly feel I shall never get there – and stop.

'Make for my plimsoll,' he says, and he grips my hand. We do, seriously intent on the shoe still wedged in the fallen tree, as if having an aim gives us the will. The moment he reaches out and pulls his gym shoe free, he says, 'Don't want to get into trouble for losing a shoe,' holding up his arms, dripping black ooze back into the bog.

For a moment, we both pause. Then he laughs outright, but I'm afraid of my laughter. It doesn't feel right, trembles somewhere in my stomach. It tries to come, but, then suddenly I am crying, sobbing, shaking. 'I thought you were going to die.'

'What, me? Me and my dad, we're survivors.'

I can hear myself sobbing in great shuddering gasps. He grabs the back of my dress with one hand and pushes me forcibly along the side of the log. Soon we are only ankle-deep, then we are standing on solid tufts of reedy grass, safe. He holds my hand again, then begins to giggle as he looks down at himself, then at me. 'You know what my dad calls it when you do something wrong. "Putting up a black." It's Air-Force slang.' Then he looks at his feet. 'I've lost my other plimmie! Well –' he turns and addresses the swamp – 'You might as well have the pair.'

We both watch as the bog accepts it, gobbles it. That stops laughter and tears.

'Best go home, I suppose,' he says. 'No way we can hide where we've been.'

'No,' I say, and think of the disapproval on my father's face. How can his daughter be such a fool?

We walk back to the edge of the trees around the lake. In the middle of the clearing stands Mr Paget with his gun levelled at us. We stop. I feel we probably deserve to be shot. Well, I do. After all, I've been told about not going into the spinney. I can now vaguely remember being told why.

'Keep walking. Keep coming on,' he shouts at us.

As we go nearer, he asks, 'So, where's your dog?'

'He's at home,' I answer. 'Chained up.'

He seems surprised and takes a few steps towards us. 'Bess?' he queries. 'Bess Bennett? What are you doing in my spinney? Was there another dog? What frightened my geese?'

'It was me, sir. I stood up too quick when I saw the swans,' Ian tells him.

He pokes his face forward. 'You're that pilot's son.' But he lowers the gun now he has identified his trespassers.

25

'Bess was just taking me to see the Red Pool . . .'

'There's supposed to be a path,' I say accusingly.

'And *I* suppose your father says that, does he?' He clears his throat, makes a performance of it. Colleen says he does this before he preaches at the Methodist Chapel. 'I think the best thing is for you to lead the way and we'll go and see what he has to say.'

'He's out,' I say.

'I can wait, and I dare say your mother'll be in, busy in the kitchen, no doubt.' He pauses to look me up and down. 'You'll be just what she wants to see this night.'

The way back is a problem. I don't want to let him know that we pushed through a hedge, another sin for a farmer's daughter. I feel Ian hesitate as we reach the spot but I catch his hand and we walk on together. It's a long way to the gate, and the gate is very near Mr Paget's farm. He makes a kind of disbelieving humph in his throat as I lead the way through, then all the way back down our side of the hedge, until we reach the path leading to the footbridge.

We cross the field to the plank bridge and my heart begins to pound as I see not just my father, but my mother and Ian's mother all coming to meet us.

My mother is carrying our socks, as if she believes it is all she has left of us. Isabella Sinclair looks very strange. If she *was* having a good day, she certainly isn't now. My father hurries forward, looking at us in disbelief, staring at the two black creatures holding hands. My father has blue eyes too, a kind of blue which becomes icy, and can look hard like marbles when he's angry. They're hard now.

'Dan,' he says to our neighbour.

Three

I 'm in bed, under the bedclothes, hungry. My hair's still wet *and* I have a tender spot where my mother hit my head on the stone sink as she scrubbed at my hair for the third time.

Pa asked what he had done to deserve a daughter like me. This hurts more. I had thought him on my side when Mr Paget started shouting and mentioned the wrath of God. My father had said, if any wrath was needed, he'd supply it. Then they went from rights of way to trespassers.

I wonder about the Lord's Prayer and *Forgive us our trespasses.* I wonder if there's a mistake and it should be tresspasers? On Mr Paget's behalf, I also wonder about forgiving *Those that trespass against us.*

Ma waved the socks about and said it was not the time to quarrel, all that mattered was that we were safe. Ian tried to make things right too – he smiled at his mother. The trouble was he looked like the pictures of *The Black and White Minstrel Show.* I wanted to laugh but Mrs Sinclair stood with her hands clamped over her ears. Ian went to her but she backed away. He was trying to explain that he was alright, but she suddenly screamed, flailed about with her hands, and then swooned. Everyone was then too busy straightening her out on the grass to listen to Mr Paget still ranting away. Colleen says no one listens to him when he preaches at the Methodists.

Once Ian's mother had recovered sufficiently to stand, Pa put his arm around her and practically carried her along. She flopped about and leaned her head on his chest. Ma flapped the socks at Ian and me to tell us to follow, while she had a last

27

go at reasoning with Mr Paget. I heard him say the Bennetts had better keep everything off his land, *Be it sheep, cow, dog or daughter*.

Pa stopped and swung round, but he was a bit hampered, so he shouted back that he would be having a word with his local councillor about the state of public footpaths in the area. Ian and I had stopped too. Pa gave me a tremendous glare before he went on again. Ian gently put his chest behind my shoulder to make me take the next step and whispered, 'He doesn't bite, does he?' I shook my head at him, censoring such a remark about my pa as much as answering the question.

Pa gave Ian a first rinse-down standing in a tin bath in the wash house. I had to wait outside, while Ma gave Mrs Sinclair brandy. Then Ian was wrapped in a blanket and Pa drove him and his mother home. I watched Ma in the sideyard, even when the car was out of sight, she still stood there. Then she turned back, and seeing me, pounced. Then it was all action and no more time to spare thinking about anything other than the trouble I'd caused and the work still to be done.

'Celebrations! I'll never be ready!' she exclaimed, not talking to me. I was just something that had to be undressed, pulled about, like some unfavoured doll. So, I just let it happen, flopped about.

My clothes were thrown in a pile on top of Ian's, and I was scrubbed within an inch of my life and half knocked-out on the sink. But I know the difference between a faint and a swoon. I know my ma would never swoon, she would never pretend like that. I know other things as well.

I know I am never going to lie in bed and make up stories about Red Pool Spinney again – even though I see the moonlight come and go as the wind scuds the clouds over the moon, and there's an old screech owl hunting. I'm free of those thoughts. I've been there with Ian, and come back. I remember the funny things: him throwing his plimsoll back into the swamp; his grinning white teeth in his black face; his jokes. I remember how he had thought of his father when all the waterbirds flew up into the air.

It is with a shock of real disappointment that I realize that I still haven't seen the Red Pool. I must have been so near yet so far. I think I'll keep quiet if he talks about it, as I do when I don't know the answers to all Pa's questions. Then I think that, after all, I *will* tell Ian, and he'll say, 'We'll have to go again,' and we'll both laugh.

The thought makes me draw my feet up into the warm centre. In my balled-up stillness, there is room for another notion which needs much thinking about. It has to do with Pa and Ian. It has something to do with sharing, like the plate tart I shared with Ian, equal shares, exactly. I feel sleep taking me just as I find the question. If my love for Ma and Pa was equal shares before, has a bit of Pa's share gone to Ian?

My bedroom window overlooks the kitchen garden and when I wake I can see Ian's and my vests pegged out next to each other, flapping madly in the morning breeze. All our clothes dance side by side, even our socks. Another thing I know is that Ian is a quite different friend to Colleen. I think it's because, even if a cow just steps in our direction, Colleen grabs me, screws up the back of my dress and uses me as a shield. If Ian had panicked like that, there would not have been any washing to do. Noel, I know, would call this a *sobering thought*.

I am starving but go downstairs slowly. The house is quiet, no one in the kitchen. On the table are a bowl, cornflakes with a cartoon of Sunny Jim leaping over a stile on the packet, milk, sugar. I help myself and eat beneath a row of flower vases filled with red and yellow dahlias, blue cornflowers and spiky ears of barley. These will be for the long tables in the barn. I suppose this is where everyone is, putting the finishing touches: tying sheaves to the uprights; putting up paper streamers, throwing long white sheets over the trestle tables.

I'd really like to help doing these things but am unsure of how I'll be received by my father. Ma may pull a face at me, pretend she's still annoyed, but it won't be real. I wonder about carrying the vases of flowers into the barn. I select one and carry it out into the yard. When I reach the barn door, I stop, then step back as my father says, 'You just don't understand. You should have seen the state she was in when I got her home.' I lean against the wall, holding the vase, recognizing the tone of voice, the same testiness that edges in when I don't really know what he wants me to say or do.

'Tell me then!' Mother sounds tetchy too. 'It all took long enough.'

'When she saw the boy, she thought he'd been burned.'

'Oh, come on. If he'd been burned black all over, he wouldn't have been standing there grinning like a Cheshire cat!' She sounded impatient. 'I thought she was a sensible woman, but going off into . . . *vapours*, like some Victorian melodrama . . .'

'Well, you'd know about that!' Pa exclaims.

'And that is supposed to mean . . . ?'

'Books, magazines, cycling to the cinema. You know about those.'

'I do know when things are real and when they're not!' Ma retorts.

'What that woman has to put up with is real enough.' There is a grim note in Pa's voice.

'I would have thought the last thing her husband needs is hysterics. I *hope* they don't come this evening.'

'Very charitable,' Pa says.

'I can do without her play-acting any time, and others might stand a chance of some attention if Isabella Sinclair is not around.' Ma sounds reckless.

'What do you mean?'

I know just how his eyes will look. I can't hold the vase any longer, so I put it down in front of my feet.

'I mean, she's the sort of woman who can twist a man round her little finger – any man. But when it comes to the *For better, for worse* bit, then, if it's not for the better, *she* will not want to know.'

'I talked to her husband. He said he had practically lived at East Grinstead hospital since 1940, and his wife's been with him.'

'I heard she was in London.'

'East Grinstead is not far from London. She could have been staying with a relative.'

'Living it up, was what I heard. A good-time girl.'

'Hearsay. They've not been in the village five minutes. Mrs West at the shop, I suppose.'

'Your mother, actually.'

I decide to go, and nearly fall over the vase. The trouble is, I feel Ma and Grandmama Bennett are probably right about Mrs Sinclair, though I usually try to be on Pa's side.

I carry the vase away and go to find Noel in the yard.

'Where are you going with that?' he asks when I find him sitting in the yard near the log pile sharpening thatching pegs for the last rick.

I put them down next to him. 'To the barn, of course,' I say, nearly adding, *Silly*.

'Going the pretty way.'

I know this means the long way round to anywhere, so I just nod.

He moves up on the log.

'You've cleaned up nice after last night,' he says.

'Nearly scrubbed away.'

He laughs in his belly for a minute. 'I hear you saw old Dan Paget's pantry?'

'Yes.' I tell him enthusiastically about all the birds, then pause.

'Noel?' I begin.

He stops sharpening the pegs. 'Now what?'

'What's *living it up*?'

Noel begins to puff and blow, which he does most times when I ask him questions, but the next moment, my father appears out of the neighbouring wash house. 'Alright, Noel,' he says, which means he's taken over.

31

'Why is there a vase of flowers out here?' he asks, but doesn't wait for an answer, just shakes his head in despair, picks them up and gives them back to me. 'When Mr and Mrs Sinclair come this evening, you can apologize for causing them both worry and trouble.' He looks at me as if *that* is all I am about, worry and trouble.

For the rest of the day, none of us Bennetts speak to each other very much. In the afternoon, the house is full of women helping, so we talk to them and they talk to us. It is only when they have gone and we are all changed into Sunday clothes, and everything is ready, that Ma's temper is restored, mostly because Pa's out in the barn drawing off pints of beer for Noel and our own men, who by tradition come about half an hour earlier than their wives and everyone else.

I hang about in the doorway of Ma's bedroom as she sits before her dressing table and powders her nose with the swansdown puff from her powder bowl. She's wearing a deep-blue satin dress with a pearl necklace and earrings, which make her creamy skin glow.

'Why did you go to Red Pool Spinney?' she asks, bending to see that she hasn't too much powder on her cheeks.

'Ian wanted an adventure.' I am surprised into telling the truth. 'And he *was* a visitor.'

'Yes.' She stays leaning forward, and looks at me through the mirror. 'Tonight we have lots of visitors to entertain. You'll help me.'

I go to stand by her, resting my hand on her thigh, and we look at each other in the mirror. This is not rude, not staring, because it's like looking at a picture. We're quite still, noticing things about each other. 'Do I have to say sorry to Mr and Mrs Sinclair?' I ask.

'I think so. Just go quietly to them after supper.'

Ma raises her eyebrows a touch and we both know it's more Pa than anyone else who's our problem. We try to please him because we love him so. Tonight we must be correct, but now it isn't just Mr Sinclair and all the operations that's a problem for me. There's Mrs Sinclair and her swooning.

'I'm glad my name's Bess,' I say.

'Oh . . . good!' She smiles at me. 'Just always be Bess, won't you?'

I nod. That, I think, will be easy.

'Ian will be with them, if they come. He seems a nice boy, so it shouldn't be too bad.' She turns from the mirror, gives me a quick hug. 'Come on now. People will be arriving any second.'

I can hear a car, and when the engine has stopped, I can hear ponies and traps coming, a brisk excitement of trotting and crunching wheels. Ma takes my hand and we go to the front door, stand under the portico. Here, a recognized division takes place. Fellow farmers, landowners, descendants of the yeomen of England, like the Bennetts, are welcomed inside, where they will be served sherry, whisky, whatever they fancy, from our sideboard, while the workers and their families go straight to the barn. The early arrivals are ushered on their ways, but later arrivals know their places anyway.

I help Stella, our regular woman from the village. We show the guests where to put their coats and hats in one of the large spare bedrooms, and where their bathroom is. Most know. They come every year, and say the same things: I've grown; what a lucky young lady I am; some ask what I've been up to. I don't answer anyone really, just give different kinds of smiles, then, like Stella, ask, 'May I take your coat?'

After about half an hour, when most people are here, mother comes and says, 'We'll go to the barn now, Bess. You carry on here, Stella, then be ready to help your sister in the kitchen.'

We get delayed a bit on the way, as Lady Philipps arrives driving her own trap and accompanied by her grandson. We rent some land from the Philipps estate, and while the invitation is sent every year, only rarely does anyone come. Greville Philipps is fifteen. His grandmother greets my mother with, 'Thought it was time Greville here got to know some local people again. There's been little chance with him away at school, and the whole caboodle evacuated to Scotland for the duration.'

'Hello, Greville. Nice to see you home,' Ma says. 'You remember Bess?'

I nod and hold out my hand as Pa has taught me. Greville smiles, touches hands, nods down at me. 'You've grown,' he says.

'And you,' I answer. He looks surprised and his grandmother laughs.

'That's the spirit,' she says to me, then turns to Ma. 'You've a bonnie daughter, unlike our gaggle of girls. Go ahead to the barn, Greville. We'll follow you.'

'We shan't be staying to eat, m'dear.' Lady Philipps tells Ma and Greville's retreating back. 'Just wanted to show my face. How's Mrs B senior? I must drop in and have a proper chat with Jessie soon.'

'She should be here any moment,' Ma says. 'She's had a letter from some friend you both knew as girls.'

'She was always the one who had time to bother with people. I've been slack, I'm afraid.'

'You've had other things to do. The estate . . .'

'The wars, and the men all wanting to go off and be bloody heroes, or martyrs . . .' She pauses for a moment as if paying respect to her lost husband and son, then says, 'Yes,' and accepts a large glass of sherry, adding, 'What we need in our family now is for our female ugly ducklings to marry well and clear off, then Greville to marry someone like Bess here and take over the whole caboodle, tout suite. How did I get blessed with such plain granddaughters, I often ask myself.'

Lady Philipps has a kind of hooked nose, but my glance is intercepted. 'Go after Greville,' Ma orders. 'Tell your father we're on our way.'

I go. But I'll not marry Greville Philipps. I know this for certain as I go towards the barn, with its crowd of people and the long tables lined with vases of flowers, the cold stuffed joints and poultry arranged, turn and turn about, all down the middle. Too much cooking and bother. I think I'd rather be shut in the old pigsty with Patch. I'd certainly rather be in the stable with Captain or, best, out with the hunters. I'll not marry anyone.

There's a crowd in the nearest doorway, drinking, raising glasses to each other, most greeting each other, some pretending not to see people. I walk past this doorway and the crowd, along the path at the back of the barn. I can hear the hubbub inside. I put my ear to the wall and it sounds just like a great beehive, buzzing and humming with chat and laughter.

I press harder to the old bricks, still warm from the day's sun, and I can hear Lady Philipps's booming voice. The general hum of talk dies a little as people realize she is there. I can hear her talking first to one then another. I move along the wall, listening hard, trying to keep level with where she is inside. I get to the place where bricks are set in a herringbone pattern with air gaps between. I put my mouth to it and whisper, like Grandmama Bennett says you should do to the bees when there's family news. 'Greville Philipps thinks girls should be seen and not heard.'

Inside, I hear Lady Philipps greeting Grandmama, and after a few minutes, raising her voice to wish the assembly good health and good harvests. She'll be going soon. Pa will walk her out to her trap. I decide to wait out of sight until they've gone.

I'm to sit next to Pa, who takes the top of one table, Ma the other, with Grandmama Bennett on her right. Pa never allows there to be a separate top table. He says we are all workers, and because the Church says, *We are one body because we all share in one blood.*

On the other side of me is Noel, his wife, Dawdie, and grandson George, who's good with animals and is coming to work for us next year when he's fourteen. Noel piles things on my plate and says he'll only sit next to me provided I don't ask any questions.

Stella, her sister, and two other helpers rush in and out with huge tureens of hot potatoes and brussels, mashed buttery swedes and carrots to add to the cold meats already all along the tables. There's salads too, but most people pour hot gravies and sauces over their meat and vegetables to make it a proper hot meal.

Then come the puddings. These are my favourites, and Ma's speciality: trifles, junkets, cold custards with nutmeg lavished on top; fruit pies, tarts made with a sweet pastry that melts in your mouth, and great jugs of cream from the dairy.

George bets he can eat more than me. He's winning when I hear Pa clear his throat meaningfully. I eat more sedately, but as soon as my plate is empty again, Pa bends over me.

'I think it's time we had a word with Mr Sinclair,' he says quietly.

'He's not here,' I say, hoping it's true.

'He's here, with Mrs Sinclair and Ian,' Pa says with certainty. 'At the far end of our table, on the same side you're sitting.' I lean forward to look, cautiously going from person to person until I come to Ian, and the flowery sleeve of a dress next to him. I stop there. 'Remember,' Pa says close to my ear, 'he *feels* just like you or I, no matter how he looks.'

He pushes his chair back. His words are like great stones weighting my feet as we begin the walk to the other end of the table. Pa has one hand flat on my back. I lean, but he propels me along. There's a lot of people getting up now, off either to the lavatories in the yard or in the house, before the speech and the singing begins.

I'm sorry I had the eating race with George. I feel sick. I press back harder on Pa's hand, but he steers me on. Pa stops when we get to Ian, so I slip in to stand by his chair. Ian immediately says, 'Dad, this is Bess,' and he makes it sound as if I am someone special as he stands up and displays me with a wide sweep of his arm. Mrs Sinclair, next to him, exclaims as she sees my father and rises to catch his arm, exclaiming, 'What would I have done without Mr Bennett! What would I have done?'

36

She stands in front of Mr Sinclair and it is not until she has gushed and exclaimed some more that she is persuaded to sit down.

'Oh! Ken . . .' she turns at last to her husband. 'Here's Mr Edgar Bennett – Edgar. We can thank him all over again.'

'And Bess too, I understand.' Mr Sinclair's voice sounds a little as if he has something in his mouth, but cheerful, with a laughing note like Ian's.

'And for inviting us all tonight,' Mrs Sinclair goes on.

'Bess has something to say about *last* night,' Pa says.

My eyelids feel as weighted as my feet have done, but I look now. I have never seen a face like this, raw and mangled. I think I only look for three seconds, because I know immediately more would be staring.'

'Hello, young lady! I'm pleased to meet you. How are you after *the adventure*?'

He does look how Noel said, as if he's been *put to the knife* many, many, many times – and stitched up many times.

Ian takes hold of my wrist where no one can see, and says loudly, 'My dad's won a medal. The Distinguished Flying Cross.'

In one eye socket there's a gold bar, as if it's propping up the place where an eye should be.

Looking down at the table, I see Mr Sinclair's hand come over and hold Mrs Sinclair's on the table, as if he needs reassuring as much as I do. The worse thing of all is that I see she pulls hers quickly away from under his fingers and plucks at my father's sleeve. Ian sees too, and his hand is tighter on my arm. This, I know, is all much worse than his face.

'I'd love to see a Distinguished Flying Cross,' I say. 'That's really something.'

'Wizard!' Ian exclaims. 'That's what you say.'

'Wizard!' I repeat and, looking at Mr Sinclair again, I see he can smile. It's sort of twisted, but his eye smiles too, and I like him.

'I'm sorry I caused so much trouble taking Ian to Red Pool Spinney yesterday,' I say unprompted.

37

'I tell you what,' he whispers as his wife preens next to Pa. 'It sounded a splendid adventure.'

'It was,' I tell him. 'But a bit scary.'

'It would not have been a true adventure if it had not been scary.'

I smile and go closer so I can see the gold prop more clearly.

'They're going to give me a new eye,' he says. 'Do you think I should have it to match the one I've still got?'

I remember a collie pup with one blue eye and one brown. It had been run over by a waggon. 'I'd have them to match.' I look at his remaining eye. 'That one's a nice brown.'

He nods. 'I shall take your advice. Shake on it.' We shake hands and Ian puts his arm around my shoulders.

Pa is still being talked at by Mrs Sinclair, so fast he can't disentangle himself, but I see everyone is back in their places, waiting for him. Soon there is a general pause in conversations, heads are all turned our way. I see Grandmama Bennett touch Ma's arm. In a moment, Ma gets up and, while she talks to some on the way, there is no doubt it is Pa she is heading for. She touches his arm, nods briefly to Isabella, then takes Pa back to his duties.

There is no need for him to bang the table as he usually does. Everyone is paying attention already. Pa stands to make his speech. He thanks everyone for all their hard work during the year – 'Which has brought a successful harvest home once more.' He thanks everyone for being there, his wife for all her hard work, and all those who have helped, then he says, 'We have an added attraction this year . . .' My eyes are not the only ones that go to Mrs Sinclair, but Pa is talking about a gramophone. 'It comes straight from duty with Kenneth Sinclair's squadron and will be playing dance records, outside on the yard behind the barn here, after our usual sing-song and, of course, our soloists.'

I had seen George sweeping the rear yard earlier, but thought it was just Noel, or Pa, finding him a job.

Mr Riddington, who is leading bass in the Church choir, is

always first soloist, and sings 'Trumpeter What Are You Sounding Now'. I don't know whether he makes his voice tremble like a trumpet on purpose, and I can't tell from people's faces. Then Mr Thompson, who is choir master, rolls his 'r's, wipes his brow and beats his breast as he recites 'The Death Bridge of the Tay', which is when 'The night and storm fell together upon the old town of Dundee', and a train full of people die as the Tay Bridge collapses into the river – and everyone laughs. Mr Thompson is serious and makes it really come to life. I don't think anyone understands how frightening a storm at night can be.

Noel wipes his eyes, but it's with laughter, and Pa too, as he rises to ask if we have any more brave soloists.

I think it is the *brave* that makes Ian call out that his dad knows a poem. Ian's voice is so clear and confident, but there is a pause, an embarrassment, and some fiddling with glasses and other things on the tables.

'Come on, Dad,' Ian urges.

A stern woman, Mrs Oldham, wife of the verger, whispers, 'The boy shouldn't push his father into the limelight like this.' I feel Pa hears and is about to announce general singing, when Mr Sinclair gets to his feet. People begin to be still, to watch and listen.

He stands very upright. He has a handkerchief kind of balled-up in his right hand. Ian's gaze is fixed on his father, full of pride, while Isabella Sinclair sits, head bent, plucking at the flowers on her sleeve.

'This is a poem written by a young American airman. It's called High Flight'. I learned it from a fellow guinea pig at East Grinstead Hospital. I think it expresses what many pilots feel about flying.'

I can't make out every word, as he struggles to free them, to send them ringing up into the beams of the barn, I just net phrases. *I have slipped the surly bonds of earth – I've wheeled and soared and swung – I've chased the shouting wind along.*

I remember the waterfowl rising from the lake, circling, and I wish I was sitting next to Ian. I see that, no matter what's happened to him, Mr Sinclair wishes he was flying still, while Mrs Sinclair would rather be anywhere than next to the man struggling to make his words clear. He wipes his mouth quickly when he has finished.

Pa leads the applause, and some of us, me especially, cheer. Then Noel, who I do love, gets to his feet and begins 'For He's A Jolly Good Fellow', and everyone gets up and sings at the tops of their voices. Dawdie cries, and others wipe their eyes, but not me, or Ian . . . or Mrs Sinclair.

Then Pa announces our usual sing-song, and we're all relieved to launch into 'One Man and his Dog Went to Mow a Meadow', with the choir descanting away, just like they do when there's an anthem at Church. Then there's harvest hymns. 'We plough the fields and scatter the good seed on the land', and on to 'Come Landlord, fill the flowing bowl until it doth run over, For tonight we'll merry, merry be, and tomorrow we'll be sober'.

As we finish this one, we hear the gramophone is playing 'Coming In on a Wing and a Prayer' outside. I rush outside and find Stella and her sister, Mary, with a storm lantern on a table by the gramophone and a pile of records, which they are excitedly going through. 'Oh, Joss Loss! "In The Mood",' Mary exclaims. 'What a pity the Yanks aren't invited, could do with a bit of jitterbugging.'

Lots come outside now, some carrying their drinks, but they find ledges to put them on and are soon dancing, people I never thought of as being able to. Mr Thompson dances with the verger's wife, Noel does a kind of clog dance in front of Dawdie, but she tells him off until a progressive barn dance, then she agrees to dance with him. Pa takes me in. We go round and round, in and out, then *stamp*, *stamp*, we bang our feet. Ian's dancing too, and his mother, of course. I see Mr Sinclair and can't wait to be his partner. When I am, he swings me off my feet, flying, flying. He's fun. Ian calls to him across the circle and his dad waves back to him.

Then comes the Gay Gordons. The men whoop and yell as they spin their partners around. It's exciting to watch and, as I walk slowly around the outside of the dancers, I feel as I did in the harvest field, as if it is all unreal, a golden dream, only this time it is a sun-coloured harvest moon and several storm lanterns that light the picture. The dancers whirl and it seems to me the night is all about flying, about soaring and chasing the wind. I like this moment of looking on as much as the dancing. I feel I am drifting on the brink of many things. I whirl all by myself.

I am like a moth, a moth drawn sometimes into the light, sometimes retreating out into the darkness to watch with big globe eyes that see everything. I feel I *could* fly if I concentrate, try hard enough. I am brought to earth by a sharp crack, a noise like a slap, though no one cries out. Then I can hear someone whispering, hissing low and fiercely.

I flatten myself to the wall, not to overhear, but to steady myself. I'm giddy, like a moth fascinated by brilliance, finding instead something hard and cruel, sent spinning to the ground.

'Showing me up in front of the Bennetts.'

I recognize Mrs Sinclair's mean, tight vowels.

'Go back to the bloody house. I'll see you in the morning.'

There is another sound, a gasp, a clatter of shoes as someone tries to keep their balance. 'Your precious dad's not going to be around all the time, remember that.' This is a threat.

'Ah, Bess.' My father is coming over towards me. 'About bedtime. Stella's . . .'

He does not get any further, for Mrs Sinclair emerges from between the outhouses. 'Edgar, you promised me another dance.' She takes his arm, but he questions her with a frown.

'I was looking for the old house you told me about, your machine store that was your family's original home,' she says.

'Not a very good time for that,' he says, but he seems to have no option but to take her in to the dance. He only has time to remind me of bedtime with a nod.

I wait until they are on the far side of all the dancers, then am

41

about to see if I can find Ian, but he's standing by my side in the shadow of the wall.

'Are you alright?'

'She can't slap Dad, so she slaps me.'

I can understand that no one could slap Mr Sinclair's face, but we are quiet as Pa and Ian's mother circle back towards us, pass us. She is laughing up into his face. We both turn away and slip back into the shadows between the buildings. We walk on until we are in the stable yard, where the traps wait, the ponies snuffling and pulling at hay nets.

'We won't stay here,' he says. 'We always keep moving on. We never stay anywhere long. Mam decides its a *dead end* or *dull as ditchwater*, no one interesting. Then she persuades Dad to move.'

The thought makes me sad. 'Everyone loved your father's poem,' I remind him.

'Dad's alright wherever he is, and I like it here, but . . .'

'You can't be sure.' I want to fight on his side.

'I've seen the signs. The only thing that might put her right is a trip up to town,' he says. 'And Dad has got to go to hospital for another operation, so you never know. I'll go to my aunt's in Peckham and Ma will live it up in town for a night or two.'

'Live it up?' I ask.

'Go to shows and dances. Visit her old haunts, she calls it. My aunt says she shouldn't, being married and everything.'

'What did your mother say to that?'

'She said, "Married to what?", and that she wouldn't have married if she hadn't had to.' His voice is very low. 'They didn't know I was listening.'

'Doesn't she love your dad anymore?' I think she should love him more, to make up. 'Anyway, I think he's smashing.'

We reach the lane. 'You go back now,' he says.

He begins to walk away. I don't want him to go, I need to do something for him to make him feel better.

'I've never seen the Red Pool,' I call out, and he stops, then turns and comes back to me.

'But you took me there. You knew the way.'

'Yes, but I'd never been to the middle of the spinney, only watched fox cubs on the edge.'

His face is as bright as a new painting as he looks straight up to the moon. My heart begins to thump, his answer is so important to me. 'I wonder if there's another way in, perhaps a drier way,' he says, his face eager, smiling properly as he looks at me once more. 'We must go again.'

'See you at school on Monday,' I say, free now to go back, now he's said what I expected, no recriminations, no questions, just the expected promise.

I run home, sure the Sinclairs must have stayed. I retrace my steps through the yard, come near to the place where I heard the slap, and George stumbles out from the same place. He grins and shrugs. 'Just looking,' he says, and goes off into the barn.

I go quietly round the corner to have a look. I have to go right to the end of the long narrow gap between the out-buildings before I find anything or anyone. Then I can *hear* something, voices, and round the corner under the eaves of the machine store, I see Mrs Sinclair's pale dress, then Pa's dark suit. He is holding the lantern that hangs outside the machine store and opening the door for her to go inside.

'Ooh,' she breathes, all excitement. 'I just love old buildings.'

'Pa!' I exclaim and run to him.

He raises the lantern. 'Thought I told you bedtime,' he says, but smiles as I lean against him. I look up into Mrs Sinclair's face and see she would like to do worse than just slap me. I shrink back behind Pa's legs for a moment.

'I'm sure it's time little girls were in bed,' she says in a little-girl voice.

'Come and tell Isabella the story of the beams,' Pa says. 'Then it's off you go.'

I shake my head. 'I just wondered where you were.'

'Alright then, off you go.' He squeezes my hand.

I turn and run then, I don't want to tell Mrs Sinclair any-thing. Turning the corner, I slip down and bang my knee really hard. I keep running towards the open space and the dancing. I don't stop to look who's there, I just go on towards the big barn, where I can hear Noel reciting 'The Village Blacksmith', and others clapping and urging him on. Before I reach the doorway, I meet Ma.

'I was just coming to look for you,' she says. 'Have you seen your father?'

I stoop down to peer at my knee. 'I fell down,' I say. 'I think my kneecap's been knocked sideways.'

She tuts. 'You wouldn't be running if it had. Where have you been?'

'Mrs Sinclair sent Ian home. I walked him to the lane.'

'Oh! Why? Where is *madame*?' She looks around.

I'm not sure why I don't tell her.

'Never mind. Come on, I think it's time for a good many of us to call it a night.'

From inside the barn, we hear Noel call out, 'Time, gentlemen, please!'

Ma laughs and says, 'That's from the man first here and always last to go.' She leads me by the hand. We go through to the hall and I look towards the portrait of Great-Great-Grandpa Bennett. Silently I remember that he started this harvest supper thing.

Upstairs, Ma says, 'You're very quiet.'

I finish undressing and climb into bed.

'I thought you were enjoying yourself. Apologizing to Mr and Mrs Sinclair wasn't that bad, was it?'

This will take some thinking about, but I remember something Pa explained the other day. 'It was like that curate's egg,' I say.

'Oh! Bess!' she exclaims, but she agrees the evening has been good in parts and, if not bad in parts, a bit shaky.

'Don't forget your prayers,' she says as she tucks me in.

'No, like a boat,' I beg and she laughs, protests she is too tired, but she reaches over me as I lie straight and still in the middle of my mattress. She pulls all the sheets and blankets and tucks them tight in the far side, then she hauls up the nearer side of the mattress and tucks the other side in just as tight, so the mattress curves up around me in a boat shape, like a hammock.

Rocked in the cradle of the deep. When I'm alone, I whisper the line from a hymn. It is how I feel, rocked in a safe cradle against any storm, protected, all unease pushed away.

Four

'**M**ornin', Bess. Good harvest supper?'
I had not heard the horse coming up behind me on the verge. I stop, balancing my bike with one foot on the grass. 'Mornin', Greville.' I reply in kind, but envy him his cob, which I haven't seen before, and which must have been bought specially for him. 'You'll be hunting, then?'

'Whenever I'm home. And you?'

He seems heartier on a horse, or perhaps more expansive because he's not under his grandmother's eye. 'Sometime,' I answer.

'No mount yet?'

'I could always ride Ma's.'

'Doubt it.' He circles the handsome cob in front of me. 'I hear your ma had, in her day, one of the best seats in the county, and likes her horses with a bit of spunk.'

I resent the phrase *in her day*. She may not be as young and flighty-looking as Isabella Sinclair, but she's not *old*. 'Isn't *spunk* rude?' I challenge.

'Ah! Sorry, school talk. Should say *spirit* to sheltered lassies.'

'I'm not a sheltered lassie, and I'll ride as well as my mother one day.'

'First catch your horse, lassie.' He raises his cap, then touches the cob with his heels. 'Mustn't miss the best of the morning.' He trots off waving his riding stick in what looks like a scornful farewell.

I swallow the urge to shout after him, remember Pa saying he could well be our landlord for the good valley land one day.

I listen to the hoof beats quicken as he begins to canter, turning off the lane to ride the bridleway. 'I've got more spunk than you'll ever have!' I wave my hand airily, mimicking his gesture with his silver-knobbed stick, then pedal on towards the village.

'Hiya!' A call comes as I cycle round the first corner into the Main Street. I had expected this to be deserted, with everyone already in Church for the morning service, but it's Colleen, with the elder of her two brothers, Roy, who's carrying a bucket. I skid to a halt.

'We're fetching water for old Mr Lyons,' she says. 'His rheumatism's bad.' Mr Lyons is one of the few villagers left who have to rely on the village pump.

'I'm taking . . .' I indicate the roll of magazines, *Woman*, *Woman's Own*, *Woman's Weekly*, tied to my handlebars. She knows Ma buys the magazines for the stories, but Grandmama and her companion, Miss Seaton, often knit from the free patterns. The Bennetts all have jumpers and cardigans that have been on the covers of magazines.

'To your gran,' she finishes for me. 'Why aren't you at Church?'

I had asked much the same question at breakfast. Usually it was all talk after guests, particularly after a party, and I had never known the ritual of Sunday morning service after harvest supper to be broken. This morning my question had brought an uneasy silence. Pa had cleared his throat, but it had been Ma who'd said, 'We'll go to evensong.'

Then Pa had accused me of hardly speaking to Grandmama the evening before. 'You can use this morning to make up,' he had told me.

I had appealed to Ma, but she had just said, 'You can take the magazines.'

'George ses you 'ad dancin' last night.' Roy sets the bucket down. Colleen's family live next door to Noel. Roy's older, but he and George are friends.

I nod.

47

'Saw him early on, he can't talk of nothing else – the dancing, . . . and things.'

Roy is the one member of the Rawlins family I have never been comfortable with. Now his fresh red lips look as if they are watering for more details as he stares at me.

'Mr Sinclair brought his gramophone, and—' I break off as Roy's grin widens.

'—and Mrs Sinclair,' he says, his grin becoming a leer. 'Mrs Sinclair likes dancing, and that with your father, George ses.'

I do not answer, remembering the loud clap as Mrs Sinclair struck Ian, and the look on her face when Pa raised the light.

'George ses you and 'im had a competition to see who could eat the most.'

'So?' I challenge, thinking George says far too much.

'George ses he followed Mrs Sinclair round the back of the sheds.' He pauses to look up, poking his face near to mine. 'And guess who she was with?'

This has echoes of stories Colleen has told me about what goes on behind the bike sheds at the big school. But any doubts about how I feel about Roy Rawlins have gone. I hate him.

'I'll tell Noel what a gossip his grandson is, *and* my pa. He won't want him to work on our farm.'

'I'm only telling you what 'e said.' The threat to George's employment makes him defensive, but then he nods at me, pushing his head forward again. 'Your father – he danced with Mrs Sinclair.'

'I danced with *Mr* Sinclair. So what!'

'George said it was your pa who went off with her –' he pauses, sneers – 'in the dark.'

'Pa had a lantern,' I tell him, and he roars with laughter.

'Wants to see what 'im doing then, don't he?' He advances his face at me again. 'Not all he's made out to be, your *pa*, is he, Miss Bennett?'

I throw my bike down, and finding his bucket in my way, I kick it hard. The heavy zinc thing crashes and rocks, loud in the quiet street, while in Church, voices are raised in sing-song ritual responses.

'Stop it!' Colleen suddenly shouts. She stoops to pick up the bucket and thrusts it at Roy. 'Come on. See you, Bess.'

'And one thing quickly leads to another,' Miss Maude Seaton, Gran's companion, is declaring as I walk slowly towards the kitchen door. 'According to Mrs Oldham, what began as a good Christian celebration became almost a pagan rite. It was a sad day for this village when the Sinclairs decided to come here.'

Miss Seaton would have seen Mrs Oldham at eight o'clock communion. She had been the one who had said Ian shouldn't push his father into the limelight.

'That man flew Spitfires for his country, and is still suffering. How could you, or anyone, say such a thing?' Grandmama asks.

'Anyone who's seen his wife, with her wandering eye and floozy clothes.'

'There was nothing amiss that I was aware of.' My Grandmama's reply is, for her, quite sharp.

Miss Seaton makes a noise like a snort, and she adds, 'You'd be too busy attending to the conventions, what the Bennetts *should* be doing and saying. Don't sound like Edgar was worrying what people thought, either at the table or later – dancing with her time after time. You must be afraid he'll turn out to be his grandfather all over again. These things often miss a generation.

'Maude! There are limits beyond which even you must not go. You really should not voice such things.'

There is both shock and anger in my grandmama's voice. It makes me rush to the open doorway and shout, 'No, you shouldn't! You're as bad as Roy Rawlins.' Miss Seaton's face stiffens in indignation, then she steps back with a cry as I hurl the magazines at her feet. 'Ma's sent those.' Before she can recover, I run back to my bike, the wooden blocks on the pedals rapping my shins as I miss the fixed pedals on their first circuit.

I can hear Gran calling, but I keep going, back along the Main Street, round the church corner, out of the village. I don't stop until I reach the lane to the farm and the field where our hunters have been put out.

I lean miserably over the gate and watch the big beautiful animals. Having gone to make up for something I had not really done, I have now committed a much worse sin. I lean my head on my arms and feel life will never be the same again.

I can hear the horses coming to the gate. I wait until I feel a muzzle touch my hair. This is Pa's horse, Ebony. He snorts gently. I know he understands I'm in trouble. I climb the gate and he waits for me to slip from the top bar on to his back. We often do this. I lie there, my arms around his neck. 'I love you, Ebony. I love you a lot better than nearly all people.'

As I lie there trying not to think, the horse lowers his head and begins grazing again. With my ear to his neck, I can hear and feel the chomping of his teeth, grinding, grinding the grass.

Pa's grandfather? Not his *great* grandpa Bennett, whose portrait hangs in the central place on the hall wall, not the man who began the harvest suppers. My mind locates a portrait in the dark place at the far side of the door into the dining room. His name was Alexander Bennett, and he has a central parting in his heavily greased hair, a waxed moustache and a silky maroon cravat. I try to remember more, but Alexander Bennett is not much talked of. I do remember Gran explaining that, *He was my father-in-law, your father's father*, in a voice that fell into such a heavy silence that I couldn't ask more.

I am still wondering about this when I see George scuttling along the lane. I slip from Ebony's back, run to the gate, leap over and on to my bike, soon catching George up.

'If you say another word about my pa, I shall tell him, and he won't take you on the farm when you leave school.'

He shrugs. 'I didn't—'

'Well, just don't!' I tell him, echoing many an unreasoned telling-off from Miss White. 'Where are you going anyway?'

'To the farm,' he says hesitantly. 'Your grandmother wants

to visit. Miss Seaton asked me to come and fetch the pony and trap right away. Is that alright?' he asks me, and I know we'll never have another eating competition, or ever be casual friends again.

'I suppose so,' I answer. 'If that's what you've been told, you'd better go and do it.'

He gives me a quick glance under his eyebrows, touches his cap, and walks on.

As he disappears I know everything *has* changed. There will be people I can give orders to, like George, others I must be friends with, like Greville, and those I want to be friends with, like Colleen and Ian. Ian is becoming a very special problem. I am sorry all over again about throwing that pink and golden pear away. I stand irresolute, flicking the lever of my bicycle bell so it just tings to the beat of the nursery rhyme about the King of Spain's daughter who *came to visit me, and all was because of my little nut tree* and nothing would it bear *but a silver nutmeg and a golden pear*.

George will be at the farm now, going to the kitchen door, cap in hand, then harnessing Bonnie to the trap and coming back to fetch Gran. I'm not sure what will happen after that. I turn my bike and ride back to the village. Seeing a group of people outside the church, I turn off towards Colleen's home and meet a group of ladies in Sunday clothes coming from the Methodist morning service. Before they are near, I knock at the door of the terraced cottage. Colleen opens the door before I have time to wonder what I will say.

'Been to your grannie's?' she asks.

I nod.

'You're alright,' she tells me. 'Roy's round George's.'

'Oh!' I nearly say I know George is not there.

'Hello, Bess.' Her mother comes in from their backyard. 'Surprised to see you on a Sunday. Not at Church?'

'We're going tonight instead,' I say.

'Good idea after a late night. Colleen can make the two of you a cup of cocoa, if you like.'

'Yes please.' The excuse to stay more welcome than the drink. The smell of our cocoa is soon joined by that of the Sunday roast beef, and all too soon the oven door is opened and the first course of Yorkshire pudding and a huge basin of gravy are placed in the centre of the table. Mrs Rawlins scoops up a few stray leaves of thyme from the table and cleans her hands of them over the gravy, so these too add to its fragrance.

For the first time, my presence is silently queried by the other children as chairs are filled. Mr Rawlins comes in beaming, red-faced, and jovial, and throws his cap on top of a pile of mending on the dresser.

'To the minute,' Mrs Rawlins greets him.

'Timetables must be adhered to,' he answers, then looks at me. 'Come to call for our Colleen, 'ave you?' But before I can reply he says, 'Set the child a place, then. Don't want her watching us eat.'

'I should go,' I protest, but Mrs Rawlins says, 'Well, I'll cut you a slice of pudding. You might as well have that before you go.'

' 'Course!' Mr Rawlins exclaims, and pulls a chair in next to him, then asks, 'Where's our Roy?'

'He went to see George,' Colleen says, nodding for me to eat the puffy slice of Yorkshire pudding covered in aromatic gravy that has been put before me.

'Well, he knows what time Sunday dinner is. If he can't make it . . .' He pauses mid-forkful and looks down at me. 'You're here. You can eat it.'

Colleen nods eagerly at me. 'Then I can walk Bess home afterwards,' she says.

'Bess had better go after the Yorkshire. Don't want her in trouble at home. Then you'll go to Sunday school,' her mother says cheerfully.

'It's lovely,' I say between mouthfuls, and it is, and I wish with all my heart I had brothers and sisters, and was not the only Bennett the future rests on. I decide to stay as long as I can, but Mrs Rawlins eases my chair out from under me as soon as the pudding course is over.

'See you at school tomorrow,' Colleen says, not leaving her place.

I'm not too confident about this, but thank her mum again. She nods back, and Mr Rawlins begins to hone the carving knife on the steel, as a very moderate joint of beef is put before him.

I ride to the top of the street. There are not many people coming out of the Sir Robert Peel or the King William IV, which face each other across the village square. Not too many think more of their dinners than their Sunday beer.

I *have* to go home. It's just a question of waiting for the moment when I can't put it off any longer; then I guess I'll cycle back as fast as I can. I see myself arriving, putting my bike in the machine store, being greeted by Patch. Animals are always pleased to see you, no matter what.

Then I see Roy Rawlins. He is lurking inside the wooden porch built all around the pub door in the war, so no light showed as the door was opened and closed during blackout hours. A man comes out of the pub and hands him a bottle of beer, drops some change into Roy's hand and goes back inside.

I cycle over to his side of the road and just stand looking at him.

He has the bottle to his lips when he sees me. 'What d' you want?' The beer froths from his lips, runs down his chin. He wipes it away with the back of his hand.

'You won't be the only one who can tell tales. I could go and tell your pa where you are.'

'Clear off.'

'You're expected for dinner.'

'*Expected for dinner*,' he mimics.

'Bess!' I spin round and see my father in his farmyard trousers and open-necked shirt, standing within a few yards of us. 'Wait there.' He indicates a spot across the road, then turns to Roy. 'You're under age. You'd better put down that bottle and get to your home.'

Roy advances with some bravado. 'We're not beholden to you Bennetts.'

I am across the street on the spot indicated. Pa does not move as Roy approaches him. For the first time, I feel a touch of admiration for Colleen's older brother, but not for long. Pa waits for him to come nearer, then reaches out and takes the bottle from him, turns and marches into the Sir Robert Peel with it. Roy and I stand as if transfixed, then, as the sound of the door opening comes again, Roy moves away, but shouts, 'I'll get my own back. You see if I don't.'

Pa walks the opposite way, towards Grandmama's. I see our car is already there, and the worst thing to me is that it is Sunday and Pa has come into the village dressed only in his farmyard clothes – no jacket, no tie.

I hesitate as I reach the yard. He stands by the kitchen door, waiting. He shakes his head at me as I open my mouth. I lean my bike where I left it before, and go to the step just as I had before, and half expect the magazines to be still on the floor, but they are gone.

Pa leads the way to the parlour. The fire is lit in here in the afternoons, but with the two upholstered armchairs occupied by Grandmama and Miss Seaton, to sit down means the black horsehair sofa which pricks the backs of your knees. The only thing I have ever liked in this room is the wild bronze horses whose reins are stretched for by helmeted warriors. These rest on the mantelpiece either side of a large bronze clock. It is ten minutes to two o'clock.

'So, now,' Pa begins. 'We'd better have some explanations and *another* apology. We'd better begin with the magazines. That seems to be the start.' He looks at me.

'No,' I protest. 'It was Roy Rawlins who started it . . .' I begin. 'Then Miss Seaton was saying . . .' I stop as I see the expression on Gran's face. She looks as if it is *she* who is in trouble. She looks stricken. In my head I hear Noel's voice: *She do look like a whipped cur.*

'So, what did Roy say?' Miss Seaton asks.

'I don't think we need concern ourselves with what Roy said,' Pa interrupts. 'It's what happened here that I'm concerned about.'

'He said Pa took Mrs Sinclair to the machine store in the dark.' I need to vindicate Pa. 'And it wasn't true. Pa had a lantern.'

I look from his set features to Gran, who is quite still, to Miss Seaton, who nods as if this confirms the truth.

Encouraged, I go on. 'And Miss Seaton said that Pa was like Grandpa Alexander Bennett, who's in the dark corner of the hall, and that things skip a generation.'

'What!' Pa exclaims.

Miss Seaton now looks as though she wishes I did not remember quite so well, and Grandmama gets up very quickly, comes to take my hand. I stand by her side as she turns to Pa. 'All this child is guilty of is defending you.'

'From what!' he exclaims. 'From what?'

No one answers.

'My dear boy, for goodness' sake,' Gran says at last, then pauses. I feel her take a deep, deep breath. I even imagine I can hear her heart pounding. 'Maude heard things at Church this morning, petty tittle-tattle, that's all, about last night.'

'And Alexander Bennett, my grandfather. How does he come into this?'

'He was guilty of some minor indiscretions years ago,' Grandmama says and stares straight at Pa. It feels as if she is not breathing at all now. 'Some have long memories and loose tongues.'

I know she means Miss Seaton, but Pa rounds on me again. 'My daughter's indiscretions have begun early. I come in answer to some garbled message you send by George. I find my daughter standing outside a public house with a young under-age lout drinking beer from a bottle, and my own mother defends her.'

Again no one speaks, so he goes on. 'All I *do* know is that Bess is getting into trouble, at home and at school, keeping the most unsuitable company – and something has to be done about it.'

The feeling I had earlier that everything is changing, that my life is about to be turned upside down, swamps me. It's like the moment I fell into the bog, only this may be worse. I have no hero, real or mythological, to pull me out. I squeeze Grandmama's hand, so she looks down at me. 'I *was* on Pa's side,' I tell her earnestly.

'I know that, dear girl.' She looks hard at Pa and leads me from the room. In the kitchen, I ask, 'What did Miss Seaton mean when she said about things skipping a generation?'

Grandmama shakes her head for a moment, as if thinking hard. 'Perhaps,' she says, 'it's looks. Perhaps Maude thinks your pa looks like his grandpa. That does happen sometimes.' She smiles and lifts down the cake tin, but I can't think Alexander Bennett's portrait resembles Pa one bit.

Shortly afterwards, Pa loads my bike into the back of the car and we go home in silence. Questions from Ma are met with the adamant decision, on Pa's part, that I am perfectly unharmed, that there's been too much talk and not enough do already, and they will thrash it all out later.

We have a very late Sunday lunch and we go to evensong. At this time of year, when it grows dark during the service, I usually like the feeling of standing between Ma and Pa, particularly when we sing hymns like 'For Those in Peril on the Sea', and the wind and rain beat on the great stained-glass windows above the altar candles. The inner light seems to run over the surface of the glass so the colours are dark and sombre.

Later that night I hear a long discussion going on downstairs.

Five

T he muffled voices, the rising and falling cadences, are like distant waves finally lulling me to sleep, while they are changing my life.

Too soon I learn that my father's plan is to send me immediately to the City Girls' School. I don't believe this, think it's just a threat to keep me on the straight and narrow. My parents talk, but I'm not included and they don't see eye to eye as they argue the merit, or not, of sending me early to my mother's old school as a weekly boarder.

They won't listen to me, and my hurt is responsible for the things I do, and Miss White tells me that, anyway, she would rather have my room than my company.

It's as if my parents too are practising being without me. My father keeps me at a distance, sending me back to the house when I attempt to follow him into the yard or the fields. I feel rejected, and suspicious when Ma meets me from school and we go to the village farm on the day Miss Seaton is away. Every Friday she goes on the bus to town, shopping, having lunch with a friend, then tea in the Turkey Cafe, which smells of fresh ground coffee and has an enormous elaborate turkey, in brass and coloured enamels, above its window.

I am right to be uneasy. This visit is to be like a pebble thrown into a lake. It makes ripples that go on and on.

'You've heard what Edgar proposes.' The words fairly burst from Ma's lips as soon as Gran has hugged and kissed us. Then I'm offered the chance to go and look at the postcard albums. These are kept in the bottom of the huge glassed bookcase in the parlour, and are a treat usually reserved for Boxing Day afternoon when we go for high tea.

I sit before this cupboard, pausing, unwilling to pass up on this treat, but aware just how desperate even Gran is to be rid of my company. The postcard albums are huge fat books, which have to be lifted carefully or the pages, each loaded with six postcards, easily split from their bindings. I carry each one carefully to rest on the highly polished table.

I know the contents of the first two almost by heart. There are photographs sent from Jersey in the 1920s, by Gran's brother, who was a seed merchant, went to live in Jersey and died during the German occupation of the Channel Islands. There are charabancs of people in top hats, trilbies, caps and hats going on outings; a coloured one from the 1930s, Blackpool Illuminations, with Blackpool Tower leaning to one side. On the back is my father's writing: 'Dear Mother, It did look a bit like this, especially to Bert. Your loving son, Edgar.' There are postcard pictures of some of the Hunts – the Quorn, the Fernie, the Duke of Beaufort's; some film stars of the silent screen; views of abbeys and cathedrals. Left to help myself, there are other albums I have hardly looked at. These are even bigger. When they are opened out, one views twelve postcards, and these are not just views, holiday-place postcards. Many of them are birthday and Christmas cards, with real lace and silk, tassels and intricate cut-out paperwork like marvellous doilies.

There is another book, more ponderous than any of the others, placed at the bottom of the cupboard because it is the heaviest, with its brass hinges and clasp. This is the family Bible. It has been so long undisturbed that it is stuck fast on the bottom of the cupboard. I can't move it, and perhaps some-thing of my own troubles transfers to this book. If I have to be uprooted, so does it. I push my fingers right to the back and prise and struggle until it gives – suddenly leaving me sitting on the floor with it on my knee. Where it has come from the shelf is much darker.

I porter the book to the table, and, unlatching the brass clasp, lift the front cover. Here the Bennett family tree is set out. The handwriting is large on the first flyleaf, the ink faded to a faint buff colour on the ivory-grained paper.

My finger traces the words and names:

> Samuel Lionel Bennett purchased this Bible on the same day he added the Main Street, Counthorpe, land and farmhouse (in the tenancy of one Samuel Cox) to his family holdings. October 30th 1839.

'And,' I add, 'began the harvest suppers.' On the next line I trace his name again:

> Samuel Lionel Bennett married Louisa Clowes, March 24th 1840.
> Edgar Paul born 1841, died aged three weeks.
> Edgar Samuel born 1843, died aged four months.
> Charlotte Mary born 1844, died 1846.
> Alexander Edgar born 1845, died 1922.

Alexander, the one in the dark place, my father's grandfather, the one Miss Seaton had talked about with a spiteful note in her voice. His name is written in again in larger writing.

> Alexander Edgar Bennett married Harriett Edna Spiers, April 8th 1865.
> Lionel Harry born 1865, died 1942.

My grandpa. I remember him: a kind stooping man. I can remember my gran sitting with her hand over his as he moved gently to and fro in the rocking chair that stands in the far corner of this room.

Underneath is another line of proud copperplate writing and I think Grandpa would have written this in.

Lionel Harry Bennett married Jessie Augusta Barton, 1888.

Grandmama.

On the first line underneath this marriage is my father's name:

Edgar James born 1900.

Below this is a name that is scored out, not born and died like all the poor Edgars and Charlotte of the 1800s, but *struck off the register*. I'm not sure where I know these words from, but they have a dire and dreadful ring in my head.

The next entry is my father's name again, then my mother's, and mine at the end.

I like seeing my name, but I find the heavy scoring-out just below my father's name more intriguing. It is done with such thoroughness, I can see the indentations made by the side of the nib. A thinner paper would be sliced through. I turn the page to see if there is anything readable underneath. I think I can make out an *A* and a *b*. Perhaps someone wrote in *Alexander Bennett* again by mistake. Bennett with a small *b*.

I go to the door, wondering if I dare to ask. Perhaps I could come when my gran is alone on another Friday. Then I hear my mother say in an intense voice, 'Edgar insists she should be sent at once. I've tried to convince him that the right time would be when we planned for her to go, *after* she's finished primary school next September. The age when weekly boarders always go,' Ma agonizes. 'She'll be the odd one out if she's sent now. Would you try to talk to him?'

'My dear, don't you think I've tried? He just recites all his so-called reasons: wrong company; bad behaviour; troublemaking; unsuitable friends; impressionable age.'

'She doesn't deserve this,' Ma says in a low voice. 'He'll break her heart.'

I go back to the Bible, run my fingers over the crossing-out, then go to the little desk and, from the drawer where the notepaper and envelopes are kept, I take out the bottle of ink, a pen and blotting paper.

With a well-loaded pen, I score out my name, then blot it. I have to do it four times before it is as well blocked-out as the other name. Then I put the Bible and all the albums back and sit and wait at the table.

As we walk from the house, we are both very quiet and are quite startled when someone runs up behind us.

'Hello, Mrs Bennett. Hello, Bess.' Ian has been to the shop, the Co-op, and is carrying a basket of shopping: bread, a tin of cocoa, and two other items which have been weighed up into the Co-op's stiff blue paper bags, the ends neatly mitred by Mr Cox, the manager, or his wife. I am a bit surprised at Ian's nonchalance, because to be caught in the village carrying something – a bag, basket, bucket, bundle – can lead to being ridiculed by your schoolmates, something it takes days, or weeks, to live down. *Gotcher basket?* I can hear the gibes. Ian doesn't seem to mind at all and swings the basket to and fro. No one who passes could miss it.

We walk together to their cottage. 'Come and see Dad. He's in the garden,' he invites. Then, looking at me, he adds, 'And we have to go for another operation.'

Though I see Ma was going to refuse, she now changes her mind. Mr Sinclair is sitting in the garden, his face turned up to the afternoon sun. He doesn't hear us.

'Dad.'

He turns, then springs to his feet. 'Excuse me, ladies. Just hardening-off the old scars ready for the next session.' He beckons us to the garden bench. I let Ma sit there. I perch on some large slabs of stone with Ian.

'We're going to build a rockery. I'm drawing the plans,' Ian says, and he and his dad exchange smiles. 'We found masses of rocks under weeds at the bottom of the garden, but' – he looks away – 'we might not get it done now.'

'Ian was saying you were off to London again,' Ma says.

'Much sooner than we thought. The hospital has an unexpected slot, so we whizz off tomorrow. Isabella wanted to thank you again for the harvest supper, and –' he pauses to wink at me with his one eye – 'for Ian's adventure.'

'I think, the less said about that the better,' Ma says.

'Isabella felt it was the right thing to do,' he says. 'And, in fact, she left to visit *you* about half an hour ago.'

'You mean—' Ma begins.

'She's on her way to your farm. You're jolly old paths must have crossed.'

'We've been to my gran's,' I supply.

'In that case,' Ma says and gets up, 'I shouldn't want your wife's intentions to go to . . .'

It's as if we all wait for the right word.

'. . . waste.'

'My dear lady, you must stay for a cuppa.'

'I'll make it.' Ian leaps up. He keeps surprising me: shopping, making tea. Not the kind of things my father often, if ever, does.

'Thank you, but I won't. I've had tea with—'

'Can I stay, please?' I beg. 'I didn't have tea, and I won't see Mr Sinclair or Ian again for ages. Shall I?'

'Why not let Bess stay. We'd love to give her tea. In fact, she can butter the bread, and Ian can walk her home afterwards.'

Ma agrees, wishes him good luck and is away. Ian and I go in to make a cup of tea. I take Mr Sinclair a cup outside, so he can stay in the sun. Ian shows me his drawings of the rockery. 'That's the ground plan, and this –' he turns the page of his drawing book – 'is how it should look in a few years, when the plants have grown.'

We both stare at the watercolour impression, both thinking that in a few years *everything* will be different. Even next week will be different. Ian will be at school in Peckham, but I'll be going away for the longest time. School, school, school, until I'm at least sixteen.

In the street, someone screeches and calls, 'You're on!' They'll be playing *tick*. It could be Colleen. She'll never have to go away. She'll go to the local Modern School, leave at fourteen and get a job in the village hosiery factory with a lot of our schoolfriends. They'll be together and friends for all their lives.

'What do you think?' Ian asks.

'I wish we were older,' I say, and tell him about being sent away to school. 'I wish we were grown up.'

'We will be one day.' He closes the drawing book, puts it in a drawer and pulls out a cloth, which he throws expertly over the table. 'Are you being sent away because of Red Pool Spinney?' he asks.

'Not exactly.' The memory of what Miss Seaton had said about his mother makes me rush on. 'There are other things.'

'Like?'

'I don't think they like me talking to Roy Rawlins.'

'Who's he?'

'Colleen's big brother.'

'Do you talk to him?'

'Not if I can help it, but Pa saw me talking to him when he was drinking a bottle of beer.'

'Oh!' He looks at me with a kind of puzzled respect. 'How old is he then?'

'Sixteen.'

'He's not old enough to drink beer.'

'No.'

He fetches jam from a cupboard, and I butter the pieces he has taken off a crusty cottage loaf. It doesn't seem to matter that his mother is not there. She is not mentioned again.

'I've taken your advice,' Mr Sinclair tells me when we are at the table. 'I've ordered my new eye to match the one I've got.'

'Are you going to get your eye this time?' I feel excited about this. 'Wizard!' I exclaim. 'That's wizard. Does it take long?'

'There's a bit of reconstruction to do first,' he says. 'We shall be away for a couple of months at least, probably until after Christmas.'

63

'Bess'll be gone too.' Ian tells about my being sent away to school.

'A weekly boarder means you will be home every weekend,' Mr Sinclair consoles me, pushing the jam pot my way. 'You must come to tea again the very first Saturday we come back from London.'

Mr Sinclair shakes hands when I leave, and we both wish each other good luck. Then, as Ian walks me home, he says, 'You know Dad won't be able to see with his new eye? It'll just be artificial, a glass eye.'

'Are you sure?' I shall feel devastated if this is true. 'They can do wonderful things nowadays.'

'Quite sure,' he answers. 'He'll be able to take it out.'

This, I thought, only happened in stories. I recall one where a white hunter took out his glass eye to frighten a tribe of cannibals. I am still worrying about this when we reach the horses' field. I stop at the gate, and Ian's astonished when the horses come neighing and squabbling up to me.

'I've never seen horses do that before.'

I know he's not watched many horses.

'They're jealous of each other! They both want to be closest to you. Which do you like the best?'

'I love Ebony.' I introduce him to both the horses and laugh when he jumps back as Glenda tosses her head.

'I'm not used to them.'

'You lifted your hand too quickly, that's why she jumped. She's skittish.'

He smiles and grimaces at me.

'You're not afraid of cows.'

'No!' He is emphatic about that.

'Colleen is. She's scared to death.'

'Will you miss . . . your friends?' he asks as he comes more circumspectly to touch and rub Ebony's nose.

'Of course.'

'Me?' he asks.

I nod.

'I'll miss seeing you around at school and that.' He pushes his hand into his pocket and brings out his penknife, it's blue, with a blade at each end. 'Look.' He pulls out the larger blade and shows me where he has scratched his initials on the base of that blade – *I.S.* – and, opening the other, he points to where he has more neatly inscribed *B.B.* on the opposite blade.

'My initials.' I feel as if I have been initiated into something very important. There I am, engraved in metal, not just written in ink. 'That's really nice.' I think about our initials folded into the knife and in his pocket while we are at different schools so far apart. Then I realize he is giving me the penknife and my heart thumps. This is too much for him to part with, his knife. All boys have knives.

'You don't really want me to have it, surely?' I ask.

He nods, but I think he feels sad doing this. He closes the blades, then reaches for my hand and puts it into my palm. 'Look after it, won't you?'

'Of course, I will, always.' My gratitude knows no bounds. 'And I'll always give it back if you ask me.'

He smiles down at me, shaking his head, and I know he is kind and brave like his dad. 'I wouldn't want you to do that. It's a present – for Christmas.' Swiftly he stoops and kisses my cheek. 'You'll be alright from here, won't you?'

I stand holding the penknife, not really taking in the fact that he intends to leave me at that very moment.

'See you, then,' he says, and his voice makes a funny broken noise as he first walks, then runs back along the lane.

When he is out of sight, I realize how bright his hair was against the autumn colours of hedges and trees, brighter even than the flower colours of his rockery picture. I ache for him to come back. I need to hear again that he really does want me to have this present.

This is my second gift from Ian Sinclair. I won't be throwing this away, and I realize I shall always think of it as his, or perhaps as ours, belonging to both of us. I feel better when I have this clear in my mind: belonging to both of us. Ours.

Carefully I pull out the two blades. I'd love to carry it around with me always, use it every day, but I can't take chances with a sacred trust. Perhaps I could use it just once, then put it away for ever, hide it. I push the larger blade back into place, then cut an experimental notch out of the top rung of the gate with the smaller blade. It's really sharp and makes a very satisfactory cut. I suddenly know what I will do. This one and only time, I will use this gift, but I have to work on the third rung down because the horses are too inquisitive.

It takes a time, but soon I have cut the two sets of initials on the gate. The curves on the *S* and the *B*s are the worst to do. I sit back on my haunches well pleased. I have crossed myself out in ink, been etched in metal, and now carved myself in wood. I fold away the blade and take a vow never to use the knife again.

By the time I reach home, I know exactly where I shall put the gift.

I am surprised to find Ma in the orchard by herself.

'Have you seen Mrs Sinclair?' she asks.

I shake my head. 'Isn't she here?'

'She couldn't have been coming here after all.' She smiles, holds out her hand to me. 'Nice tea?'

I nod and am almost quite happy, the penknife in one hand, Ma's hand holding the other, but when we reach the kitchen, I see there is an unopened letter on the mantelpiece. Ma sees me looking and turns away, so I know it's from the school.

I run upstairs. I have something important I must do. I find a piece of brown paper left from covering a book, and a piece of ribbon left from the pincushions. I make a really neat parcel of the knife, folding the brown paper neatly, getting the ends of the ribbon level and tying a double bow. Then I cut a piece of paper out of the back of an exercise book and write on it, 'Bess Bennett's most precious penknife.' Then I add, 'Please note, this also belongs to Mr Ian Sinclair,' in case anything happens to me and I'm not able to tell anyone. I fold and tuck the note beneath the ribbon.

Ages ago I hid a rabbit's foot I had begged from Noel – which Ma said was disgusting. If that is still where I hid it, I shall put the knife there. I pull out the top left-hand drawer of my chest and carry it to my bed. I search in the wooden cavity where the drawer came from, and at the back I feel the foot. It is disgusting now, more shrunken, with the bones sticking out. There's a stone too. A brown, smooth rock with white lines that look like matchstick men. I had forgotten this. I put the knife in with the foot and the stone and slide the drawer back and close it.

When I go back down, my father is in the kitchen, standing with the letter in his hand and saying, 'You weren't here, so I just made her a cup of tea, showed her round, then walked her part way back along the footpath.' He stands tapping the letter on his fingertips.

I am mesmerized by the letter. Please, please, God, make my father love me again and not send me away.

'Showed her round' – Ma's voice is tight – 'the house?'

The letter is still being waved about. I bargain: God, if you could just manage for there not to be a place until after Christmas, that would give me a few more months. I could be so good, Pa would change his mind.

'No, not the house.' Pa scornfully dismisses the idea.

'So, where?'

'She wanted to see the machine store . . .'

'The machine store!' Ma exclaims.

'It was the original farmhouse,' he reminds her, but looks at me. I know he's thinking I've said enough already, so keep quiet. He goes on: 'She was interested when she saw the family portraits. You remember.'

'She pretended to be interested. She is, in case you are *still* unaware, scandalizing half the village.'

He shook his head. 'What do you mean?'

'Her attitude to her husband is despicable. Then there's her flirtatious manner. Mr Faulkner, the butcher, hardly feels safe, I'm told.'

Pa hoots with laughter. 'Dennis Faulkner! He'd be like the cat with the cream, lapping it up.'

'Edgar!'

'You're a prude, Fay,' he says, but his voice is quite gentle. 'That's your trouble.' He looks at me as if he is quite surprised I exist, then goes on: 'This is not the time for such a discussion.'

I grip my thumbs in my palms and want to crouch down as he thrusts his forefinger under the flap of the envelope, tears it open, then says, 'Bess can start immediately. We're to take her to see the headmistress on Monday at four thirty.'

All kinds of reassurances come my way in these last two days at home. Ma is going to learn to drive the car so she can fetch me home every Friday.

'And take me back!' I accuse her.

'You'll only be going nine months early,' Ma reassures. 'It is where I went to school, you'll like it.'

'It's nearly a year! All my friends are here.'

'You'll make new ones very quickly.'

'No. No, I won't,' I sob. 'They'll all hate me, and all the teachers will be like Miss White.'

They tell me all kinds of things, promise all kinds of things, except that I need not go. No problem of any kind is allowed to stand in the way. I go to the City School, where I am shown photographs of my mother as a girl in a hockey team. These hang near the doorway of a gymnasium named after my mother's family, The Topham Gymnasium. I'm to be allowed to go home each Friday, but must be back in school by five o'clock on Sunday evenings.

I think longingly of the village school, which will soon be full of painted robins and snow scenes. At St Catherine's we have a proper crib with plaster figures in the school chapel, and we learn descants to the carols and our parents are to be invited to a service of nine lessons and carols. I just long for the holidays.

On Christmas morning, before anyone is up, I pull out my dressing-table drawer and take out the small parcel. I wonder if Ian is home. I think of the other desperately unhappy girl at St

Catherine's, who cut off her hair with a pair of dress-making scissors thinking she would be able to go home early, but they just tidied her up, and she looked awful as well as feeling awful.

But Christmas does have one glorious surprise: a pony, my parents have bought me my first pony. He's dappled just like a rocking horse, with a silvery mane and tail and is called Sparkle. Noel says he's *a picture-postcard pony*. I'm to ride to the Boxing-Day hunt, which always meets in the centre of the village.

'When you see Lady Philipps at the meet, remember to thank her for helping us find Sparkle. Without her, we might not have found anything half so nice.'

Greville is at the meet on his handsome cob, and edges his way over to us through the crowd. 'Mornin', Mr and Mrs Bennett, mornin', Bess. You made it then! He's fine, isn't he. Just right for a . . . young lady.'

'He's beautiful,' I say, laughing at the tease. He knew I would think he was going to call me a lassie again. 'He can jump too. I'll show you.'

Then, among the crowd of villagers, I see Colleen waving. All her brothers and sisters and Mr and Mrs Rawlins are there, nearly all the village is there, even Mr Collins, the headmaster. It's quite thrilling with everyone together laughing and talking, waiting for us to move off. I feel it's like the end of a pantomime when all the cast come on stage to wave goodbye. Then I see Ian standing with several other boys, but we are moving, the master is calling us in. 'No stragglers! Come on, young Miss Bennett, you've got to live up to your mother's reputation in the field.'

'She'll do that,' Pa says, seducing me back into loving him, but I so urgently need to tell Ian his penknife is safe, I need to talk to him, but I have the awful feeling that I may not be able to do that for a long time, perhaps years and years.

Six

1947–53

T he next six years is a strange time. The depths, and the
heights, are mine.

It is a time when I am compressed within boundaries, fenced
in as effectively as any farm animal. I am corralled at school,
where I am educated, groomed – and restricted to being just the
part of me that the system approves of.

I am happy when from time to time the wonder of learning
takes me over; happy when, that very first harsh winter, I learn to
ice-skate. In a few months I am an expert. The feeling of flying
across the frozen lake in the city park is perhaps that of escape.

Skating brings more than this. Towards the end of that first
long frosty season of 1947, my housemistress waits for me as I
glide to the bank. 'If you carried yourself off the ice as you do
on, you would look and feel a totally better person. Your
mother is a Topham, for goodness' sake. Put your shoulders
back, hold your head up, have some pride.' She delivers her
quiet rebuke and leaves me.

When I find a moment alone, I practise standing against a
wall and pushing my shoulders back to it. At first, just the
roundy top of my back touches the brickwork, and I have to
push fiercely back for my shoulders to square up on the
lavatory wall. I stand as if nailed there, trying to memorize
how it feels so I'll know if I ever slouch again. I'll remember the
scorn in my housemistress's voice, as I remember our village
headmaster reminding me who my father was.

70

So, I try to remember that I am not after all just Bess, but a Topham, *and* a Bennett. Yet, in assembly at St Catherine's, we were given the maxim, *This above all: to thine own self be true.* At sixteen I do not find it easy. So many emotions pull me in so many ways. I have to pretend to be a different person depending on where I am, and who I am with. It feels less than honest.

At home at weekends and during holidays, things are not the same. The old moments of closeness are rare. With my mother they come when she picks me up from school on Friday nights and we go to a theatre, or the cinema, before we drive home. We are both animated and chatter on about the dramatic performance of Flora Robson, or the comedy of Wally Patch, or the thrill of the film *Phantom of the Opera* with Claude Rains, but we fall silent as we near home, our enthusiasm for the arts kept within the confines of the car.

The close moments I share with my father come when we have chance encounters in stable doorways, but most precious are the times when we ride together, me on Ebony and Pa on Glenda. Then we forget there is less laughter than there used to be, that three used to be close company.

It seems to me that the differences are embodied in a new collie, Bracken, which goes to sit by Pa's knee if I try to fuss him. At these times, in the farm kitchen with the three of us, and the dog pressed tight to Pa, there is an atmosphere as if my parents are trying harder because I am there, and I wonder if only the dog is being honest and that they'd all be more at ease without me.

Only Noel is the same, and I think he is happier now his grandson, George, is in the Army doing his National Service. I certainly am, for encountering George had become a constant embarrassment, his decorum awkward and ridiculous every time he tugged his forelock to me. I hope the Army will change all this. Everyone says it makes men of boys.

The strangest thing is that I've come to feel most at ease when I am at the Hall, although not with anyone in particular, because the two girls are both at Cheltenham Ladies' College.

71

When they leave soon, I suppose they will either become part of life at the Hall and in the county, or go off to finishing schools somewhere abroad like Switzerland, or do a Cordon Bleu cookery course.

Greville is around a lot of the time because he is learning to manage the estate and the farms when he comes of age. Lady Philipps says she can't wait to have things out of her hands, but Pa says she'll always be the second pair of hands on the reins.

Perhaps I feel at ease because I have never paid more than short visits to the Hall before this time. I have no comparisons to make between then and now. So, very happily, I take up the invitation to skate on their lake whenever conditions are right, and often when Greville is busy I am quite alone, spinning and speeding between boathouse and willows. This is freedom, the release of the mind from everything, the wonderful moments when my body, my brain, my life is in perfect equilibrium. I try to ensure I skate when Greville is busy. He is a competent skater, but never transverses the lake, skating round and round the circumference like a goldfish in a bowl. I see him at other times, of course. There are always two hunt meetings at the Hall during the season and tennis parties in the summer, when Anthea and Daphne are home from Cheltenham.

Then what seems like a chance encounter with Lady Philipps at Gran's results in an invitation to go and ride a *brave young mare* she has bought, which needs *a brave young lady* to bring it to its best and then show it. Tommie, their groom, is to give me lessons to polish my jumping style.

A course of jumps is set up at the back of the Hall. Noel, who thinks Irish Tommie is good for the mucking out but little else, comes to watch. He soon warns me to, 'Mind what you point that animal at. She's a flighty piece – she'll jump anything you set 'er 'ead at. You mark my words.' I toss my chin up at him. 'Aye, I know all about your new haughty ways,' he shouts at me. 'But don't you take too many risks. Don't you give your mother more grief.'

I soon know he's right about the young grey mare, for if I

don't get Phoebe straight at the jump, she'll take the side supports just as willingly. It's exhilarating and heart-stopping. Eventually I think about the other thing he shouted after me – my mother can't have *more* grief, unless she has grief already. I shall ask Noel when the opportunity comes.

By the time the City Agricultural Show comes around, I am registered for the junior showjumping, and I also beg to be allowed to show Ebony in the ridden-hunter class. That horse and I have spent so many hours together, I want him to have a moment of real glory before he is put out to pasture with no more hunting to look forward to. I know it's possible to do well, for his groomed coat shines like his name, and when he is plaited up, his hooves blackened and oiled, he's so proud of himself, he arches his neck and everyone's heart warms to him.

Ebony is kept in the stable all the summer night before the show, so he knows something different is happening, and I creep into the warm straw and dungy smell of him well before Noel arrives.

'Hi, hi,' he greets me. 'Trying to get my job.'

I've made a start but Noel takes over and soon he is hissing and sucking over the most thorough grooming I've ever seen. I plait up and stitch the mane, which I am good at. Pa says it is stitching all those pincushions for Miss White.

'Noel?' I begin as we reach a state of readiness when I know he's about to send me off for breakfast.

He drops a brush back into the box. 'Don't I know that tone of voice,' he says. 'Now what have you got on your mind?'

'What you said when I was jumping Phoebe.'

'Mind what you're aiming that grey at? Aah, glad you took heed.'

'No, about not giving my mother more grief.'

He turns away, stoops to pick up the brush again. 'Broken bones take a long time to heal. Don't want you in that infirmary.'

'*More* grief, you said. To have more, there must be some already.'

73

'Teach you *something* at that posh school, then.'

I am determined that he will not escape that easily. 'There *is* something. It's not the same at home as it used to be.'

'You're growing up.' He pauses to look at me, then looks away quickly and adds, 'You're grown-up – a young lady. It's not for me to make comments about my boss.'

'About Pa?'

'About things that are none of my business.'

I wait, but he does not add *or yours*, and the grief, whatever it is, feels more ominous.

When I go into the kitchen, the new collie whines as if unsure of me, and Ma tries to ply me with a cooked breakfast. 'Everything ready?' she asks.

'Noel's finishing him off.'

'And Tommie will be getting Phoebe ready. What excitement!'

I do not answer.

'Bess?' she queries. 'You *are* alright? Not too much for you?'

I want to say no, it's not too much, I could ride and jump all day, it's you and Pa I'm worried about. 'Noel said—' I begin.

'Noel said what?' Pa comes into the kitchen already in shirt and tie, hair slicked down, rubbing and clapping his hands as if eager to begin the day.

'He wondered about the horsebox.' I lie, unable to risk making this grief Noel knows about worse.

'Everything's arranged, he knows that. Tommie's driving over from the Hall. You and I'll go with him and Noel in the horsebox with Ebony. Your mother's driving the car in. Then Noel and Tommie will come home with Ebony when the hunter classes are over, and they'll come back with Phoebe for the showjumping in the afternoon.'

'What could be simpler!' Ma exclaims and we laugh. I see the glance between them hold for a second, cling hesitantly, then slide away.

'Is that all OK with you, Ma?' I ask.

'Of course, dear.' Her glance questions the need for the enquiry.

The part of the showground reserved for competitors is like a separate world, an encampment full of lorries, jeeps, cars, horseboxes. Many have already unfolded tables and umbrellas, claiming sites for later picnics. Most people know each other – most know Noel and greet him with booming good humour. One or two comment about not thinking to see *that old horse in the ring.* Noel winks at me. 'Take no notice. We've got 'em worried.'

Pa fusses, anxious about me and about his old horse. He needn't. Ebony and I understand each other. When we're both ready for the ring, and I'm as smart as my ride, we have a private word. I mount and lie briefly on his neck, as I do in the fields and whisper that this is his day. He knows it. When I sit up and adjust my heels and knees and hips in line, I catch Pa's glance and it makes my mouth fall open, for I see pride, love and almost a sense of awe in his eyes.

'You'll walk it,' he says. 'Off you go.'

Noel has told me to think of it as a hunt meet, only with a bigger crowd, but I am resolved to think only of the horse, of showing him off. We walk into the ring with his neck arched like an arab stallion. I feel, if I just knew the magic word, he would break into a kind of *pas de seul.*

There are fifteen of us in the class, most of whom I recognize from local hunts. The man who is acting as announcer on the loudspeaker is Mr Pacey, the Philipps' land agent, whom I see whenever I hunt.

We parade around in a walk, then trot and canter; then we are called to stand in the middle in a line. The two judges, a man and a woman, both in immaculate hacking jackets and jodhpurs, walk around and inspect horses and riders, pulling a strap here and observing a jacket and stock there. I look straight ahead, and so does Ebony. The woman pauses and looks at his teeth, then asks how old my horse is. 'He's twenty,' I tell her proudly. She steps back and views him all over again. 'Then he's an even bigger credit to you and your groom,' she says, and moves on.

Then six of us are picked out and we have to trot and walk around again. Three more are sent out of the ring. My excitement mounts as I realize we are in the last three, we will get a rosette. Already I imagine how proud he will be, say with the yellow ribbons of third place attached to his brow band. But it's first we get, a red rosette, and Ebony tosses his head as if he loves the glimpse of the ribbon ends by his eye, and I pocket the envelope with the prize money.

'Give them another circuit.' The lady judge smiles and nods me on my way. We go almost in extended trot, he is so proud, but as I reach the far corner and prepare to come down before the grandstand, Mr Pacey on the loudspeaker system calls out: 'Come on, Bess! Let's see what he can really do.'

I circle Pa's hunter in the corner, squeeze with my knees, then tell him it's to be all-out with my heels. We pass the main stand at full gallop and in a wild enthusiastic storm of cheering and hallooing. Then, as we thunder on, I hear cries of alarm from the less knowledgable crowd at the far rails. They're wondering if I can stop.

'That was wonderful,' Mr Pacey cries over the loudspeaker. 'I'm sure you'll agree when I say we shall look forward to seeing more of this young lady.'

Now we have come to a halt, people all around clap and cheer, and I hear one voice adding my name. 'Well done, Bess!'

I catch sight of a tall blond boy. He towers above the children on the ropes. He waves for a moment quite wildly, then, as if remembering about horses, he points in the direction I shall leave the ring.

Once back in the collecting ring, Noel holds the bridle while I slip off into Pa's arms. 'What a girl!' he exclaims. 'Well done!'

'Done what you set out to.' Noel holds out his horny old hand and we shake.

'*We* did it.' I pretend to wipe sweat from my brow, then lean forward and give him a kiss. He becomes overwhelmed and mumbles something about may I always be as happy as I am at that moment.

'I'm so proud of you both.' Ma comes hurrying from the ringside. A man I don't know comes by and pats me on the shoulder. 'Her mother's daughter,' he says, touching his hat to Ma. 'I remember you giving a similar display at about the same age.'

Ma laughs happily. 'Nice to see you.'

'Who is that?' I ask, then only half listen to her reply about it being some friend of Grandpa Topham whose name she cannot remember, because I can see Ian hovering.

'Won't be a minute,' I say, and run over towards him.

'Hi!' I exclaim, aiming for the screen aplomb of Bette Davis, but I'm too excited to be cool.

'You were wonderful,' he says, and for a moment I think we will grasp hands, but instead he makes a shaky upwards, throwaway, gesture. 'Thundering along without moving a muscle on that great charging horse.'

I laugh. 'It doesn't feel like that, it feels like a great charging half ton of horse, and me bouncing about on top.'

He laughs, and it isn't like Ma and Pa's tentative laugh in the kitchen. Our laugh meets, melds. There is no bother about the Bennetts, or Tophams or Sinclairs. I am Bess and he is Ian, and our only history is a pear, Red Pool Spinney and a penknife. We walk over towards my parents, aware they keep looking our way, but just before we get there I say, 'I've still got your penknife safe.'

'After all this time,' he says, and there is wonder and laughter in his eyes now.

'Do you want it back?' I ask. 'I always promised I'd give it to you.'

He looks down and smiles, in a way that makes my knees weak. 'I'd much rather know you are keeping it for me,' he says in a very low voice just before Ma greets him.

The greetings and the talk are very formal, and soon Ma and

Pa are kind of summing up Ian's life to date, his scholarship to a public school, and approving of his ambition to become an architect. The conversation flows smoothly until he says, 'I just love old buildings.' The words draw my gaze from Ian's golden hair to Pa, as they trigger a memory, the first harvest supper after the war and a lantern held aloft. Wasn't that exactly what his mother had said about our old machine store the night I found her and Pa going into the old outbuilding. Pa's eyes are not wide enough for scrutiny.

'Will you stop and have some lunch with us?' Ma asks.

'I'm meeting my dad,' he says and, glancing at his wristwatch, adds, 'I should go. He'll wonder where I am.'

'How is your father?' Ma asks, but Ian only smiles as he turns to go.

'See you around, Bess,' he says. 'Perhaps before the holidays are over. Colleen was asking after you. I often see her walking home from the factory.'

I think he looks cool in every sense in slacks and open-necked shirt. I think about his mother, and the sound of the slap she gave him at that same long-ago supper.

My images of the day are to be mainly of Ian, so casually dressed, and that gallop past the grandstand, then later the ignominy of the swing around the same corner in the afternoon's showjumping. It is as if, distracted by the speed of that earlier lap, I come round too fast and there's no time to straighten Phoebe for the double in front of the stand. We hit the side supports of the first and cannot take the second. I circle out from between the fences, go back and rejump it perfectly, to applause, but it is the end of my competition.

Afterwards, Lady Philipps comes and congratulates me on the ride and says we'll do better next time out. Greville, who never shows or competes, is dignified but consoling. His suit, his bearing and his immaculate manners succeed in making me feel like an assistant of Tommie's who's failed on her part of the job.

It also succeeds in irritating me, particularly when he stands so close, wanting to help, and I catch the smell of perspiration and hot tweed.

'Why don't you take your jacket off?' I ask.

For a few seconds he looks astonished, then he makes a half gesture to the bundle of official shield-like badges dangling on red silk cords from his buttonhole. 'It would not be right, would it?' He pauses and glances at my black hunting jacket. 'Not for me, not for us.'

His mild and very reasonable reply makes me feel a bit ashamed and I let him help after all, let him take Phoebe's saddle as I pull it off.

'Put it in the horsebox.'

Noel comes hurrying from his place at the far side of the grandstand, near the double, and dismisses him, before going on to give his opinion of my performance. 'Too fast, not thinking what you were doing.'

It's true, for, turning to ride down the line of jumps in front of the grandstand, I remembered seeing Ian after my gallop. The thought had been enough for me to lose concentration for a few seconds and put myself out of the competition.

It is not something I do the following Monday, when I calculate exactly at what time Colleen will leave the village factory and walk the two hundred yards to her home. A short walk. Timing is more than important here.

I announce that I'm going to visit Gran, which I intend to do afterwards. By taking a detour through the fields and lingering outside the post office, I manage to be going past the factory just at six o'clock, when the workers begin to come out. Two older women come first and retrieve bicycles from racks. One, in the act of pedalling away, is waylaid by a young boy. She is not best pleased, talks angrily to him, then opens her purse and gives him a coin. Then a whole group of girls and young men come out, laughing and calling to each other like children released from school.

'Yeah, yeah, yeah!' a girl with her arm linked in Colleen's calls to a tall youth. 'We've heard it all before, haven't we?' She turns back to Colleen and pulls her closer to her. It makes me feel like a ghost from the past, a poor shade watching new people enjoy village life. I feel a pang of pure jealousy.

Then Colleen notices me. She waves, frees her arm from her new friend and comes running across. I hold out my arms, for Colleen has always grabbed me in moments of emotion. 'It's been ages,' I say as we laugh and hug.

'Bess! I *thought* you'd be here today.'

'Why?' I ask and smile over her shoulder at her new friend. I recognize an even keener jealousy in the look the girl now gives me, and there is spite there too.

'I have something for you,' she says, with a swift glance at her new friend, who obviously does not mean to be ignored.

'You'd better introduce me to your *friend*,' she demands.

In a few moments I learn her name is Hewitt, Adeline Hewitt . . .

'Adeline?' I query, thinking it's a nice name.

'We call her Addie in the factory,' Colleen tells me. 'Her mother worked for the Americans.'

Addie slaps Colleen quite hard, leaving a red mark on her forearm, and tells her off for saying such a thing.

'Ouch! Now what have I said wrong? She's so Bol-shev-ik.' Colleen pronounces one of Noel's favourite words in exactly the way he does, as if it's three words, and we share esoteric faces.

I wonder about Adeline. After all, there is still a big American base nearby. It was much bigger during the war, when the Flying Fortresses were based there, but a lot of local people still work on the base, and are the envy of many, with their handouts from the PX store.

'So?' Addie suddenly demands of me. 'What are you thinking?'

'That it's a nice name. It sounds American.'

'Yeah, So?' Addie's voice is full of aggression now. 'So what?

You're like a few more in this place, all hats and no drawers.'

'Hey!' I protest, but Adeline makes a dry spitting noise and nods to indicate someone behind me. I turn to see Mrs Sinclair just leaving her house.

'Y' know what I mean, kid?'

The fake American accent and the approach of Isabella Sinclair make two words leap to my mind: *more grief*. Colleen protests that Addie is just talking stupid and has always got a chip on her shoulder. Addie, meanwhile, is on a steamroller course to discredit me as an unworldly idiot, no rival to herself as a best friend for Colleen.

'Y' know, dearie, just like playing mums and dads.'

'Addie, stop it,' Colleen orders.

'Talk of the factory, it is. Don't know what we'd talk about if it wasn't for Mrs Is-a-bella Sinclair.'

'So, who is she supposed to be *laying*?' I hope the word will shock her, but she just answers the question.

'Oh! The butcher, for one.' She pauses and laughs. 'And you *are the* Bess *Bennett*, aren't you?'

I glance quickly towards Mrs Sinclair, but I need not have worried. Far from recognizing any of us, from the expression of set fury on her face, it is more likely that she has not even seen us.

'What do you mean?' I demand of Adeline. I feel my face blaze, my fists clench, but *whatever* I may be reading into this statement does not worry Adeline, who is screeching and staggering about with uncouth laughter. Next moment she is pushed aside as Mrs Sinclair strides between us, heading across the Main Street towards the bus stop, her eyes staring blind with anger.

'Hey!' Adeline protests, but I want to know what Adeline means.

'What are you insinuating?' I demand, but Colleen intervenes, as is her wont, by grabbing my dress, but this time to drag me out of the way and put herself between us.

'Come on,' she says. 'Our mam'd love to see you.' She takes my arm now and turns her back on Addie.

81

'Just a minute . . .' I begin. 'I want to know what she's implying.'

'Leave it, Bess,' Colleen implores. 'It's only what she hears at the factory. Go on, clear off, Adeline Hewitt.' She begins to march me forcibly away.

'See you tomorrow, then.' Adeline, addressed by her full title, is at last convinced that Colleen is not to be re-enlisted on her side this time. She struts away with a loud sniff, and hurt at the rejection in every line of her body.

'Adeline *Hewitt*?' I emphasize, for there are more Hewitts in Counthorpe than any other family.

'Exactly. The whole story's in the name.' Colleen's turn to sniff now, but she goes on quickly: 'I've got a message for you from Ian Sinclair.'

'A message?'

'Come up our entry.' It's always been one of our places for telling secrets.

The black gate to her entry is next to their black front door. Colleen unlatches it quietly, we both step in and walk to the middle point, which we know from long experience is the safest place not to be overheard by anyone either from front or back. She grabs my hands and gives a little shiver of excite-ment. 'He wants to meet you.' She nods affirmation of the statement, and her gesture over her shoulder into the distance gives the clue.

'Old Brig?' I ask.

She nods and gives a little thrill of excitement. 'He's going to be there at half past.'

'Half past six.' I bite my lip as my heart thunders about at random. 'It must be nearly that now.' Just as I go to look at my wristwatch, the church clock chimes the short four chimes of a quarter past the hour.

'If anyone asks, I'll say you were with me,' she supplies.

'Thanks. I should go, then . . .' And when I still don't move, she giggles.

'Your first proper boyfriend,' she enthuses. 'You've beaten

me to it. Go on.' Her voice drops to conspiracy level to ask, 'Tell me all about it afterwards?'

'I'll meet you out again tomorrow.' I make it sound like a solemn vow.

Then she pushes me out of the entry and I run past my grandmama's like a blinkered horse, not wishing to be distracted, and telling myself I don't care if Miss Seaton is on her usual street watch.

Some fifty yards past the last house, the roadway splits. I take the left fork, which leads to the tiny hamlet of Packman some three miles away.

I am soon in sight of the Old Brig. The bridge is ancient, narrow, originally constructed for packhorses to carry produce to distant towns, given a name when it became a meeting place for boys and girls – who collect wherever there is running water – and in the evenings by sweethearts, or clandestine lovers.

A stile next to the Old Brig drops back from the line of the hedges, so that anyone walking in the lane cannot immediately see those meeting there. In fact, it is possible, if need be, to slip over the stile and lie low behind the hawthorns, but many of the lovelorn have found time to stand and cover the stile with carvings of initials, hearts and arrows.

Now it is my trysting place. The thought takes my breath and I have to pause as I come within twenty or so paces. I wish to appear like a young woman, not like a child rushing to play in the brook.

I walk now, no slouching, hardly breathing. I wonder if Adeline Hewitt has delayed me too much, or am I too early? Such sweet anguish. I stop at the point where I can still be seen from the lane, but also by the one who is waiting at the stile.

He is leaning on the top rail, but straightens when I come into view. Then I have the strangest feeling that I am on the brink of some new journey, that if I take just one step, that first step, I am beyond recall, committed.

Ian holds out his hand and I go to him.

Seven

I t was the moment Edgar helped his daughter dismount at the City Show that he knew a major new consideration had come into his life.

It was the sensation of his hands sliding over her slim hips until they found purchase in the hollow of her waist. By the time he had steadied her on her feet and kissed her cheeks, he was in a state of bemusement. She had laughed, probably thinking his expression was still one of amazement at the red rosette on his old hunter's brow band. But it was stupefaction he felt. The girl he had helped on to his horse – the daughter he adored, had tutored, done all as he saw best for – had undergone a transformation, had come back from victory in the show ring a young woman. He had seen, week by week, how she was becoming so, of course he had, but it had taken the run of her sensual litheness through his hands to shock him into accepting the fact.

He had watched her lean over to kiss the equally bemused Noel, found himself clearing his throat to fend off tears for the lost child. Fay had come running from her seat in the centre stand, and he had reached out automatically, as if to take her into his arms, as if he needed comfort, something to hold on to. 'So, what do you think of our Bess now?' At least he was sure of their mutual celebration at her success. These days it often felt she was all they had in common.

As Fay gave their daughter a great hug of congratulation, a bright glance came his way, though it was probably accidental, as she was beaming all around, but he saw again the girl he had fallen in love with twenty years ago. He felt a stirring of hope that things might be better between them. Perhaps he might again find the patience and the energy to do all she needed of him – every time. Then a man walked between them, breaking the spell as he made some comment about Fay as a girl.

The next moment, Bess was off across to the entrance gate, and when eventually she began to walk back, he recognized young Ian Sinclair. The boy hadn't been around much, he couldn't remember the last time he had seen him. He was quite the young man. 'Jesus Christ!' he blasphemed under his breath as the thought linked with his discovery of his daughter as a young woman. He was overwhelmed by an impulse to go and punch young Sinclair on the nose that minute.

'Edgar!' A low exclamation made him glance at Fay, who was watching him intently. Her voice was audible only to him. 'The boy is innocent, whatever you and his mother have done.'

'Done?' he queried, but she held his gaze steadily, stared him out. How long had Fay known, or was she guessing, assuming that because their love life had stalled, Isabella Sinclair was the one he was going to?

When he looked back, she turned away from him and looked towards the young couple laughing together, and coming slowly towards them – but not before he had seen the hurt and reserve come back to her eyes.

He'd like to have told her. Yes, that's always been your trouble, your bloody reserve. Never let your heart rule your head, always under control. A deeper part of his mind adds dourly, regretfully, Not like me. *Not like me.*

He watched with a growing sense of apprehension as the youngsters strolled closer, and he wondered whether Bess would take after him, or her mother? How would she respond to her lovers, her husband? What disappointments and traumas lay ahead for her?

'No.' He said the agonized word aloud, then, seeing he had startled Bess and Ian, he exclaimed with loud and false heartiness, 'So, young man! How are you?'

*   *   *

In the afternoon he watched Bess dismount again, after not such a successful event. This time it was Greville Philipps whose hands reached up to help her. He wondered how strongly this young man felt the sensation, as he stood so close helping Bess untack, taking the saddle from her. Noel had walked over to him, jerking his head at this second young man of the day. *Flies round a honeypot, they'll be.* He had shown his displeasure by not looking at his man, who had muttered some stupid remark about pardoning him for breathing.

This young man with his daughter struck Edgar very differently from young Sinclair with her, not nearly so disturbing to his equilibrium. He felt no desire to punch young Philipps on the nose. These two were more natural together, more of a natural pair. What, in time – in perhaps no more than a year or two – all in the county might call a good match – and all the better if the deal he was contemplating came to fruition.

Howard Pacey, the Philipps' land agent, had tipped him the wink that Dan Paget's farm was to come on to the market, and his employers were not looking to enlarge their properties at that time. Adjoining his own land, it would be a natural enlargement of his property. It would certainly stretch him financially, but he had land enough, buildings enough, for security and he knew his bank manager well enough. It would give Bess a better standing, for it would all be hers one day – hers and the man she married.

He watched the attentive Greville, and the idea of the Bennetts' and the Philipps' acres joined gave a mental image of pasture, arable and woodland as far as a man could imagine. Then another aspect of the situation struck him. Was Bess already being considered in the same way by Greville's grandmother? Her reputation had for many years been that of a woman who got her way in most things, one way or another. There was a lot to suggest it might be so.

His glance rested on the young grey mare, steaming and restless after the excitement of the ring. Had this been bought on a whim, as Clara Philipps said, or had it been bought solely for Bess to ride, to take her more often to the Hall? Then there was the long-standing friendship between his own mother and Clara, and now this tip-off from their land agent.

He had been wavering about the land, largely because of the extensive and totally neglected Red Pool Spinney, which had even daunted the local wartime agricultural committee. It would need much time and money, both of which he would be pushed to spare, and he would have to be seen to make movements to reopen the public footpath. This had risen to the level of a public scandal, with a national ramblers' association taking up the same protest he had himself made years ago. If he bought, he would have to put his money where his mouth had been. He would probably have to get in contractors with some kind of a bulldozer to clear the footpath through. He could put right the general neglect through the rest of the woodland later, a section at a time. There was in any case, he told himself, no farmer worth his salt who would want a large spinney in such a state of bad husbandry.

He straightened up, he'd have a word with Pacey, tell him he'd decided. He smiled to himself. He had done the hard part, made the decision. He would buy.

He nodded with satisfaction as he watched Greville taking the reins from Bess while she threw a sweat rug over the young mare's back, good to see them working together. He must check with his mother where the family Bible was. It would soon be his turn to enter the purchase of another farm, another extension to the Bennett fortunes. The last one must have been – he remembered with some excitement – the last one had in fact been the very first entry, for hadn't Samuel Bennett bought the Bible and the Main Street property at the same time? 'In 1839.' His lips moved and he tried to calculate how many years ago that was, 1839 to 1953. Time there was an extension of the Bennett properties, time to move on.

He drew in a deep breath and looked up to the sky, to the future.

'I've been watching you,' Fay began.

'Ah!' he exclaimed, but softly, and holding back the words, *Nothing new there, then.*

'You've just made a decision.' She paused, turning statement into question. 'To buy the Paget farm?'

'How do you come to that conclusion?'

'I've known you long enough. Some kind of weighted look fell away, your brow uncreased.'

He nodded.

She looked pointedly from him to Greville Philipps and Bess, as always, protective of Bess and her sensitivities. 'I hope it's for the right reason,' she said.

'I think so. Yes, I know so.'

'You'll have to clear the spinney,' she added. 'After all . . .'

'I've thought of that.' It had sounded sharper than he intended, and he regretted that. They fell so easily into the way they had developed of dealing with each other these last years – remark and immediate retreat, sniping at each other – and, these days, not usually bothering to return the fire.

It always came back to that bloody spinney, he thought. It had been wood from the spinney that had been responsible for his first real involvement with Isabella Sinclair. It had been that dreadful winter of 1947, when coal was at a premium, with roads impassable and the coal sent south by boat frozen in on the Thames. Trees from the spinney bordering his land had fallen, flattening his boundary fences. He had become concerned about his mother's fuel supplies. Noel too had run out of coal, so the men had gone to the spinney, sawn away the branches then dragged the trunks back to the farmyard with chains, the shire horse and the trap pony. Here the tree carcasses were sawn and split into mountains of logs, which they hauled into the village, filling many an old person's empty coal hole. Dan Paget had come tramping through the snow to try to claim payment for the wood, but when Edgar retaliated by threatening to send him a bill for damaged fences, no more was heard.

At the end of one afternoon's work in February, they took a

final load into the village. Edgar had told Noel to go home, for the old man looked weary and was full of cold. He determined to deliver no more, just to call on his mother then return home. Driving the tractor and trailer past the Sinclair home, he was hailed by Ken Sinclair. The man looked terrible, the cold making his new facial scars livid purple. 'Any of those logs to spare?' Ken had asked. 'I need to buy something to burn before we all freeze to death.'

Isabella had asked him into the kitchen as her husband and son stacked the last of the logs under the porch. He had wondered if he had misheard when she said to him, 'No need for a chap like you ever to be cold, there's always a warm welcome for you here.' She had opened her cardigan as if to enfold him under it.

He had been shocked, but there had been no time for any other reaction, as her husband had come back and insisted he had a tot of whisky, because he would take no money for the logs. A month later, when a thaw had set in, but when it seemed the cold clung closer to the bones, he had received a pathetic little note asking if there was the possibility of another load of logs. It had been signed *Mrs I. Sinclair*.

'What do you think?' he had asked Fay. She had shrugged, then remembered: 'You said how pinched with cold Ken Sinclair looked, with his poor face all discoloured.' He had supposed he could spare more logs.

There had been few passers-by on the village street, which was a series of treacherous icy mounds under varying depths of water. He threw the logs under the back porch, where Ken had stacked the first load, and was half intending to leave without knocking on the door. The memory of Isabella's swift sentence as she opened her cardigan speeded the stacking of the logs. Since encountering Den Faulkner, the village butcher, in the noisy bar of a local cattle market, he had come to believe the stories of her living it up in London, while her husband was at the East Grinstead hospital. He had no wish to be involved with this woman.

He had barely put down the last log when he realized the kitchen door was open behind him. A voice called, 'Come in! Tea up. I'm all ready for you.'

He could hear teacups rattling on saucers. A cup of tea would be welcome, and would give him time to work out what he would charge her for this load. Free logs were not intended to be a regular thing for this woman.

As soon as he stepped into the kitchen, closing the door as told, he knew he had been conned, for the kitchen was not just warm, it was hot, a great fire glowed in the grate and Isabella Sinclair was dressed in a short-sleeved pink jumper knitted from some long haired wool. Around the neck, sequins sparkled. Her hair was a bright tumble of blonde curls, and a wide pink ribbon, which matched the jumper, rested on the top of her head like a child's bow.

'Have we time for tea?' she asked, and when he hesitated to answer, she came slowly around the table to him. He had not moved, and she very carefully slipped her arms under his jacket and around his waist. 'There, now,' she said.

He was aroused immediately and she knew it.

'Thought I might have a bit of trouble with you,' she said, her voice falling to low seduction. 'Neither of us needs a fire, do we?'

'Seems you've got all the fuel you need,' he said, trying to encourage a flame of anger which flickered at her blatant deception.

'More than enough.'

'Where is your husband?'

'Where d'you think?' The tone was suddenly sharp, dismissive, but her body was pressed closer. 'Things went wrong with his last op.'

'I thought you stayed in London when he had to go back to hospital.'

'Fell out with my sister, didn't I, interfering old cow.'

The conversation seemed to him to be going on at a great distance, diminished by the movement of her body, her hips hard against him now. 'And Ian?' he asked, his voice husky.

'Still with her. They'll think I'm still in town with other friends.' As she spoke, her hands went under his waistcoat to his trouser belt. He felt it tighten for a second before she loosed the buckle. 'No one knows I'm here.'

He tried to draw away as her hands went to more intimate parts. 'Does your wife give you the come-on like this?' she asked.

The question made him give a brief grunt of laughter and she gained more access for her fingers.

'No, I thought not,' she breathed.

'What can *you* know?' he asked.

'I know a frustrated man when I see one,' she told him. 'Heavily frustrated, I'd say.'

'Some men,' he began, but he let himself be led by the trouser top to a great fluffy rug in front of the kitchen fire, a rug which surely belonged in a bedroom. Once his foot fell on that fluffy fake sheepskin, he knew he was beyond recall. It was his last coherent thought as this woman roused him to such swift desire, he felt he might come like a youth before he got anywhere near her.

When, afterwards, she'd said, 'You can give me the train fare if you like – not cheap, London and back', he had put a pound note on the table. He had not gone to check on his mother, and as he drove the tractor and trailer homewards, he became convinced he might be sporting either white hairs from the rug, pink from her jumper, or some betraying long blonde hair. He stopped the tractor, leaving the headlights on full. Hurrying into their light, he fell knee-deep into a half-frozen rut. Kneeling in the freezing water, he had the urge to throw himself bodily down into it as penitence or purge, he hadn't been sure which.

Fay, he remembered, had been concerned about him when he arrived home blue with cold. She had brought him dry clothes, heated milk and laced it well with brandy, then gone out to make sure he had remembered to cover the tractor engine against frost.

Some twelve months later, he had again encountered the village butcher in the same bar at the same cattle market. Den Faulkner had leaned companionably next to him and asked how he was getting on with you know who.

He had sipped his whisky and answered, 'OK.'

'Thought so. Don't cost me near so much in steak these days.'

He had not replied, but had waited until he saw the butcher driving homewards in his big black Riley before going to meet Isabella. She had devised a routine of going into town 'shopping', then riding out on other buses to some village he could drive to after the market. They would spend time together, she would catch a bus back into the city and he would drive home. Sometimes, in bad weather, she even managed to hire a room in the market town, and her discretion on these occasions he could not fault, for she always met him some distance from the boarding house, and when they went to the room, he saw no one.

His gratification was each time quick and effortless, because she too was roused and satisfied easily. This was her fascination. This and the way she had of saying, 'Ooh! Thank you, Edgar, thank you,' as she reached her own peak of satisfaction. Compared with his wife, this woman was nearly a nymphomaniac.

Fay had always involved him in a lengthy courting ritual before she could accept his intimate touches. Each time he left Isabella, the person in his mind was Fay. He often drove home silently explaining why he went to Isabella, and arguing that he felt Fay found more satisfaction from her films, and the scene of the waves crashing up the beach to indicate the act of love, than the real thing. *You've got no appetite for love. You're more comfortable in a cinema seat than in my bed.* He often ended his litany muttering aloud as he drove into his farmyard. In the dark watches of the night, he acknowledged that the woman he met was little more than a prostitute, one becoming ever more expensive. 'There's the fares . . . and I like nice things, Edgar

. . .' But she had awoken an appetitite in him which had all the addictive powers of a drug.

But even drug addicts reached the end of the line, either killing themselves with their habit – if they could afford it – or giving it up. He watched Greville and Bess talking quite quietly together, as they dealt with the young horse, and made yet one more decision. He would break with this woman, put her firmly in the past as from that moment. There was no way he wanted to harm Bess's future prospects. He would buy the Paget land and try to breathe life back into his marriage.

He thought of the Bennett family Bible again as Greville came striding towards him. There might be a marriage to pen in, then later the addition of children with double-barrelled surnames, the Bennett-Philipps. It had a ring to it.

Eight

I feel this step towards Ian must be like my first step ever. It is a venture. I am like a child who has viewed walking, watched others do it, but never known the sensation.

I have seen moments such as this in films like *Brief Encounter*, eyes meeting, lingering looks, knowledge dawning. Now is my moment. I am in this role, taking part. This is being on the brink of life, with everything to come. I won't need *this* step caught in a snapshot, me in dress and bonnet, ten months old, and left fading by a parent's dressing mirror. This step I shall never forget.

I don't realize I have a hand extended until Ian touches my fingers. It's like an electric shock, the touch of God and Adam on the ceiling of the Sistine Chapel.

'Colleen gave you my message?' he asks as our fingers fall back, hands drop to our sides.

I nod and reach out to the stile, needing a reality to steady the world. I can feel the many carved initials, deep hieroglyphics under my hand; all those other lovers, all feeling like this? All thinking they are unique, that no one had ever loved as they did – as I do. I feel as if I belong to some immortal band, have joined some esoteric club.

'So, no trouble getting away?'

'Visiting Gran,' I answer, and feel we have to say mundane things to each other to hold on to reality.

'As long as you're here. . .'

'I do intend to look in on Gran,' I add, babbling on. 'I'll have time, it's not as if you want to go gallivanting off to Red Pool Spinney or anything.'

'Well, not now,' he says, but straightens up like the blond hero he is, ready to go when the moment comes. 'I don't think we'd make it there and back before midnight.'

'Some other time, then.'

'You promise that?'

I nod again. 'We *will* go again one day, and I really *will* see the red pool.' I imagine us finding a new way, a new path, but still one where we can watch, as much for Mr Sinclair as ourselves, as the waterbirds take wing.

'I had to see you today. Could we walk for a bit?' he asks, and there is a change in his voice that stops all flights of fancy. 'I have to talk to you. It's easier to walk and talk.'

I remember Noel says everyone should always walk if they have problems. He says it saves wear and tear on wives and furniture.

'What's wrong?' I ask. 'You're making me feel as if we're about to go down into that old bog again.' I try to make a joke, but my laugh is tremulous and he doesn't deny that I am right. 'It *is* something awful, isn't it?'

He nods. 'But remember we did get out of that quagmire.'

Just, only just, but I say this in my head as we begin to walk along the lane towards Packman. He takes my hand, casually, almost as if he does not notice that the swing of our arms has brought them together. His hand is warm compared with mine. 'What is it, Ian? Tell me,' I urge, afraid of what my imagination might conjure if I am not quickly told the truth. I grip his hand a little tighter, so he knows there is nothing lax or casual about how I feel.

'When I saw you at the show, I felt everything in the world was wonderful. We're always so right together, immediately, as soon as we meet, aren't we?'

This is true. Of course we are. But I don't have time to find my breath, and the words to agree, before he goes on.

'But, as usual, my mother has spoilt everything.'

His mother? I remember the look of fury on her face as she went to the bus stop not an hour ago. 'What's happened?'

95

'My dad and I are leaving Counthorpe,' he says quickly, as if delivering the blow as mercifully as possible.

'Leaving?' This is worse than anything I might have imagined.

He nods. 'Not that I blame Dad. I suppose I'm just surprised he's stuck it as long as he has. We've stayed in this village longer than we've been anywhere.' He squeezes my hand. 'You remember I told you how we've moved about.'

My mind is in a turmoil. I am in such a state of revolt against this news his voice seems to come from some obscure distance, and reaches me only as an echo.

'When he came back from hospital last time, she finally reduced him to tears.'

This I grasp, this brings me back to reality, to anger. 'She made your father cry.'

'I'd never seen him cry before, not with all he's suffered, all the operations . . .' His voice is low. 'Not even when he peers in the mirror to shave the parts of his cheeks and chin where his whiskers do still grow.' He swallows hard, regains control. 'That's when I want to cry.'

The graphic picture of his father trying to shave – to put on a brave face – keep up such appearances as he has left, there is much more suffering here than just my disappointment, my heartbreak.

'I've never seen a man cry,' I whisper. I try to imagine my pa crying and can't.

'If it were not for you, I'd be pleased to go,' he says. 'Dad should have left her years ago. She's been no comfort to him, no kind of a wife.'

'No.' I remember his mother pulling her hand away from her husband's before he recited the flying poem. He had needed support then. All Adeline Hewitt had implied also flicked like a snake's tongue into my mind, but I push the gossip away. I feel an unlooked-for tear run down my nose. 'Ian, what are we going to do?'

He stops, steps in front of me, holds my forearms. 'I'm sorry. I didn't want to upset you, but . . .'

I shake my head furiously. 'No, no, you can't help it, it's not you, it's . . .' I look up at him, gritting my teeth, trying to stop being so weak and self-centred. Pa and St Catherine's would think this a very poor show. 'It's just so unexpected.'

Quite slowly, as if he will stop the second I make any protest, he puts his arms around me. We just stand still in the middle of the path. I am lost in this my first embrace from any man except my pa. It is such a gentle embrace, such a tenderness, so correct. One arm is around my waist, the other is angled upwards towards my head, as a mother holds a small child. I draw myself up taller to be closer to him, and as I do, his arms tighten a little more. I breathe in deeply, pressing my ribcage up against his chest, and he holds me tighter still. I wish I could go on holding my breath, so he would hold me ever more firmly to him, but when I breathe out at last, he looks down at me. 'I shall come back, Bess,' he says. 'When you're older, I shall come back for you.'

'I feel old now,' I say, looking at him intently, willing him to read how much I love him. 'Very old. Old enough to know what I want.'

'Me too,' he answers, but his face is solemn, set to face difficulties. He turns and we walk on.

'So, where are you going?' I ask.

'About as far as you can go and still be in this country. Not far from Land's End. My great-aunt lived at St Just. Dad's inherited her house. We're to go there.'

Cornwall! I heard someone at a tennis party at the Hall exclaiming that it was easier to get to France than to Cornwall. And it's stupid to wish he hadn't mentioned Land's End, because the name sounds so final; stupid, too, to say I shall miss him, for I've hardly seen him more than a dozen times in six years, but I swallow hard and say, 'I shall miss thinking I *might* see you.'

We both laugh, not very loudly, not very convincingly; swing our joined hands a little higher for a moment.

'Do you have to go?' I ask.

97

'I can't let Dad go on his own. He needs company, needs me.'

'But you'll be going back to school.'

'No, I'm finishing. There's the possibility of a place in an architect's office in Penzance, someone Dad knows through East Grinstead hospital.' He gives a little ironic laugh. 'I shall stay there until I have to do my National Service next year, then I'll begin training seriously. I hope to be able to work and have days off for college. We'll need the money. Dad says he'll have to pay *mother*' – there is a bitter sincerity in his voice as he adds – 'and I'd pay not to have to live with her.'

Until today, I believed everyone loved their parents, had natural love and affection to some degree or other for mothers and fathers. I could not imagine either my father or my mother ever doing anything that would make me say, or even think, such a thing. 'When do you have to go?' I ask.

There is a long, long silence. 'Dad was all set to go today, but I said I wanted to explain to you and say goodbye. I know he understands how special you are to me. He always has.'

'So this is—'

'To say goodbye for the time being, but we could write, couldn't we?'

I imagine letters coming to the farm when I'm at school.

'I'll want to know everything that's happening, everything you're doing,' he adds.

I can see his letters waiting on the mantelpiece. There would be curiosity, tactful enquiries, then perhaps comments – questions. I remember that first letter from St Catherine's, propped so conspicuously for all to see. I would need complete privacy for letters from Ian. 'Perhaps it would be a good idea to write care of Colleen,' I say.

'If that's what you want.' He looks surprised, but when I nod, he says, 'OK. Then, when I've done my National Service – when we're older – we'll get together again, you'll see.'

'It's twenty-one, isn't it, before you can do as you like. Five years for me,' I say, full of despair. A moment of desperate panic comes over me. 'It's too long, isn't it!' I exclaim.

'Nothing and no one will separate us for ever, Bess. We won't let it happen. Say you believe that.'

'I believe you mean what you say, but . . .' I feel so apprehensive. 'Will you ever come back to live here, do you think?'

'I shouldn't think so,' he answers. 'Once we've made the break, I won't want to come and live anywhere near my mother. I never want to see her again. When I'm earning, I'll be independent, live my own life.'

'But things happen, don't they . . . So much can happen. Your mother could move.'

He shrugs as if he no longer cares what she does. 'As soon as I leave the forces, I shall come back for you, Bess. I'll take you right away from here.'

I feel a bit like Alice and the pack of playing cards. I feel as if all the portraits of the Bennetts are trying to harass me, beat on my head. I try to imagine what Pa would say if I told him I wanted to go and live in Cornwall.

'But, if your mother wasn't here . . .' I try to find another way, something that will please everyone.

'But she *is*,' he states. 'And my dad has had more than enough. Bess' – he stops walking and steps in front of me – 'before I go, I just need to tell you that I love you. I know I'll never love anyone else as I love you, ever.'

Like Ian, I think you do know when you find the right person, and that age really does not matter. 'And I love you,' I say, looking up into his face, his pale skin, the angle of his cheekbones and chin; at his shining hair, at this young man who has sprung from the pages of a book of mythological heroes to real life. I stare, layer and store the memories: the Ian I first met in the harvest field; the Ian at the village school; the growing Ian winning scholarships, and Ian the young man. I hear Colleen's excited *Your first proper boyfriend. My* young man – who is leaving my life.

'Time will pass,' he says.

I want to tell him I feel it already has, for I feel so much older

99

than when I walked down this lane to meet him, a lifetime older, a different person.

'It will,' he urges.

'You won't forget me?' I ask.

'Never, never, never.' He pulls me close, and I see he is going to kiss me. I close my eyes, and his lips touch mine – full, sweet, sensational.

After a few seconds, we draw apart, both shaken, and my lips are tingling.

'I think you should go now,' he says. 'I'll wait here for a bit, give you time to get to your gran's.'

I remember he turns me and gives me a gentle push on my way. I know I walk a few steps and then look back, but he has turned away. He is standing by a gate, very upright, only his clenched fists rest on the gate and he is staring up and ahead, into the far distance. I want to run back. I want to put my hand on his arm, so he'll seize me and say wild things about never letting me go. I want to be in his arms, holding myself in, seeming to contract in his arms, so he holds me tighter and tighter.

I must have run in the other direction – I have no recollection, and am certainly not out of breath, even though I am back in the Main Street, and slightly past Grandmama's house. I stop, stand close under the churchyard wall, try to regain some kind of composure, try to stop my mind racing with new experiences, new ecstasies, new agonies. New wild plans of going back and saying, Let's run away together, or, Let me go with you. I can't imagine five years ever passing. Five years ago, I was eleven. I'm so much older *now* – and in *another* five years, I will be old – old enough.

I become aware that there are quite a few other people in the street, when I would have expected them to be indoors, finishing their evening meal. I wonder if my excitement has given off waves, like wireless waves, which they have all picked up, bringing them out to see what was disturbing their sixth senses. I glance back. Thank goodness it has not brought Miss Seaton out. My intention of making some truth of my white lie by looking in on Gran fades at the thought of her housekeeper. Then I hear other unusual things, some commotion, some kind of disturbance ahead. There's shouting, banging, crashing, as if things are being thrown about.

I walk on and see that the commotion is outside Ian's house. Mrs Sinclair is transferring an assortment of cases, furniture drawers and clothes from below her bedroom window, over the garden wall, into the street. There is a small crowd of onlookers, some shouting encouragement, some crying shame. The next moment, Colleen is by my side. 'Where's Ian?' she asks.

'But what's she doing?' I ask, though I can see very well. 'She went off on the bus.'

'She must have got off at the first stop. I saw her running past our house like there was a fire or something. I came out to see what was the matter. Then I could hear her shouting in the house. The next thing, the bedroom window opens, stuff comes flying out. Then, not content to have it all in the garden, she's throwing it all out into the street. It's all Mr Sinclair's stuff.' She runs out of breath as she repeats her first question. 'Where's Ian?'

'He's coming,' I say. 'He said he'd follow me.'

'I think you should run back and get him. She's gone mad.'

I remember how Mrs Sinclair had violently pushed Adeline aside on her way to the bus stop, so furious she had neither seen nor cared about any of us. 'Where's Mr Sinclair?' I ask, then gasp as I see a uniform lying on the debris. Mr Sinclair's RAF uniform, with wings and medal ribbons. I start forward, but Colleen restrains me.

'Go and get Ian, that'll be best. He can go inside and see what's happened to his father.'

I turn and run as fast as I can, and I find him on the edge of the village. He sees my alarm even from a distance and begins to run to meet me.

'What is it? What's happened? Are you alright?'

I tell him it's his father everyone is worried about. We

both run back, hand in hand. He lets go as we reach the crowd, which has grown, and I hear someone has gone off to fetch the police constable. I also hear other muttered comments. *She'd a b'n tin-panned out of the village, years ago. It's 'er things as want throwing out. She's been nothin' but a nuisance since she set foot in the village. Aye, but mind what you say.* I turn in time to see a woman's head nodding in our direction.

Ian heads for the back of the house, and I follow. I notice the rockery now resembles the drawing Ian made, then we are in the kitchen. Mr Sinclair is sitting at the table, looking like a man waiting for bad news, but when he sees us, he smiles and stands up. 'Ah! My boy. Been waiting for you, and your young lady.' He gives a half bow, but staggers a little as he stoops to pick up a small attaché case by his feet. 'The other cases are already outside, I believe.'

Wordlessly, Ian takes his arm and I pick up the case. There is a sudden silence as we emerge into view of the crowd, then his mother's voice screams out again.

'No one treats me like this, no one!'

'You've been found out, lady, that's your trouble,' a man shouts from the back of the crowd.

She shakes both fists at the spectators, then towards her husband. 'No one deserts me and gets away with it. D'you hear, you burnt-out bloody war hero.'

There is a wave of protest from those standing around, and one or two move nearer. She advances on us. She looks like a wild creature, her blonde hair in a great disturbed mass about her head, her face contorted, ugly and hard under her intense red lipstick and black eye make-up.

She stoops, picks something up, then leaps towards us, brandishing a coat hanger. I see how her hands are clawed so her red fingernails show like long talons as she hurls herself towards her husband and Ian.

'Leave me, would you? Leave me! You'll pay! I'll make you pay! Look at him. Look at him! Call yourself a man!' If she is

102

capable of judging anything, she has certainly misjudged the mood of the villagers.

Many of the crowd come forward and close around us, some shout back at her. *You're a wicked woman! Go back where you came from! Clear off, we don't want your sort here.*

Even in the confusion, I want to urge Ian to stay in Counthorpe, let his mother go; for surely, after this, she will have to leave anyway.

Then, as we reach the far side of the crowd, someone says, 'I've got your uniform safe, Mr Sinclair.' I recognize George's voice and see that, in addition to the uniform over one arm, Noel's grandson has collected and reclosed a suitcase. He joins our party. 'Where are you going?' he asks.

It is a good question. I've no idea, and behind us we hear a final shouting duel between the crowd and Mrs Sinclair, then there is a change of mood and I realize she has had the sense to retreat, slamming the house door defiantly – just as 'Bobby' Burnett arrives on his huge black bicycle. 'Late as usual, Tom,' someone shouts to him. 'It's all over.'

I see the village policeman swing his leg over the back of his enormous black bicycle, survey the scene and ask, 'Just a domestic, was it? Anyone hurt?'

Then Colleen is close by our side. 'Come to our house – sort yourselves out,' she says, and at the same moment, her father is there, taking the attaché case from me and the suitcase from George, leading the way into his home.

The kitchen and the table are crowded as usual, but Colleen's mother has only to look at her husband's face – the cases and loads of clothes people are bringing – to size up the situation. 'Come on, children, we need the table.' Just as I have seen happen before, the plasticine and cutting out disappear from the table like magic, and cases and clothes are loaded on to it.

'Tea, Mum?' Colleen asks, lifting the kettle.

'Sit down, old chap.' Mr Rawlins brings forward the many-cushioned carver chair. 'We'll soon have things sorted.'

'You're very kind,' he begins, but his voice breaks a little and

I hold my breath, willing him not to cry again. He clamps his lips in a tight crooked line and nods his thanks.

'Come on, Dad,' Ian says, taking his arm and seeing him back into the chair, lifting cushions to fit around him. I see only too well that he does need Ian. 'We'll go for the next bus into town,' Ian tells him.

'But you won't be able to catch a train until tomorrow,' I protest.

'We can probably get as far as London, then stay the night there.'

'The eight thirty, but you'll be late in,' Mr Rawlins confirms.

'We'll be in good time for the Cornish Riviera express tomorrow, then,' Ken Sinclair says.

I hear a little gasp from Colleen, and her lips form an angonized *O* as we exchange glances.

'That where you're off to.' It is not a question, just a statement by Colleen's father as he cuts into a newly made cake. 'Very nice. Very nice indeed. I suppose, once you're in London, it wouldn't be that many hours to wait before the Cornishman pulls out tomorrow. You have to change stations, you know that.'

Mr Sinclair nods and, talking so matter-of-factly, Mr Rawlins has given him breathing space, time to regain his dignity. George is quite a revelation to me as he neatly folds and restores Mr Sinclair's clothes to the case, while Colleen's mother finds a strap for it and Colleen pours the tea and offers the cake, which no one takes except George and her father.

'We could put you up overnight,' Mr Rawlins offers. 'Soon double the children up.'

'Thanks, you're more than kind, but I think the sooner we're gone the better,' Mr Sinclair says. 'We probably wouldn't sleep much tonight wherever we are.'

Ian and I exchange glances. 'I'll walk Bess to her grandmother's. That *is* where you were going?'

I nod, go to Mr Sinclair and hold out my hand. 'Goodbye and good luck.'

'Goodbye, my dear. For now, anyway.'

I stoop to kiss his cheek.

'The next bus is in twenty-five minutes,' Mrs Rawlins adds, then calls, 'Bye, Bess! Come again soon.'

We walk from the cottage to the village square and turn left. 'You see what she's reduced my dad to,' he says and, as we walk past on the opposite side to his house, he adds, 'And I'll never forgive her – never.'

I can understand that. I can see why he has to go.

All that remains of the sensational event is PC Burnett's bicycle propped outside the Sinclairs' garden gate and a trio of men still talking nearby. As we pass, one calls, 'Your father alright, is he?'

Ian raises a hand and nods, but we do not stop until we are opposite the old farm. I have forgotten all about Miss Seaton, but she is there at the gate and calls across the road. 'Not holding hands this time, then?'

'No,' Ian replies, but immediately takes my hand and makes a play of kissing it. 'Just saying au revoir. I'm sure you can't object to that.'

We part before she has time to, and before she can raise her voice again.

Nine

1953

'You were in the village last night,' Ma says the moment I enter the kitchen, then begins again. 'Morning, Bess, but you did go to the village, didn't you?'

All night my mind has been filled with scraps of conversations, either soaring with memories of Ian's declaration of love and his promise to return, or plummeting with his departure, our separation. In between, I heard Adeline's voice – *You are Bess* Bennett, *aren't you?* – and I keep coming back to the fact that Isabella Sinclair is still in the village and Ian has gone.

I learn that the news of the fracas has reached our farm via the early morning cowman and George.

'Yes,' I reply. 'And before you ask, yes, I saw it all. Saw Mrs Sinclair throwing her husband's things out into the street, behaving like a madwoman.'

'You didn't say anything when you came home.'

'No, I couldn't talk about it.'

She doesn't harry me, turns away, laying rashers of bacon into the frying pan, while I fiddle with the packet of cornflakes. Her silence seems to force me to fill the gap, to explain. 'Pa was listening to the news, and it would have caused upset for you, and I didn't want to talk about it. Anyway, it should be the other way round. She should be thrown out.'

'I wouldn't argue with that,' she says, and for a moment her voice sounds weighted, as if she is talking to a contemporary, then she adds, 'Ken Sinclair doesn't deserve such treatment,

106

that's for sure, or poor Ian. George tells me Colleen's parents came to the rescue.'

'Until it was time for the next bus into town. Ma,' I begin, yearning to take her hand, lead her upstairs, sit her before her dressing table, then kneel by her side and talk – and talk. I wonder how very much we'd both learn if we were as honest as could be? Then I hear Pa talking to someone outside. His voice sounds animated, excited. We hear him laugh, give an order.

Ma's voice almost has an edge of command as she says, 'I wouldn't mention the Sinclairs if Pa doesn't. He's not into melodramas, as we know.' She puts her hand gently on my shoulder as she leans to place toast on the table. 'Did you see Ian before he left?' she asks.

I nod and she gives my shoulder a squeeze. It makes me wonder what my decision would be if I really had to choose between my parents. Ian's choice was never difficult, but mine – to go off into the blue leaving either my father or mother behind, for ever – that would tear me in two.

Part of me still feels I failed Pa by not being a boy to carry on the family name. I still feel I have a debt to pay for that. Deeper is the knowledge that, even if he was proved to be utterly in the wrong, proved to be the most awful sinner, I might still take his side, follow the long-ingrained pattern, dogging his every step, mood and word.

I've always echoed his opinions, even when my instincts were on Ma's side. I've often echoed his *Oh! Oh!* when he successfully goaded Ma into a passionate outburst. I remember when Pa's hero, Winston Churchill, failed to carry the country with him after the war – Ma, getting breakfast, as now, had said she had expected him to lose the election. She had argued that the working man who had fought for his country did not want to go back to his forebears' heritage of subsistence wages and tied cottages. 'It's wrong,' she had declared.

Pa had winked at me and nodded slightly towards Ma, implying the leg-pull to come, then said, 'They know the system.'

'They don't have any choice!' Ma had risen to the bait, and, when she realized, had for once not laughed, but had become even crosser. 'And you may rule your daughter's heart now, but you won't always, or her head when she's out of your shadow.'

'Oh! Oh!' he had exclaimed.

'Oh! Oh!' I had echoed.

I find I am still ashamed of that. The truth was, and I think may still be, that I have always been more eager to share the joke and the laughter with Pa than overtly to take Ma's side.

'Are you going to eat that toast or just butter it to death?' Pa's voice makes me jump. I hadn't realized he had come in and is sitting next to me at the table. I laugh shakily at this pun, but I am becoming ever more curious about why he is in such a good mood. His eyes are shining and he is smiling all over his face. He picks up his knife and fork and holds them upright, reminding me of a nursery-rhyme character waiting for his pie.

'Shall we tell this heiress the good news?' he asks Ma, accepting the plate of eggs and home-cured bacon which has filled the kitchen with the aroma of its frying.

My heart leaps. Ian must have come back.

'I have just agreed to buy Mr Paget's farm,' he says.

I stare at him. He could be speaking in a foreign language, for I can grasp no meaning in his announcement, yet he is looking at me for a response. I ask the only question that forces itself into my head. 'What for?'

'What for?' Pa's exclamation makes me realize I have certainly misunderstood. 'What for?' he repeats, and he swivels on his chair to see me better. Then the word *heiress* and all that implies for a Bennett sinks into my brain. I look at Ma, silently appeal to her.

'They say larger farms will be more profitable to run in the future.' Ma's voice is high, sounding like a speaker asked to extemporize. 'There's so much machinery coming into agriculture . . .'

'What for?' Pa repeats, as if Ma has not spoken. 'If you have to ask, then I'm damned if I know.' He puts down his knife and fork. Bright orange yolk runs from the knife to the table.

'Edgar!' Ma exclaims. 'Give the girl a chance. At sixteen, one's concerns are not about buying land and property.'

'I've suddenly lost my appetite.'

I concentrate on the egg yolk, as the chair next to me is scraped back. 'Nothing I ever do is right for any of the women in this family.'

I look up then, and he glares down at me.

'And you are as bad as all the others.'

He gives me that look when his blue eyes become colder than polar ice, the look that tags me a failure.

'No – no, I'm not,' I deny vehemently and automatically.

'Don't upset yourself,' Ma says as the door slams. 'He doesn't really mean you.'

'Who does he mean, then?'

'He will certainly mean his mother and Miss Seaton.'

'As well as us,' I add, and into my mind comes Miss Seaton's judgment about my pa being as bad as his grandfather – as bad as Alexander Bennett, whose portrait is in the dim part of our hall.

I watch as she takes Pa's breakfast and puts it into the Aga. She looks as distracted as Grandmama had done when her father-in-law had been mentioned.

'Are you upset?'

She does not answer, but stands very still. Her knuckles gradually turn white as she holds the rail where the tea towels hang. 'Why should you think I am?' she asks carefully.

'Things are not the same, are they, and . . .'

'And?'

'Ian and his parents,' I begin, but can't go on to compare Ian's real trauma to mere suspicions.

I watch her knuckles gradually lose their tense whiteness. She is consciously – self-consciously – in control again now. 'Bess, I shall never ask you to choose between me and your pa, but—'

'But?' It is my turn to prompt now.

'But don't let him ever push you in a direction you don't want to go.'

'I won't, don't worry!' I say very firmly, and don't mean ever to allow it to happen. When I leave the kitchen, I look back as the door closes and see Ma sink to a chair. She normally tries to clear breakfast away before Stella arrives, so the day's work can go smoothly, with the kitchen as headquarters.

Later in the day, when I am in the yard carrying back saddle and harness after my ride, Noel comes from the barn. I am taller than him now, not that he lets that impress him. 'What you done to upset your father? One minute he's top of the world, then he's right down, snapping at everybody all day, deserve it or not.'

'I only asked him why he wanted to buy Paget's old farm.'

'Ah! That'd do it,' he says.

'So, why exactly does he want it?'

'Well, it's for you, ain't it, to enhance your standing in the county.'

'Noel,' I begin, and hear him draw in a long breath. 'What do you think would happen if I wanted to go quite a long way off to live?'

'You'd break his heart,' he said without pause.

'So, I've no free will then?' I ask sharply.

'No, that's not what I said.' He takes my bridle and saddle from me and walks ahead to hang it in an old stable where the tack is kept. 'I said you'd break his heart if you did.' He pauses and looks at me hard. 'That's not the same thing, is it?'

'No,' I admit, 'just –' I hesitate between *impossible* and *harder*, then I think of Ian and finish – 'Just much harder.'

'You thinking of leaving us, then?' he asks with a grin.

I toss up my head and tell him, 'Not at the moment.'

'Good,' he says. 'Anyhow, should have thought you'd be glad to have Red Pool Spinney. You and that young Sinclair can go swimming there anytime now.'

'He's gone, Noel,' I remind him heavily.

'Oh, aye, but he'll be back, I reckon.'

'You really think so?' I exclaim, but he just cocks his head at me and winks.

The thing about Noel is that everything he has ever said, even ridiculous old adages like *Rain before seven, fine before eleven* is usually right – as he always points out to me. He kind of gives me hope that things will come right, so after that, the day doesn't seem quite so dour.

When the time comes to walk to the village again, I tell my mother where I'm going. 'Give Colleen my love,' she says. 'And ask her when she's coming to the farm. Now she's a working girl, I never see her.'

I wonder whether that's because Colleen is at work, or because she hears too many tales at the factory and might be embarrassed to come to the farm. I hope Adeline won't be hanging around again, and I remind myself that I need to ask, belatedly, if it will be alright for Ian to write care of Colleen's address.

Tonight I feel self-conscious, as again I wait around. I could almost wish I was at school. There I could lose myself in the ordered routines, there my peers know more about my mother's family, the city-based seed and corn chandlers, who have been school benefactors for years – generations – than about the village, the farm, the Bennetts.

The factory doors swing open, release the inmates. Some look up, breathe in the summer evening, and I find myself mimicking their deep intakes, imagining how good it must be to come out of that atmosphere, redolent with the smell of wool, which lingers so strongly on their clothes. Some leave with heads bowed, brows furrowed, home on their minds, problems to scurry back to. Adeline comes out with several youths, most of whom obviously feel awkward as she laughs outrageously, throwing herself about like a ball bearing in a game of bagatelle, ricocheting first off one, then another – and she is so aware of me standing there. When they come level, Adeline gives me a triumphant look from the centre of her entourage, turns up her lip in derision and does not answer my greeting.

Colleen is one of the stragglers tonight. This will be to avoid Adeline, and *her* behaviour was probably to show me she doesn't care.

We greet each other and smile.

'Alright?' she asks, and I shrug.

'They went on the bus last night?' I ask.

She nods, then adds, 'What a performance.'

I too think of Mrs Sinclair. 'Right. Surely *she'll* have to move now.'

Colleen shrugs. 'Our mam thinks she'll stay, says she's too well in . . .' She trails off, as if what she is saying is leading her in a direction she does not mean to go.

'Could we go for a walk? I need to talk to you.'

'Ian asked me about the letters,' she says.

'Oh, good.' I'm not sure why I'm surprised. Surely I hadn't thought all the talking would stop when I wasn't there. The truth is, I hadn't thought about it going on. 'Do you want to go home first?' I ask.

She doesn't answer for a moment, and I see by her face she has some reservations about this walk. 'We'll always be friends, won't we, Bess?'

'Always,' I say, though the fact that she needs to ask the question makes my heart sink. 'No matter what.'

She runs home while I wait on the corner, from where I can see both Mrs Sinclair's house and the beginning of Gran's white wall where it begins to curve and form the far corner of the village street. The smell of a freshly cut lawn is in the air, but there is no sound. The street is deserted. The factory workers have disappeared into their homes and, though the next bus from the city will bring another load of office workers and the like home, for the time being it is still. Then another evening racket disturbs the village. From the rookery high in the churchyard elms suddenly erupt black, cawing, squabbling birds, a tumble of disquiet; alarming as they tumble in the air, like acrobats missing their trapeze, then swooping up underneath their neighbours, shouting insults. Then just as quickly it is over, the birds feather their wings to land on nests and branches. I wonder if there is still any niggling or under-beak grumbling going on I can't hear. I guess the story of Mrs Sinclair's exploits will be retold for years among us humans.

I wonder where Ian is now. Would he have reached Cornwall yet? How soon will he write? Will I ever see him again – and when? Then Colleen comes running and I ask again to make sure she really doesn't mind about the letters. She doesn't, she says she's pleased. 'What a shame your first proper date had to be like that.'

'It'll be my last if he doesn't come back.'

'He will.' She takes my arm and presses it to her side. I know we will always be friends, best friends, no matter what.

'Colleen,' I begin, and for a moment she giggles, so I stop. 'What's to laugh at?'

'It's just that George says his grandad always expects the worst when you begin with his name.'

'Noel?' I'm surprised he talks about me to George, but I am not to be put off. I want to know what the world thinks is happening between my father and that woman, what the gossip is. Somehow this extra loading of property on my shoulders, the purchase of Paget's Farm, Pa's use of the word *heiress*, makes me need ammunition for some fight I can only vaguely imagine. 'Ian's mother,' I ask. 'Her men friends, who are they?'

She draws in a long breath and expels it noisily, but does not answer.

'Or who do people *think* they are?'

'The butcher for sure.'

'Mr Faulkner?'

'Are you surprised?'

'Just that I couldn't imagine anyone fancying Mr Faulkner.'

'I know,' Colleen agrees. 'He's so beefy and . . .'

'Suety,' I add. 'But then, I couldn't imagine anyone fancying Mrs Sinclar.'

'Oh, yes!' Colleen contradicts. 'She's like a doll in a box, all sparkly bits and cooey noises. You watch chaps' eyes when they look at her – not yesterday of course.'

'Surely men can see through the tinsel?' But I am in danger of letting this become gossip, just a chat.

'Colleen.' I use her name again, but this time she does not laugh. I think it's called biting the bullet. It feels like it could prove fatal, my world might really be shot dead.

'Colleen.' I look down at her left hand as it lies along my forearm. I see her first finger is a mass of tiny needle pricks, and I know the miniscule wooden handled hook she uses to pick up stitches in the hosiery still hangs on a string around her neck. She is quite proud of being chosen to train as a mender. Women do these jobs until they marry, and if they don't marry, carry on doing them for forty, fifty years. My heart lurches with a sudden and desperate wish that she will find someone really good and kind to marry and be happy with. 'Adeline seems to suggest my father is one of them.'

Her fingers hold my arm tighter. 'That's what people have been saying for a long time now. I'm sorry, Bess. I always tell them it's all rubbish, that no one has ever seen anything.'

'No, that's right!' I exclaim, seizing the fact. 'When could he? He never goes anywhere.'

'They say she meets him in the fields, that they walk and find secluded barns.'

'How ridiculous! My pa's a bit more sensible than that. There's Noel and George, and everyone, about the fields and farm all the time.'

'Not all the time,' she corrects me. 'Not in the evenings.'

'Pa's at home in the evenings.'

'When you're at school, you wouldn't know that, and Fridays you often stay to see a film or a show. Sunday evenings your ma is taking you back to school.'

I feel my face flaming. My first instinct is to ask if everyone knows our business, to turn on Colleen as she argues on the side of the gossip. My second thought is to remember that it was Pa who wanted me away at school. 'Oh, no,' I breathe. 'Surely not.'

'Does your ma know, d'you think?'

'You mean, *if* there is anything to know?' My voice sounds hard, but even as I half listen to Colleen apologizing, saying that, of course, no one knows for certain, I have the sinking feeling that I do know. I know that things are not right at home, nothing is as it was between my parents. Real laughter, spontaneous joy, died in our house long ago. I know that.

'Of course, people are jealous, that makes them spiteful,' Colleen is saying.

'Jealous? What of?'

'The Bennetts, of course. You.'

'Me?'

'Of course. You've got everything going for you, haven't you?'

'Have I?' I think of her home, the big table with everything happening on it, all her brothers and sisters, even 'orrible Roy. I envy her them most of all.

'You're not mad with me, are you?' she asks. 'You said you wanted to know?'

'I had to know what was being said, and now I want to go back.'

We both look along the lane towards the Old Brig. We haven't walked very far.

'That didn't take long,' she says and catches the little hook as it swings around her neck. 'Back to my dinner then.'

'Yes, and I'm going back to make sure Pa doesn't go off to any secluded spots – not while I'm at home, anyway. And if I catch him . . .'

'What will you do?' Colleen's hand flies to cover her mouth as she asks.

'Embarrass him, that's for sure. Shame him, I hope – if it's true – and infuriate *her*.' As I say this, I see her face distorted in the light of a lantern held aloft by Pa.

'One thing,' Colleen says. 'We can rely on Miss Seaton to keep an eye on this end.'

I think it is quite strange how a friend always tries to leave you on a lighter note, no matter how dour the situation. I wonder if this is one way of knowing who your true friends are?

Ten

I am woken suddenly, startled by a sharp noise. I lie a few seconds and it is repeated, a sharp crack at my windowpane. I go to the window and blink in disbelief. There in the pale grey light of pre-dawn is George. Immediately I appear, he beckons and pulls something from his pocket, waves an envelope. A letter!

I grab my navy school dressing gown, pull it on as I tiptoe towards the stairs. I try to avoid the floorboards that creak the most. The corridor still holds yesterday's heat and is blissfully silent, Ma and Pa still sleeping. Colleen knows George would be here for the milking an hour before Pa rises, and that only my bedroom faces the back. How she persuaded him to bring the letter and throw stones at my window is something else. I wonder about this as I creep down through the kitchen, angrily shushing Pa's collie, which growls at me.

By the time I have the back door open, George is round to this side of the house waiting for me. He hands over the letter, whispering, 'It came yesterday, in the afternoon post. Colleen couldn't get up to the farm last night, so I said I'd bring it.'

'Thanks, George. Good of you.'

'Right.' He nods and grins.

I wonder why Colleen couldn't come to the farm last night. George's grin seems to suggest it was something to do with him. Are those two going out together?

I nod again and he moves off, a low-lying morning mist swirling around his legs. I go back through the warmth of the house to my bedroom, breathless with anticipation. I read the envelope as if I have never seen my own name and address before. I have never seen them in Ian's handwriting before. I decide it is neat without being small, very masculine, the kind of handwriting that will look good on blueprints for wonderful buildings, for cathedrals and such.

I insert a nail file under the envelope edge. I pause just a second to thrill to the moment, this brillant beginning to the day. I had not expected a letter so soon, had disciplined myself not to fret until the end of the week. Now I feel so wonderful, I would not be surprised if a great light came out of the envelope as well as the folded notepaper.

> Mrs Robinson's Guest House
> 33 Morrab Road
> Penzance
> Tuesday 22nd September 1953

My Dearest Bess,

It's been a long journey – I feel a long, long, way from Counthorpe and you. We finally arrived at my great-aunt's cottage this morning. We had to ask when we arrived in St Just, and received very strange looks standing in the middle of our luggage enquiring about the cottage. What Dad didn't know was that Great-Aunt Emmie had been in a nursing home for five years before her death, and part of the roof of her cottage has fallen in!

So, we have to find a local builder, and in the meantime are staying in this boarding house – clean, good meals, cheap.

Until I can begin work properly, I am looking for some kind of casual work. Maybe I can labour for the builder on the cottage. I'd like that. What I haven't told you is that the cottage is actually on a cliff path, halfway between sea and sky, with spectacular views – bet it's awe-inspiring when the sea's rough. Storms are probably responsible for the roof being partly dislodged. I am working on a strong design of roof timbers and the local tradition of cement-washed tiles.

I keep thinking of how we parted – and before – and hoping there was no more trouble. You must never blame anyone, but my mother— Things like this – well, maybe not quite like this – have happened ever since I can remember. Like I say, my parents should never have married, though where I would have been without my dad, heaven knows! Never blame anyone else, Bess.

Colleen said it would be fine to write care of her. I think we *both* have a good friend there. Dad and Mr Rawlins had quite a heart to heart, and when the time comes, Mr Rawlins is going to help Dad get some furniture down to Cornwall. This has been in store for years after some other debacle in another place!

I am building all my future hopes on coming back for you, Bess. You are the most precious thing in my life.

Write me care of this address – soon. We will be here for a few weeks at least, even if we find a builder straight away.

Your loving,

Ian.

There followed kisses.

My loving Ian. I moon long over the love and kisses, over the beginning and the end of the letter. Still dreaming, I put the letter carefully away under my drawer, silently replace the drawer – then must have and read my letter again.

I read and reread, recreating him through his words, and, eventually, begin to take in the body of the letter.

Never blame anyone else must mean don't blame my father – but surely, if you love someone, you are faithful to them, and if you *marry*, you make vows . . .

I put the letter carefully aside and stretch over to my bedside cabinet. Inside is a small fat red and gold book of prayers Gran gave me. It has a name in the front and a date: *Louisa Clowes, her booke. September 27th 1827.*

I find The Form of Solemnization of Matrimony.

119

It says that marriage *Is not by any to be enterprised, nor taken in hand unadvisedly, lightly, or wantonly to satisfy men's carnal lusts and appetites, like brute beasts that have no understanding, but reverently, discreetly, advisedly, soberly and in the fear of God, duly considering the causes for which Matrimony was ordained.* Then the vow my father took: *Wilt thou have this woman to thy wedded wife, to live together after God's holy ordinance, in the holy estate of Matrimony? Wilt thou love her, comfort her, honour and keep her in sickness and in health; and, forsaking all other, keep thee only unto her, so long as ye both shall live?* Under that is: *The man shall answer, I will.*

'No margin for error.' It is a phrase Pa often uses about driving tractors, accounts, calving heifers, horse dealers. No room for doubt either. These solemn vows leave nothing unsaid.

I can hear movements. Pa will be getting up, getting ready to go to market, pleased his harvest is finished once more. He'll probably buy in some young steers to fatten for the Christmas markets.

I put the book of prayers handy on my bedside cabinet, and Ian's letter carefully back into its hiding place. My first love letter. When I have enough, I'll tie them with ribbon; with the thought comes the realization, as devastating as an omen, that a bundle of letters will mean months, years, of separation. I wish Colleen was not shut up in that factory with its smell of oily wool. I wish *she* and not George was outside, so we could go off together to walk the lanes, and I could be openly lovelorn.

I hear my parents' bedroom door opening and Pa going downstairs. I stare at the red and gold prayer book, and know I *would* blame him if any of the rumours proved true. If my father and – I cast around for a way of describing Ian's mother to myself – Mrs Sss, that makes the kind of echo that seems right – if my father and Mrs Sss have committed acts of carnal lust, 'I'll –' I leap from the book of prayers to Noel's parlance – 'be down on them like a ton of bricks.'

When I go down for breakfast, expecting the bright greetings

120

for my benefit, then the silent breakfast, I find something almost uncanny has happened. My parents act like they've made a huge fresh start, almost as if *they* are the children and have listened to *my* threat to *behave themselves or else.*

Pa is like a man reprieved and Ma flits around the kitchen like a songbird released from a cage. There is even a little banter between them at the breakfast table.

'So, I'm not going to market again for the time being,' Pa announces, as if summing up a discussion we've all been involved in.

'Not even today?' I ask. I had thought I would answer Ian's letter while he was safely away at the market.

'Not even today,' he replies. 'I realize I've been making quite a few mistakes . . .' He pauses, looking at Ma, one of those glances which leaves me outside the full meaning of what they are saying to each other. It gives me a warm glow. I haven't seen one of those looks for years.

'I've been wasting a lot of time going so often, when I'm neither buying nor selling. I thought it paid to watch trends, to see who was there and so on.' He trails off a little as he finds me watching, listening to an explanation that went on too long.

It is usually my eyes that move away, but this morning he picks up his double-size breakfast cup and drinks. He emerges as if he has made another new decision. 'We're going to look over the Paget Farm this afternoon. The house is empty now. Will you come?'

'No,' I say too abruptly, then add, 'Thanks, not this time. I've some writing to do.'

'Can't you do that this morning?' Ma asks.

'I need to ride over to see Tommie about the autumn cross-country, and I've promised for ages to show my face at The Hall.' I stop, see the amusement on Pa's face. I know I am manufacturing things he will regard as a valid use of my time, and *he* knows I am just making excuses not to go with him and Ma, though he can have no idea why.

I spend the morning checking where Pa is, but he never goes

further than the horses' paddock on the lane, and he speaks to no one but our own men. At one moment mid-morning, Noel asks me what I'm about.

'She's off up to the Hall to see Tommie,' Pa answers from behind me.

'Could've fooled me,' he answers. 'Under everyone's blamed feet.'

'When she's done some writing,' Pa adds pointedly.

'I'm just going to do it now.'

'Tell your mother I'm just off with Noel to find out what new fencing we need in the lane, then I'll be in for lunch.'

After lunch, I decide I'll answer Ian's letter first, then I can post it on the way to the Hall. No one is about as I go upstairs, and I remember the matching azure Basildon Bond paper and envelopes in Ma's stationery set, and there are stamps in the farm desk in the kitchen. I could borrow some for this first reply, then buy some of my own.

I go to Ma's bedroom, find the stationery set on the small table beneath the window. Ma quite often writes letters to her friends and relations abroad. I open the box and slip three sheets of paper from beneath the ribbon and then an envelope. The next moment I hear Ma calling, first outside, then up the stairs. 'Bess. Bess, if you can hear me, we're just off to Paget's Farm. Sure you don't want to come?'

I don't answer, because I am in her bedroom, then I hear her say, 'She'll be gone to see Tommie.'

I have a small table in my room, but I shall write my letter kneeling on the floor by my bed, using my atlas to rest the notepaper on.

From my room I can see Ma and Pa walking off across the fields. They walk quite close together, very involved in their conversation. The two of them are just beyond the gate dividing our orchard and paddock when a man's voice calls out. They stop and turn. I wait to see who comes into view. A young man in uniform – officer's uniform. They both look delighted to see him. Pa shakes his hand, Ma too, and he stoops to kiss her

122

cheek – then I recognize him. Greville. Home on leave from the Grenadier Guards, where I understand he has undergone officer training and is now a Second Lieutenant. His National Service will end in about twelve months, and he will be home again. Greville. He of the skating around the edges of the lake; Greville of the upright bearing; the noble birth; the fun parties; the haughty sisters; the good sport at tennis, and the super gran. Greville, a place-for-everything, and everything-in-its-place, all's-right-with-the-world and God-in-his-heaven kind of chap. I might have gone happily out to talk to him at another time, made a foursome for the outing to Paget Farm, but now, as he glances back at the house, I draw back, clutching my purloined notepaper.

There is some discussion, more looking back towards the house. I wonder if he's come straight from the Hall and would know I was not there. No, I think not. They would assume I had gone a different way, our paths not crossing. Then Greville decides to walk on with Ma and Pa. I see he is explaining something and there is a sudden hearty burst of laughter, then they are out of sight.

I had felt concerned for my letter writing as they lingered, wanted them away. Now their departure disturbs me. Why should Greville bother to go with them to see Pa's new acquisition? He surely has more interesting things he could be doing. He should be spending his free time keeping up to date with his own affairs, helping his ever-busy grandmother. I hope they don't go to the spinney and find the lake, make the birds fly. I don't want them intruding there.

I have to reread Ian's letter twice before I can get back into the proper mood to answer it. I feel in two minds about telling him that we have bought Paget's Farm – but I do.

I am amazed when I return from the Hall quite late in the afternoon to find Greville and Pa, jackets off, with maps spread out all over the kitchen table. Greville rises as I come in, and for a moment I am amazed to see his colour rise from his neck to his short cropped hair. Even his ears glow pink. 'Hello, *Bess*, good to see you. How are you?'

For a moment I wait for the *m'dear* at the end of his rhetorical question, then acknowledge him. 'Greville. You're looking well.'

'You missed a good outing this afternoon. We've all been exploring,' he says, looking towards Pa, who immediately rises from the table.

'Yes, come on, Bess, talk to Greville. I want to see Noel before he leaves.'

Greville retrieves a note in his handwriting from the table and hands it to Pa before he leaves us.

'Your father doesn't want your man to go off to the timber yard with the small waggon. He needs about ten times more fencing since he saw the far boundary of his new land.'

'Is it a mess over there?'

He nods. 'I'll show you.' He looks down at the maps spread over the table and with a gesture suggests we sit down. 'We found these beautiful old things in a cupboard in the house. I told your Pa he should have them framed.'

We sit side by side as he points out the section where the boundary fences are practically non-existent.

I am more fascinated by the old names of the fields written in a script with many curlicue flourishes. I wish it was Ian sharing this. Tiptree Hill, Spoil Bank, Jollity – I read out the names, which must have stories behind them, as well as the more mundane Top Pasture and Leys Land. I am completely fascinated when, in the middle of Red Pool Spinney, I see Eye-Spa Pool. 'What does that mean?' I ask, reaching my arm over Greville's to point.

'Because –' he begins very slowly, as if he needs time to recollect – 'it was believed the minerals in the pool were good for the eyes, particularly the red eyes old stockingers used to get because of all the close work they did. People used to go there to bathe their eyes and bring back bottles of the water.'

'Oh, like a shrine!' I exclaim. 'I didn't know that. I've never heard that. How interesting.'

'Yes, I suppose, just like a shrine.' And he looks down at my arm still crossed over his. I move it away.

'How did you know about it?' I ask, meaning, how come he knows when I didn't.

'There are several really ancient books of local history in the library at the Hall. Fascinating reading. You'll have to borrow them.'

'I would like to.'

'One of your father's first tasks will be to re-establish the footpath through the spinney. I should imagine, if the traditional track is found, it will go to the pool.'

I remember all the trouble the neglected footpath has caused over the years, but I no longer want it opened up, and I heartily wish Mr Paget had not died.

'Things have to be put in order,' he adds, as if he senses some of my reservations.

I remember he likes to have matters orderly, doesn't like people – girls – stepping outside their allotted roles. 'Of course,' I oblige, but I'm not going to talk to him about this subject any more. 'So, how is the regiment treating you?' I ask.

'Not often, is the standard guardsman's reply, I believe,' he answers, stretches, then intertwines his fingers behind his head, and I catch the scent of a woody kind of men's toiletry. 'I'll just be glad to be finished and home. It's a weird way of life.'

'Weird? What's weird about it?'

'Everything, from day one on.'

I wait and he sighs as if conceding unwillingly to some oft-requested recital. 'For instance, when we went to our officers' training depot, we were told by the sergeant major that, while we were there, he would call us sir, and we would call him sir.' He tucks in his chin and his voice is deep as he proclaims: '*When you were born, the midwife threw away the wrong bit, sir! Physically deformed, are you, sir? Answer my question, sir!*

125

No speaking in the ranks, sir! And every *sir* he could make sound like *cur*. It was amazing.'

'Weird!' I burst into laughter. 'Is it true?'

He is laughing too, nodding. 'Of course, that's just a few examples.'

'Character-forming,' I suggest.

'I remember that being said to me when I was first sent away to school.'

I have a sudden memory of him on a railway station, clutching a small suitcase, and I suppose it would have been his father seeing him off. He put his hand on the seven-year-old's shoulder as he boarded the train and handed him a small wicker basket. He was directed by the guard to a first-class window seat. We were seeing off my uncle but I was more interested in watching as the guard waved his green flag and Greville's pale ghostly face passed out of sight.

'That was just training, though, wasn't it. You've sort of graduated now.' I want to pull us both from early and bad memories of schools.

He gives a hoot of laughter, pushes out his lips and nods with ironic vigour. 'Sure. I've got a clipboard now. I follow people around and take notes.'

I frown at him and he shrugs, but nods his head. 'I follow officers round when we do inspections, make notes of discrepancies in behaviour and general standards around the camp. Occasionally I am sent, all by myself, to note down the condition of the latrines.'

'But—' I begin a protest.

'Oh, my dear Bess, there are no buts in the Army. You do as you are told, particularly when everyone knows you are just a National Service conscript. There's only one thing worse, and that's an officer who's passed his basic officer's training and *still* has no interest in *getting on a bit*. I'll be out next summer, thank God, though at the moment it feels like a life sentence.'

I think of my lonely times ahead without Ian. 'I can understand that.'

'Can you, Bess?' he says, letting his hands come gently back to rest on the map. 'Can you really?'

'Really.' I nod with certainty as Pa comes back into the kitchen. 'I really can.'

'Fay says stay for supper,' Pa says to Greville.

'Thanks, but –' he looks at me as if he doesn't want to push our state of agreement too far – 'not tonight, I think.' He picks up his tunic and begins to put it on. 'Bess and I have been talking about the footpath.'

'Ah, yes! First job, I think.' Pa turns to me with enthusiasm. 'Just like we always said it should be. Finally get the best of old Paget, hey, Bess.'

Greville nods agreement. 'Settle a long-standing public dispute.'

They are both on the same side, want the same kind of things, there's no doubt about that. My eyes go from Greville's smiling face to Pa's and I wonder what it must be like to live in a cottage halfway between sea and sky – like being suspended in a dream, I imagine.

Eleven

1954

E dgar judges that the dancing at Greville Philipps' demob party is reaching the stage where anyone over twenty-five would do well to retreat to the terrace or the conservatory.

The big band is reaching a pitch of sound which has risen ever since the leader triumphantly announced 'rock and roll'. In the centre of the ballroom the youngsters are doing what looks to him like stylized gymnastics. He catches spasmodic glimpses of Bess, her black hair bouncing as she gyrates with the two Philipps girls, their current beaux and Greville.

He stands near to the open terrace doors, angling his face to catch a cooling breeze. It has been hot all September. He is apart, yet still near enough to be judged with his group. Fay stands laughing with two of her brothers – *the Tophams from town*, as they are collectively referred to. This Topham generation, as their fathers and grandfathers before them, do business with most of the landowners in the Midlands. Edgar feels their inclusion in the invitation for this evening is an extra gesture of friendship, a tightening of the bonds between the families. He would say it gives the nod to trade with the Tophams continuing when Greville takes up the reins of the estate. He has a great respect for Clara Philipps and the way she has for so long overseen the family's business affairs. Edgar would expect this extravagant celebration of Greville's return to have practical meaning as well as just being a splendid festivity.

His gaze goes to his wife. She looks splendid. Her soft dark hair has been set free, falling like a girl's to her shoulders. She is in a deep-blue gown with a pattern of silver embroidery, leaves and stems climbing up to a concentration of flowers over her breasts and shoulders. It had been made for the county ball to celebrate the accession of Queen Elizabeth II just over a year ago. Fay had worn her hair up then – high, more formal.

He sees her become aware of his attention. She smiles, makes his heart move. He believes he probably loves her more now than he has ever done. He believes their marriage has been strengthened by the test it has survived. She has only once verbally berated him, she only once showed her real anguish – and he his – when his guilt and his needs had spilled in a great flood of confession.

At the end of his story of the Isabella Sinclair affair – the sordid liaisons, his knowledge that Faulkner, the village butcher, was also involved making it seem even seedier – he had tried to explain, and this had felt like ploughing to the very depths of his being. He told her how he ached for *her* to make an advance to him instead of always having to go through the rituals of lengthy and uncertain courtship. 'I'm never sure of you. It always feels like a gamble as to whether you'll let me make love to you.' He remembers saying that. She had been astonished. 'I rather thought it was wrong, somehow brazen, for the woman to make the advances,' she had told him. 'Not when it's your husband, Fay,' he had replied.

She had gone to the window, stood with her back to him. He had thought his marriage finished. 'I didn't know,' she had whispered after a long time. Turning to face him, she had repeated it over and over. 'I didn't know.' Then she had cried as if her heart was breaking – and so had he.

Then, wonderfully, slowly, and often with an air of studied determination which was comic on occasion – and the laughter helped – she had set herself to break her inhibitions. They learned together that the strict reserve had been rehearsed at the knee of a puritanical nanny. Fay realized this same wooden-faced woman had also restricted her contact with her brothers, kept them most unnaturally apart for years. She had grieved over that too, but it had been an awakening, a new beginning, for the two of them.

Fay and her brothers all give a sudden guffaw of laughter. He smiles too. There is an element of making up for lost time in Fay's manner these days. She looks his way and he has to quell an impulse to seize her and rush her out into the garden, make mad passionate love to her in some isolated spot in the gardens. He knows quite a few possible places. He sucks in his cheeks and raises his eyebrows at her speculatively, so she loses the thread of the conversation, and half turns her back on him.

Then he notices Harding, the Philipps' butler, who is threading his way discreetly between the guests, brushing past side tables burdened with huge displays of mostly roses and stocks. Their perfume has become heavier during the evening. He is, Edgar sees, coming around the room with very deliberate intention and tactful speed. He has a mission, it seems, for he passes Lady Philipps and comes around to their side of the dance floor. He frowns as it becomes obvious that Harding is coming to him. The butler gives a single discreet nod and moves close to his side. He leans forward and Edgar automatically inclines an ear.

'There is a –' the butler hesitates, then decides – 'a woman wishing to see you, sir.' He clears his throat before adding, 'Mrs Bright, the cook, is detaining her in the kitchen.'

'Detaining?' Edgar draws back to frown at the man.

'What is it, Edgar?' Fay is immediately by his side.

'Is it something at the farm?' she asks Harding. 'An accident?'

'Nothing like that, madam,' Harding replies, but adds no further explanation. Behind him the dancing comes to an end and the young people come laughing, feigning exhaustion, from the floor. The Philipps girls go to join the party grouped around the High Sheriff of the county, whose son is Daphne Philipps' latest young man. Bess and young Greville come towards their

130

group just in time to hear Harding explain, 'Mr Bennett is asked for downstairs, that's all.'

Edgar and Greville exchange frowns. 'Shall I come with you, sir?'

'It's just Mr Bennett—' Harding begins.

'Oh! I'll just go and see. Won't be long.' He is beginning to feel annoyed with Harding and ushers him ahead.

Once they are in the panelled passage leading from the hall to the kitchen, Harding races ahead but he calls to him, 'Just a minute, man, tell me what this is all about.'

'It's Mrs Sinclair. You know, the ex-pilot's wife . . .'

'Yes, yes, I know who she is.' He wanted to protest that he had put all that behind him. 'What about her?'

'She was on her way to the front door, asking for you. Shouting your name, sir. One of the maids was outside collecting glasses and came and fetched me.'

'What the hell does she want?'

There is a pause and Harding glances at him with a cynical man-to-man look, merely adding, 'She's the worse for drink, and nasty with it.'

When they reach the kitchen door, Harding tries to push it open but it is stayed from the other side. The door is heavy, lined with baize both sides. The old soundproofing is good, but Edgar can hear shouting. Harding puts his shoulder against it but calls before pushing again. 'Mrs Bright, it's Harding with Mr Bennett.'

The door is released and they enter behind the ample back of Mrs Bright. In front of her is Isabella Sinclair. Edgar draws in a hissing breath of disgust through his teeth. She is unsteady on her feet, reeling about, bent from the waist like a rag doll, looking likely to fall any second, but no one moves to support her.

The blonde hair is dishevelled, a bow of red ribbon has tumbled from its high perch and her dress is twisted around her as if she has violently wrenched herself away from someone. Her stockings are laddered and swarf-stained. Just as they enter, she straightens herself up for a second, then launches herself forward and, meeting the obstacle of the cook, kicks her hard on the shin.

'Let me through, you bleedin' old cow!' She paws at the bigger woman, but Mrs Bright, face red enough for apoplexy, retaliates with a push that sends her sprawling back on to the table, where piles of clean dishes wait to be put away. A young girl, who still has a tea towel in her hand, gives a little whimper as a pile at the far end of the table slides, wobbles and falls.

'That's family-crested,' Harding wails, diving to the far end of the table to stop any more falling. 'Do something, for Gawd's sake, Mr Bennett.'

'No use trying to reason with her,' Mrs Bright shouts. 'She's beside herself.'

'Mr Bennett.' Isabella Sinclair pauses to focus, then comes swaggering up to him. 'My, aren't we –' a belch interrupts – 'in your whistle and flute.' She flips a hand at his bow tie. He fends her off, more disgusted with himself than her, that he had ever found her attractive enough to deceive Fay for.

'Why are you here?' he demands.

'Wanted to see Mr Edgar Bennett, didn't I?'

'How did you get here?'

She lifts a forefinger and wags it at him. 'Wouldn't you like to know.'

'The maid said she thought she heard a motorbike.'

'That would account for the swarf all over her legs,' Mrs Bright comments.

'You shut up, you!' The venom in her voice makes the girl whimper again and stuff the tea towel into her mouth.

'Keep well away, Jill,' Harding tells her. 'In fact, you go get your coat and hat and go home.'

The girl hesitates.

'I'll see you don't lose any money.' He nods her on her way.

'*I'm* losing money,' Isabella declares. 'Can't go to London now – no money. No money.' She advances on Edgar.

'Stand no nonsense from her,' Mrs Bright intervenes, infuriating Isabella, who seizes a large dinner plate, raises her arm and throws it in the general direction of the cook. The plate hits the baize door, falls to the stone floor and breaks.

'She's got to be restrained,' Harding shouts. 'Come on, Mr Bennett, it's up to us.'

'Mr Bennett! Mr Bennett! T'aint Mr Bennett to me,' she says forcefully. 'It's Edgar, dear old Edgar. Don't be shy, darling. Keen enough for me once, wasn't you? What's changed, then? Your hoity-toity friends don't approve – perhaps they don't know – yet!' She pauses to laugh, adding triumphantly as she remembers, 'Yes, that's why I come, to tell them.'

Edgar is suddenly icily angry. No use now trying to hide anything from the servants. He gives a nod to Harding and the two of them move around either side of the table. She retreats a step or two, then picks up another plate. Harding is making a lunge to save the family china just as Greville and Bess walk into the kitchen.

'What the devil's going on here?' Greville shouts.

'Oh, look!' Isabella Sinclair calls. 'It's Miss Hoity-Toity. See you going to your gran's, don't I. This your young man, dear? Know about your father, does he? About your father and me, I mean, dear?'

Edgar sees his daughter step back as if she has been struck, Greville putting out an arm to keep her behind him.

'Can you manage here?' Greville demands.

Edgar nods and Greville turns Bess around and takes her back through the baize door and out of the kitchen.

'Go and tell everyone else, shall we?' Isabella tries to push past Edgar to follow.

'Everyone who matters knows now,' Edgar mutters as he catches one flailing arm and Harding grabs the other.

Greville is back in seconds. 'I'll fetch my car,' he says. 'The three of us can see this lady home.'

'Oh! Lady!' she exclaims, but as she struggles, they hold her tighter and her language slips into real broad cockney. 'Tek your bleedin' 'ands off me! You're bleedin' hurtin'!'

'I'll have my car in the stable yard in five minutes. Harding will show you the back way. Keep her in here until then, there's a lot of people on the terraces.'

'I'd like to go on the terrace—'

'You're going nowhere, madam,' Harding says and suggests, 'We could gag her.'

She struggles and shouts so loudly, Mrs Bright stoops, picks up a floor cloth from near the sink, and holds it in front of the other woman. 'Shut your cakehole, or I'll ram this in it,' she tells her. Isabella stops shouting and Mrs Bright explains, 'You've got to talk to 'em in language they understand.'

'Five minutes can seem a bloody long time,' Edgar comments as they hold on to the blaspheming, kicking woman. Harding gives him a quick grin, a momentary flash of fellow feeling.

The five minutes up, the struggle to get her past the various small pantries and storerooms adjacent to the kitchen becomes ugly, just a matter of brute force, as she sticks her legs out to catch at every wall and door and her cries echo alarmingly. As they finally reach the outside door, Harding puts his hand over her mouth. They have to walk past the far end of the back terrace to reach the stable block.

Above them, the lights gently illuminate couples, sparse groups, and the music comes with melodious softness now from the distant rostrum. Their progress is awkward. Harding stumbles and she again tries to scream. Edgar mutters, 'I've got her,' and takes both arms, pinioning them hard behind her back, while Harding now keeps one hand firmly clamped over her mouth.

Their progress is still hardly quiet as they propel her across the gravel, both anxious to reach the cobbles of the stable yard. Then Edgar realizes they are being watched. Someone is standing under the ballustrades of the terrace, the bars of light falling across her. Bess. She stands so still, as if turned to stone herself.

He can imagine how it looks, the brutal way he is holding and pushing this woman about. The perspiration on his forehead prickles like icy needles, and he has no heart for this physical battle, there seems little point.

'Come on, sir,' Harding urges. 'Nearly there.'

They reach the cobbled entrance. The large gates are open and, inside, a sports car stands with its door open but hood up.

'You drive,' Greville says, holding out his keys. 'Harding and I will go in the back with her.

'Thanks.' He is grateful not to have to sit by her, to struggle with her all the way back to her house. Once in the back of the car, she seems to quieten a little and they must have relaxed their grip, for the next moment her hands claw at Edgar's face. As she is pulled away, he feels her nails take skin from either side of his neck.

There is a swift melee in the back seat, then Greville orders, 'Drive, fast. There'll be nothing on the roads at this hour.'

The village street is deserted when he pulls up outside her cottage. 'Where's your key?' Harding demands. 'Your house key. Where is it?'

'It used to be under the flowerpot near the rockery,' Edgar says, not caring now what conclusion they draw from this knowledge. 'I'll get it.'

'No, you stay in the car. I'm sure that's best,' Greville says. 'Harding and I will manage.'

'Hold her, sir,' Harding says as he gets out, then goes round to open Greville's door. So much of this would be comic, Edgar thinks, if it wasn't so heartbreaking. Thankfully the woman now seems exhausted and the two support her rather than drag her to her own back door.

He moves to the passenger's seat and all he can think of is Bess's still figure barred by shadow, motionless and judging, assessing the situation, as he has always taught her to do.

The way back to the Hall seems much shorter, as return journeys often do. The whole incident had probably not lasted three-quarters of an hour. Harding turns to go back through the kitchen, and Edgar hands him a pound note. 'Thank you.

That's just for your help.' Not for your silence, it's not hush money, he wants to add.

When they enter the porch, Lady Philipps is there and is obviously aware of what has happened.

'Edgar, Fay has driven Bess home, and I suggest it's best if Harding drives you home right away. I've sent a message down to him.'

'I'll take—' Greville begins.

'This is your party,' she reminds him. 'I think less questions will be asked if you return to the rest of your guests without further delay. Some are looking for you to make their good-byes.'

Edgar nods to Lady Philipps as Harding reappears on cue. Nothing more is said. The Philippses, grandmother and grandson, turn back into the house and the door closes.

At home, he finds Fay waiting for him in the kitchen.

'She's gone up to bed,' she says as he enters and looks at her.

'What made them come after me?' he asks.

'She got it into her head that something had happened to the horses.' Fay shrugs. 'Greville said the way to deal with that worry was to follow you and find out.'

He had gone to the Hall feeling all his stars were back on course, but now it's as if the whole damn solar system has fallen on his head. He grips the back of a chair and feels like a man in court, in the dock. 'What did she say?'

Fay looks down, frowns. 'She didn't speak all the way home in the car.'

He knows there is more. 'When you got home?'

'She wanted to know how I could stay with you when I knew, then ran upstairs without waiting for an answer.'

'I've lost her, Fay.'

'She's too much a part of you for that ever to happen, and I'm afraid too much like you to make it easy.'

Twelve

I tear off my red party gown and throw it on my bedroom floor, then like a dog unearthing an old bone I find out the small fat red book of prayers.

I crouch in my window seat nursing my hurt, my disbelief, my anger. I wonder why I am gripping this book until my knuckles show white. Do I think God might be some help, or if I squeeze hard enough, he will take time backwards so tonight never happened? Or do I want to confront Pa, stab my finger at the pages of The Form Of Solemnization Of Matrimony, face him with the holy oaths he has broken? Do I want to go to their bedroom and ask my mother how she can bear to be in the same room with him? He is, after all, the beast who has lusted after carnal knowledge of another woman.

When I followed Greville into the kitchen, Pa's eyes had been hard blue ice. 'But I can be angrier than that,' I whisper. I had seen his anger startled away for a moment when he saw me there, witnessing his guilt. Then, standing below the terrace, if the first moment made me feel superior, grown up, the second made me feel sick at heart. I've never seen him treat an animal with such harshness as when he and Harding were bundling Mrs Sss along. The dimly glimpsed figures had been like a scene from a war film – someone picked up in the streets of Paris, a spy perhaps, being bundled away to be tortured at Nazi head-quarters.

Outside, a shadow passes between moon and ground, grow-ing larger as a great barn owl comes down to the edge of the orchard. I see its white moonchild face as it drifts in. Then, so swiftly that fear clutches my heart, it swoops down, and is away again with a mouse hanging in its claws. I can see the victim's limp form, head down, tiny feet dangling, long tail trailing. The owl's hooked beak will not be merciful. I hope it's already dead.

I remember the Sunday afternoon when Colleen's horrible brother, Roy, had swooped around in front of us on his motorbike, scattering gravel, skidding to a halt just in front of our legs as we strolled towards Packman. He had tried to goad me with information I already knew to be true. It was a fact that for over twelve months Pa had sold his beef cattle direct to Mr Faulkner, the local butcher, instead of sending them to market. I had already asked Pa about this, for I had been watchful and curious about everything he did, everywhere he went. He had said that it saved him time and transport costs, and gave Mr Faulkner more profit. 'Better for both of us.'

When I repeated this to Roy, he had sneered. 'You believe that, you'll believe anything. It'll be hush money,' Roy had told me triumphantly. 'He's being paid in kind to keep his mouth shut!'

At the time, I had told Roy that I wished he'd keep his mouth shut. To which he had replied that I'd better be nice to him, or he'd tell about the letters that came addressed to their Colleen. It's been an uneasy truce, and soon no doubt he'll be able to really gloat, for this kind of story never stays secret, and it will not want in the telling.

Villages can be good places, or narrow spiteful places, full of gossip, but one positive thing could come from this. It will all make it much easier for me to leave home, and I know immediately what I intend to do. In just two weeks' time, at the end of term, I shall leave school, no going on for any further education. I am seventeen and I intend to begin earning some money. I shall save, then when Ian comes out of the Army in about eighteen months time, I shall go to Cornwall, or if not then, as soon as I am twenty-one, when *no one* can tell me what I can and can't do.

I'll write to Ian, tell him what I intend. I take out my

notepaper and put Colleen's address at the top and begin, *My dearest Ian*, and then I can't go on. In spite of all my father's done, I find I can't write the words which will utterly condemn him in another's eyes. So, do I love my father more than Ian? Or Ian more than my father? Neither seems true; these loves are different. One is where I come from and the other is where I want to go to. And love, I learn, may have nothing to do with liking.

I write about my plans, nothing else. Perhaps when we meet, whenever that may be, I'll tell him. Then, I suppose, I sleep, I cry some, and in the early morning, all that is left is anger.

I don't want to see anyone, but I always look after the horses when I'm home. I certainly don't want to encounter Noel; he's too astute, too tuned in to my moods. I might just blab out the whole affair to him, probably finish in tears on his shoulder, and that would be ludicrous; I'm about eighteen inches taller than him now.

I am returning to the house when I hear Noel's nailed boots in the yard. I lengthen my stride to be inside before he comes into sight and, stepping quickly into the kitchen, I find Pa pouring boiling water into a teapot we never use. He looks up at me, his eyes are steady enough, but wary, and he is making tea. The whole world has gone mad.

I turn away to the sink to wash my hands.

'Take this tea up to your mother,' he says and before I turn I hear the back door close behind him. So quickly does he go, his collie is left behind. It stands and whines at the door, rolls its eyes in my direction. I feel a pang of empathy for this slave of my father's, and open the door. It skitters around the edge and is away.

I take the tray upstairs because I am curious what has kept my mother in bed, and my father making tea. I tap at the door and Ma raises herself from the bed.

We exchange looks and she sighs deeply.

'You're alright?' I ask and she nods. I turn to leave.

'This is none of your business, you know.'

I stop, shake my head and swing round. 'None of my business!' I exclaim. 'He's my father, isn't he?'

'He has never failed in his duty to you as a father,' she says, staring straight back at me.

'Only to you as a wife.' I have in my mind to quote the marriage ceremony, to fetch the prayers, throw the book on her bed. 'How can you bear it? How can you be here?' I indicate their bed and the gesture seems crude even to me.

'Because I love him,' she says simply.

'And Ian's mother? All that is true?' I still need someone I trust to confirm this thing.

'Yes, Bess,' Ma says unequivocally. 'It's true. It's no use trying to hide from the truth. But I came to realize the faults were not all on one side.'

'How can you say that? You've not been unfaithful.'

'No,' she shakes her head, then smiles. 'You may understand more when you're older, when you are married. You know what Noel says – *You can't put old heads on young shoulders.*'

'Bugger Noel!'

'Bess!'

'His sayings get on my nerves.'

'Because they are usually right, you mean.'

At another time I might have unfrozen and laughed, but this is too serious. This has all changed my life. I go to the window and tell her I do not intend to stay at school, or continue my education. 'I shall learn to pay my own way. I may go and live in London; there are always jobs there.'

'No, Bess, don't even think it!' Pa slams his hand flat on the kitchen table. 'No daughter of mine is going off to London on her own. What are you thinking of?'

'Well, I am not staying here,' I tell him. 'I'll ask to stay at school for next weekend, then when I leave in a fortnight—'

'You will come home,' he says heavily.

'We will see,' I answer.

'We *will* see.'

140

Ma's voice intervenes and I spin round to her, shocked to see how pale and tense she looks.

'We will see,' she repeats. 'In two weeks we will discuss the matter properly. There are a good many options we can consider if Bess no longer wishes to be here with us, her parents.'

That hurts. I want to protest it is not her that I object to, that it is my father who is, or will be, the public disgrace as soon as this latest episode gets out. He is the one I put high, high on a pedestal and defended, he is the one who has fallen. My fallen idol.

'What options?' Pa demands.

'We both have families, Edgar, connections. Something can be found for Bess to do if she doesn't want to continue at school.'

'And what about here, this place?'

'That is something else that must wait,' Ma says, and she goes from the kitchen and leaves us together. I hear her walking slowly upstairs.

'You are making your mother ill.'

'Me!' I exclaim. 'I hardly think so.'

'Your mother and I settled our differences a long time ago.' He pauses and spreads his hands, then throws them up a little as if to include my mother in the bedroom above. 'Can't you tell?'

I stand, dumb, drowned by too many emotions. I cannot come to terms with this less-than-perfect father, this man who says things are better when it seems to me they have just been hidden, covert – a covert affair. I've seen such headlines in Mr Rawlins' *News of the World*.

'So?' he questions. 'Why let an incident spoil everything like this?'

'An incident!' Now the words burst out. 'It doesn't feel like an incident. I wonder if Mrs Sss thought it was an incident – or Greville, or Lady Philipps, or Harding, or the cook, or the maids, or the village.'

'You're like your mother, you can always dramatize a situation.'

'Situation! Incident!' I exclaim, feeling the words from prayers tumbling about in my head. 'It's more betrayal and heartbreak. I trusted you, but you're no better than the beasts in the fields with your lusting.'

He draws in a long breath, his face blazing.

I stand my ground, staring him out, but brace myself for some kind of retribution.

He catches at and grips a chairback as if to steady himself, and I hear his breath being let out slowly, raggedly. 'There was a time I might have put you over my knee for such talk.'

'Pity you didn't when I was small. Pity you took me every-where. Pity I was always in your shadow. What a pity! Then I wouldn't have loved you, or respected you like I do.' That last word slips from my lips but I snatch it back with a shout; 'Did! Did! Like I did!' I rush to the door, then turn to add, 'And I wouldn't have made a fool of myself defending you all sum-mer.' I run up to my bedroom, slam the door.

When I am back at school, I write to Ian, tell him I won't be going home for two weeks, and that, when I do leave, it will be permanently, and after that I am not sure *what* I shall be doing.

That my first weekend at school should also be my last is very strange. Perhaps it's not so curious that the final week of real security rather hurtles by – for the end of the week promises only some rather sad goodbyes and afterwards uncertainty. It becomes obvious I do have to go home in the very first place, but after then, I don't know. I think I am a little surprised that Ma took me at my word and has left me completely without contact from home for these last two weeks. So, she and Pa stand together. I suppose I admire her for such loyalty, but Pa has taught me my standards to judge people by, and he must accept the consequences.

On the final Friday I have taken my last case of belongings down to the hall to wait for my mother when one of the old gardeners – whom I've often talked to because he remembers my mother at school – beckons me from the front door.

'There's someone waiting to speak to you at the front gate.' He looks behind himself conspiratorially. 'I'd get out there quickly if I were you. Don't think I'd dare tell you if it wasn't last day of term.'

'Oh! That sounds intriguing. Thank you.'

'That's alright, miss. Just be careful.'

He touches his cap and I go out wondering what this could be about. There have been one or two end-of-term pranks. This could be a belated one. I stop against one of the huge stone pillars capped with seated lions and can see no one I know at all, just passers-by, a couple, a soldier. I think perhaps it is a mistake.

'You don't recognize me?' a voice asks and, striding across from the other side of the pavement, comes the soldier.

'Ian.' My lips form the name but no sound comes the first time. 'Ian.'

He holds out his hands. I feel my face and the whole world light up.

'Bess.' I take his hands and we pull together, each to the other. He puts a kiss on my forehead. I smell the wool of his uniform, like a sheep with mist on its back, feel the hard peak of his cap peck my head. 'Thank goodness I didn't miss you,' he says. 'I've only just got off the train. I walked straight up from the station.'

I can't think what to say. I laugh from pure excitement. I stand with my mouth open, shaking my head in disbelief. He looks taller. His stance is certainly that of a soldier, though it always has been, always upright. Then I ask, 'What have they done to your hair?'

He laughs. 'You should see me without the cap! And you, I thought perhaps you would be in school uniform.'

'Not on the last day. Well, not for the last few days really.'

'You're all ready to go home?' he asks

'Ma won't be here just yet.'

'But you *are* leaving.'

'Good as left,' I tell him. 'Ready to get on with my own life, earn some money, as I said in my letter.'

Then we kind of lapse into what our hearts and minds are saying, and it's an effort to ask, 'But what about you? This is such a surprise.'

'Just passing through,' he says quietly.

'Passing through?'

'Well, sort of.' He looks rueful, then smiles. 'Could we walk, or find somewhere to have a coffee, sit and talk for a while?'

'Why not,' I would agree to anything, I am so happy to see him; so fearful, from what he says, that it will not be for long. 'Ma won't be here to collect me for ages yet.'

He does not answer, but catches my hand and pulls it through his arm. We walk like a couple. We exchange smiles, and as we go along, it is as if we silently renew all our memories, all our golden moments, in fields and brooks, in dreams.

The way is downhill, so the pleasant prospect of the city spreads out before us – like the life we are going to make together, I tell myself, a broad sunny canvas. It is a wonderful walk; the pavements are wide; there are old arched gateways through to tree-lined walkways made in Victorian times. Quite soon we can see the ornate brickwork of the railway station, its archways and brick cupola with a huge clock. I never noticed it was all so pleasing before.

We walk in a maze of unsaid things, of sentences half thought-out, but waiting until we are still, settled to the task of catching up. There is much to say, much to learn from each other. I am tormented by the question Noel says you should never ask a soldier on leave: *How long have you got?* But perhaps that was only in the war. I look up at him. The angles of his face seem harder, as if spare flesh has been trained off him. He does look older, like a real man. His whiskers glinting in the sun look quite stiff and strong.

Then I realize that, as we are looking at each other and smiling, other people are glancing at the two of us and smiling. We must be glowing with a very special love and happiness.

'There's a milk bar just past the station. Ma and I used to go there sometimes before we went to the cinema.' I feel a touch of regret that those outings after Friday school are over.

He nods and soon we come to the bright blue and yellow facade of Banty's Milk Bar. There are high steel stools with blue seats at the counter but in alcoves there are small tables. We both look towards the far corner.

Ian brings over two coffees and two long glass dishes with double scoops of vanilla ice cream. He sits opposite, takes off his cap.

'Will you please stop looking at my haircut,' he pleads.

'Your lovely hair! How could they? Couldn't you tell them?'

He pulls a dire face. 'One chap made some quip about *just a short back and sides* and the barber ran the clippers straight over the top of his head. I kept quiet.'

We laugh, but then, as I pull at the first wafer pushed into the ice cream, I feel as if it is all pretence; I feel I want to curl over the ice cream and cry tears on to it.

'Are you alright?' he asks, and his hand covers mine.

'You said, passing through.'

He nods at the ice cream, which I will eat because he's bought it for me.

'Not sure you can pass through Leicester going from Penzance to London. More of a diversion.'

'You shouldn't be here.'

He shrugs. 'I'll be late reporting back.' He uses his spoon to shave a layer of soft ice cream from the outside of the mounds.

I do the same and, blurring the outlines of our ice creams, we put cautious questions and give gentle answers to each other. There are much longer gaps between some questions and some answers. We play at eating, but our glances devour each other in greedy snatches, searching out old selves in new images.

'Will you be in trouble?'

145

He shrugs. 'I had to see you. I had to go see Dad and make sure he was going to be alright, and I had to see you.'

'Your dad?' I remember the distressed man in the village street.

He nods. 'He's creating a cliff-side garden in between redecorating the cottage. The building work's finally finished. I guess he'll be fine now the locals know him a bit. They don't seem so shy down there about asking him questions about his face.' He fakes the Cornish accent, '*What happened to you then boy?*' though I notice there's tact enough not to use their other expression, *m'andsome*. He pauses, quizzes me. 'You won't forget how to laugh, will you, Bess?'

I shake my head, lips pressed tight against laughter that could easily spill into tears if I let it out.

'I was worried he'd feel even more lonely when . . .' He pauses to look quickly at me. 'But he'll be OK. The locals have really taken to him now they know his story – bit of a local hero – and he's joined the village cricket team.'

'Lonely when?' I pick up the uncompleted sentence.

'I'm on embarkation leave.'

He grips my hands, and I concentrate on khaki sleeves, his hands, my hands, navy cardigan sleeves, blue formica table top. 'Well, I was,' he murmurs. 'But I've been recalled.'

'To go overseas?'

'Singapore.' He goes on, talking about a communist uprising in Malaya, and British troops fighting Chinese guerillas since 1948.

I'm not overly sure I remember where Singapore is. At the end of some distant peninsula? 'But it's the other side of the world,' I decide.

'About a month on a troopship.'

I think about him going further and further away for a whole month. I've only just got him back. I want to accuse him of always going away. 'How long will you be gone – out there?'

'To the end of my National Service, I guess.' He gives my hands a little shake, trying to distract me from the misery which must be written large on my face. 'We must think about when I come back.'

I think *if*, just like I'm in some wartime drama, but this isn't the films, this is for real. The lights won't go up and I'll walk away. This is my particular misery, no one plays this part but me. I look down sharply so he cannot see the idea, this fear in my eyes. *When*, I tell myself. *When* he comes back. He startles me with the same words.

'When I come back, we can tell your parents how we feel about each other. I'll be nearly twenty-one by then.'

That magic age. 'No one will have any further say in my life when I'm twenty-one.' I hardly know whether I speak aloud or not, and Ian is rushing on, just as he did when we went to the Red Pool. He is rushing on and I am, just as then, lagging behind.

'I promise,' he is saying, 'I shall come and take you away, pluck you from the bosom of your family.' He laughs, sounding reckless, challenging, the knight on the white charger.

Perhaps it is the word *pluck* which brings the memory of Ma's ball gown, flowers massed on her bosom; then of Pa frogmarching Mrs Sss. I make my own vow with all the fervour of someone with their hand on a pile of Bibles: 'Nothing and no one will stop us being together one day.'

'I do love you,' he says.

'I love you,' I reply, then thrill at such talk in public. I could wish I wasn't always so aware, didn't always see myself doing things. I'm like my own audience, watching my own performances, always self-critical. Then it's as if some masochistic urge takes over. 'When do you actually have to go? I mean' – and I ask that question – 'how long leave have you got?'

'None,' he replies and watches my face, then adds quietly, 'I have to catch the nine o'clock train back to London.'

'Tonight?'

He nods. 'I just came to see you.'

'Nine o'clock.' My misery feels complete.

The waitress comes over to collect the dishes and cups, waits with a cloth to wipe the table. We see that the milk bar is filling up: city workers coming in for a quick snack before evening classes, theatres, cinemas, dates. They're happy.

'Come on, let's go,' Ian says. Outside, as if the traffic reminds him, he asks, 'What time will your mother come to the school to pick you up?'

I have not given this another thought. She could already be there, but there is no way I am giving up these last three hours. 'If I walk back to the station with you for your train, I'll be in time.'

'Sure?' he questions, and I see the words *That's late* hovering on his lips, and though I nod emphatically, he goes on: 'There's the park near the station, we could go there, then I could walk you over to meet your mother, say hello . . .' He trails off, leaving the *and goodbye* in our minds.

I don't want him involved in another family argument when I'm hours late, and I don't want to share his remaining time with anyone. 'No, let's jump on a bus and go to the Abbey Park. It's much nicer there.'

The Abbey Park is ablaze with autumn flowers, multicoloured asters and dahlias, great massed beds of red salvias. At this time on a Friday evening there are not many people. The pavilion is open, but we take the path to the left and go towards the abbey ruins, the pattern and plan of the ancient building told by low but well-maintained walls and the plinths and circles where pillars once stood. A sense of history still clings here in this quiet corner: a drama of conflicting religious faiths, foolish popish ambitions. Here is the tomb of Cardinal Thomas Wolsey – charged with high treason, but who died in 1530 before he could be brought to trial. I came here years ago with the history mistress, wrote my essay, and have never been back until today.

This time there is more history – history being made – and it feels larger than life, more colourful than technicolor. Here, while they are sitting on the sun-warmed walls of the old Abbey, Ian Sinclair asks Bess Bennett if she will become engaged to him when he comes back from abroad. She says yes, and until he can ask her father and officially buy a ring, he gives her a small black velvet box.

'Open it,' he urges.

'I haven't bought you anything.'

'You couldn't hardly' – he grins at me – 'not knowing I was coming, but I shall expect you to make up for it in letters to your soldier.'

'My soldier.' I indulge in the words. Inside the box is a small locket, gold-chased with a design of lilies.

'Oh! It's beautiful. Does it open?'

'Yes, but there's nothing in it.'

'I could put some of your hair in it. Well, I could if you had enough to be cut off.'

'Oh! I reckon I could spare a bit off the top.' He takes off his cap and holds up the longest piece of hair he can find. 'Look at that, must be two inches at least.'

'But we've got nothing to cut it . . .'

'I've got a knife.' He feels in his pocket and brings out a small clasp knife.

I take it from him. 'I've still got your other knife,' I tell him and for a moment we look at each other with happy nostalgia. I think this must be like when you are old and have lived together all your lives and have lots of such memories to share, happy yearnings for times past.

'Go on then.' He offers me the top of his head.

I open the knife and, standing in front of him between his knees, hold the tuft of hair up straight. He curls his arms around my middle. 'I need something to hold on to,' he says. 'In case it's painful.'

'It could well be,' I say as I begin sawing. 'And it could take some time.'

'I don't mind.' One cheek presses close to my chest, and my heart doesn't know where it should be. 'Take as long as you like,' he says.

I saw away.

'You are allowed to breathe,' he says. 'Are you breathing?'

'No, I don't think so. I don't think I can.' I feel that if I stop sawing away at his hair he will let me go, and if he let's me go, I shall probably fall over. 'Oh! That's it!' A triangular wedge of hair comes away in my fingers. I hastily rough over the place I had hacked it from so his scalp shows less readily.

'Sure you don't need any more?'

'You've not a lot to spare. I mustn't drop this, I'd just lose it in the breeze.'

I intend to put his hair under the tiny heart-shaped frames on both sides, but he says that my hair should be on the other side. 'And please can I have a piece to take with me?'

So, we hack a piece of my hair off. This is easier, and Ian puts a sizeable chunk of curl into his army pay book. 'Now I'll always have a bit of you with me,' he says.

'And bits of us will always be together,' I add, looking at the blonde and black hair in either side of the locket. I stand in front of him again and stoop to put my cheek next to his, then turn a little so I may kiss him. I wish I was experienced enough – or brazen enough, Miss Seaton would say – to kiss him on the lips. 'I shall treasure it all my life,' I tell him.

'And I shall treasure you all mine,' he says, and holds his hand over his heart where his pay book is. Then he asks, 'Are you hungry?' I shake my head, then I realize he must be, just an ice cream since he travelled from London, and at nine he has to travel back again.

'You'll need something, though. I could smell cooking when we came by the pavilion. We could have something there. Come on.'

We have fish and chips, bread and butter and huge cups of tea. The room seems massive, like an enormous cricket pavilion, but with many tables and a mere scattering of customers. It smells of frying but of other things too: long summer days; dry dusty wood and nets; mown lawns and the evening smell of a river. The River Soar is wide here in this park, people swim in parts of it, and I can hear the weir. I think of our home brooks rippling along into these waters, and then, like us, finding themselves suddenly involved in bigger things, rushed along willy-nilly, out of control.

I glance at my watch. Five minutes past eight.

'It can't be.' I feel as if we've been cheated, robbed, we can't possibly have used up over two hours.

'We'd better start back for the station,' he says and takes my hand, carrying his cap in his other hand. We walk to the bus stop. I am half anxious for the bus to come, half hopeful it won't. It does, of course. We alight at the stop nearest to the station and it is twenty-five minutes to nine o'clock. My heart does a kind of nervous dance, the word *palpitations* comes fleetingly to my mind.

'My kit's in the left-luggage office,' Ian tells me.

By the time we're on the platform for the London train it is seventeen minutes to nine. You can't escape time on a platform: there is a huge clock; people looking at it every few seconds, or at their wristwatches, and asking and telling each other the time. After a few minutes have worried themselves by, he props his kitbag and case against the end of a bench, and we walk away from the main groups of waiting passengers.

It is getting quite dark now, clouds have blown in and the moon has not risen. We walk on and on with slow measured tread, until we reach the point where the platform ends, slopes down to the railway lines. 'That's it, then,' I hear him say as we hesitate, teeter, one step short of beginning the descent.

Someone is shouting from further along the platform, but we take no notice, until the voice becomes louder, angry. 'Oi! Oi! You two!' Then we turn to see a porter gesticulating at us, bent forward in an urgent half-running stride.

Ian lifts a hand and draws me away from the slope and into the shadow of the last shuttered office on the platform. 'He must have thought we intended to walk down on to the line.'

'A suicide pact. . .' I begin to say, but stop because it does not seem such an improbable idea. I suddenly understand why people might be driven to such things.

'I want to live with you, not die with you,' Ian says. 'We have everything to come.'

'Yes,' I say into his shoulder, for in spite of all the attention we have drawn to ourselves, we stand unashamedly, wrapped in each other's arms. 'Together we have everything to live for.' I know this is true, because I realize when I am with him I am more myself than at any other time, I am like Bess Bennett *buffed up*, as Noel would say, to be at her very best. To be with Ian is what my life is all about.

'I'll write first to give you my army post office address.'

I press my forehead against him, then worry my cheek into his jacket, wanting to keep the feel of him, the memory, breathe in the male smell of wool, soap and, faintly, of our last meal together.

'Will you get mail on the boat?' I ask.

'I'm not sure. Perhaps they take it overland to places like Gibraltar.' I feel him shrug and I hear a train approaching. I pray it is not this platform, that his train might be late, delayed – but they never are.

'You promise to write?' His voice is suddenly anxious, and his shoulders tense under my hands.

'Of course, of course.' My voice is thick but urgent. 'I love you, Ian.'

'I love you, Bess Bennett. Never forget . . .' His voice is lost in that of the porter, who raises his voice again. 'Leicester. Leicester station. Leicester.'

We are sluggish players in all the sudden activity, arriving where his bag and case stand as the last of the others climbs aboard. Doors are slamming, while steam surges, hisses and roars from between carriages and under footplates. The whole station is roaring in expectation of departure, and we are holding it up.

Our porter comes and takes Ian's case. 'Come on, young chap. All aboard!' He puts the case inside the train. Ian throws his kitbag inside, then turns to take me in his arms a final time. He kisses me on the lips and I kiss him back with all my heart and mind. There is more shouting, a deafening succession of swifter surges of steam from the fired-up express, and Ian leaves me.

For a moment I stand, arms half-outstretched where he has left them. The porter moves between us, slams the door, then stands by my side as if he expects me to hurl myself after the train. He does not know how bereft and enervated I feel as the train begins to lurch forward. But Ian is still by the window, kissing his hand and throwing the kiss back to me.

I move along, run, but it is too late, there is no objection from the porter, for the train is well out of my reach. Still I wave and call all kinds of things. *I love you. Write soon. Goodbye. Goodbye.*

'Don't go too far, Miss,' a voice by my side says, and I think it must be the porter, but it's a policeman.

My attention is fixed on the final sight of Ian's arm and hand as the curve of the track takes him out of sight. I lower my arm, and I suppose I would have lingered on that spot, but this tall robust officer seems determined to accompany me.

'Seeing your young man off?' he asks.

I nod.

'Worse in the war,' he comments.

'He is going to a war, in the Far East,' I tell him. 'He's been recalled from embarkation leave.'

'Ah, so that might account for it then.'

I focus on him properly for the first time. He is a tall, robust middle-aged man, and I realize he is taking in my appearance with shrewd and knowing eyes.

'Account for what?' I ask. 'What do you mean?'

'If I'm not mistaken, you are Miss Bess Bennett. Left St Catherine's School this very day.' He looks me up and down again and nods as if satisfied with his guess, and my silence.

I nod as the awful truth dawns on me. I have been reported missing.

'There are a lot of people worried about you, young lady,' he goes on. 'Your father reported you missing about two hours ago.'

'My father . . . But it's my mother who comes to pick me up from school, always.'

'Not today,' he says. 'Not today. We'd better walk back to St Catherine's now and put his mind at rest.'

'I . . .' I stumble over the surfacing realization that when Ma comes to meet me we are so often late back home, I had half believed she would be accomplice to hiding the real reason for my lateness. The thought of immediately encountering my father appals me.

'Unless,' the policeman adds, 'you'd rather accompany me to the police station.'

Thirteen

'Thank God.' Pa's voice is low, husky, as I walk into the headmistress's study, but he does not move. Another time, all other times, he would have taken me into his arms, I had only to graze a knee. Our eyes meet for a few seconds, we see and understand how we used to be, and how this has changed.

He stands, grey-faced, to one side of the desk, leaving the blue Persian mat free for me, I suppose. I step to the other side of the desk and leave this posh mat to the policeman. It obviously doesn't bother him, I like him, the way he stands so crushingly on it.

The constable becomes my new champion as he tells of finding me on the railway platform, leaving the story at that, making no mention of Ian.

'The railway station?' Pa queries.

'It is a place we always keep an eye on in these cases,' the constable adds. 'And the bus stations.'

I see the idea come to Pa's face that the policeman caught me just as I was on the point of running away, of catching the London train. 'Of course,' he says.

'You do realize how much concern you have caused?' Miss Smith asks, shaking her head in disapprobation. 'Have you any explanation to offer your father?'

'Before explanations, I think an apology is due to Miss Smith,' Pa intervenes, straightening up, preparing to deal with me now I am safe.

I think he probably does not want too many explanations about why he thought I was running away to London.

'You have delayed Miss Smith's departure for her holidays,'
he prompts me. 'To cause trouble like this at the very end of a
term is unforgivable.'

His pomposity infuriates me. Why has he come? Why is he
here instead of my mother? I clamp my teeth tight; anything I
may say will only cause trouble, will probably – I glance at the
policeman – be taken down as evidence and used against me.

My father steps forward as if to urge me again to an apology,
but Miss Smith raises her fingers an inch and she is in control.
Now I do feel ashamed for causing my headmistress concern.
She has been a distant, but kindly, figure all through my time at
St Catherine's – short, rotund, grey-haired, walking with a
pronounced limp, she controls the whole school and staff with
her dignity, her air of seeing all, and her expectations of the
highest standards in all things.

'I am sorry, Miss Smith, to have caused you concern. It was
not intended, not planned.' I wonder if I am going to spend my
entire life apologizing for things I do not intend or plan, but
that just seem the right and inescapable thing to do at the time.

'So, it was a whim that took you to the railway station and
wasted four and a half hours of everyone's time,' Pa states.

The constable clears his throat. 'The young lady seems
unharmed, sir, so unless you wish the police to take any further
action, I'll be about my other duties.'

'Yes, of course, officer, thank you for . . '

He does not finished the sentence.

'That's alright, sir. Goodnight to you, and you, ma'am.'

Pa goes to open the door for him and I send my silent thanks
after him. My respect for the police was high before but has
now gone up a lot of notches. Perhaps knowing more than they
tell is part and parcel of their job.

Once the door closes, there is a pause, as if none of us is quite
sure how to close this drama. Then Miss Smith leans heavily
forward on to her desk as she rises, so heavily I wonder if her
hip is hurting more than usual.

'It is Bess's last day here, and I should not like her to leave under any kind of a cloud. I think, my dear, on the whole you have been happy with us?' She smiles and her questioning is gentle, not compelling me to answer.

'It's been good for me, Miss Smith, I know that – and thank you for everything.' I go forward and take the unexpectedly proffered hand.

'God go with you,' she says.

We are out of the city before Pa speaks to me directly again. 'So?' he questions and demands all in the one word.

'Why did you come and not Ma?' I ask my question, then another idea occurs. 'She's not ill, is she?'

'So, that might concern you? It wouldn't concern you to have kept *her* waiting for four and a half hours. Where the hell have you been?'

It had been hell watching that train go out, hell after heaven in the park, so brief a time.

'Bess!' he shouts and bangs the steering wheel with the palms of both hands.

'Is she alright?' I demand.

He does not answer.

'Is my mother alright?' I shout at him, swallow hard at my audacity, then remember that I have lost all respect for him anyway and don't care any more what he thinks of me.

'She has worried about you solidly for a fortnight.'

'I was fine at school, she'd know that.'

'And now? How about *now*?'

'I thought I could go and live with Grandmama until I find a job.'

For a moment I think he is going to drive straight into the back of a coal waggon. I realize he meant how would Ma be feeling when we were so late back.

'You could have phoned,' I say. 'Let her know.'

'Miss Smith was telephoning,' he shouts, then controls himself, drives much slower, but demands, 'So, what is this new madness?'

'It's not new. I told you before I went back to school, I am going to earn my own living, be independent.' I add a silent *of you!*

'You will come home and talk to your mother in a civilized manner.'

'There's no point, my mind's made up.'

'And so, Bess, is mine.'

I think of my conversation with Ian. I knew being twenty-one would be crucial to our future together. I glance at Pa without moving my head. I wonder what he would say if I told him the truth, the whole truth.

'Why did you go to the station?' he demands. 'Your luggage was still all at the school, as far as I know you have little ready cash, your Post Office Savings Book is at home.'

'You've been in my bedroom, looked in my drawers!' I accuse. My concern is for what's in the space under the drawers. 'Is there no privacy even in my own bedroom?'

'You seem to hold little store by your own bedroom, your home, or your parents.'

'My filial duty, you mean.' I never realized I could sound that ironic, that rudely scarcastic. It shocks me, makes my heart pound.

'Yes, I did look,' he goes on, ignoring my remark, 'to ease your mother's mind. She was desperately upset when you didn't want to come home for the weekend, then worried you might do something stupid, like running away.' He glances over at me, as if judging the child again. 'But even I didn't think you'd be quite so stupid as to think of running away without clothes or money.'

The denial, my own defence, is on my lips, but I bite it back. Those days, I tell myself, are over. I don't need to justify my actions or weigh my answers. I'll go home with him – but I shall not stay.

'I don't think you realize how hurtful you've been,' he adds.

'Or you,' I say through clenched teeth. If he hears, he does not reply, but his knuckles grow whiter on the steering wheel.

When we arrive home I find Ma does look pale and drawn. She does look as if she has spent two weeks worrying.

'Are you alright?' she asks me, holds me at arm's length, then embraces me. 'Really alright?'

I nod against her shoulder, knowing she is at the same time silently quizzing Pa.

'So, come and tell me what happened.' She pulls me towards a chair and sits next to me. Pa stands at the head of the table like the presiding judge. The old court hearings round the kitchen table, all we need is a gavel to call for order.

'The horses,' I ask, 'did George exercise them?'

'He gave them good exercise, all fortnight, riding his bike and leading them.' We exchange a small smile. It is a wonder to us both that someone so good with horses is so terrified of getting on one's back.

'In fact he took Ebony up to Tommie a couple of times and he put him around the manège.' She puts a hand over my arm. 'Bess, where have you been?'

'Just in town, that's all. Down to the park, a drink in a milk bar . . .'

'Are you hungry?'

'No, I had fish and chips in the park pavilion.'

'You went to the Abbey Park, then?' She is silent, and I know she guesses there is more, much more.

'Why don't you just tell us the truth?' Pa says.

'Alright!' I stand up, pushing the chair violently back, and tell them – some of the story I tell them, but not about the locket or our promises to each other.

'For goodness' sake, why didn't you explain before?' Ma says. 'Everyone would have understood.'

I see she does, but I laugh at the idea. 'Oh, yes, I'm sure! Miss Smith would have said, Off you go and I'll explain to whoever comes to pick you up.' Then I am appalled at how like Pa I sound.

'So, you're telling us that this boy came specially from London to Leicester to spend a few hours telling you he's being sent overseas!' he exclaimed.

'Saying goodbye,' Ma intervenes.

'Saying goodbye!' He swings round on her.

'You could have telephoned, Bess.' Ma ignores his outburst. 'Even from the town to the school would have helped. Your father need not have involved the police.'

'The time went so quickly.' I sound on the defensive and that's not what I want, it's not the way to begin asserting my independence.

'But you did realize that one or other of us would be waiting, wondering, worrying? For four hours, Bess.'

'Four and a half, Pa said.' But I remember how grey he looked.

Ma gives a tut of exasperation and Pa throws down his jacket. 'Are you doing and saying everything you can to annoy us?'

'Not really, and whatever—'

'Whatever?' he prompts, shouts, 'Whatever, what?'

'Whatever I do is as nothing compared with what you've done. You've torn this family apart.' The words of the marriage service could easily trip from my tongue, but Ma distracts me as she gets up from the table looking stern but shaky.

'I think,' she says, 'we shall all discuss this more calmly in the morning.'

'I'm sorry, but there's really nothing to discuss.'

'You mean you'd sooner spend your time with a sergeant pilot's son than discussing your proper future with your parents?'

I feel as if my lungs have ceased to work. The unexpectedness of this remark rivets me. My *proper future* – and it is the first time I've heard the phrase *sergeant pilot*, but obviously it is meant to be derogatory, a put-down. I suppose I had assumed Ian's father was an officer, but had never thought about it, it had never been mentioned. I can't believe my pa, *my pa*, would stoop to such a tactic to try to discredit Ian. My chest hurts, I feel as if even my body has gone wrong, I seem to be still inhaling when I should be exhaling. My voice is nothing but a

160

gasp. 'I expect his face burnt, and hurt, just the same whatever rank he was.'

I think Ma murmurs, 'Yes'.

'And whatever he is' – I see no reason to hold back my feelings now – 'I love Ian, so you never will be rid of the Sinclairs, will you?'

For a moment there is a stunned silence, then Ma says in a low, low voice, 'Bess, you're seventeen.'

'And it's four years before you come of age,' Pa states.

'Four hours, four years, it won't make any difference,' I tell him. 'When he comes back, we're going to get engaged.'

Pa takes in a deep breath, but Ma raises both hands quite suddenly and shakes her head violently, as if she can take no more, and this distracts him.

I am surprised when without looking at or speaking to either of us she leaves the kitchen. She is obviously going to bed, without a kiss or even a goodnight. For a moment Pa and I stare at each other, then he too turns and follows.

I stand and try to recognize what I feel. Triumphant or abandoned? Lonely? If Ian is not to be approved of, ever, this may be what it will always be like. Independence, striking out for what I want, may have to be like this, solitary. But only, I tell myself, until Ian comes back. Then there is the cottage by the sea, where the sergeant pilot lives. I remember now that the uniform George rescued from the street had stripes on the sleeve as well as the medal ribbons and the wings.

Over the whole weekend, Pa and I are like circling tigers. I come to feel we would be happiest actually tearing at each other, instead of just prowling around. Ma weeds the kitchen garden for a long time on Saturday; on Sunday, telling only Noel, she goes for a long ride alone, so no one goes to Church though Pa gets ready, then changes back into his everyday wear.

'Taken on the boss agen then, 'ave you?' Noel greets me on Monday morning.

'You know nothing about it,' I tell him.

'Don't I, though?' he replies. 'How do you think your mother feels about you wanting to go live with your gran? You bide your time a bit, young lady, that's my advice.'

'I don't want anyone's advice,' I say, spacing the words. 'Thank you.'

'We'll see, but I'll tell you something for nothing.' Then he stops and I have to ask. 'Neither of you will win.'

'Thanks, that helps a lot,' I tell him.

'If you tear each other's hearts out, neither of you'll win, will you?'

He goes off, lifting his cap from his head as if to let the air in, then pulling it back down again. He will be around all day, coming and going between yard and stackyard, clearing and tidying ready for the new wheat stacks, leaving me torn between a wish to find out just how much he does know, and a need to be alone.

By late afternoon I am standing on the bridge leading over to the Pagets' land, now ours. The watercress is dark-green under the bridge and grown tall with bobbly green heads. I walk on. There is a new gate close to the place where Ian and I squeezed through the hedge. Somewhere in the near distance I can hear the sound of new fence posts being put in, and I wonder if there has been any start on the footpath through the spinney. I think not because Pa has decided the fences must have priority.

I wish I could have a timetable, a sequence of things to do. Instead it feels like – like I've pulled out the old Oxo tin from the bottom of my book cupboard and am trying to make a picture of all the odd jigsaw pieces preserved there over the years: thick three-ply wooden pieces, thin wooden pieces; big simple cardboard sections, small complex shapes with their round interlocking sections bent and twisted. It is not possible. I should throw all the old, odd pieces away. The puzzles they belonged to have long gone. It's like Pa trying to make the new me fit into his old picture.

If I lean over, I can touch the tallest of the seeding watercress, stir its rank brook-bed odour. I need to be with someone who will really listen to me. Colleen doesn't even know yet about Ian being sent abroad, and above anything else she will understand how I feel about that. Ian's journey to the other side of the world has not begun, or I don't suppose it has, and my ache for him is greater every hour, every minute.

I walk back towards the farm just in time to see Grandmama's trap arriving at a brisk trot, and I am surprised to see she is driving herself. She sweeps into the yard at a much faster speed than George ever drives her. I go to take the pony's head and Noel is immediately there to open the little door and help her alight.

'Time someone came to sort this lot out,' he tells her.

She shakes her head at him. 'Noel Wright, I've been telling you to mind your own business for fifty years.'

'Feels like mine,' he mutters grimly, taking the pony's head.

'Are you off somewhere, Bess?' She kisses my cheek and pulls off her gloves.

'Where's Miss Seaton?' I ask.

'Having a holiday,' she answers in a tone which suggests she might have dismissed her, sent her packing.

I follow her into the house. Her greeting to Pa is perfunctory, while she holds Ma for extra seconds as they kiss. She takes off her coat *and* hat, drawing out a long pearl-ended hat pin, then thrusting it back through the felt. This indicates a longish stay, and she has our immediate attention as she says, 'I have had Clara to see me.'

I feel my eyebrows rise, and as always, mention of Lady Philipps immediately has Pa's attention, but I guess their last encounter would have been at Greville's party.

'What did she want?' His question sounds abrupt, rude.

'She is my friend, Edgar, and has been for many more years than you've been my son.'

There is something so meaningful in the way Gran uses the words *friend* and *son*. I find myself remembering the saying about friends you choose, but relations you suffer. I go to sit out on the old settle beneath the inner opaque window to the wash-house, hoping to be ignored there, but as I sit down I find every eye on me.

'Clara wants to help. She *is* helping.' Gran pointedly does not make herself at home in the kitchen.

'Come through,' Pa says. 'Tea, or sherry?'

'I think a sherry,' she says. 'A little Dutch courage.'

I get up and follow.

'Sounds ominous,' Pa says, then, making an effort to lighten the situation, adds, 'What have you and Clara been up to?'

I see he knows he has said the wrong thing the moment the words have left his lips.

Gran clears her throat with a double falling note of censure and sits down. 'It is not my intention to go over what has been done. The past can't be altered.'

I hear echoes of more than our present troubles in Gran's voice. I remember the crossings-out in the family Bible – someone effectively scrubbed out something in *their* past, even before I tried to eradicate myself from the Bennett lineage.

'But it can be forgiven,' Ma says. 'Edgar and I have solved our difficulties. We're fine.' She glances at me. 'We'll all be fine.'

I shake my head.

'As you see, Bess thinks otherwise.' Pa gives a humph of disgust.

'Yes, I do,' I confirm. 'How can it ever be *fine* again?'

'There are things that will help,' Gran says. 'For one thing, Mrs Sinclair will shortly be leaving the village.'

We all do a kind of mental blink, and no one recovers quickly enough to comment before she adds, 'Clara knows the owner of the property very well.'

'That may be so,' Pa says, 'but you can't just evict someone . . . She will have paid her rent.'

I wonder how he would know that for certain.

'Clara and her friends have effective ways of dealing with life's unpleasantnesses.'

'Paying them off, you mean?' Ma speculates.

'She appears to be a woman who can be bought,' Gran says.

There is a stunned silence as we all three absorb the full implication of that statement. I glance at Gran with admiration. She finishes her sherry, her Dutch courage.

'It's her who should have gone in the first place,' I interject passionately.

'I guess no one will argue about that,' she answers quietly. 'But there is something else. A proposition.'

'A proposition?' I glance at Ma and Pa, but they obviously know nothing of this.

'Yes. Clara, Lady Philipps, has made a serious business proposition to do with you, Bess.'

I can feel Ma and Pa's approval, like warmth from a fire, because of the source of this proposal, even before we've heard it!

'I understand you have left school.'

'Yes.'

'For good?'

'Yes. My school days are over.'

'And you are going to do what?'

'Find work, be independent.'

'She will, of course, do no such thing!' Pa intervenes.

'I shall, sooner or later.'

'There's plenty to fill your time here,' he begins, his tone more irate.

'Edgar, would you let me talk to Bess on her own? There is no point in continuing any discussion if what's proposed is not to Bess's liking.'

'That seems a good idea to me,' Ma says, and leads the way out of the room. Gran prompts her son with a raised eyebrow, a long in-drawn, and slowly expelled, breath.

'I presume we shall have the opportunity to hear this proposition eventually – whatever it is.'

'Yes, of course.' She nods reassurance and Ma puts a hand under his elbow. The gentle touch twists my heart. How can she?

'I'll have another sherry, please,' Gran says as soon as we are alone. 'And I think half a glass won't hurt you.'

'I don't want his sherry.' I sound like a petulant child, but Gran gets up and helps herself and brings me a small glass. She nods at me to take it and sip. I do. I've no quarrel with Gran. Haven't I stood, her arm around me, feeling her heart pounding when she has taken my side on other things.

'How do you know about school?' I ask.

'Your mother came to see me yesterday, while she was out riding.' She leans right back in the chair, her head resting on its high cushion. 'Bess, what she says is true. Your Ma and Pa have settled their differences.'

'I don't see how they can, how Ma can forgive him.'

'In a way, Bess, it is really none of your business. It is just between husband and wife, and no one should *ever* try to interfere between them.'

'What he's done just makes me feel I don't care any more about him, or the Bennetts, or anything.'

'Oh! You have to go on caring no matter what.' She closes her eyes and repeats, 'No matter what.'

'Has something else happened?'

She opens her eyes, quickly, looks startled. 'No, no, child, of course not.'

'A long time ago?'

The eyes are shuttered now. 'A lot of things happened a long time ago.'

'Will you tell me some time?'

'I wouldn't think so,' she says, laughs a little and shakes her head. 'No, at your age things are either all black, or all white. When you're as old as I am, you'll know there can be a lot of grey, matters neither all right nor all wrong. Things happen between men and women, sometimes it's no one's fault, some-times – sometimes it's beyond their strength to prevent them.'

The way she clenches a fist makes me wonder if she means physical strength.

'Pa is his own master, no one forces him to do anything.'

166

'Lady Philipps too is her own person, no one forced her to come to see me. What she proposed came as a complete surprise to me.'

I am suspicious but certainly listening.

'Clara says you have talked of setting up a livery yard, and developing a riding school.'

'Dreamt, you mean. I know that's out now . . .' I am about to elaborate but she holds up a hand.

'In exchange for you caring for the horses at the Hall and giving a hand with the office work, which is becoming a real burden, she will let you have the stables block there rent-free for as long as you like. What do you think?'

I think, yes! For two years, or perhaps for three years, until I am of age I could do the work I love most, looking after horses, teaching young riders. It would not be a bad deal for Lady Philipps either. Tommie needs supervision, and as wages go up, labourers on the land are being replaced by machines – but you can't tend horses with machines.

'So?' Gran prompts.

I am thinking that Lady Philipps is also no fool – but neither am I. I have not fogotten that she has two less-than-appealing granddaughters, and one very elegant grandson whom she said years ago she would quite like to marry me off to.

'You know about Ian Sinclair?' I ask. 'I wouldn't like there to be any misunderstanding if I took up the offer.' She looks at me very solemnly and I see she does know. 'This is to help you, Bess, not for the good of the Bennett lineage.'

'Gran, did you make that crossing-out in the family Bible?'

Her hands swing out in alarm, as if she has lost her balance, and our two glasses go flying from the small side table, the delicate etched bowls and twisted stems splintering as they bounce between rug fringes and wooden floor.

'No!' she exclaims. 'No, never think that, never.'

Fourteen

'It's usually the innocent who suffer.'

The bitterness in his mother's voice makes him turn away, makes the anger that seems so futile against Bess's obstinate resolution seethe very near to the surface. 'That'll be a woman you're talking about, of course,' he mutters.

'Fay, I'm talking about.'

'Fay? It's Bess who's refusing to see reason.' What Bess was refusing to do was live under the same roof with him. She saw him as the ultimate betrayer, the fornicator, the arch-enemy, he knew – he had opened the ancient book where a school protractor kept the place at The Solemnization of Marriage. She would have read the vows. 'She's got a lot to learn about life,' he mutters.

'I'm very afraid she has,' his mother agrees. 'But Fay is the loser, whatever she may *say*. She doesn't want Bess to leave home, not now, not like this. They've grown to be more like sisters than mother and daughter.'

The remark makes him pause. Both she and Fay have this unsettling knack of revealing some aspect of a situation he has not seen before. 'The thing is,' he goes on, 'if she doesn't come here to you, we're afraid she may do something worse. She's adamant she'll only take up the offer of the stables, *stay in the area*, as she puts it, *provided* she doesn't have to live at home.'

'There'll be gossip enough to boil pump water.' The local saying echoes his own unease. 'Then there's Maude,' his mother adds. 'More explaining to do.'

'I trust she won't gossip.'

'Maude can keep a still tongue when necessary.'

'I hope you make sure she knows it's necessary now.' He looks fixedly at his mother but she does not answer. Her relationship with her paid companion is always a bit of a mystery to him. He has a vague memory of Maude Seaton coming to the farm when he was a boy, of a long earnest conversation with his parents. He has no recollection of her being in their lives again until after his father had died, and his mother had needed a companion – then there had seemed no problem contacting the woman.

'It'll only be for a time,' he adds. 'Just until Bess gets over this nonsense.'

'Nonsense?' She shakes her head at him. 'I remember a young farmer's son prepared to incarcerate himself in a City office *for ever* if it meant getting what his heart was set on.'

'I'm not sure it's just young Sinclair.' He hears the tone of his voice moderated by his mother's memory of him as a young man courting Fay Topham. 'It's me she doesn't want to be with.' He comes to a halt, his unfaithfulness not a subject he can converse with his mother about.

'I'm not going to pretend I don't know what you are talking about.'

He feels he has never seen his mother's face so thin, so etched with deep harsh lines. She certainly does not regard him as innocent.

'No, it's Bess.' She extends the name, letting the sibilants linger, making him consider the whole physical being and spiritual concept of Bess Bennett, his daughter.

'You've made her.' She pauses, shakes her head. 'Ever searching for the truth – the right way. The girl could model for everything that is good and noble, like a great French heroine of the revolution.'

He visualizes the figure standing high on the barricades holding aloft a tattered flag. Bess bloodied but unbowed. 'I've made her too good for this world,' he hears himself say. 'You're right, so she'll never forgive me.'

169

'You misjudge her if you think that. Her heart's big enough to forgive, it'll just take time.' She draws in a deep breath. 'And of course she can come here whenever she wants, for as long as she wants. Provided you and Fay are both in agreement.'

'I never want to relive those hours before she was found on the station,' he admits. 'I don't want to be chasing her to Cornwall. Fay and I both think she might try to go there if we don't all agree to this ultimatum she's delivered. God knows, I've nothing against Ken Sinclair, he's had enough to bear, but . . .' He remembers his reference to the *sergeant pilot*, a low unthinking ploy. 'But I curse the day any of them came here.'

'Not many in the village would contradict that.'

He thinks of Faulkner.

'Clara has something in hand,' she says confidently. 'She's not managed the estate all these years without knowing a lot of influential people, a lot about human nature and even more about ways and means.'

'Let's hope she's right about Bess,' he says, not wanting to dwell on Isabella Sinclair.

'Her wish to work with horses? There's not much doubt about that.'

'And the boy'll be away a couple of years. A lot can happen in that time.'

'Indeed, lives can be changed in minutes,' his mother says enigmatically.

He is reminded of her words as Fay greets him on his return. He nods his mother's acceptance of Bess's terms for beginning her working life at the Hall, then sees her start, flinch as from a blow, as Bess rises from the kitchen table and, not looking at him, asks, 'Can we take my things now then?'

He wonders he can feel such intense dislike for someone he loves. 'I'll take your things tomorrow morning,' he says. 'I've wasted enough of one working day.'

'I can take them myself,' Bess says shortly. 'I could use Gran's trap, *she'd let me.*'

Fay's laugh is brief, startled, hurt. He wants to mimic, *I could use Gran's trap, she'd let me.*

'Apart from your clothes,' Fay is saying, 'which will need some sorting, there's things like harness, grooming kit and so on. I presume these will all have to go with you and your horse to the Hall.' Fay's voice is businesslike, her back erect. He reflects that she rarely loses control, never shouts, never loses her dignity, the perfect lady at all times. Perhaps that *had* been one of the problems with their lovemaking, too much the lady – but now . . . He instinctively raises his eyebrows – her new skills in the bedroom still surprise him.

'Oh! I hadn't thought of all that.' Bess sounds almost enthusiastic. There's a couple of old tea chests in the attics, I could fetch those down, use those – there's my books as well.'

'I'll see what clothes are in the wash,' Fay says.

'She's not going to Timbuktu,' he puts in as he sees the effort it costs Fay not to turn away too soon and show her hurt. 'She can come back for things.'

Bess looks as if she never intends to.

'Oh! Get your things together and I'll take them over in the waggon this evening. I'm sure there'll be plenty of people around to help.' He adds in a mutter, 'And enough gossip to boil pump water.'

Fay says something as he leaves the kitchen, but he doesn't hear. His collie bitch follows but he senses the dog's ambivalence. It knows his mood is not right, that though he walks quickly away from the house, there is no aim and purpose to his going, no mission. He is uncaring as to direction, except perhaps to avoid his men, Noel in particular. He needs no platitudes, and is in no mood to come under the old boy's discerning eye.

He goes through the long meadows, where only the already-milked cows will wonder at his presence. He walks on towards the brook and, as he steps up on to the plank bridge, he stumbles. His irritation with his own clumsiness makes him scuff his boots along like a recalcitrant child. He stops in the

171

middle of the bridge and leans over the handrail. This place, this brook, is always redolent with memories of Bess fishing with bent pin and worms, falling in when she lifted her line to find two fish clinging to her worm: *Two fish on one worm! – Splash!* Bess and Colleen making all kinds of things, damming the water up; getting wet feet in the winter trying to walk on the cat ice; Bess helping him haul out a sodden sheep, trying like a desperate little washerwoman to wring the water from its fleece, crying when it was dead.

Bess never scuffed her feet, no matter where he ever led her. She never dragged behind, never questioned, never complained.

Good God. He can't remember the last time he cried. She had followed him willingly everywhere. He tries to push the willing little sandalled figure in the gingham dress out of his mind – tries to find some fault.

She had also followed young Sinclair, of course – or had she led? Six years on, the question holds an added importance. They had come back hand in hand; two filthy children, two children who had come close to dying, according to the boy's lurid account. Childhood adventures made adult bonds – and young men, husbands-to-be, would always displace fathers. He gives an ironic laugh and pushes himself up from the handrail, roughly brushes the tears from his cheeks. Such conclusions didn't help much.

He draws in a deep breath, the dry air of midday, the fall of the year approaching. The land smells exhausted: the harvest taken but the soil not replenished, that wouldn't come properly until the huge steaming piles of dung were carried from the middens and spread before the ploughing. Now is the fall time, *the convalescence*, his father used to call it. *Now's the time for convalescence, and after that, all's well again.* Unexpectedly, the memory comes of a look his parents exchanged as this was said; on his father's part, a look of steadfast reassurance, and on his mother's, he was not sure, but suddenly he realized it had been a significant look, saying much more than he had understood as a child. Had his brain harvested it now to remind him how much less of the true situation Bess could know?

Bess is certainly enervating him far more than the time of year. He takes in the shoulder-high willowherb, and the many places where it has keeled over into the water. The first tangles to trap the debris the winter rains will bring; like this first serious rift with his daughter, an entanglement which, if not dealt with, will build up, flood, turn placid stream to drowning torrent. One real storm and it could happen overnight. He stands and stares at the trouble he could avert, and wonders if he even wants to try, if he cares any more.

You have to go on caring, Jessie. His father's voice comes again from the past, an overheard answer to his mother, to her despairing, *I feel I don't care any more.*

You have to go on caring. It rings in his brain like a discipline from the past. What else could he do anyway? He could either give up, let his land, his family, everything, go, or he could harden his heart, or thicken his skin, whatever it took, to try to accept Bess's decision, her rejection of him.

There were certainly things he was putting off: with the acute housing shortage in the country, he could hardly let the Paget farmhouse remain empty; and there was the spinney and that damned footpath.

Noel had reconnoitred with young George and reckoned the best thing was to get contractors in with some machinery first. 'We'll waste a lot of man hours trying to make a way through that lot on our own. You want men and machinery, and they'll best come in from the far side.'

He guessed the old boy was right – and perhaps now was a good time to go and make a decision. Work on the footpath would at least give the villagers something else to think about besides Bess leaving home.

It takes a good hour to reach the lane on the far side of the spinney, and as they reach it, his collie stops, her muzzle and one paw raised, looking first at the trees, then back at him. He gives her a nod. The dog might as well enjoy herself. She disappears almost immediately, snaking her way under and between the stile and into the neglected woodland. For a moment or two he can hear her passage.

He surveys the stile, the remnants of a foot plank, sole clue to the fact that a footpath ever existed here. He pushes at the uprights – sound, stout oak, worth using to build a new stile on – but beyond is a tangle. He has come without a walking stick, with nothing to knock down the seeding grasses, hold aside the intruding bramble.

'Bracken!' he calls, and there is a crack of wood and snap of twigs as the dog hears and comes towards him. Some forty strides in, he turns to look back towards the stile. It is just possible to see there has been a path here, for while there is a greater growth of grass, the canopy of saplings is less dense. Ahead, the path is less clear.

He visualizes the old map found at Paget's, how the path angled through the spinney, and calculates that if he keeps the sun slightly to his right there should be no problem. Then, in the shadows, he glimpses the coat of a fox lit to auburn as a glint of sun catches it; seems Brac is disturbing more than the rabbits.

He recalls the awe in young Bess's face the dawn he woke her early to watch a vixen bring her cubs to the edge of the spinney, her wide-eyed delight as they played, tumbled, quarrelled. She had said nothing all the way home, her hand pushed into his. She had just given him a smile of thanks every time their eyes met. Years later he found she had written a full report in her school English book. 'I wish I had been there too,' the teacher had commented.

'The foxes are still here,' he breathes, as if it might be a comfort, then starts as, from close by, comes the scream of an animal in abject terror. He tuts at his alarm, only a rabbit made vocal by extreme panic.

He wonders if he trained Bess only to speak out in answer to questions, to the little tests he used to make up to teach her things? Surely he was never that oppressive – and she'd been vocal enough recently.

There is a crackling in the undergrowth and he thinks of

recalling his dog, but is distracted by the realization that no sun at all is filtering through the canopy where he stands.

He must be nearing the Red Pool, tries to remember how long it is since he stood on the huge smooth cobbles which surround the gently seeping spring. Going back to his grandfather's day and before, when stockingers spent long hours over their looms, the pool had been constantly visited, its water carried to the houses of those too old, too frail, or too poorly sighted to go themselves. When he came to the pool he would take a new bearing.

The smell of the pool reaches him, metallic with an underlying hint of sulphur. He pushes on, his boots sinking deep into the accumulation of decades of putrefying leaves. He wonders what young Bess and Ian made of the place as he comes in sight of the stones, deep rust-red where the water runs from the ground. The natural layer of cobbles which underlies great stretches of his land is near the surface at this point and has restricted the growth of saplings, so the sun still slants through. In two generations, or three at most, this has gone from a local resource to a deserted wilderness, but with the woodland properly managed, it could be a magical place. Though he wonders if the present generation would feel his own reverence.

He acknowledges his own reluctance to open it up to all and sundry. Rambling, that was the new craze hitting the country – freedom to walk and cycle, youth hostelling. Banned during the war, everyone was now able to buy maps showing all the footpaths from any stationer.

He whistles to Bracken and moves on, keeping the sun to his right, noting that even at this tailend of summer the ground is very soft, his boots sinking occasionally up to the lacings. He whistles again and from ahead to the left his dog whines.

'Brac!' he commands, and the dog yelps its distress.

'Alright girl, I'm coming,' he calls and pushes his way towards the sound, and is soon over his ankles in black ooze. He reaches up, takes his weight on any sound branch, and steps as near to the trunks of the trees as he can. He calls again and the dog cries back. It sounds in real distress, and as a branch snaps off in his hands, landing him up to his elbows in mire, he has no doubt of his dog's predicament.

'What's happened to the damn drainage?' he demands as he creeps and scrabbles along using a fallen tree as support. 'More expense!' he exclaims. Brac whines – and he locates her. He can see her head, hears the suck of the morass as she pulls a forepaw free and strives to come to him. She sinks faster, disappearing sideways, her peril extreme, one paw free, but her head going down.

He launches himself, dives, seizes the dog's scruff and heaves – pulling her partially out before he wallows, trying to get his feet back under himself. For an eternity he swims in a nightmare of black porridge, then one foot finds submerged cobbles. He lifts himself and the dog and throws her with all his strength towards firmer ground. It is enough, the dog's front paws paddle frantically and she is out, bounding up on to firm ground, shaking, swinging her mud-weighted tail as he manages to stand, crotch-deep, then wade out to join her.

The trauma over, his knees give way and the dog licks his face. He puts an arm over her back and they sit and recover together. He feels the chill of the thick filth on the dog's coat and her uncontrolled trembling as Brac leans on him. He stares at the bog as it reestablishes its surface, swallowing up all trace of their presence.

He remembers young Ian Sinclair swathed in a blanket in the back of his car, his young treble over-high with the telling of the story. He had let Isabella Sinclair shut the boy up, tell him he was worse than his dad with his ridiculous stories.

He calculates the length of his own leg and imagines a child, the two children, caught in the same depth of mire. It was not safe for anyone to walk here. The boy's story of near tragedy had been true. Bess had once before nearly been lost.

The feeling of hopelessness, of being unable to deal with Bess wilfully leaving home, overwhelms him. How can he cope? His thoughts race, but he finds no answers.

The dog beside him shivers convulsively. He gives an exclamation of disgust at his thoughtlessness and, stirring himself, lays a hand on the dog's head. 'Come on, home!'

Fifteen

There's much noise and activity in the back kitchen, Miss Seaton preparing to light the kitchen boiler for wash day. 'Good morning.'

She does not look up. This is the first time the two of us have been alone together since I moved in on Saturday night.

'Good morning, Miss Seaton.' I give her the benefit of the doubt as she kneels, rattling the poker in the bottom of the boiler, drawing out the clinkers.

'Should have thought,' she says between savage thrusts with the poker, 'there's enough people living away from where they should rightly be, without this!'

'What do you mean?' I neither understand her vehemence nor what she means. Who else has left home?

She does not answer, rises stiffly, carefully balancing the ash pan to take it outside. I hurry to open the yard door for her and the wind sweeps in and blows streaks of ash across her apron. She reaches quickly for a sheet of newspaper she has obviously laid ready for the purpose and shelters the ash as she goes out. 'Bennetts!' she proclaims, spits the names as if it is a blasphemy. 'Bennetts! Act first, think later.'

I've noticed on other occasions, when heavy chores have to be done, her temper is short. She feels more like Maude, the domestic help, when she wants to be Miss Seaton, the companion.

She jerks her head, indicating I should close the door after her. Hand on latch, I pause, listening to early-morning village life. I can hear people talking in the street, a man running,

178

calling for someone to hold the bus. I'll be part of this, of real village life, for the first time, able to pop in to see the Rawlinses whenever I want. I won't have to rely on Miss Seaton to know the gossip. I might even be home from the Hall in time to meet Colleen tonight! We'll both be working girls, swopping stories, secrets – and *both* with serious boyfriends, if what I suspect is true. I wonder if Lady Philipps will lay down strict working hours?

There are a lot of uncertainties about this day, mainly because everyone at the Hall has been away for the weekend. a shooting party in Norfolk. This was hosted by Colonel Hugh Ratcliffe, High Sheriff of the county, whose son, Roger, Daphne Philipps is now betrothed to.

There are no more exchanges between Miss Seaton and myself. Gran comes down and tuts about my meagre breakfast of toast and marmalade, though neither of them have anything more. I collect my cycle and ride round the yard to give Gran a final wave, as she stands at the kitchen window. Her hand rises high in response, as if she is seeing me off on a long journey.

I want to have my horse over at the Hall as soon as possible, fit it into the routine of care and exercise straight away, but I can hardly arrive on the first morning with another horse. I must see Lady Philipps and possibly Greville, but I also want to speak to Tommie. I want him on my side. He's been running the stables with only casual help ever since the war, ever since I can remember.

'Time he had someone with a bit of knowledge around,' Noel had complimented me unexpectedly when he learned I was going to take over the stables at the Hall. I didn't tell him I intended to live with my grandmother. I still have to face his judgment about that, made much worse now because I really should have told him right away.

Cycling gives me a sense of leaving such troubles behind, of freedom. I sweep along, tyres hissing on the still dew-damp lane. The trees and hedges are of every shade as their greens die back to yellow and all the shades of browns and rusts, briar leaves brilliant red shields, the autumn palette spectacular.

The air is sharp, clear, but with that under-scent of damp autumn. Somewhere in the distance I can hear a sound I love, a horse – no, more than one – coming along the roadway.

This time of year will always be my special time, mine *and* Ian's. It was harvest time when I first saw him. I remember his bright hair dappled with sunlight as he stood in our brook. I remember how he held me as I hacked off a piece of his short blond hair, and it is like electricity shooting deliciously, piquantly, through every part of me. I am kind of sensitized by this feeling, every piece of me aches to be with him. I remember as a child thinking that if I willed things enough they would happen – but I am older now.

I must do adult things, throw myself into running the stables and working for the Philippses in the estate office, then time will pass more quickly, not hang so heavily. I still have not had a letter from Ian. Perhaps they are not allowed to write for security reasons, like the war, when a poster had urged, Be Like Dad – Keep Mum. As soon as that first letter does come, it won't be so bad.

I imagine new bundles of letters tied with ribbon, then with a pang of excitement I wonder if I dare tell Ian to write to me at Gran's direct. Surely there will be no reason why not. Gran would not mind, is on my side, but I'm not sure what time the post is delivered and who picks it up from the letterbox.

The sound of the horses is close now, coming towards me. I brake – don't want to career into them around the next bend. I recognize the horses and riders as soon as they come into sight; Daphne and Anthea Philipps. I'll not be on my own, either in the stables or riding, while they are at home.

I stop my bike to greet them properly.

'Hello, both. How are you? I'm just on my way to the Hall.'

They look at each other. Anthea says something and they rein in.

'An early visitor, then,' Daphne says with a laugh, her face flushed with exercise and happiness.

'Congratulations in order,' I begin. 'So pleased to hear—'

'Not a visitor,' Anthea corrects, cutting in. 'Not any more. Don't you remember the Hon telling us Bess is going to work for us?'

I've never liked this label they use about their grandmother, Lady Philipps. They never say it to her face.

'Really?' Daphne's exclamation has hauteur and she pretends to look at me in an entirely different light. 'I couldn't have been listening.'

'It's a business arrangement,' I begin, knowing I am being ridiculed, knowing they are both fully aware of the facts.

'Goodness!' This time the exclamation is full of real derision. 'At your age.'

Her tone makes Anthea laugh loudly, her horse fidgets, she puts her heels into its sides and they begin to move away. 'We'll see you around, then. In certain quarters anyway.'

'In the stables.'

They laugh down their noses, like horses, but as I stand looking after them, shocked and humiliated, I realize I, who have danced at their parties, played tennis, swum in and skated on their lake, am out of their thoughts in seconds.

So, the Bennetts are out of favour then, not to be entertained if their father is disgraced, if they work in one's stables. I want to turn round, go back – to Miss Seaton's disapproval? I feel like one of those displaced people in the war, going from country to country, place to place, belonging nowhere, toting and pulling their worldly belongings along endless, cheerless roads. The comparison makes me ashamed. I do, after all, know where I belong. I belong with Ian, and it could make matters much easier if *all* the Philippses now regard me as an employee. This patronage, I remind myself, is a means to my own ends. I touch the locket, which has become like a talisman. I've sworn never to take it off until Ian comes back.

The clock over the stone arch into the stable yard shows ten minutes to nine o'clock as I ride in. Late for a stable hand, early for a boss – as time goes on I will get it right, get my role correct, know where I stand. Tommie comes from one of the stables, raises and waves his cap. The arrangement is known to him and it gives me a real lift to see him looking so pleased.

'We'll whip 'em into shape, miss, and no mistake,' he grins, then inclines his head to someone who has just entered the yard from the direction of the house. 'Mornin', m'lady.' He touches his cap as Lady Philipps comes smiling towards me.

'Wasting no time, young Bess. That's the idea.'

'I was coming to talk to you about everything, to say thank you and—'

'Start straight away I hope!' Clara Philipps exclaims and, taking me by the arm, 'Come on, m'dear, the office awaits.'

The office awaits. She laughs as, for a second, I do not respond to her gentle pressure. 'Don't worry, I'm not going to set you to work in the office straight away – that'll be Greville's pigeon. No, I thought we could have a proper chat in there. The house is all taken over with the girls and Roger's lot. We all came back from Norfolk last night, you know. All of us,' she emphasizes. 'Didn't bargain for that!'

'Gran said you were in Norfolk, or I would have come before.' I do not mention having seen her two granddaughters. 'This is a wonderful opportunity.' I glance around and, though I know the place well, now I calculate how many free stables there might be, how many horses the stalls in the barns will take.

'Built when the horse was truly the king of the road.'

I nod, feel myself blushing. Clara Philipps is well aware of my new proprietorial interest.

'Be hard work with the hunting season upon us. Jessie alright, is she?'

'Fine, thanks.' Though this is not quite true. Since the episode of the broken wine glasses, Gran has been withdrawn, often unaware when spoken to. I had been startled to glimpse the family Bible in her bedroom. Nothing has been said about my crossing out – or the earlier one she had so vehemently denied doing.

The estate office is more than warm. A gas fire, radiant orange, pours heat into the room. 'Mustn't disturb any of these.' She makes a pass over the huge old desk which faces the door, where letters cover the side of the desk behind an ornate brass inkstand and files take up most of the rest of the space.

'Greville has set up a desk under the window.' She gestures to where a smaller modern desk is positioned beneath a view of the side lawns, copper beeches and one corner of the lake where I practised my skating. On the desk is a smaller silver inkstand, and a leather blotter with clean pink blotting paper. Left to his sisters, I would probably have been doing the office work in the tack room.

'You come with the highest recommendations. Noel says you're the best horsewoman he's ever seen, and that, m'dear, includes your mother.'

'Good heavens! He's never said anything like that to me.'

She laughs. 'The old devil.'

The dear old devil, I think. 'I've learned so much from him,' I admit. 'Almost everything I know about looking after and caring for horses, which I love as much as riding.'

'That's just what he said about you.'

'Who said what about young Bess here?' a voice inquires from the doorway. Greville stands smiling. He looks older out of uniform, or perhaps the cares of the estate are more onerous than his stay in the army, which he hardly took seriously. His tallness, cords, Harris-tweed jacket – the kind of formal uniform of an estate manager – makes the bowl of bright maroon and yellow asters he is carrying more incongruous. 'For your desk,' he explains. 'A welcome.'

A welcome, flowers – for a moment he joins Noel in my heart.

'That's nice, dear.' Lady Philipps approves. 'Really, now you are here, perhaps you should show Bess a little of the estate work you need help with.' She gestures to the laden desk. 'That might be more practical, because really Bess knows what's needed in the stables.' She takes the bowl from her grandson.

Greville and I exchange smiles acknowledging we are being organized.

'We've six hunters here at the moment,' she goes on. 'Tommie knows about the state of play with those, then there's the trap pony and the old Shetland, who is obviously going to live for ever. That leaves several stables and all the free-standing stalls in the barns for your livery, lessons, or whatever you wish to do. Pony Club contacts might be useful.'

'I wondered about Tommie. Will I pay part of his wages?' One thing I know I have learned from my father is how to be fair in business and a good employer. 'I mean, when I begin to have other horses here and he is helping me.'

'Good gracious, no. That will come from the estate as always.'

'You may need to employ someone extra later,' Greville says. 'As you begin to be established.'

'I suppose we might just like to know who you intend to set on, when the time comes,' Lady Philipps says in a more sombre tone, which suddenly makes me remember the incident in the Hall kitchen, Greville and I walking into the fracas.

'I'm sure we can rely on Bess to choose the right person,' he says.

'Unlike my father, you mean.'

There is a moment's silence as the words I had not intended, not even consciously formed, surface.

'Your father!' Lady Philipps exclaims, and sounds, well, not exactly best pleased, before she declares, 'Oh, that's in the past. Dealt with.'

'You're not your father's keeper.' Greville urges acceptance of his comment with a quizzical nod.

'No, but I . . .' I break off, my mind a confusion of blood ties and the red prayer book's 'lusting beasts'. 'How can you be sure about me?' I see Greville's lips twitch and I think of his sisters. He and they are all of the same mould, the same blood, so I'm game for him, just as much as I am game for them.

'No.' I censor any amusement he might feel, but my voice is not steady. 'How can you?'

He looks as if he has much he would like to say, which he is thinking better of, but his face is serious now. Perhaps he sees his new assistant leaving before she has begun.

'Let's walk round the lake. Pity to waste the sun. I can tell you a bit about the office work as we go.' He sweeps out an encompassing arm to shepherd me out of the door.

'There was no need,' I begin.

'Every need, my dear.'

'No, I really don't want to . . .' but I hesitate over the word *stay*. I really don't want to stay, but while I could deal with Anthea and Daphne, and their snide remarks, real kindness, which I sense here, is something else. I watch Lady Philipps place the bowl on the smaller desk with infinite care, then, turning back, she nods to me.

'Off you go,' she says.

I walk out quickly, need to be away. All this time, I have not cried – at home, at my grandmother's – so why here, for goodness' sake? The worst possible place. I am nearly running by the time I reach the beech trees at the edge of the lake, but I am aware that Greville has kept up with me without much trouble. A hand appears in front of my face holding a large, very white handkerchief. I stop, let the sob in my throat escape, take the handkerchief and near cover my face in it.

'Bess, you do want to come here and work the stables?'

I am very still, face cowled in the whiteness of the handkerchief, thinking of why I am here, of Ian two years distant.

'I mean, if you don't . . .'

'I do,' I assure him. 'I really do need to. It was the thought of trust and – my father. You know everything that's happened.'

'Your father succumbed to a temptation, that's all. It happens.'

'That's all! My father's married, he took vows.'

'Bess, come on. I understand your parents have settled their differences.'

'You don't understand. I'll never settle mine. I've *lost* my father, my pa.' I feel myself swirling my hands about as if I'm searching in some morass for my beloved father, the man who is no more, perhaps never really was, except in my imagination. 'He's gone.'

Somewhere quite near, a mowing machine starts up. Greville takes my elbow and propels me towards the boathouse, then to the seat under the far wall, sheltered from the breeze.

He leans back, sighing, relaxing as if totally contented, while I perch on the edge of the bench.

The smell of the mown grass comes quickly, mingles with the smell of the wooden boathouse as the sun dries it off. I remember Abbey Park and the smell of the river and the pavilion and fish and chips.

'Do you remember I said we had some books about the Red Pool in the library?'

Diverted, as he intends, I drop my hands and the handkerchief to my lap.

'I was going to put them on your desk, make a pile, by the flowers, but you came earlier than I thought – your first day and all.'

'A pile?'

'There's three, and I feel there's a fourth with some references, if I can lay my hands on it.' He pauses and pushes at the gritty path with a well-polished brogue.

I suddenly wonder why he does not have a dog, and ask.

'Get too fond of them, then it hurts too much when something happens to them.'

I remember Patch, the first dog in my life, and how I had come upon him, run down, lying on the side of the lane. 'Oh, Patch!' I had cried. He had lifted his head, wagged his tail and died. Tears come again, for something else irrevocably lost.

'Bess, you have to put this behind you.'

'You don't understand.'

'Perhaps I do. You know, when you were small, we used to say, "Look, there are the BBs". That was you and your father, inseparable. What you have to accept is that he is not an idol, he's a man. Just a man.'

'Fallen off his pedestal.'

'Yes. And you are grown-up, a young woman.'

'So, I should accept infidelity!' I exclaim, leaping up. Stepping away, I trip on the grass bank.

'You should accept that adults are fallible,' he says. I think it is more because he does not fuss after me as I stagger to the brink of the lake, one shoe going into the water, that I look back at him.

'I nearly fell in the lake,' I tell him.

'I think it would have done you good,' he says. 'Calm you down.'

Then he laughs and gets up, offering a hand. I hesitate, then take it, and he pulls me back on to the path.

'You want to talk any more about your father?'

'No, we'll never agree.'

'No, it's a gender thing,' he says.

'What's that mean?'

'You're a girl and wouldn't understand.'

'Oh! Really!' I turn on him, furious. 'Now say that *time will tell* and go on about *life's little lessons* and *I'll understand when I'm older.*'

'Well, you might . . .' he says, then immediately holds up his hands as if in surrender. 'Shall I jump into the lake, will that help?'

'Are you never serious?'

'Very, very often,' he says, and the look he gives makes me feel that seriousness is something he keeps for private moments. It reminds me that I have seen him in many different roles over the years: the obedient grandson; the arrogant youth riding and hunting; the reluctant army officer making mock of his own position . . . and now? He is a more complex man than casual acquaintances might believe, a man whose true nature is probably only revealed in snatches, as when he admitted he could not bear to own another dog because of the grief of losing it. That had been both surprising and real.

'The office work,' he begins, as if we have just set off to stroll

187

and discuss the topic. 'I was going to suggest you might learn best if I just give you jobs to do as we go along. So, for instance, this afternoon for an hour or so, I could really use your help with a pile of letters from tenants. If you could just read through them, make a list of names, addresses, their requests and complaints, perhaps even put them in order of date or urgency, or something, that would be really helpful. Later in the week, we might visit a few.'

Sixteen

Noel and my father are talking on the far side of our yard
as I climb out of Greville's car. The conversation stops
but there is no acknowledgement, no raised arm, no movement
towards us – just riveted attention.

'See you later,' Greville says as I close the door. I think that
unlikely – he won't be back from London until I've left the Hall.
I watch as he turns the car, stopping again briefly to speak to
the other two. I know both of them have reason to ignore me,
and Noel's stare over the top of the sports car is so fixed and
aggressive I think for a moment he is going to shout at me from
across the yard.

'Hello, my dear,' Ma calls from the back-kitchen doorway
and comes to envelope me in a hug which makes me feel as if she
has said, *Hello my love, my darling, don't ever go away again* –
but it's in my imagination, for she goes on, 'I guessed you'd be
here for Ebony this morning. I told Noel to leave him in his
stable, so he'll be feeling tetchy, still shut-up when the others are
out.'

'Noel knows about my living with Gran?'

'Did he glare?' she asks with a laugh. 'His famous glare. I
always think, what a pity we didn't have dozens of children, he
could have scared them all in turn with that glare.'

There's a strange note in her voice, something almost hyster-
ical-sounding, but then she asks, 'Like some toast? We could have
a cup of coffee and some toast together before you ride off.'

Why does my mind add *into the blue*? 'You alright, Ma?' I
ask.

189

'Fine. Why shouldn't I be?'

'I thought you looked pale.'

She turns with some concern to look into the mirror hanging near the window and makes a noise which sounds like agreement.

'I was thinking,' I say, though it only occurs to me at that moment, 'that we could still go to the cinema if you'd like. You could pick me up in the village. It's on the way either to the local flicks or into town.'

'That'd be nice. We must arrange something,' she says, smiling, so that I feel better.

'Find out what's on where,' I add, smiling back.

'Yes.' For a moment we are both as if nothing has happened.

'Where's Greville off to?'

'London. His grandmother is signing the Hall and estate over to him. She came to him in the office last night and just announced that now the girls were "sorted" she was signing the "whole caboodle" over to Greville, "thank the Lord", and he could go up to London to their solicitors today.'

'She's never wasted time,' Ma says, 'but I didn't know the girls were *both* settled. Knew Daphne was engaged; wonder if there's some news we haven't heard about Anthea. Greville never said anything?'

'Just that he knew something was in the wind, but wouldn't like to comment, as he thought it a most unlikely match.'

'Curiouser and curiouser, though I suppose we'll hear soon enough. There'll probably be an announcement in *The Times*, then a double engagement party.'

'I don't suppose we'll be invited if there is.'

Ma considers this possibility, shifts her stance uneasily and considers it as a real possibility, and I wish I had said nothing.

'Why would she want to sign it all over to Greville anyway?' I ask.

'Probably the only way to ensure it stays in the family. Death duties can be crippling. It's only been Clara's wonderful man-

190

agement that kept it all together up to now. It must be a relief to pass the responsibility on to Greville.'

Over coffee and toast I learn that, in any case, death duties will only be completely avoided if Lady Philipps lives seven years from the date of the gift.

'That's why she'll be in a hurry, then,' I say.

'Guess so.' She laughs at the remark. 'Though I think she's the sort who'll live to a ripe old age.'

'I do hope so.' And I do, for I feel Lady Philipps is my one link – as well as my buffer – between our two families. I would be very uneasy without her presence.

Ma comes to the door to see me off. 'We won't forget the cinema, or the theatre,' she calls. 'And I'll be up to Gran's sometime soon.'

My horse really is champing at the bit by the time I have him saddled up. He certainly resents not having been put out at the usual time, and is showing me so. I am just preparing to mount when Noel's voice comes from behind me.

'Off then, are you? Is this for good?'

'You startled me.'

'Reckon somebody should startle you,' he replies, nodding over my shoulder towards the house. 'Are you really leaving your mother?'

'No,' I reply. 'I am leaving my father.'

'Not much to choose between one sort of leaving and the other, is there?' he demands.

I swing up into the saddle, and the horse circles skittishly as I struggle to pull myself aboard. Immediately, Noel is at the head. 'Think what you're doing, girl,' he says in a harsh undertone, and I know he does not mean getting on the horse.

'I don't need this, Noel. I thought you might understand.'

'I understand you're breaking your dear mother's heart. You should stay home for her sake.'

'I always thought you were on my side.' I gather up the reins.

'Everyone's on your side if you did but think straight.'

Out of the corner of my eye I see him walking towards the

191

stable, closing the door I have left open. *You're breaking your dear mother's heart.* Well, my pa has broken mine, and more, he's ravaged my mind, torn up my trust in him by the roots. I shall never get over it, never understand, never come to terms – to love one person, or to say you love them, swear vows, then have a relationship with another. I remember seeing a young soldier on top of an ATS girl in one of our hayfields during the war. I had no idea what he was doing to her. At just seven I had wondered if I should run for help, but then they sat up and, after a few moments, walked away hand in hand. I suppose that must have been a casual carnal relationship. I wonder if they were hurting other people, whether they had made vows to others?

I put Ebony on the grass verge and push him gently to a trot, then, reaching the bridleway, I urge him to canter, steady him enough to take a small fence into a field which is good for a gallop around. He immediately tosses his head and takes the bit. I let him go for a few minutes, taking pleasure in his cheek until it gets alarming. I come to my senses as I am thrown about in the saddle, lose a stirrup for a moment, and know I must take back control. I press with my knees and touch his flanks with my heels, urging him on, and now he wonders about whether it is such a good idea to take charge. He had thought he wanted to gallop off with me, that this was his will, his show, now he's confused. He slows and releases the bit, wondering what it is all about.

This is something I learned from Noel years ago. For all his moralizing, all his poking his nose into the family business, I shall really, really miss him. In fact, I secretly hope he will come busybodying up to the Hall. He probably won't be able to resist coming to see what mistakes I am making.

That thought is really cheering, and now we both have our breath back, I put Ebony to one of the worst jumps the Hunt has in our area. A hedge marked with red and white wooden flags as suitable for jumping but well known for bringing riders down, the width of the hedge often causing a horse to baulk as it reaches the point of no return. It is notorious enough to have a name: Baffty's Leap. Ebony flies over as if it is nothing at all.

I feel the joy of the stretch, share the grunt of expelled air and of satisfaction as we land. Horses, Noel says, enjoy a clean jump just as much as their riders. I wonder how much I shall see of him in the village. Noel giving advice about horses will be a very different experience to Noel living next door to Colleen and giving advice about my life whenever I encounter him.

There is no cure for that problem. He won't move, and I cannot imagine anything changing my mind about living at home.

This ride may be the best part of the day, for there is obviously some big family announcement to be made at the Hall. I wonder if it will be made tonight when Greville returns, a kind of special private settling of family affairs. Intending to make sure I am away from the house early, I decide to do the office task Greville has left me first. I am very surprised to encounter a man in purple vest and clerical collar coming out of the office with Lady Philipps. I am being introduced to The Reverend Norman Wallace from Norfolk when Anthea breezes into the hallway and, cutting across the exchange of names, whisks them both away 'to where the others are'.

I retreat to my list of tenants and their requests, feeling efficiently relegated by Anthea to my place. I ponder the Reverend whoever from Norfolk and I wonder if he is anything to do with Norwich Cathedral. A cathedral wedding would be very much in keeping for Roger and Daphne, Roger being the son of a high sheriff. I wish I was going home, so Ma and I could have a good girly gossip about all this. Gran would be just as willing, of course, but there's Miss Seaton. Now a Miss Sss instead of a *Mrs* Sss, blights my life.

When I cycle back towards Gran's, my spirits lift as I see Colleen standing on the village square, and I have my foot on the ground before I take in the fact that she is with George. He stands leaning against the wall, she on the edge of the pave-

193

ment, dangling one foot into the gutter to draw lines in the dust. I feel they would not be so far apart if it was dark.

'Hello, you two. Wondered if I could come round to see you later, Colleen?'

'We're going to the pictures,' George answers.

'Oh! Are we?' Colleen pretends to be pert. 'First I've heard about it.' She comes to put her hands over mine as I stand holding the handlebars.

'What's on?' I ask, thinking of my mother.

'*Zorro*,' he answers, looking at me doubtfully as if he wonders if he should include me in the outing.

'Oh, good! I love the sword fights. I'll tell Ma. We may go later in the week. She likes a bit of swashbuckling.'

George looks relieved.

'Nothing's come yet.' Colleen squeezes my hand. 'I can pop over as soon as anything does. Be handy for that, you living in the village . . .' Her voice trails as she looks beyond our group. We both turn to see her brother, Roy, coming out of their house in Church Street. He sees us, changes direction and comes swaggering towards us.

'Going across to the King Bill later?' he asks George, who shakes his head.

'Could go on the bike and have a drink at the Cock at Packman,' Roy suggests as an alternative.

'*We're* going to the pictures,' Colleen tells her brother.

'*We're going to the pictures*,' he mimics with a sarcastic sneer.

He is dressed, as he always is after finishing work at the local dye works, in knee-length leather boots; long, rather dingy, white silk scarf with tangled tassels, and gauntlets which seem to have brought on the habit of balling one fist and punching it aggressively into the palm of the other hand. The smell of leather hangs in the air as he does this repeatedly, changing hands each time.

'You're not going out with 'er, are you?' He looks at his sister again. 'Nah! Course you're not, not 'er.'

I think he must be very dense to be living in the same house and not realize his sister and his friend next door are sweet on each other. I guessed ages ago.

'Why shouldn't he?' Colleen demands. 'Shut your spiteful face!'

'Our Colleen!' Roy scoffs. 'You must be bloody mad.'

'Leave off, or . . .' but Colleen's voice is shaky. 'Coming spoiling things.'

'Go 'ome, y'baby, our mam wants you.'

'No, she don't.' Colleen is really becoming upset now as her brother shows her up in front of her boyfriend. 'You're just jealous you've not got a girlfriend.'

Roy swings round so aggressively, George, who has leaned listening intently to these exchanges, now pushes himself upright and stands protectively near to Colleen. 'Reckon she's about right,' he says.

'Huh!' Roy exclaims, and pulls his scarf tighter round his neck, as if preparing for action; but as George raises his chin, as if inviting an opening attack, Roy begins to turn away. His eyes meet mine as he does so, and he reads my scorn. 'Don't fret,' he tells me. 'I'll teach you a lesson, just like I taught your precious father.'

'Clear off,' George tells him. 'Before we *all* start saying things we don't mean.'

'He's always like this, these days,' Colleen says. 'Except when he's going off on his motorbike, and –' she breaks off, then raises her voice to shout after her brother – 'you can't get a girl even with a motorbike.'

Roy stops in his tracks, stands rigid, not turning, but something in his stance sends a chill dancing up my spine. I sense the remark is a mistake, that there will be a price to pay.

'It's alright, he daren't do anything, he's too scared of our dad,' Colleen reassures us.

'I don't know where he gets it from,' George says as we watch him go through the Rawlinses' gate, 'but there's a bad streak coming out in him.'

'He'll be off on his bike in a minute,' Colleen says.

'Enjoy the film,' I say as I take my leave, and as Colleen looks at me I mouth, 'With your boyfriend.'

'See you,' she says, her cheeks flushing a brilliant red.

Odd words from the exchange link in my mind: a lesson he'd taught my father – the motorbike – a bad streak. A kind of awful knowledge swells like excitement in the pit of my stomach. Roy Rawlins delivered Mrs Sss to the Hall kitchen the night of Greville's demob party. I remember someone saying a motorbike had been heard – didn't someone else mention swarf on the woman's legs, the state of her stockings? I come to a halt outside the cottage where Ian lived. I can see one end of the rockery he and his father built, still shrouded in blue and white aubretia. The cottage is definitely empty and being cleared out ready for the next occupant: a dirty white fake-fur rug has been thrown out over the dustbin, and there are a few very unsavoury metal saucepans, all well patched, alongside.

Later that evening when I try to write some cheerful newsy pages to Ian, the encounter with Roy keeps getting in the way. At last I give up. I know Gran will listen to the play on the radio. Miss Seaton will pretend to listen, but Gran says she'll be asleep in minutes.

We are well into a seafaring drama when the old front door bell jingles noisily on its spiral spring. *This* noise wakes Miss Seaton, who has slept through storm and shipwreck.

'Half past nine, late for callers,' she says, but refuses to let me go, as she blinks herself awake and straightens her skirt. She returns very quickly, followed by Greville looking large and military in a camel overcoat with leather buttons, but holding two bottles of champagne. He brings the smell of cold night air in with him, then a hint of his ferny toiletries, and of whisky or brandy.

'Will you forgive this intrusion, Mrs Bennett, ladies.' He half bows to us all. 'I wanted to come and ask you all to celebrate with me.'

'Celebrate?' Miss Seaton feels impowered to ask as she is obviously included in the event.

I remember he said he would see me later, but had not expected him to come here. Reluctantly, I twist the wireless knob to off, just when the play was really gripping. I hope there'll be a repeat.

'Glasses, Miss Seaton.' He places the bottles on the small table from which Gran swept the glasses the last time we drank in this room.

I glance at Gran, who is watching him intently but so far has said nothing. Miss Seaton places the crystal bowls on the table and asks again, 'What are we celebrating?'

'I think,' Gran says, 'we are looking at the new owner of the Hall. I think the new squire has officially taken over.'

'You, madame, are correct, and I wanted to come here, because—' he stops suddenly, seeming at a loss for words, as if the impulse that has brought him here has run out.

'Because you feel your life is taking shape, and with Bess now working at the Hall, it seemed appropriate,' she suggests.

'That's it exactly. Life begins here.' He laughs triumphantly as he loosens the wire on a bottle and eases the cork with his thumbs, pops it recklessly. Miss Seaton has to duck and, though it hits the glass of the bookcase hard, we all laugh. He pours the champagne, which froths and bubbles in the bowls, then adds, 'Everyone else at the Hall is too busy celebrating other things.'

'What other things?' Miss Seaton asks promptly.

'Charge your glasses,' he says, 'and all will be revealed.'

'But first a toast to you, my dear Greville,' Gran says as we all stand to drink his health, clink our glasses. 'I saw you the day you were born and you've grown into a man your father, and your grandfather, would have been proud to see inherit their properties. Greville Philipps!'

'Mr Greville,' Miss Seaton echoes.

'Greville.' I find his glance meeting mine over our raised glasses.

197

'And the other celebration?' Gran enquires now. 'You can't keep us in the dark any longer. Is it . . . ?'

'Anthea! Yes!' he exclaims. 'Engaged to the vicar of some tiny parish in Norfolk. But plans are afoot for a double wedding in the spring at Norwich Cathedral.'

'Goodness!' Clara must be like a dog with two tails,' Gran exclaims.

I remember the long-ago conversation between Ma and Lady Philipps about her two *horsey* granddaughters, and echo Gran's sentiment. 'She must be pleased,' I say. 'And I did meet a Reverend Wallace briefly this morning. I thought it might be all about a wedding, but never guessed that was Anthea's father-in-law to be.'

'No, that was her husband-to-be,' Greville corrects. 'She is marrying the Reverend Wallace.'

'But . . .'

'I know.' Greville grimaces. 'There is quite an age gap, and I think he's quite . . . well . . . unsuitable for Anthea – his lifestyle, his background, his age, everything – but apparently he is the one she's set on.'

'Goodness!' The exclamation sounds lame even to me, but I labour on. 'A double wedding. There'll be a lot of toing and froing to London for dresses and things.'

'I must . . .' Gran begins. 'Well, *you* must tell Clara how delighted we all are for her, the girls, you, everyone.'

Somehow we don't seem to be getting these congratulations right.

'One more glass and I must go,' he says. 'Or my grandmama will begin to worry, think I've driven into a ditch or a tree or something.'

'Perhaps I should get you a sandwich, or a biscuit or two, soak up some of this alcohol,' Miss Seaton suggests.

'No, I'm fine, not far to go now.' He puts down the glass with studied care and I'm sorry we've not made a better job of celebrating with him. He had looked flushed and happy when he arrived. Now, in spite of three glasses of champagne, he looks more sober.

'I'll see Greville off,' I volunteer.

Outside, he says, 'So we'll start visiting my tenants tomorrow afternoon, if that's OK with you.'

We share a laugh at the *my*, then I tell him that I've found some of *his* tenants have been waiting a very long time for repairs and answers to their enquiries.

'I know. I do know, and we can't keep blaming the war, can we? No, m'dear, it's not good, but together we'll begin to put things right, hey?'

'I'll do what I can.'

I watch him drive away, standing quite still as he gives a toot on the horn and waves out of the window. The way he said *m'dear* has made me feel quite old, and as if he intends to put too much responsibility on me. Once I have horses in livery, and hopefully riding lessons to give, I may have to remind him that Lady Philipps did originally say one or two afternoons a week in the office.

It does seem Greville is expecting rather more of my time than that.

Seventeen

There are many calculations about the voyage out to Malaya. We pore over the Rawlins family atlas, and Colleen runs her finger across the world, making comforting reassurances that Ian will never let me down, she's *sure*. He will be posting letters when the ship reaches Gibraltar at the west end of the Mediterranean – then it is to be Port Said at the head of the Suez Canal, then Columbo on the island of Ceylon – then the options become a bit thin – her finger wavers below the Bay of Bengal.

'Never mind. When he reaches Singapore, he'll post masses. You'll have bundles come!'

Colleen, at her mum's prompting, has started her bottom drawer *in earnest*. Clothes rationing is over, but bedlinen and household linens are only just beginning to come back into the shops and, according to the newspapers, people are still queuing and fighting for things like carpet squares and rugs. Colleen has joined a linen club someone runs at the factory, paying a little in each week, then, when a certain level of savings is reached, she proudly carries home brown paper parcels of sheets, pillowcases or towels.

It is an event as each item of precious new linen is carefully laid into the bottom drawer of the chest in her tiny back bedroom. A little crowd of us gather on the landing, the younger girls, May and Mavis, and Mrs Rawlins are always on hand to witness the ceremony, often her father too, though he pretends to be just passing. We all gather to witness the new acquisition being put aside, put to rest 'until', Colleen says.

'Until when?' either one, or a chorus, demands, but the house-wife-to-be just replies, 'Oh! It'll be ages and ages.'

'But we know who!' May shouts.

'Georgie-Porgie from next door,' Mavis sings, and Colleen tries to say rubbish, or never, or some denial, even *Not if he were the last man on earth* – but never makes it sound convincing, and everyone falls about laughing.

Every time she rearranges the contents to make room for the new item, or takes the whole lot out to count and smooth, and gloat over the growing collection, I feel it is another stone on the coffin of my hopes, a coffin smelling of lavender bags.

After the first weeks, and then months, have gone by with no news, no letters from Ian, I come to feel that, as my friend blossoms, I shrivel inside. She suggests that perhaps he has been sent straight to a jungle – we have read that it is a jungle campaign – and there has been no time to write. I shake my head and concentrate on caring for the six hunters I now have in livery, and am thankful that weekends are practically fully booked with riding lessons.

I decide not to go to Colleen's on Fridays, the usual day if there is to be a parcel, and talk to Gran about this bottom drawer. She tells me that the village girls, working girls, have to make lengthy preparations against the expense of beginning a household from scratch. 'Another year or so and she'll be looking to store bits and bobs of furniture people offer her, wherever she can. I've often had pieces in my attic for someone or other.'

'Well, you would have room now you've given so much away to our man in the cottage.'

'That's true,' she says and her smile is gentle, her eyes inward looking. The man in the cottage where Ian lived is obviously rather backward, but Gran and Miss Seaton have taken him under their wings. He comes from the village where Miss Seaton was born and has apparently just lost his elderly mother, leaving him alone.

Gran, Colleen – they seem happy. My mother and father

seem happy, though I know Ma would rather I was at home, even her enthusiasm for driving to the theatre or to see a film is not quite so overwhelming.

'She's grown listless – like you. If you've the time to notice,' Noel informs me on one of the many occasions he bats remarks at me as I pass him in the street, or in the entry they share with the Rawlinses.

I do fill my time as much as I can. Greville is always taking me off in the afternoons to see some aspect of the estate, and has offered to teach me to drive. I shall take him up on it as soon as I am old enough. Why not? It will help me along this endless, wearisome road that has to be got through before I am twenty-one – and free. I need to take my mind off Ian, need to do other things. It would be pointless me beginning a bottom drawer.

'What are you thinking about?' Gran asks. I am telling her about learning to drive when a motorbike roars past and Gran tuts. 'No prizes for guessing who that is.'

No, no prizes, and I know just how he will have banged out of the house, his father shouting after him to 'take your time on that bike'. I would have spent more time at Colleen's house, even just keeping Mrs Rawlins company, if Roy had not been there, but since he has lost his best friend's regular company to his sister, most evenings he sits morose on one side of the fire with his father on the other. Mr Rawlins alternately reads then shakes his newspaper at his only son, prompting him to go out if he's going, not leave it until it's dark. But this, as now, he always seems to do, roaring back into the village in the early hours of the morning. Sometimes, Colleen tells me, only just in time to go to work.

At school we were instructed how to read and judge a newspaper. It had seemed a silly exercise – we had made it a bit of a lark – but it became one of the useful things in my life. Each evening now, I scan the newspapers for war news from Malaya, but Korea has long ago taken over as the current battle zone.

Malaya seems to be an emergency only for those living and working out there. The politicians and the general public have forgotten we have troops there.

Just before Christmas 1953, I write to Ian's father at the boarding house in Penzance where they first stayed. I know he cannot still be there, but I think the letter might be forwarded. I print the request on the envelope – *Please Forward* – and underline it, twice.

Then, in the New Year, I write to an address made up from all the information Ian gave me in that first letter from Cornwall. The envelope reads:

> Mr Kenneth Sinclair
> The House on the Cliffs (formerly the house of one Emmie
>   – surname perhaps Sinclair)
> St Just
> Penzance
> Cornwall.

I confide in Colleen and this time we study a walking map of Cornwall I bought in town, from one of the big new shops now devoted to walking and cycling, which stock just about everything one needs to follow such pursuits. We find there are at least two St Justs, and doggedly I rewrite the letter and send it to *St Just in Roseland*, which, if one was journeying through Cornwall, would be reached first. These letters I send from Gran's address, putting my name as sender on the back of the envelope and her address. I feel I have covered all eventualities.

I hear nothing, I become obsessed with the lack of any kind of reply. I had thought that at the very least *these* letters might be returned *Not Known* or *Gone Away*. There is a missing child story running through the newspapers, appeals from the parents for news. The father is quoted: 'We just need to know what has happened to our daughter, whatever it is, we need to know.' I feel I really, really know how this parent feels.

Colleen is the one friend I lean on. She believes as totally in

Ian as I do. I encounter Roy one evening as I open their gate and walk up their entry. He blocks my way, coming on instead of giving way and turning back. 'Should think your chap's found himself a Chinese girlfriend by now. Susie Wong, I bet.'

I have to back away to avoid coming into contact with him, moving out into the street again to let him pass. 'Let's see, you were too flat-footed to get in the army, weren't you?' I say. 'I wonder why that doesn't surprise me.'

It sounds like he snarls.

The following day I walk into the estate office to find a copy of the *Malay Straits Times Magazine* on my desk. On the cover is a photograph of a young woman, attractive, in one of those wide-brimmed straw hats, looking up and smiling from her work in a paddy field. I am not sure if she is Malaysian or Chinese.

'Where's this come from?' I ask Greville as he follows me into the office. My heart thumps as I suspect some devious trick of Roy's. Yet how could he possibly have got it there?

'Oh! It was an old friend of father's, his son's a rubber planter out in Malaya. Just been to see the Hon. He must have left it behind. Take it, if you'd like.'

He stands watching me, smiling. 'It won't bite,' he adds as I move away from the desk.

'Don't call your grandmother *the Hon* – it's disrespectful,' I counter. 'I thought it was only your sisters who did that.'

'Naughty bad habit. Sorry.' He seems to ponder, watching me closely. 'How about this first driving lesson, after you've finished here. I need to see your father – we could astonish him by arriving with you driving.'

'That seems a bit unlikely on a first lesson, and, of course, there is the fact that I'm not eighteen until February.'

'We could swop over just before the gateway, and –' he does an expansive flyaway gesture, arms in unison – 'you can sweep in, astonish old Noel!'

'He'd probably report me to the police.'

'We'd be on private land, which is why I am going to teach

204

you to drive here around the Hall grounds, and your licence can be my eighteenth birthday present. Then you can drive the estate jeep.'

I open my mouth, not sure whether I am going to protest or agree.

'A real asset to any employer,' he goes on. 'Some extra bod who can drive.'

'OK,' I agree.

'That's great,' he enthuses, and for a moment I think he is going to kiss me on the cheek, but instead he leans over, pokes at the magazine, then turns and nods. 'See you in about an hour then.'

When he has safely gone I sit at my desk and draw the magazine to me. The magazine opens as if of its own will to reveal a picture of a yet more beautiful young woman. She is definitely Chinese – she wears a silk cheongsam and has an hibiscus flower behind one ear. Her smooth high-cheekboned face is stunningly smooth and perfect. Her dark eyes look enigmatic, full of secrets. No one, no one at all, could be indifferent to her charm. I see her in colour, the hibiscus flower red, but in truth all the photographs in the magazine are sepia.

I turn the pages, more so I no longer see her flawlessness than to study pictures of water buffalo at the edge of paddy fields, smiling tappers working amongst the rubber trees, the magnificent Gothic post office in Singapore, the Raffles Club – but inevitably I come back to the Chinese girl. I know it cannot be Roy who has manoeuvred this magazine on to my desk, so it must be fate showing me a picture of the girl – or if not this girl, someone much like her – whom Ian will undoubtedly have fallen in love with.

I leave the magazine on my desk and next day it has gone, but the Chinese girl's photograph is engraved on my memory. If something like this has happened, and he cannot bring himself to tell me, then I have to take steps, more steps – more drastic steps – to find out. I am like the parents of the lost child, I have to know. I feel my life has come to a standstill, I cannot move on until I know for certain – even if it is the worst.

If I could find his father, the man who brought his gramophone to our harvest supper, recited the poem about flying, I'm sure he would help me, answer my questions honestly. I would know once and for all whether or not I am wasting my life waiting for Ian to come back to England.

With the double wedding in Norfolk fast approaching, and much extra work to do at the Hall – plus I have promised my mother and gran I will go to the wedding, for we are all invited as a family – I make myself a promise. I will go to the wedding, but when I come back, I shall take time off and go to Cornwall – stay in both St Justs if necessary and find Ken Sinclair, not come back until I do. I have money saved from the six horses I have in livery and the increasing number of children who are coming to me for riding and jumping lessons.

We are all to go to Norfolk on the Friday morning. The wedding is the next afternoon and we are all due to come home on Sunday afternoon. Noel and Dawdie are to move into the farmhouse for the weekend, and I have hired two extra lads from a neighbouring Hunt stables to give Tommie a hand with the livery horses. I have cancelled the lessons.

I realize arrangements are the easy part, it is making up your mind that is difficult. Now I have decided what to do, the measures taken for this weekend away are like a rehearsal for my expedition to Cornwall.

Greville offers to take me to Norfolk with Lady Philipps, but Grandmama and Ma think it more proper for me to go with them. 'We've been invited as a family, we should go as a family.' Then I catch a silent plea from my mother and agree, though it would have been far more fun motoring with Greville.

In the event, with Grandmama in the car, everyone is polite, if restrained. We arrive at our hotel, which is large, rather splendid, if a little ridiculous, with part of it having a turreted roof like a pseudo-castle. Another time, Pa and I would have had a joke about this, but as it is, we both get out of the car and stand taking in the view of this city which looked so confusing as we drove through twisting streets with medieval names, a tangle of yards and public houses, often glimpsing the cathedral, its spire dominating the city.

Our cases are collected from the boot by a stooped but obviously strong porter, and we are shown to our rooms. Gran on the ground floor, me in a single on the first floor and Ma and Pa on the second floor. 'Shouldn't get on each other's nerves, then,' Pa says after we have seen Gran to her room and reassembled in the lift.

Ma laughs, briefly, and I see her cock an eye at Pa as she sees my poker face. I am thinking that this weekend, possibly after the wedding, will give me the chance to tell my mother that I intend to go to seek out Ian's father. Pa moves aside as we reach the first floor and, as I move to step out of the lift, Ma catches my hand and gives it a squeeze. 'See you at dinner.'

Greville, Lady Philipps and her two granddaughters join us at the hotel for the evening meal. Daphne is expansive, Anthea is to my mind quite strange, at one moment the life and soul of the party, the next silent, brooding almost, watching her sister as if taking the lead from her how to behave on this night before their marriage.

I have a new costume for the wedding, blue linen with a rather beautiful multi-toned blue chiffon blouse and a broad-brimmed hat trimmed with the same material. I suppose I don't mind dressing up occasionally, but am wondering whether to put on trousers and sweater and go for a walk along the beach before having a shower, when I hear someone in a great hurry outside. I start as there is an urgent rapping on my door. I open it and find Pa in dressing gown, his hair wild, his eyes full of concern. 'Can you come to your ma, she passed out on me.'

We run up the stairs, much quicker than the lift. In their bedroom Ma is sitting very still in a basket chair near the window, wrapped in her woollen dressing gown.

'Here's Bess,' Pa says. 'Now I'm calling a doctor.'

'Edgar, *please* don't, just go and have your bath and let me talk with Bess. I'm sure I'll be fine when I've had a rest. It's happened before, I just told you.'

Pa goes out into the corridor and I have no doubt he is going to reception to call a doctor. Left alone, I am really alarmed. She is pale as ivory and when I take her hand it is so cold. I go to fetch a blanket from the bed and, though I hear her say not to, I pull it off, disturbing covers and sheets. There is, I realize, a bloodstain. I turn the clothes back further and gasp. The stain is extensive and bundled in the middle of it is Ma's nightgown half-soaked in blood.

'Ma?' I am fearful.

'It's just my monthly curse, it's nothing to worry about, but it's . . . it's just worse than it has been.'

I stand holding the blanket, my gaze first on the bed, then on my mother. Is this why she has looked so pale, been so tired?

'They've been heavy, and go on a long time,' she admits.

'Pa said you fainted.'

'I did get out of bed quickly.'

'Oh, Ma, come on, you're used to being active all day long, then going out in the evenings and enjoying yourself.' Now I understand why the outings to the cinema had been so few. I also guess something else. 'Pa didn't know, did he?'

She exhales like someone who has finally had to face a very difficult situation. 'Not until just now when I passed out half in and half out of the bed.' She smiles ruefully. We both know Pa will not now give up on this, it will be dealt with, put right, no excuses allowed. I tuck the blanket round her as the door reopens. 'Oh, well!' I say quietly. 'Here we go.' We exchange brief esoteric smiles.

'The doctor should be here in about twenty minutes,' Pa announces. 'I'll get dressed.'

I nod to his unspoken request for me to stay.

'I've asked for some tea in case you feel like it,' he adds.

'I do,' Ma states. 'Tea more than the doctor.'

'Hmm.' Pa's grunt is non-committal, welds Ma and me closer. We are all on a second cup of tea when the doctor arrives.

'You go and get dressed now.' Ma smiles and nods me away. 'Pa will come and tell you when the doctor has gone.'

He does come some twenty minutes later, looking paler than I've ever seen him. He comes into my room and closes the door. I hear him swallow hard as he passes me on the way to look out of the window. He stands with his back to me, head hunched down, his shoulders rounded. His black silhouette against the bright reflection from sea and white sands looks like no one I know.

'Pa?' I feel stricken, heartsick. I want to go and wrap my arms around him, to restore him to the man he used to be, the man who when I was little I would have flown to, grabbed his knees, clung on until he took me up. But the taking up is now for me to do, and I do not know how to begin.

'Your mother has to see a specialist. The doctor is ringing through to our own doctor and making arrangements. She is to stay in bed until we leave for home.' He shakes his head, then lets his chin fall back on to his chest. 'She wants us all to go to the wedding while she stays here in the hotel.'

'So, it's urgent.' It is the thought of the telephone call to our doctor that concerns me.

'Yes, from what the doctor said, and he seems a good man. Your mother has let things go on far too long.' He turns to face me. He was pale when he came into the room, now he is ashen.

'I'll stay with her, Pa.'

He nods and we seem to look directly at one another for the first time in a long while. 'Come up in a few minutes, we must have a family conflab.' In my head I hear Noel's voice say *about time*, and one of the many other remarks he has made come to mind: *You should see your ma first thing in a morning, she don't look so rosy then.*

When I go upstairs again, Gran is there too, looking worried but already in her navy and lilac wedding suit. Ma is in a clean nightgown, in a newly made bed raised at the foot. From being so pale, her face is now flushed, feverish colour topping each cheekbone.

'I want you to all go to the wedding. We'll deal with me afterwards.'

'Hmm!' Pa's grunt is now a meaningful censorious noise in his throat.

'I'll stay with Ma, that'll be best,' I tell Pa. 'That's what I'd really like to do. You and Gran go.'

Gran looks from one to the other. 'I think Bess is probably right. Fay will rest better with one of us here. We can fulfil our obligations, let Greville know what has happened, and come away.'

Pa has to be persuaded. Finally Ma says, 'Edgar, please just go, you are wearing me out rootling around.'

Once they have gone, she has some fruit juice and toast and as I sit by her bed she falls into sleep. I watch with such fear in my heart. She lies so still and the colour leaves her face as a full half hour goes by. I peer closely to make sure she is still breathing, she is so quiet and still. A little later, as I sit staring out of the window, she makes me jump as she says my name.

'Sorry I startled you.'

'Will you have another drink?'

'Not fruit juice, but I could drink lots more tea.'

I am quickly down to reception and back. 'Won't be long,' I tell her. 'And they say they are having telephones installed in the bedrooms soon.'

'Very up-to-date,' Ma says with a smile. 'Next time you won't have to keep running up and down stairs. Bess, I wondered if you have heard from Ian recently?'

I shake my head, the question catching me off-guard.

'I didn't think so. I could tell by your looks and your manner that something was wrong. When did you last hear?'

'I've never heard since he left,' I whisper.

'Oh! Bess, why didn't you tell me? That's so long ago, that's awful.'

'Why, Ma, why, do you think . . . ?'

She studies me, shakes her head. 'I know no more than you do, but he seemed a kind, genuine boy. I liked him.'

I loved him. I do love him, but I don't say it aloud.

'You have written to him?' she quizzes me, just making sure.

I tell her – everything, all the letters, those to his father, everything.

'And you've had no replies at all?' Her colour has come back again, but it's not a normal healthy flush and I feel I should not be worrying her like this, but I'm not sure how to stop now we are embarked on the saga.

'I don't even know if he's safe,' I agonize. 'There have been quite a few casualties out there.'

'There must be something we can do,' she says. 'Some Army organization – or the Salvation Army – we could contact.'

I tell her then what I plan to do. She listens carefully and agrees I must go as soon as we return home.

'We'll get you back and sorted first,' I tell her.

'You sound so like your Pa sometimes,' she begins with a smile. Then a cloud passes over her face, and, suddenly fearful, she asks, 'Bess, will you come home? Just until you go to Cornwall. It would help me – and your Pa.'

'Of course.' I go to the bed and kneel, holding her hands. 'Of course I will. Don't worry about anything, Ma. I'll be with you.'

Pa comes straight back from the cathedral. 'I've explained the situation to Greville,' he says, 'and persuaded mother to stay for Clara's sake. Don't want too many empty seats at the wedding feast.' He takes a professional kind of stance to face Ma. 'The doctor is coming again after his evening surgery. There may be the chance of an ambulance transfer to the Leicester Royal Infirmary tomorrow. If not, there is that private clinic.'

'No, Edgar, no!' Ma pulls herself upright. 'I won't have that. I am going home in the car with you, Bess and your mother. I'll see a specialist but I am certainly not being taken straight into hospital.'

Nothing he says will change her mind.

'I came here yesterday in a car, for goodness' sake. I can certainly go back in one tomorrow.'

Eighteen

H e awakes with a start of terror, a feeling of falling off the edge of the world, knowing neither where he was, nor what beast of the night menaced him. Had he shouted out?

Then the truth, the reality of his dread, falls on him. This is his own bed and Fay – his worries about her health – is beside him. He feels he has hardly slept until the last few unguarded seconds, has tried all night to keep still for her sake, when his body ached to move, rake about.

'Edgar?' she queries softly. 'You awake?'

'I jumped in my sleep. Sorry.' He pushes a hand over and hers is there waiting. He turns on to his side to be nearer. 'Can I get you anything? A drink?'

'No, you'll soon be up for the milking. I'll have something then.'

'What's the time?' He feels like sleeping now, feels drugged and drained with the need.

'Half past five.'

He groans and she laughs gently and snuggles to him. *Wriggling in*, she calls it, but to him it is sheer eroticism. He pushes an arm under her shoulder and pulls her close.

He can smell the new talc she began to use a few months ago, a pleasant sharpish eau de cologne kind of scent. Blue Seas. The name suits it. Then, with a pang so sharp he has to discipline himself not to spring up and question her, another idea forms. Had she begun to buy this stronger-smelling powder to conceal another odour?

He remembers waking in the Norfolk hotel, remembers the

heavy redolence he had only subconsciously recognized as he
ignored Fay's frantic plea for him to 'Just fetch Bess, or your
mother', and pulled down the bedclothes she had gripped to her
chest. Farmers were used to the smell of blood, of birth, and it
had been that smell. He had recognized it but not believed it
until he saw for himself.

From that moment, he had not felt at ease until they were
home. Now all he wanted was to hear from their doctor about
the appointment with the specialist. He hoped no one was
dragging their feet, trusted there was no lax secretary, no
recalcitrant nurse, no golf-playing consultant delaying matters
even for a second. He supposed he trusted old doctor Hughes;
they had known him long enough. He had helped deliver Bess
in this bedroom, but if there was no phone call by lunch time . . .

Fay eases her head into the crook of his shoulder. 'Alright?'
he asks.

'Hmm.' She breathes and is still again.

He lies wide-eyed, watching the room reveal itself as the light
grows behind Fay's flounced curtains. She has made this room
very much a lady's chamber. His heart aches with his pride in
her as they lie so snug in friendship and love.

Leaning over so his cheek touches her hair, he imagines it
smells of his hay fields, of the phlox and old-fashioned pinks
she cultivates near the house. He feels stirred, then wonders
whether their new, more intense love-making has made her
condition worse. Now he has the feeling of falling from some
waking cliff, tipping, tormented, so he must move, must get up.

'It's not time yet, is it?' she asks.

'No, I'm just awake. I'll make a start. I'll bring you—'

'No, we'll have tea when you've finished.' She raises a hand,
waves, but before he can take it, she pulls it back under the
covers.

He is surprised to hear noises in the kitchen, opens the door
rapidly as if he expects intruders, or the dog to be about some
mischief. 'Bess!' he exclaims. He had even forgotten his daughter was at home. 'You startled me.'

'I thought I'd go up to the Hall, help Tommie out for a couple of hours. I'll be back before eight. Ma alright?'

She watches him closely, as if testing him for more lies.

He turns away, angry. By the time this girl understands, it will be too late, it'll be all over. All over? God! What makes him think that?

'Ma is alright?' Bess questions.

'She's had a good night,' he states. 'Stay as long as you like, nothing's spoiling. I'd be surprised if the appointment with the specialist is today.' He had not meant it to sound quite so abrupt.

'I'll be back by nine, then,' she says and turns to go, then turns back as if she has more to say.

He waits but she pats the dog's head, startling it, then leaves.

George has the cows all in their stalls when Noel arrives, swinging down from his old black bicycle. 'Met young Bess cycling over to the Hall. She's home, then?'

Edgar nods curtly. 'See you later.' He scowls to discourage chatter. 'I'm off back to the house.'

'Ah, no!' Noel contradicts. 'The wife's sent something for Mrs Bennett.' He fumbles with the straps of his bike bag. Edgar is caught between the niceties of gratitude, for whatever it is, and the wish to be away, feeling quite unable to undergo one of Noel's ordeals by proverb.

He takes the small brown earthenware pot, its paper cover secured by string, and Noel nods acceptance of his thanks.

Before he enters the house, he can hear the wireless, and he finds Fay tipping coke from the hod into the Aga. 'Damn me!' he exclaims as he takes the hod from her. 'Woman!'

'I'm not staying in bed until the doctor chooses to come,' she tells him. 'I rested all day yesterday, and it has stopped. I'll be myself again in a day or two. It was just a heavier period than usual, that's all.'

'Fay.' He catches her hand and pulls her to a chair. 'This is what you've been doing for months, isn't it. Convincing yourself it's nothing to worry about, and it's been getting worse. So, will the next time be worse than last? Do you really think you can carry on like this?'

Elbows on the table, she holds her head in her hands. 'No,' she admits.

'I blame myself,' he says, and when she protests he shakes his head. 'I should have realized. I knew you didn't have so much vitality, but I thought it was because of Bess leaving home.'

'That's one good thing that's come out of this,' she says. 'We are all together again, all under one roof.'

'You think she'll stay?' he asks, and wonders if at that moment he wouldn't rather swop that for Fay being well.

'I do,' she nods. 'But you must be patient with her, and—'

'And?'

'And . . .' She pauses to pull a face at him. 'Think of her as a kite you have to let out bit by bit on her string, let her feel the wind gradually.'

He wonders for a second if her brain is affected, then he sees the grin. 'Noel,' he groans.

'His advice to parents with growing children.'

'I escape him in the yard but get the maxims anyway. The old b—' He lets the word end with a puff of air through his lips. 'He's like a Nazi infiltrator brainwashing us. Anyway' – he snaps a finger at her and takes the pot from his jacket pocket – 'he's sent you this.'

They look doubtfully at the squat brown labelless pot, with its thick brown paper cover carefully cut round with pinking shears.

'It'll be Dawdie's special honey and herbs,' she guesses. 'She decants it out of a big jar.'

'Stirred into your tea, he said.'

'Ahem. I don't think so. You have some, keep your strength up.'

'*My* strength up?' he asks, then Brac begins to bark furiously at the door, looking to them to understand the warning.

They both see a black car draw into the yard and together they suggest, 'The doctor?' Edgar goes out to meet him.

A small grey man, who Edgar always said could be mistaken for a City businessman until seen in action, Dr Hughes is ushered into the kitchen. They both notice the absence of his medical bag. Fay offers him tea and he accepts. They both wait on his word.

'Made you my first call,' he says as Edgar pulls out a chair for him and he sits at the table. 'Oh! I see you have some of Dawdie's honey. Cured many a case of hayfever round about. Local pollen curing local allergies.'

Both of them regard the pot with surprise and he laughs. 'Take it, it'll do nothing but good.'

Edgar moves the pot to one side and sits down facing the doctor.

The doctor nods and continues. 'I rang Mr Meyer's secretary and he telephoned me himself later. He's an old colleague of mine. He is coming out to see Fay this afternoon. I'll bring him over. We should be here about four o'clock.'

'Good, that's excellent, thank you.' Edgar is both shocked and pleased with the speed of this. It is what he wants, of course it is. He glances at Fay.

'So soon,' she breathes, and the doctor nods, finishes his tea and rises.

'So, I shall see you good people later. And now I must be off to begin my rounds proper.'

Edgar walks with him to his car and extends a hand. 'Thanks for all you've done. It is very quick.'

'Unfortunately,' the doctor says, taking his hand, looking him straight in the eye, 'it should have been months ago.'

Nineteen

Since our return from Norfolk, though a scurry back to the farm might better describe it, surprisingly it is Ma who has taken control. She insists all is normal again, and that everything is to carry on as usual. This, and the realization that there is nothing either of us can do until she has seen the specialist, helps me on my way to work at the Hall that Monday morning.

One of the hunters is already tied up outside its stable, head down, too busy eating his breakfast to acknowledge my arrival. A barrow load of dirty straw has been pushed out, and inside I can hear the clean straw being forked in around the sides to help with the next night's bedding.

'Morning,' I call, expecting it to be Tommie who answers.

'Bess?' It's Greville who comes from the stable, pitchfork in hand. 'Good morning to you. Didn't expect to see you here this morning.'

'Where's Tommie?'

'At the other end.' He indicates the far end of the block, and as he does so, a second well-loaded barrow is pushed out into the yard. 'I said we'd meet in the middle. How's your Ma?'

'She says she's fine. We're waiting for the doctor to ring about the appointment with the specialist.' I gesture towards the fork he holds. 'Shall I carry on here?'

'You feed and we'll muck out, then we'll have a coffee break.' He too must be mulling over our troubles as we work, for when we pass some time later, he says, 'Good thing your mother finally agreed to the telephone.'

We share a brief laugh. Ma had been very reluctant, saying it made the farm seem like a business instead of a home. Greville had pulled her leg, saying she had only changed her mind because Mrs West had finally removed her chipped, white and blue enamel sign – *You May Telephone From Here* – from the village shop. Pa had also made the point that he felt his mother and Miss Seaton needed a telephone.

Pa? I lean with one hand on the neck of a horse and remember how Pa had staggered as he came into the kitchen that morning, bumped into the table, looked thoroughly startled, convinced me that there was another emergency, another haemorrhage; but he had said no, all there was to do was wait for the doctor's call. I can never remember him unbalanced like that, never remember him stumbling; even jumping the widest stepping-stones in our brook, he never faltered. This morning he had looked so uncertain, a man stripped of his confidence, looking at me almost as if he did not know who I was.

A hand falls gently on to my shoulder and I start violently. 'Sorry,' Greville apologizes. 'We both spoke to you.'

Greville takes my elbow as if to steady me and I look up to see Tommie standing in front of me, face full of concern.

'Alright, miss?' he asks.

'Thanks.' I nod. 'Sorry. Lost in thought.' I unloose the horse's halter, preparatory to leading it out to pasture, but Tommie takes it. 'I'll do that, miss, you go and have your breakfast.'

'Have you had anything?' Greville asks.

'I'm going home. I said I'd be back by nine.'

'You've oceans of time. Come on, let's see what's on offer. At least a coffee.'

I nod and we walk together from the stable block towards the kitchen quarters. I suddenly think of Mrs Bright, the cook. I have, of course, often seen Harding, their butler, since the night of Greville's demob party, and he treats me with his usual circumspection. I think of him, and respect him, as a true professional. Mrs Bright I have not seen. I only know she is still

218

at the Hall because I hear her name mentioned from time to time.

It is something of a shock to precede Greville into the kitchen and see Mrs Bright looking exactly the same as she had more than two years before, the same broad expanse of white apron, the same rubicund face presiding over a pan of bacon.

'Hello, Mrs B. Can you manage breakfast for two?' Greville asks.

'Just coffee for me, please,' I amend.

'Some toast then, Miss. That won't take much eating.'

I nod, giving in. 'Please.'

At that moment the baize door from the house opens and Harding comes in. It does feel like a repeat reverse performance, particularly when it is me he addresses.

'Ah! Miss Bennett, your mother is on the telephone, wants to speak to you.'

'My mother?' This seems so contrary to anything I might expect, he has to prompt me. 'It does sound urgent, miss.'

'Come on.' Greville leads the way out of the kitchen, along the servants' passage into the hall, where the receiver lies alongside the telephone.

'Hello, Ma. What's wrong?' I listen intently to catch every inflexion.

'Oh, Bess! Thank goodness. Can you go to Noel's house in the village? You're nearer than us. It's Dawdie – we've just had a call from the doctor, some kind of collapse. Your father's taken Noel home. George is somewhere the far side of the spinney with the contractors.'

'Are you—?'

'I'm fine, except your pa insisted I stay at home. Go to Noel, my dear. He will be distraught if it is anything serious. Do what you can.'

'I heard,' Greville says. 'Come on, my car is ready.'

We are in the village in no time, but already there is a small crowd grouped around two cars, the doctor's black Ford and our green Riley. The Rawlinses' front door is wide open, Noel's door closed.

I go to Dawdie's front door, which is strange – always before I have gone up the entry and through the back door. Colleen's mother opens the door. She steps back to let us in but shakes her head.

Upstairs there are voices, Noel's voice ragged and desperate and, as we look to the stairs, my father comes down. He too shakes his head. 'George should be here,' he says.

'I'll fetch him,' Greville volunteers.

'Far side of the Red Pool with the contractors.'

Greville nods and goes.

'What happened?' I ask.

'I heard such a bump when I was up straightening my bed,' Mrs Rawlins says. 'Our bedrooms adjoin over the entry. I put my ear to the wall and could hear the most dreadful noises, like someone . . .' She pauses, looks at me, then at Pa, shakes her head as if unable to describe what she heard.

'Dawdie's had a massive stroke,' Pa explains. 'The doctor is not hopeful.'

'I don't know what'll become of Noel,' Mrs Rawlins says very quietly. 'The pair of them live for each other.'

I want to protest that it is my mother who is ill, having to see a specialist, not Dawdie, not Noel's Dawdie. I see him teasing her, see him dancing a little dance before her at a long-gone harvest supper. This is too much, I tell God. Not fair.

Then, upstairs, there is a sudden noise as of a chair knocked over and we hear Noel cry out, 'Dawdie, no! Don't leave me! Don't leave me.'

While we stand stricken, Colleen's mother turns immediately and goes upstairs.

Pa suddenly sits down at the table, which is covered with a green velour cloth with bobbles, matching the old-fashioned mantle cover. Dawdie's house is immaculate.

'Pa? What do you think?' I ask in no more than a whisper as the voices swell upstairs, as if trying to contain and calm Noel's cries.

'She's gone,' he says.

'But that's not fair. Not fair.'

'Life's not,' he says and looks at me briefly, as if to say I have still that and much more to learn. 'Life's not,' he repeats. 'Best put the kettle on.' He pulls the silver flask he uses on hunt days from his hip pocket and stands it on the table. 'Noel will be down in a little.'

I am not sure how he knows this, and, feeling an intruder in Dawdie's kitchen, I put the kettle on the gas stove. Each brass tap is bright and worn smooth with polishing.

The tea is made, the pot under its patchwork cosy, when George comes bursting in, cap in hand, mud on his boots. His glance skims over the two of us as he passes through and up the enclosed stairs. We listen to his heavy tread, and realize it has been quiet upstairs for some minutes now. He comes down quite soon and stands at the bottom of the stairs. There is a tap on the door. I open it to Greville.

'I was too late,' George tells him, then sits slowly down at the table, staring down at the cap he still holds in his hands, as if he is the visitor, not us. He swallows hard, then says with low fierce anger, 'I told the old man he should have retired years ago, had some life with her.'

'He wouldn't have been happy,' Pa tells him.

George looks up, throws his cap violently to the floor. 'I know that, damn it! I don't need you nor nobody else telling me.'

'No, course you don't, boy.'

But it is Mrs Rawlins who, coming downstairs, diverts his anger. She goes to him and takes him in her arms. The same age as her children, she is comfortable with him.

'Your grandad is coming downstairs in a minute or two. The doctor'll need a few minutes with your gran, settle her down neat.

I realize she means lay Dawdie out. I've no idea what is done – pennies on the eyes to keep them closed, or more personal things? I pour the tea and Pa adds brandy.

Greville holds out a hand to George, who looks up but does not take the hand. 'I think it will be more fitting for me to see your grandfather at a later time. I intrude here.'

George stands up and slowly takes his hand.

'I'm so sorry, George.'

George nods and crumples back into the chair, openly crying now.

'Will you stay, Bess?' Greville asks.

'We'll see Noel,' Pa says.

When he has gone, Mrs Rawlins draws me into the tiny back kitchen. 'I wondered if you would run down to the factory and fetch our Colleen.' She nods back towards George. 'She'll be the best comfort he can have.'

It seems strange that this is the first time I have been into the factory. I have to pause just over the threshold to catch my breath, stand on a mat as long and broad as a school's. There is an office behind a glass partition, but that is empty. Beyond, there is a general concerted busyness, almost a cosiness, as if each noise, each buzz of machinery, each raised voice or laugh is part of the same thing; and it is, of course – making a living. I've lived so close, my best friend has worked here for years now, but I'm a stranger to this village factory. This, I also remember, is Adeline's territory. I wonder if the aggressive girl still works here.

'Hello.' A man in a brown smock comes from the double doors at the far end of the entrance hall. 'Looking for someone?'

Colleen starts to her feet as the foreman takes me to the mending room. 'What's happened?' She stands, hand pressed over her mouth, eyes growing rounder.

I tell her the full story as we hurry back to Noel's house.

'I can't believe it, I heard her at her dolly tub this morning. She always gives Noel's work shirts a good drubbing before she puts them in with the other wash.' She takes my arm, holds my forearm as we run. 'I don't know what Noel will do without

222

her.' Unconsciously, she repeats her mother's words. 'Or George, come to that.'

'He's got you.'

'Yes,' she agrees, but there are many doubts in the word. 'But no one'll replace Dawdie.'

When we arrive, Noel is insisting he must go back upstairs to make sure the window is open. 'Let her go free,' he appeals, and is agitated until Colleen's mother calms him and says she will go.

'And tell 'er I mun't be long coming after.' His loud anguished cry alerts us all.

Now it is Colleen who goes from George to Noel, takes and grips both his hands. It is also the moment Pa and I both realize that we should make our goodbyes for the time being. Noel needs to be with his grief, with his own, his grandson, his neighbours. Pa, as his employer, albeit lifetime friend, and me, for all my heart aches for him, are de trop, our continued presence not quite fitting for these first moments.

Climbing into the car, I glance up at the bedroom window, latched open on its outside bar and hook. 'It's a custom among the old villagers,' Pa tells me as we drive away. I am halfway home to the farm before I realize I was at the Hall, that my bike is there, but I never make any decision whether I should go back. I know I should telephone Greville but I never do.

We tell our news of Dawdie's sudden awful death, then I am told the news that the specialist is coming to the house this very afternoon. The rest of the day is like a series of alarm bells ringing at different ends of my life, so I scurry from one state of alarm to the other. We seem to meet in sudden anxious spurts of conversation, then spin off into our own solitary desperate worry, though soon enough our doctor comes with the specialist, a Mr Meyer – a large man, like a rugby forward, short back and sides, pleasant but unsmiling face. There is the examination in the bedroom; putting clean towels in the bathroom for him to use; Dr Hughes and Mr Meyer upstairs with my mother, Pa and I sitting silent in the kitchen, listening to the distant voices. Then the door opens upstairs and Pa goes to meet them. They take him into the parlour, talk to him behind the closed door.

When they come out, all I am privileged to hear is the forced heartiness in the voices of the medical men, and when I meet them in the hall, Mr Meyer talks to me as if I am a child. 'Well, young lady, you'll no doubt be helping look after your mother when she comes out of hospital.' The pat on the shoulder, the departure, Pa following to the car for another few words, head bent into the car, then closing the door of the sleek black Rover and watching the two medical men drive away.

'I didn't know Ma had to go into hospital.' I confront Pa in the hall, but he does not answer, looking past me to where Ma is coming downstairs.

'I'm glad they could not stay for a drink. Now we can all have a cup of tea in peace in the kitchen,' she says, leading the way, busying herself. I think I should help, but when I attempt to, Pa points to a chair. Normality is to be stretched as far as it will go.

'Hospital?' I question.

Ma nods. 'I'll explain,' she tells me quietly, but as she brings cups and saucers to the table she wonders about asking Stella if her sister Mary is free to give a hand in the house while she's incapacitated, but what may be far more trouble, she says, is replacing Noel and George. 'Do you think Noel will come back to work? George has told me he thought he should have retired long ago. He's seventy-six, and George won't want to leave his grandfather for a time. I could be very difficult for you, Edgar.'

She stops and looks at Pa. He is looking at her, following her with his eyes, but obviously not listening. I see that while my mind has been going round and round a myriad problems, trying to see what the repercussions of the day's events will be, like circles running out from a stone thrown into a lake, Pa's thoughts are different. Pa's concerns are like a reverse play of mine, a film running backwards to show the circles drawn back into the centre of the lake, the stone emerging and coming back to his hand, his heart. Pa has only one worry: Ma. I know this moment is important, that I shall remember it always, as he sits, neither hearing nor seeing, just staring at my mother. It is almost as if he realizes something no one else yet knows, and at that moment the pain in my heart is all for him.

In the past, Ma and I always felt it was Pa that was our problem, our happy problem, because we loved him and wanted to please him so much. Now I see Ma is Pa's problem.

'Edgar,' she repeats.

'You told the specialist you would not go into hospital until after Dawdie's funeral.'

'That's right. I would not dream of doing so. I shall go and see Noel in the morning, see if I can do anything. I don't think a few more days will make much difference, whatever he says. Dawdie has been part of all our married lives.'

Noel has been part of the whole of my life.

'I'll come with you tomorrow morning,' I tell Ma.

'And the horses at the Hall?' she questions.

'I'll speak to Greville. I've left my bike there anyway.'

'I can drop you off tomorrow.'

Then we both exclaim as Pa bangs his fists on the table. 'Mr Meyer told me, *and you*, as soon as possible. *As soon as possible.*'

'After Dawdie's funeral,' Ma says gently.

'Right!' He rises, strides out of the kitchen, bangs the door. We stand motionless, listening, and hear our car door slam, the engine start, and with a crash and grind of gears he drives out of the yard.

'Where do you think he's going?' I ask.

'Probably to help dig Dawdie's grave,' Ma says, then exclaims at her own words. 'No, no, I don't know what made me say that. It must be nerves.'

'But just the sort of thing he would do if he could,' I supply as we turn to each other. We hug, pat each other's backs, our shaky laughter subsiding into mourning for Dawdie, grief for

Noel. I realize we are overwrought. Then, as we begin to regain control of ourselves, my concern is for my mother.

'You said you would tell me why you have to go into hospital.'

'I need an operation, a hysterectomy, the consultant thinks. I obviously should not have let things go on as long as I have.' She pauses to look at me as if instilling some message for the future – my future – a lesson I should remember.

I am not sure what a hysterectomy is, but it's an operation, Noel's *being put to the knife.*

'Don't look so stricken.' She takes my hand and we sit back at the table. 'It means removing a part of me that I can well do without at my age, my womb. Lots of women have it done.'

'I guessed what the *ectomy* bit was. I remember Colleen having a tonsillectomy. I just wish you didn't have to have it done.'

'If wishes were horses, beggars would ride.'

Now, I think, we are back to Noel, poor devastated Noel. I wonder if *he* will weather *his* loss – his *ectomy.*

'I wanted to ask if you had said anything to Greville or Tommie about going to Cornwall.'

'Well, no, I . . .' I am so surprised she should ask this question at this moment.

'I want you to do two things for me, Bess,' Ma says. 'I'd like you to stay here with your father, at least until I'm home again. The doctor said he thought two weeks, three at the most. Could you bear to wait another three weeks before you go to Cornwall to find Ken Sinclair and your Ian?'

'I haven't made any arrangements yet, so I couldn't go for a week or two anyway.' So I promise. The only thing that really troubles me is Ma's reference to *your Ian.* My Ian? I wonder. I think of the Chinese beauty in the magazine, and of Ian's long, long silence.

Pa comes back about nine that evening to announce that Dawdie's funeral is on Thursday, and Ma is to go into hospital on Friday morning – it is all arranged. 'And I think it's fitting that we cancel our harvest supper this year.'

'Yes,' Ma agrees, but slowly.

'I'd like to offer to pay for Dawdie's wake instead. I guess all the village will attend, but I'm not sure how to approach the matter.'

'Speak to Colleen's mother,' I tell him. 'She'll know what to say.

'Good idea.' He nods approval, and I feel seven years old, basking in approval.

'I can do that tomorrow,' Ma volunteers.

On Thursday morning we all assemble at Grandmama's, piling in from the yard to find a stranger seated in the kitchen, smiling, benign. He does not rise when we enter, merely nods quite pleasantly, as if we are the strangers and he perfectly at home.

I do feel I have seen him before, about the village, or somewhere nearby. I wonder for a moment if he has ever helped at the Hall in the gardens, but then the mystery is solved as Miss Seaton comes in and, looking meaningfully at first Pa then me, announces, 'This is Mr Benjamin, he lives at Pear Cottage.'

I see Pa lift his chin, as if to take a blow, at the mention of the Sinclairs' old home, but he nods affably enough to Mr Benjamin. Ma and I both say good morning.

This, then, is the man Gran emptied her attics for.

Gran comes in, ready in black hat and gloves. She acknowledges us all, kisses Ma and me, nods to Pa, but her concern is obviously with Mr Benjamin, who rises and whose smile broadens as she comes in.

'I think you'd best go now, Mr Benjamin. We are going to Church.'

'The funeral,' he says, then grasps and rocks his head between his hands, as if in extreme agony, but then emerges looking quite calm, and glancing round at all the company, bows his way out, Miss Seaton following as if to see him off the premises.

We all watch him go, a man not unlike Pa in age and build, but in every other respect unlike. In his own village he might well have been termed simpleton, the village idiot, and I wonder again at the chance that has brought him here for Gran and Miss Seaton to cosset and care for. I notice that, as he is seen out of the front door, he is carrying a small parcel wrapped in greaseproof paper. A slice of ham for his tea, as like as not.

'Landed on his feet,' Pa comments.

'Time he did,' Miss Seaton says shortly.

'Noel was in the churchyard early this morning,' Gran tells us, 'insisting the grave be dug deeper.'

'Most unseemly fuss,' Miss Seaton judges.

Pa gives a grunt of disagreement. 'He just knows old Smith, the sexton, too well. He's a lazy blighter, wants watching.'

We pass the grave just inside the churchyard to the right of the path, and the large mound of earth, its basic message concealed under a green tarpaulin, suggests it is now dug good and deep. The tolling of the tenor church bell has sounded out the double strokes to tell of a woman's death, and now solemnly pro-pounds every year of Dawdie's seventy-two years. Black-clad villagers crowd the path, talk in low tones under the ponderous bell.

The church fills rapidly, people sliding closer in the pews to accommodate yet another one or two. Greville comes along the side aisle and squeezes in next to me at the far end of our central pew. It is a nice gesture, for he can hardly have known Dawdie at all. Ever since Monday morning he has done so many thoughtful things: brought back my bicycle; diverted a lad from the gardens to the stables for the time being, and generally made me feel he works for me rather than the other way round. When I'd told him this, he had said if it were so then he would never leave his boss's side for a moment, attend her every whim, never ask for a rise and bring her flowers every day. He did bring flowers for my mother.

He has perhaps done most for my father, coming over and

asking to be shown how the contractors were progressing at the far side of the spinney; talking at length about plans for the Paget farm; bringing the old history books he had spoken of from the Hall library; reminding him that the Hunt would like to have the traditional first cubbing on our land the following week, and taking him to walk the covert.

The quiet organ music ceases, and the whispered conversations. We hear movement at the back of the church, everyone stands. I have looked in the small red prayer book, because I have never been to a funeral before. It says that *The priest and clerks meeting the corpse at the entrance of the churchyard and going before it shall say, or sing—* And before I can recall more, the words themselves ring in my ears.

'I am the resurrection and the life, saith the Lord: she that believeth in me, though she were dead, yet shall she live . . .' And so the recital goes on, the only difference being there is no mention of *she* in the old prayer book, only *he*. I concentrate on trying to remember more rather than be affected by the sight of the coffin with its simple spray of red roses, the bearers in long black coats, with Noel and George walking immediately behind, then Mrs Rawlins and Colleen, and four people I do not know.

I remember the red book says that The Order for the Burial of the Dead is not to be used for any that die unbaptized, or excommunicated, or who have laid violent hands upon themselves. Dawdie is clear on all counts, and as the long orders are read by the vicar, I try not to listen, but the words *and be no longer seen* penetrate the control and my tears fall, though I try to pretend they do not. A hand encompasses mine and pushes something into it. For a second time, Greville has given me his handkerchief to stem my tears.

Once I begin, it is difficult to stop, though I do, as we hear the vicar give a kind of résumé of Dawdie's life in the village. I had not known her proper names were Doris Audrey, nor that she had only come to the village as Noel's young bride after being a parlour maid and assistant to a city chemist. She had, after her marriage, gained quite a reputation for some of her herbal potions, and later, when the beehives on Noel's allotment became prolific, for her special honey mixtures.

It is the nearest we get to a lightening of the service, and soon those who had been nearest to Dawdie and Noel follow from church to graveside to witness the committal. Adjacent to the village square, I see that PC Burnett has stopped all the traffic to show due respect. People in the street stand still, men bareheaded, heads bowed. I look round at the cottages and houses lining the square, and every window has its curtains closed. I am aware of the imposing granite cross to Alexander Edgar Bennett, he of the dark place in the hall, with other Bennett graves nearby. I have heard that there will not be many more burials in the churchyard, the village is to have a cemetery on its outskirts.

Noel stands at the foot of the grave, George by his side, bent so low in grief he seems smaller than his grandfather. Noel has his feet set apart, as if to keep some purchase on the earth as the final moment comes and the committal is read: 'Forasmuch as it hath pleased Almighty God . . . earth to earth, ashes to ashes, dust to dust . . .' And the undertaker lifts a spade of fine earth up to Noel. He takes a handful and, going forward, sprinkles it finely down on to the coffin. Then George. His handful falls less lightly, more startlingly, echoing like a knock on a door, not like someone being laid to rest. I see Noel stagger a little, but, immediately, Mr Rawlins is behind him, hand under his elbow.

It is not a cold day, but I am shivering when we leave the graveside. We follow as the mourners are led from the church-yard across the road to the skittle alley of the Sir Robert Peel, where the wake has been arranged. This was convenient for everyone, but seemed wrong to me. Dawdie had never entered a public house in her life, but once inside the long room, it is tastefully done, long trestle tables on one side hold the food, and on the other, chairs are arranged around smaller tables. Noel sits with George, receiving condolences from all who come. When it is our turn, I go first, but can hardly speak. I stoop to kiss him. 'I'm so sorry, Noel, so very sorry.' He grips my hand and nods, for once he has no wise words to say.

When it is Ma's turn, he looks up at her as if in alarm. 'I've heard you're going to hospital, missus. I hope all goes well for you.' Then Pa goes forward. 'Thanks for—' Noel begins, but Pa's hand falls on his shoulder. 'Noel, I wish I could do something that would really help.'

Noel shakes his head. There is nothing anyone can do to make his life whole again.

In bed that night, Pa's words as we left the funeral stay with me. 'Well, that's one thing over.'

Now we face Ma going for her operation tomorrow. I wonder if she will sleep at all, or Pa – or Noel, or George. The world seems a sad, sad place. I wonder if Ian might be dead? Would we have heard? Surely his father would have let me know – but perhaps not. I find I am still using Greville's handkerchief.

Twenty

T he following days happen in snatches, as if someone tears aside a blackout, lets in the scene for a few seconds, then blots it out again. It is as if I am the film in my old Brownie camera, in complete darkness until someone clicks the knob which opens the shutter for just a brief glimpse, recording that moment for ever on the film of my memory.

I would destroy that film if I could. It flashes its cruel pictures over and over but I hardly believe them.

On Friday morning, before my mother goes to hospital, she looks so in control, except for a wistful glance at her beloved teapot. Pa takes his tea into the yard, with a slice of toast, which I see him give to Brac.

He telephones me to say Ma is early on the list and he has to ring at two o'clock. He has decided to stay in town. He will go to visit Ma's people – her two brothers and, if there is time, her parents – who all live on the outskirts of the city. I am to let Gran know what is happening.

At two thirty the telephone rings. The operation is over but has been much longer than anticipated and he has to ring again at four o'clock.

Gran decides she wants to be at the farm, and George is despatched to fetch her.

At four, Pa rings. He can go in to see Ma at eight. It's good to have Gran there. We talk of possible complications, then decide we are foolish to speculate.

Shortly afterwards, the telephone rings again and I think it must be someone enquiring after Ma, but it is Pa from the hospital. He has been sent for.

Gran and I are wondering what to do when the telephone rings again, startling us both. It is Greville.

'Hello, Bess, how are things going? Operation safely over?'

I stammer out a rushed string of facts.

'Do you want to go in?' he asks.

When we all arrive, we are taken into a separate room behind the ward sister's desk. We are told the doctor will be in to see us quite soon.

It is Pa who comes, though for a second I do not recognize him. A few hours away have aged him ten years. He focuses more on Gran than me. 'She's gone,' he says.

Gone. What is he talking about? Where can she have gone? He brought her to the hospital, left her in their care. I jump to my feet. 'Gone?' I exclaim, then Gran goes to Pa and enfolds him in her arms. He drops his head to her shoulder. I can't accept this, watch as if mesmerized by the sight of my father cradled in his mother's arms.

She is holding him still when the specialist, Mr Meyer, white-coated, weary, looking brave in defeat, walks into the room, closing the door behind him.

Mr Meyer sits with us and tells us that the operation had been far more complex than he'd ever imagined. The invasive cancer had taken over her womb and bowels. 'The human body can stand a tremendous amount, but this was just too much. We did everything we could, but it was not enough.'

I see Ma's face, that meaningful look, and her words: 'Should not have let things go on as long as I have.' But I don't want to understand all this. What I want to do is run, leave it behind, speed back in time, back to yesterday. Then I am struck by the thought that we shall always remember the date of Dawdie's funeral.

I sit in a desolate place, people speak to me. Greville holds and pats my hand, Gran once holds my other hand, then goes back to Pa.

'Would you like to come with your father and Grandmama to see your mother?'

I look up sharply, realizing the question has been asked before, but angry – of course I want to see my mother. I nod sharply to the quietly spoken sister, who lowers her head as if accepting my anger as her due. I see Gran catch Greville's jacket sleeve as we pass, urging him to come with us. The nurse leads us to the room just next door to where we are – just next door. I'd thought my father must have walked miles of hospital corridors to reach us. He looked as if he had come a long way.

I can't believe we have been in the next room all this time. I felt we should have known, been told.

'Oh!' Pa's exclamation is very low. 'All her colour has gone now.'

She lies so straight, so neat. I want to hug her back to life. If she had been pale before, it is nothing like she is now. Now she is colourless, a cold bloodless pallor. This is someone else, they have made a mistake. So many ridiculous things tumble about in my mind as the three of us are given chairs to sit close to the bed. It is as if we are waiting for her to speak, awaiting some kind of raising of Lazarus, so intense is our concentration. Pa holds her hands and gazes fixedly at her.

After a few moments Greville gets up and moves his chair to the wall, nods to us and goes soundlessly out, closing the door.

'It's difficult to take in,' Gran says.

'I can't believe it. I made her come.' Pa bends low over the bed and his shoulders move in silent sobs. 'I should have left well alone.'

'It wasn't well though, was it, Pa?'

'No, it was not,' Gran confirms, and comes to stand between us, takes my hand and Pa's, holds them together in hers. Gran means to comfort both, and for us to comfort each other, I understand that. I also see the mirror image of my grief in Pa's eyes. Ma always says we are too much alike.

The thought that she will never say so again devastates me. I realize that, ever since I can remember, my mother has been a kind of mirror we've both used to see each other through. She got the angle right for us, so we liked our reflections as we sparked off witty remarks about things – about life, about political oafs and union causes – and about her sometimes.

I feel guilty now, Ma, for the truth is – and it's too late for anything but truth – I was more eager to share the understanding of the clever pun and the laughter with Pa than to overtly take your side. I suppose I wanted to be on both sides as a child, but when I chose, I chose the man I have – or had until lately – hero-worshipped all my life. It always seemed so important to me to be on his side.

'We must let Fay's parents and brothers know,' Gran is saying.

I see Pa's hands tighten, and I know how he feels. It is as if to spread the news will really make it true, while if we keep it to ourselves, then perhaps it won't have happened, can't have happened.

Pa lays his head on Ma's shoulder and puts an arm defensively across her. I feel appalled by his grief as he lies over the bed, appalled and shut out. I am not sure how much time passes, it could be eons or seconds. Then Gran startles me again as she comes forward, squeezes my shoulders and says. 'I am going to say goodbye to your mother now.'

She goes to the far side of the bed, leans over, whispers to Pa, then kisses Ma's cheek; stands for a moment, head bowed, then whispers, 'You've been a good girl, Fay, as good as any daughter to me. God bless.'

She comes back to me. 'I'll wait for you outside, Bess.'

I look up and she lowers her head in the direction of my father. I am not sure whether she means that I should also leave, leave my father to grieve by himself.

Gran goes out, and in a little while I too go to the far side of the bed, lean over and kiss Ma, my lips meeting her coldness with lingering shock. Then I sit down again. None of us really shared the moment of her passing, for I heard Mr Meyer say she never regained consciousness. This cannot surely be goodbye. I do not know how to leave. Some minutes later, the door opens again and Gran and Greville come in and whisper to me to say my goodbyes while they wait for me.

I go through the formality again and let myself be led out. Once in the corridor, nothing seems real. Arrays of doors stretch on either side of miles of shiny corridor. I feel like Alice, but not in Wonderland. Then I am being held, held and walked. We meet people and they talk to us, Greville answers, but propels me on into an empty dayroom, and lowers me into another chair and presents me with another handkerchief. 'Oh no!' I shake my head at him. 'Not again. I don't want any more handkerchiefs. I'm not crying.' He presses the cloth very gently to my face and I realize I must be, for my cheeks are awash.

'That was your Topham grandparents and your mother's two brothers,' he tells me.

Soon my maternal grandparents, my uncles and one aunt, are all in this dayroom with us. All tall, they seem to dominate and fill the room. My maternal grandmother is weeping in between asking questions, which Grandmama Bennett answers as well as she can. I catch odd words about other people who must be told and talk of arrangements. I do not seem to see Pa, yet I am sure he should be there by now.

'What is it?' Greville asks as I spring to my feet.

'Pa?'

He nods to the opposite side of the door, where Pa stands with Gran and Nan and Pop Topham. We move over to them, and while Gran Topham fusses and weeps, Pop Topham wordlessly tucks me under his shoulder, takes me under his wing. There is talk of us going to stay with them, but we both shake our heads. We would sooner go home, Gran Bennett says. In any case, she will be staying with us for the time being, and there are the animals to look to.

We both know things could be arranged, but neither of us wants to be anywhere but at home. Other decisions are made for us. Pa is not to be allowed to drive home. Angus Topham will drive Pa's car and his brother Ross will follow in his car, to bring Angus back to town. Gran opts to go in with Angus and Pa. Greville is to take me home.

He does not talk, just asks if I am comfortable, need more air, says I should tell him if there is anything I need as we go along.

'Bess,' he says after we have travelled in silence some way. 'I don't want you to worry about anything at the Hall. Tommie and I'll manage very well. You must look after your father.'

I wonder if he is going to mention our recent difficulties and do not answer.

'Forgive me for what I am going to say, and I promise never to mention it again.' He glances across at me as he turns the car into our lane. 'I know your mother was overjoyed when you went back home to live. I think it would make her happier still to know you will stay on with your pa permanently.'

I do not answer.

'I hope you don't resent my saying that.'

I shake my head. 'I know it's true,' I say. I also remember my mother's double request. Stay with your father until I am home, then go and find your Ian in Cornwall.

Twenty-One

I t is thought fitting that the service should be at the Tophams' place of worship, which is also the city cathedral, then my mother is to be brought to lie in our parish churchyard.

This information is relayed time and time again as the tentative enquiries as to the truth of the news turn into a flood of phone calls, a trail of personal visitors. Colleen comes in the evening with George. She weeps with me and for me, holds me for a long time when she first comes, embraces me often as we talk. When they leave she leans heavily on him, his arm about her waist. I ache for such comfort. The next day when Stella comes she brings a fruitcake from Mrs Rawlins.

I hear from many of my school friends, Miss Smith, the headmistress, and the housemistress who reminded me my mother was a Topham, gave me back my sense of pride. I need it now, need to stop lingering out of sight, in my bedroom, falling back into the shelter of barn walls, appealing for the impossible from a God I now doubt.

I take over the outdoor things Ma did, while Gran supervises everything indoors. I feed the hens, collect the eggs, wipe and stack them in trays for collection by the egg-packing station, and with Noel absent supervise the horses. I wonder vaguely if the hunters would be better at the Hall, but I am unable to think ideas through, nothing seems to matter that much any more.

I know we need to do the everyday things, the feeding round, the general animal care, but it is a wearisome business. Gran is our strength, she sees the way it has to be, the daily routine. The times we sit at the table for meals, even if we eat little, she supervises us both with gentle compassion. She is circumspect with Pa, for there is a terrible energy and anger just below the surface. It is as well there is much to keep him busy, much to arrange, but I see him nearly pull a door from its hinges as the latch sticks and impedes him. First he rattles the feed-store door, kicks at it, then attacks it with a hefty stake, swinging it up at the latch time and time again. The door finally yields to a blow and swings slowly open. In a comic film it would have had the audience rolling in their seats. I fall back out of sight, appalled.

I see the differences in our loss. Pa's loss is the end of something I have barely touched upon, though I have lost that too. My loss is the complete end of childhood. I am nobody's child, Pa has never treated me as a child: a junior partner, an equal at times, but I've never had from him the gentle uncritical love I had from Ma. I feel I have no future, just the past. I feel I am drowning in the increasing numbers of letters of sympathy that arrive each morning, when I now accept letters I have hoped for will never come.

On Wednesday morning, Gran decides I should go to the Hall. Greville has phoned or visited every day. 'I think you should make the effort. They've been so good.' Gran has had Lady Philipps to see her as many times as Colleen has come. I think Gran is as glad of her friend's hugs and pats as I am of Colleen's.

'You've taken on responsibilities, you should see to them,' Pa mutters.

I am getting my bike out of the machine store when I hear someone in Captain's stable. George can hardly be finished in the milking parlour. Then I hear a familiar hissing in and out as the dandy brush is swept rhythmically over the animal's coat. I go slowly, sidle like a child, until I can see into the stable.

Noel is facing me, standing on his crate, sweeping the brush from the head over the neck and as far down the shoulder as he can reach.

I lean in the doorway and we look at each other. 'Noel?'

'Aye, well,' he says. 'Best to be busy.'

'You alright?' I ask.

'No,' he states. 'You?'

'No,' I say, and the next moment I have flung my arms around him and we hold on, equal in stature with him on his crate. I can smell horse and straw and manure on his old jacket, and they seem like smells from a past happy life. We stand motionless, companions in grief, until a hairy muzzle explores this strange embrace, blows hot air and strands of hay over us. 'Aye, well,' he tells the horse. 'Perhaps you know best. Going to the Hall?' he asks me.

'I wish *you*'d come over some time.'

'Maybe. First things first.' He places a proprietary hand on the carthorse's neck. 'Where's the old man?'

I realize he means my father. I've never heard him use the expression before. From anyone else it would sound disrespectful. I see that real grief strips away social niceties. Death must, I think, bring honesty. So, of one thing I should be sure; whatever his sins, Pa did love my mother. 'He's in the house,' I tell Noel. 'But off into town in about an hour if you want to see him.'

'No, I'll have a word with your grandmother.'

The day before the funeral I see Noel beckoning George inside, then Gran meeting him like a conspirator on the doorstep. George leaves carrying Pa's shotguns. She realizes I have seen. 'Just a precaution,' she tells me. 'Life can be very empty when everything is over.'

The service at the cathedral is dignified, our grief not diminished, but dwarfed and amply contained beneath the great vaulted ceiling. On the right, the sun shines through the huge Gothic windows, the stained glass dappling its colours over the congregation. The central aisles are full, many people I have no recollection of ever seeing before.

I try not to let every word, every hymn, every prayer of the service cut my heart. I try not to think at all, just to stand up, sit down, kneel, at the right times. I listen to the account of Ma's life and want to say more.

The agony of the service over, we file out, Pa and I immediately behind the coffin. I see Miss Smith halfway along the central aisle and then right at the back Colleen and her mother. I feel a great surge of emotion, my legs drain of strength. I must stumble, because Greville, who is following with Gran, is suddenly by my side supporting me, arm around my waist, and Gran moves forward to take my place by Pa.

When we reach the village, I feel overwhelmed, for though I had understood the committal is usually a more private family affair, Pa must have arranged for a second shorter service to be held at the graveside. The churchyard is full of people. The church choir, male choristers in their white surplices over black cassocks, women choristers in all-enveloping black cassocks and black square hats worn one point towards the sky, stand in two orderly rows to one side.

We have to file through a corridor of people. I see Mrs West from the village shop, Mr Faulkner the butcher and the Co-op manager, Mr Partridge, standing together and wonder if all the shops are closed. Mr Rawlins is there with George, and I recognize many of the casual men who work for Pa and their wives. Noel nearer to the end of our progression. Miss Seaton shepherds Gran away from us, drawing her around so that she stands with her back to the huge cross of Alexander Bennett.

The service is short, but infinitely sweeter to me for the soft singing of our choir, the familiar country tones in the responses. Then comes the soft fall of roses, followed by the harder thud of soil on wood, the second time in my life – and in one week, in this same place – I have heard this shocking sound.

The crowd drifts away and leaves us, the family, the nearest family and then just Pa and I still at the graveside. There is no comfort we can give to each other, nothing in us to replace the loss. It is as if our relationship needed Ma as the focal point to be real at all, but in the same moment we both complete our sojourn, aware of the men with their spades standing at a respectful distance but lingering purposefully. We walk around opposite sides of the open grave, take a last look at the coffin with our roses and a scattering of soil, and without speaking move away towards our village farmhouse.

The rooms are crowded, but here I know everyone, for only the Tophams and one or two close friends have come from town, and soon there is a division such as always happens at our harvest suppers.

The Tophams are in the parlour and I glimpse Pa seated in a far corner with people going to him, talking to him, shaking his hand or patting his shoulder, moving away for another to take his or her place. The farmers are in the dining room with the village businesspeople. Sherry and spirits are being dispensed. Noel, George and other villagers are in the kitchen, where Stella and Mary are busy replenishing trays of refreshments, pouring cups of tea, carrying them wherever they are wanted.

I find myself in the hall as if I really do not belong to any group, but Greville stays by my side. After a time, he says he thinks I should sit down, takes my elbow and settles me next to Lady Philipps, who sits talking to various people, but holding my hand very firmly so I shall stay where I am. I am grateful to be organized.

At last it is over, the goodbyes all said, everyone gone except Greville, who is to drive the three of us back to the farm. We are ready to leave when, coming downstairs, I hear Miss Seaton telling Gran that Mr Benjamin keeps coming and asking where she is. 'He comes every day asking if you are back.'

'Oh dear. Explain to him as best you can, Maude.'

There is such a closeness between the two as they speak of this new neighbour, almost a gentleness in Maude Seaton as she nods at her employer.

242

Pa and Greville are waiting in the yard by Greville's car, both men look very pale, both solemn, but it is the *difference* in their expressions that makes me wish I could turn back into Gran's and stay there. Greville looks at me with some kind of watchful expectation, Pa's eyes are without light. Greville looks at me asking too much, Pa too little.

Two days after the funeral the guns are missed. Gran and I are both in the kitchen as Pa opens the cabinet next to the dresser.

'What the hell!' he exclaims, staring into the empty cupboard, then turns on us. 'So?' he demands.

'I thought it best,' Gran says.

'You should mind your own business, woman!'

'It is my business.'

I am appalled to hear him shout at my grandmother.

'You!' he exclaims. 'In fact, both of you can go back to where you came from as soon as you like. I don't need you here.'

Brac, who had retreated under the table, suddenly rushes to the back door, barking. We realize someone is knocking, a rather strange, rat-a-tat-a-tat-a-tat, like a child playing a drum.

Pa strides to the door and wrenches it unceremoniously open. We hear someone enquire for Mrs Bennett.

I think for a moment Pa is going to strike the caller, and Gran, as if thinking the same, goes forward and holds Pa's arm.

'It's me,' she says. 'It's me he wants.'

There is a kind of emotional shift on the doorstep and Gran says, Edgar, this is Benjamin; Mr Benjamin, who's come to live in Pear Tree Cottage.'

'I wondered where you were,' Mr Benjamin says, coming in to stand in front of Gran, cap in hand, smiling, waiting.

'You should not have come,' she tells him, and he looks completely crestfallen. 'This is a sad house at the moment.'

'Your lady said where you were.'

'Miss Seaton did not mean for you to come, I'm—'

'Oh, let the man come in and sit down. He's walked here. Give him tea or something,' Pa says impatiently.

'I can make tea,' Mr Benjamin volunteers.

'He likes to do things,' Gran explains, then adds with a nod to the visitor, 'He's good at doing things.'

Pa pauses to take a new measure of this man, then goes off, calling the dog, who has been smelling around Mr Benjamin's legs and wagging his tail, a reception he usually only gives to those he knows well.

I wonder if Pa is going to corner Noel or George about the guns, but the atmosphere in the house relaxes once he has gone, and Gran lifts a hand to Mr Benjamin's shoulder and urges him to sit down.

'I shall be staying here for quite a time, Ben. I think it is best if I come to the village to see you.'

I had thought the man's surname was Benjamin, but now it seems it is his Christian name.

'I like it here,' he says. 'It's a nice place.'

'You must not come again, Ben.'

There is something so dogmatic in her tone it surprises me almost as much as when Pa shouted at her.

'Surely it—' I begin, but her uncompromising look silences me and I begin to make fresh tea.

'When you've drunk your tea, you must walk quickly back to the village. It will soon be dark.'

Mr Benjamin drinks his tea, has a piece of cake and goes off very amicably considering the greeting he received.

Gran watches him go from the kitchen window and is very quiet, almost as if she has suffered yet another loss. I wonder if she knows how often and how deeply she sighs as we wait for bedtime, for Pa to come in, or perhaps just for some meaning to come back into life.

Pa does not come in until it is almost dark, and after Gran has several times wondered where he is.

'Who is that Ben? He was still lingering around in the lane. I walked him to the village.'

'He lives in Pear Tree Cottage,' Gran repeats. 'I told you.'

244

'There's something – I don't know' – he throws down his cap – 'either odd, or familiar, about him. He seems keen to come back to see you, told him he could any time.'

'I wish you hadn't done that,' Gran says.

Twenty-Two

I n my dreams I search for my mother in all kinds of terrible places: stables high in filth, woods treacherous with bogs and huge houses with endless corridors in which I become lost and terrified for my mother's safety.

I wake to a worse nightmare, when I remember she is really lost to me. The dreams become worse each night, so I try to stay awake. I begin to creep downstairs most nights to find comfort with Brac, opening the front of the aga and sitting in the slumbering glow. I feel close to my mother here. I make tea in her teapot, just for the smell of the infusing leaves and the look of the teapot inside its cosy on the table.

I don't think much, not rationally. I've gone over the same useless ground time after time. It's more as if I just hold thoughts of my mother in my hand, let them rest there. These at least I have, these at least we accomplished together. Outside, autumn is turning to winter early, with frosts, moaning winds and early-falling leaves. It feels right other things should die.

At two o'clock one morning I am balled tight in the cushions of the old carver chair when Brac goes to the door in the hall, tail swinging a hesitant greeting. Pa comes in, hushing the dog, but Brac is used to company at night. I move cautiously so as not to startle him too much.

'Who's there?' I see him stoop, his hand on Brac's head as he questions.

'Pa, it's me.'

'Bess!' He snaps on the light.

For a moment I think he is going to bawl me out, and such a

range of emotions crosses his face, I wonder one brain can survive such a storm. He recovers himself and says, 'You can't sleep either.'

'Too many dreams.'

'Ah!' He lifts the tea cosy, then replaces it.

'It'll be cold. Do you want me to make fresh?'

'No. Thanks. I thought of having a walk out. I need the air.'

'It's still pitch black.' It is only now that I take in the fact that he is fully dressed. 'Haven't you been to bed?'

He looks down at his clothes. 'Oh yes, I've been to bed.' He makes it sound a bleak and lonely place.

'I could get dressed and go with you. I'd like that.'

'Would you, Bess?' He shakes his head, his smile is grim.

'I used to go everywhere with you.'

'Those days have gone.'

'We could make some part of them come back.' I will never forget his affair with Isabella Sinclair, or her, for that matter – she makes stones in my heart – but I know I could forgive him.

He turns away and leans towards the kitchen window and peers out as if looking for the first trace of dawn. 'I have to make a move,' he says, then looks back at me. I am unsure if he even sees me, though he nods, reminding me of the nods of approval he used to give when we rescued sheep, or rubbed corn between our palms to see if it was ready to harvest.

'I'd like to come,' I persist. 'Wait while I put some clothes on?' He does not answer and I hurry upstairs.

I throw on pants, trousers, jumper, socks, but when I get down, only Brac is in the kitchen whimpering by the back door. Boots and wellingtons are left in the porch. I guess he will be lacing his boots. I pull on my thick riding jacket. Then, holding the dog's collar, I open the door. His boots have gone and, though I call and listen, there's no reply and I can hear nothing.

Strange he should leave the dog even if he did not want my company. Then I remember that George brought back the guns a day or two ago after Pa lost his temper and threatened him with dismissal, or the law, if he did not. I rush to the cabinet.

Old family guns are there; grandfather's silver-chased shotgun, the pellet gun, but the new double-barrel Ma bought him is not. My heart begins to pound. If he was hunting, looking to shoot the odd rabbit or pheasant, or scare away a fox, he would surely have taken Brac – and what am I thinking of, it's dark, still dark.

I remember Gran's words: *Life can be very empty when everything is over*. The nod he had given me was not the old nod of approval, but goodbye – goodbye. 'He is going to shoot himself, that's why he's not taken the dog. This is what Gran was afraid of.'

I run to the bottom of the stairs, think to shout up to her, but I need someone who can hurry across fields, can use force if necessary. I go to the telephone and ring the Hall. It rings for an age and Gran comes down the stairs.

'What is it?'

Greville's voice answers at the same moment. I look up at Gran and talk to Greville.

'I'll come at once. Stay where you are.'

'No, I'll take the dog—'

He interrupts me. 'Where do you think he'll go?'

'Up towards his new land, the Paget land, the farmhouse perhaps, and from there towards Red Pool Spinney.' I am almost surprised to hear myself say all this. How do I know? But I do, it's the only dream he has left.

'Wait there for me, Bess,' Greville orders.

'No, I can't.'

'I'll be quicker by the new path,' he is saying as I put down the phone.

'Grev's coming,' I tell Gran.

'Take Brac on the lead, then. She may find him – and you'll want a torch.'

I clip the stout rope lead on to Brac's collar, push my feet into wellingtons.

'Be careful.' Gran rummages in a drawer and finds a second torch then pulls on her outdoor coat over her nightgown. 'I'm going to look around the yard and sheds.' I hesitate. 'Go on, girl. I'll be alright.'

Through the yard and into the orchard I can see only the line picked out by the beam of the torch, but my eyes soon adjust and I can make out the blacker shapes of trees against the blackness of the sky. We reach the orchard gate and I wonder whether to shout or not. I decide not, or not until I am sure I am quite near. I don't want to make him feel harried, trapped, make him act more quickly than he might. *I* could not live with that.

I pound along, wondering what I'd do if I did hear a shot. My mouth goes dry at the thought of what I might find. My mind short-circuits to rabbits and game shot at too close a range, of the bloodstained bed in the Norfolk hotel.

I hear myself quietly urging Brac on. 'Find your master, go on, good girl.' Encouraged, she goes almost too quickly, for though I do know every step of the way, things look strange, out of proportion in the wildly swinging light; tufts of grass loom like bushes, bushes like great barriers, cows like hefty prehistoric beasts and the darkness weighted with the smell of them.

It feels as if I am trying to climb a steep hillside instead of just the slight rise up to the Paget land. My boots and the wet ground again make this reality much worse than any nightmare. I come to the gate Ian and I were marched through by Mr Paget so long ago, his gun hooked over his arm. I pause to listen – nothing. On we go, the dog more eager now.

I reach the Paget farmhouse. I can see much better now and, though there is as yet no line of light on the horizon, the blackness is becoming the cold greyness of earliest dawn. I try the doors of the farmhouse, peer into the sheds all around, but there are so many places someone could hide if they wanted to. I decide to release Brac. 'Go on, find your boss.' I indicate each barn, stable and shed in turn, but then as we come to the way out of the far side of the farmyard and the path up towards the spinney, she whines, looks back at me and stands with a raised paw.

'This way, is it?' I can see the dog now without the torch, so let her go. Only when we come within sight of the spinney do I call her back to heel. I go more cautiously over the last field. Brac turns towards the left, away from the wide pathway the contractors have driven so devastatingly through the woods, the soil and the debris still piled around, nothing tidied, nothing regrowing as yet.

I let her lead me towards where the mini lake, Paget's pantry, used to be, all drained away now. I stop to listen. There is a breeze rustling the leaves still clinging to hedges and trees. Somewhere nearby a sheep coughs, so like a man, my heart jumps into my mouth. Then, just as it steadies, it starts to pound again as I realize I can see someone.

A man is standing, leaning back against a tree on the edge of the clearing. It has to be Pa, and I am equally sure he has not seen me. In fact, he seems to be listening intently and looking in the opposite direction, back into the spinney.

For a few seconds I forget the dog, then I realize she is on her way to him. I step towards the hedge, close in. I want to be much nearer before he sees me.

I hear him speak. I don't catch the words, but hear the surprise as the dog reaches him. He looks around, but I turn my face away so it does not show white against the hedge, and he is still more concerned with something in the other direction. Brac settles herself down by his feet.

I move with slow deliberate strides towards him, like the childhood game, What's the Time, Mr Wolf?, drawing nearer and nearer while his back is turned.

Then, turning, he catches me, no game now as he pushes himself up from the tree. He raises a hand, as if to prevent me moving nearer, his other, I can see, is holding his gun, the way a sentry does when at ease.

'Go home, Bess,' he orders. 'And take the dog.'

'We'll all go together,' I say, still going nearer.

'Leave me be, can't you!' he shouts, suddenly out of control, swinging the gun up, first towards me, then down to the dog, then beginning to turn the barrel towards himself. 'Damn you, leave me be. I want to be with your mother.'

Many words storm around in my brain, selfish things I want but cannot have. 'Think of Gran,' I shout at him and he laughs.

Then we are both distracted. Someone is coming, running, from the opposite way. It must be Grev, I pray it is.

'What the hell?' Pa cries as Grev comes running from behind the heaps of spoil on the pathway, sees us both and slows to a walk. Pa levels the gun at him. 'Go home,' he tells him. 'Take Bess with you.'

'Nothing would give me greater pleasure than to take you both home, pour you a large brandy and we'll talk things over.'

'Keep back.' Pa points the gun at Greville's chest.

'No, sorry . . .'

'I'm telling you, I'm serious.'

'And so, old boy, am I.' He walks slowly but steadily towards the gun. Pa puts it to his shoulder, his finger curled around the trigger.

'You've still a lot of work to finish,' Greville says. 'This path, plans for your new land, the farmhouse, Bess – her future – securing a good future for your daughter.'

We reach him together and Greville grips the barrel of the gun, forcing it down, and as I stumble the last step towards Pa, he lets the gun go. I grasp him around the waist, hold on as if he is struggling, but he isn't. He does not do anything, just stands with his arms limp by his sides. I exclaim my relief, saying 'Oh, Pa! Oh, Pa!' over and over.

Greville puts his arm around me and, with no movement, no response from my father, I am so grateful for his support, so thankful for his help, his presence, his bravery.

'Come on, sir, there are people who need you,' he says.

'We all love you, Pa, and need you. I left Gran searching the outhouses at home. She'll be worried sick. She'll probably be up here any time in her boots and her nightie.'

Pa's head drops on to my shoulder, so heavy – the weight of all his loss – and so we stand until Brac suddenly gets up, shakes

251

herself and barks at us, as if to say, that's it, that's enough. Perhaps the dog senses some change we do not, for after a few more seconds, Pa lifts his head and his arms, putting one around each of us.

Without speaking again, we begin to walk, supporting Pa between us as if we are bringing some wounded man home from a field of battle.

Greville goes on supporting us. Most days I go to the Hall and he comes to the farm. He takes Pa out on all kinds of missions around the two properties. One morning he arrives with a huge hired tractor with a bucket contraption on the front, and suggests they go and begin to clear the spoil heaps the contractors have left.

'Wants doing afore the winter frost sets in hard.' Noel leaves the end of his statement high like a judgment.

Greville may not know it, but this is in itself a success, a step back to normality for Noel. It's the first time he has intervened with one of his bossy remarks since his bereavement.

After I come back from the Hall one afternoon, I walk up to where work is still going on. Pa is driving the large tractor with the bucket. Greville has a smaller one, spreading the soil into a natural hollow, so helping level the field. I stand for a long time before they see me.

Greville stops his tractor and walks over, Pa works on.

'Shaping up, isn't it. Come spring, the scars will green over and we can get into the spinney, do a little proper husbandry.'

'Thanks to you, Grev.' I'm not sure why I shorten his name, it just feels right. 'Gran and I owe you so much.'

'Bess, it is not a hundredth part of what I would wish to do for you.' I feel awkward as he asks, 'Would you do something for me?'

'Anything I can.'

'Will you always call me Grev?'

I think I almost grin, with relief really, because I had thought it might be something more than I would want to do.

Two weeks after Greville becomes Grev, Gran decides it is time for her to think of going home. 'Stella will come every afternoon at two, and stay to prepare your evening meal. Let's see if that works out. I can always come back.'

We talk about Pa as I drive the trap to the village the next Monday morning. 'I feel your pa will be alright now. He's back with an interest in the land and in you.'

'And seeing Noel getting on with his work makes you feel you ought to try.'

Then I feel she kind of tries a remark out on me, tests me. 'He's been more himself since you began shortening Greville's name, had you noticed that?'

'No, Gran, can't say I had. He's been better since he's been working out on the land with those tractors.'

'Bit of both, I think,' Gran says. 'But you, Bess, mustn't let him take over your whole life. You must follow your own star.'

I suddenly hear my mother's voice saying, *Just always be Bess, won't you?* I remember thinking it would be impossible to be anything else, but I understand more now. I see how one could become trapped, by love really, and let your own star slip away. I think of my intended trip to Cornwall. I still intend to go.

It is a strange irony that as we go into the house and find both Ben and Miss Seaton waiting with coffee cups and biscuits, Miss Seaton also hands me a letter. 'This came Saturday,' she says.

It has a Cornish postmark. I notice that much before I push it into my jacket pocket. 'Thanks. I'll get off, Gran. We've got a hunt tomorrow, don't like to leave Tommie too long, he gets fussed with so many horses in our care.'

I pull the pony into the gateway where I used Ian's knife to carve our initials and with thumping heart study the envelope. I think the postmark is St Ives. Ian's father's writing? It must be.

Slow, and with a prayer in my heart, I put my finger under the flap and tear it open, look at the signature on the third sheet. It is from Ken Sinclair. The last time I saw him was sitting in Mr Rawlins' carver chair.

> Dear Young Lady,
>   Your letter has just found me. I have moved several times since Ian and I first came to Cornwall, so perhaps it is a wonder it found me at all. I am now very happily settled further along the south coast, a community of printers and sculptors. I am living with a lady artiste friend, and would say I am happier than at any time since before the war. If Ian was close by, that would be nice, but it seems that is not to be.

I have to stop reading, terrified of what is to come.

> You ask after Ian, which surprised me. He did mention some time ago that he had not heard from you . . .

Had not heard from me! How could he hear from me, I was waiting for an address to write to. He just *never* wrote to me. One letter might have gone astray or something, but he could have written again and again if he had really cared.

> . . . and to be honest I think this had some bearing on his decision to sign on for a second term in the Army. This has meant he has stayed out in Malaya, and seems to be building quite a life for himself out there even outside his army duties.

This is not true. This can't be true. Tears are falling and smudging the ink.

> You will remember he was keen on garden design, and we did the rockery together. He has come into contact with a wealthy family out there who own a tea plantation in the Cameron Highlands (I think some of his regiment went up

into these cooler mountains for furlough). One of the daughters wants a rose garden making around her home in Kuala Lumpur – though Ian tells me it will mean shading the roses from the sun with plaited screens – so he is doing this in off-duty hours. I think it makes a pleasant change to his army duties.

I remember the Chinese beauty in that Malayan magazine. It will be someone like her, that will be why he is not coming back. It was true what that despicable Roy Rawlins had said, he had found someone else. How could he? How could he at a time like this, with my mother and everything. The two things seem to become one.

The anger of irrevocable loss comes over me more totally than anything I have known in any of the days since I lost my mother. I stand and kick the gate as hard as I can. It hurts my foot, my leg and finally breaks the bottom rung of the gate. Only then do I stop. Stop, but then remember the locket I have worn all this time, and I cannot bear it around my neck any longer. I grab the locket and pull until the chain breaks. I stand with it in my fist, the chain swinging then falling, and I hold just the heart-shaped piece of gold with our two locks of hair inside. How bitter a token now, made worse by the memory of standing between his knees to hack off his piece of hair.

So much for love, so much for waiting and trusting.

The chain glints near my feet. I put a boot over it, think of pressing it into the mud, obliterating it, but then I think of a more bitter revenge. I will let him know my disdain for his lies. I'll send it to him care of his father.

A thousand hopes, a thousand desperate wishes, all gone.

The hand on my shoulder, then warm hands holding and chafing mine, bring me back to some kind of recollection. I am sitting in the corner by the gatepost, very cold, the wet has seeped through my jodhpurs. I look up into Colleen's worried eyes.

'Why aren't you at work?' I ask, for I seem to remember it's Monday.

'Oh, Bess! It's evening. We were just coming to see you, we have—'

'Not now.' A man's voice interrupts and I realize George is there too.

'How long have you been here?' she asks. 'You look terrible. Have you had a fall? Try to stand up.'

'She's been crying, haven't you, miss?' George says. 'Natural enough.'

I remember crying, sobbing great uncontrollable gasps, sure my heart was breaking.

I still find it difficult to stand. They both help me, one either side. We're like invalids, Pa and me, having to be lifted and tended.

'George spotted the trap right along the bridleway. The pony was grazing.'

'She's perished through, we must get her home. I'll fetch the trap,' George says.

'How long have you been here?' Colleen asks again as George runs back along the lane.

'All day, I must have been. I took Gran home and . . .'

'Oh, Bess, you poor thing.'

'This came.' I pull the letter from my pocket. 'Read it,' I tell her. 'Before George comes back.'

She reads and exclaims, grips my hands, and asks as she refolds it, 'Will you write back to him?'

'Doesn't seem much point, does there?'

'He says at the end that he will forward a letter on to Ian. I think you should.'

'Colleen, all this time, he could have written – he knew my address, your address, *Gran*'s address. He could have written any time in these last years. Your Roy was right, wasn't he? He has found someone else.'

George is back with the pony and trap, and growls at the mention of Roy's name. 'Nothing but trouble, him.'

George drives and Colleen holds me in her arms as we sit in the deep tub seat. I am shuddering, beginning to realize how long I must have sat in that muddy gateway. I must have cried myself insensible, and my chest hurts.

'I should have gone to the Hall. Tommie will wonder . . .'

'I'll go and have a word,' George says. 'Don't worry about Tommie, won't hurt him to have to stretch himself a bit.'

Stella is laying the table when we arrive. 'Why, what's happened?' she asks as she looks at me.

'Bit of a mishap,' George says. 'Think she needs a cup of tea then a good hot bath before her supper.'

'Yes. We'll come back tomorrow, Bess.'

I feel totally exhausted. I think I know what people mean when they say they have touched bottom.

Twenty-Three

I hunt the next day, though when I arrive at the Hall, Tommie – ready to be aggrieved about my not turning up the day before – takes one look at me and says he can manage if I want to go straight back home.

Grev confirms how ill I look, and says *he* will take me home, but the meet is at the Hall and I do not want to let anyone down. So I hunt. Well, I sit on my horse and go with the group, it amounts to no more. I feel sick and miserable, totally removed from everything and everybody, the people I have lost more vital to me than any I meet that day, though they are more than kind.

When I arrive home, I notice George has not gone home as usual after the afternoon milking, but is standing talking earnestly to Noel, often glancing towards the house. Then, as the evening comes, he walks slowly down the lane, and comes back with Colleen.

They come together to the door and, as Colleen always does, knock, and come in.

We exchange embraces and George stands self-consciously tossing his cap a short distance from hand to hand, his eyes going uneasily to Stella as she prepares our meal.

'Your father's out, is he?' he asks.

'In town all day, but should be back any time.' I see how awkward they both are in Stella's presence.

'Ah, right,' George says, then nods meaningfully at Colleen. 'I'll wait for him outside . . .'

'Can I talk to you, Bess?' Colleen asks in a meek little voice when he has gone.

'Come up to my bedroom.' Her manner invites thoughts of yet more troubles.

'It'll be chilly up there,' Stella intervenes. 'And if you want to talk private, I can be off.' She turns to me. 'Everything's ready. The soup's simmering. Just put a light under the vegetables as soon as he comes in, they'll be done by the time you want them.'

Colleen is still silent when we are alone and some awful fear comes over me. It must be me, I must put some kind of curse on people. I make everything go wrong for everyone. Colleen never sits so, with downcast eyes, her hands in her lap. I should tell her not to be friends with me any more. I'm a Jonah, I make everything go wrong.

'Bess, I've something to tell you. I'm –' she hesitates then rushes on – 'in a family way.'

'A family way.' I repeat, only then realizing what she is telling me. 'A baby?'

She nods. 'Me and George. We're going to get married right away – registry-office job.' She looks at me, tears in her eyes. 'So, it won't be like we always planned, will it?'

We had always planned a double wedding, had bedecked ourselves in cast-off adult dresses, high-heeled shoes and paraded out into the fields and made daisy-chain headdresses, necklaces and bracelets for our double wedding.

'The only things we never thought about were the bride-grooms,' I remind her. 'But you have George.' It's me who takes her hands now, kneels at her feet. 'That's wonderful, isn't it. You have George, and he is the one you want.'

'Yes, but . . .' Tears stream down her face. 'I didn't want it to be like this, not a registry-office job.'

The familiar words used to pour scorn on a rapidly arranged village wedding make me think that, if my mother had been here, she would have seen to it that Colleen had her wedding in the village church, as she should – of course she should. 'I don't see why you can't be married in Church. Plenty have over the years.'

She drops her head as if in shame, and I stand and hug her as she has comforted me so often in these past weeks – years – ever since I can remember.

'But you can't, can you. Not that quick,' she demurs, but I have already made up my mind.

'A few weeks, I'm sure there's a way.'

'Noel said the same.'

'Noel knows?'

She is awkward again, hesitant. 'Noel has said when we're wed we can move in with him, provided Mr Bennett doesn't mind. I mean, George does work for him.' She pauses then adds, 'Noel says we can have the big bedroom. Waste of a double bed, he says, with just him in it.'

The bedroom arrangements in Noel's cottage will not be ideal. Two smaller, box-like rooms lead off the main bedroom. Noel would have to walk through their bedroom to reach and leave his own.

'But at least it'll be a roof over your head, a start.'

Just as I think this is exactly the kind of thing Noel probably said, we hear his voice outside. The door is knocked on and opened, but it is not exactly who we expect, for Noel is with George and Greville. The situation has obviously been explained to Grev, for he immediately puts Colleen at some kind of ease with a wink in her direction and the remark that some get on with life quicker than others.

'But I see that as no reason why Colleen and George should not be married in Church. I mean, they intended to anyway.' I pose the idea and Grev immediately concurs.

'No problem,' he says. 'Village people, village wedding. Just a matter of planning – forward planning, I've heard it called.'

'Not too far forward,' George says and, after a hesitant laugh, though just from the men, we all sit around the table, and Grev draws up what might be called a plan of campaign. Pa is a latecomer to the scene and is more or less told of decisions to date.

'*I'll* see the vicar,' he says. 'We want no sanctimonious demurring.'

*   *   *

260

Four weeks later I arrive at Colleen's house to put on my bridesmaid's dress of red velvet, along with May and Mavis, her sisters transformed by their long dresses from gawky school-girls to wand-like young ladies. The red velvet *dug out* by Lady Philipps, the making organized by my gran as her gift.

Colleen's dress was finished the night before by her own mother. This is of plain ivory satin, a compromise on the virginal white insisted on by Colleen. I have brought the headdress woven with the help of the head gardener at the Hall. It is of fresh flowers – white jasmine and cream rosebuds, specially nurtured over the last few weeks.

'I would have liked to have made it of daisies, really,' I tell her. She would have crushed me and her dress in a spontaneous embrace had not her mother cried out that she had spent hours removing the last creases after the making of it.

The circlet is secured over the veil and Colleen's golden hair. The finished picture enchants us all. The rosebuds, the ivory dress, her hair all combine to give the bride an aura of gold, a radiance.

'You take my breath away,' her father says as we emerge from the staircase. He stands shaking his head, laughing in astonishment.

'Don't laugh, Dad. This is serious,' Colleen reprimands.

'Oh! I know love, but if I don't laugh, I'll cry.'

She runs to throw herself into his arms, with her mother again crying out to mind her dress. They stop at comic arm's length and lean forward to peck each other on the lips. 'Nearly hit the buffers then,' Mr Rawlins says.

So, Colleen and George are married in the church we have all been so firmly linked to all our lives, all our families' lives, through the births, the marriages and, so recently, the deaths.

The one person not there is Colleen's brother, Roy, who went off somewhere on his motorbike with a mate as pillion, saying he'd be back in a day or two when the fuss was over. I'm glad, and even his father says they are better off without him, but I see Mrs Rawlins is putting a brave face on her son's absence.

There'll be many questions about it, and gossip, of course. 'One more thing for them to get their teeth into,' I hear her mutter, though her natural pride shines through in her resolve not to let anyone else take over her eldest daughter's day.

We all go to Noel's house afterwards and have cups of tea in relays and pieces of the wedding cake Mrs Rawlins has made and painstakingly iced with rosebuds.

Already there are changes in the cottage. Some of Dawdie's jars and bottles have been put away somewhere, the shed in the yard probably, and most of Mrs Rawlins' crockery is, temporarily at least, in Noel's kitchen.

Noel sits in his old wooden armchair near the kitchen range, and he looks tired. Soon Pa says he thinks it's time we made room for others who are standing about chattering outside and in the backyard, many with gifts in their hands. I mouth across the room to Colleen that I'll see her in a few days. She bustles across, much in her old manner, grabs my arm and bustles me upstairs, where my clothes are lying on Noel's old bed, now newly furnished with matching green silk counterpane and bedspread, and no doubt linen from her bottom drawer.

She hugs me tight. 'I know if it wasn't for you, none of this would have happened. You've given me my wedding day.' We hold on to each other and cry a few more tears.

'Thanks, Bess, we'll always be best friends, won't we?'

'Always, always.'

I think it best to scoop up my clothes and go, and am quite relieved to walk away with Pa. It has been an emotionally draining time for us all, not helped as our way takes us past the old Sinclair cottage. Just a glimpse of the rockery Ian and his father built makes my heart thump, takes my breath. I know I have to control this. Ian is in the past, on the other side of the world. I must do as people say you should in bad circumstances, take every day as it comes, keep busy, take over Ma's roles at home and run my business. I glance at Pa, see the muscles in his jaw flexing as he grits his teeth. They say time heals, but I wonder if our scars are not just too deep and wide.

At Gran's, we find good hot tea being poured by Miss Seaton. We all sit somewhat silent, though Gran says, not for the first time, 'You look very well in red velvet with your dark hair,' and I know we are both thinking of the long black slip I chose to wear, the mourning under the celebration, a gesture towards the true state of things, like Colleen's ivory dress, I suppose.

'There's been something I've been meaning to do for a long time,' Pa says as he empties his cup, 'and that's bring the old family Bible up to date. Now seems like a good time.'

He rises and Gran and I exchange alarmed looks.

'Don't worry, I know where it's kept,' he says. 'Don't suppose it's been moved.'

'Is now a good time?' Gran demurs. 'Surely you don't want the bother of it now.'

'I'd like to do it now.' Already he is in the hall. We hear the bottom cupboard of the bookcase pulled open, then the old postcard albums being piled on to the table, a slight pause, then the heavier old Bible. We can visualize it all, and now we wait, looking at each other, Miss Seaton shaking her head as if she too knows what he will see.

There's a sound in the doorway, past sins flash before my eyes. Pa stands holding the Bible open in both hands. He stares at me with an expression of one who has never seen me before, or, if he has, certainly does not understand me.

'Why has your name been crossed out?' he demands.

'It was when you sent me away to school,' I say defiantly, remembering all the trauma. 'I didn't want to go.'

'And the other? What other name did you cross out?'

'No, I—'

'What gives you the right to defile a family heirloom, a record going back generations? What right?' He lets the Bible fall with a great crash on to the kitchen table.

'It was not Bess,' my grandmother says quietly, but there is such a note of authority in her voice, everyone's attention is focused on her.

'You!' Pa exclaims in astonishment.

'Me? No!' Her exclamation is as explosive as the wine glasses shattering in the parlour the day I asked the same question.

This time the denial is enforced by Miss Seaton's violent lifting of her hands and shaking of her head. 'Never! Never!' she exclaims.

He's bemused by their reactions, leans with his hands spread over the pages where the inscriptions lie.

'If not you, who?' He looks back at me. 'I think I am entitled to know.'

'Not Bess,' Gran repeats.

'Who then? Haven't we all been through enough without some stupid petty prevarications about a crossing out.' Miss Seaton raises her eyebrows at the word *petty*.

'If someone died, why wasn't it recorded properly? A birth, a death, what was the problem?'

He is clearly studying not just the crossing out, but exactly where the erasure lies. He puzzles some long time before he looks up again. 'The crossing out is a name under mine.' He frowns at his mother. 'Was there another child? Why was it crossed out, put in and crossed out?'

'Because—' Gran begins.

Miss Seaton rises with officious bustle and goes to Gran's side, putting a hand on her shoulder. 'It was just a mistake – a wrong entry.'

Gran looks up into her face, shakes her head. 'Perhaps it should be told. Perhaps if it is not told now, it never will be.'

There is a strange feeling in the room, as if the two older women are quite alone, making some momentous decision.

'Will it do any good?' Maude Seaton asks.

'It may. None of us can live for ever.' She smiles up at Maude. 'We'll have to pass on the responsibility one day, or . . .' She shrugs as if to say, *or all is lost*.

He frowns, lifts the page and scrutinizes the crossing-out from the back. I could tell him he will make out nothing from that. 'So, it is a name. A child?'

'A child,' Gran confirms.

'Your child.' It is not a question, Pa is assuming this from the position beneath his own name. This had never occurred to me.

'Yes, my child,' Gran acknowledges.

'Born after me, who died . . .' he trails off into melancholy, then adds, 'So, I might have had a brother or a sister.'

'No,' Gran says.

He looks in astonishment. 'But surely, your child . . .'

'Not died,' Gran says, and Miss Seaton lets out a resigned sigh. There is another silence.

'Stillborn?' he hazards.

'Never should have been born,' Miss Seaton bursts out. 'Never!'

I imagine a monster, some poor deformed creature, hidden away – still living out a miserable existence in some asylum.

'Born, then – but crossed out?' His voice is full of the injustice of this act.

'Not crossed out by anyone here!' Maude Seaton emphasizes.

'Mother,' he appeals, but gently, seeing she is becoming really distressed. 'You can't leave it like this.'

'No,' she agrees.

We wait, but again it is Maude who makes the move. She comes to the table. 'The answers are all here.' She points to a name in the good book, points and moves her finger along as if scoring a line under Alexander Bennett.

Alexander Bennett, my great grandfather, whose portrait languishes in the darkest spot in our hall.

'He crossed out the first name,' Maude goes on, and I have the curious feeling that she is pointing out the accused, fingering a man in the dock in a court of justice. Her manner is censorious as she backs away from the table. 'I know the story,' she says. 'From the beginning.'

There is silence as Maude Seaton goes on. 'Your grandmother and I grew up in the same village. My mother cleaned for her family. Your gran's home was my refuge, her mother was my champion against my dad.' Her voice drops as she says the word. 'He was like an animal when he was drunk, and he was drunk every Friday night, when he'd been paid. As I grew older I spent every Friday night sleeping at Jessie's house, or there would have been entries in our family Bible that needed crossing out – that's if we'd ever had such a thing as a family Bible.'

So, Maude's father was a brute beast with ravening lusts even for his own daughter. So, how does this concern my great grandfather? But I know better than to interrupt.

'Even after Jessie married, I still went to her mother's house every Friday. Then my father died. You were born, Edgar, and your mother brought you to see us regularly whenever she visited her mother. Then, when you were two, she came . . .'

Gran nods her on, but Maude now finds it difficult, so my gran takes her hand and continues herself.

'I remember I went pretending it was a normal visit, but Mrs Seaton soon guessed there was more.'

'The story soon came out that your grandfather, Alexander Bennett' – Maude condemns with a second stab towards the Bible – 'had forced himself on her when everyone else was in the harvest fields.'

'He came upstairs. I thought for a moment when I heard a man's tread on the stairs that it was your father.'

'She had the marks on her arms and legs, red weals. She showed my mother when she finally broke down and told her everything. She was the right person to tell,' Maude says bitterly. 'She protected me, but suffered herself – every Saturday morning there were new bruises.'

'Rape, it's called nowadays,' Gran finishes, as if, now started, she intends to leave no doubt.

'But . . .'

'Aye, there were many bruises,' Maude says.

'But my father?' Edgar queries.

'There were those who knew and those who did not, never did,' Maude adds.

'So, my father never knew?'

266

'It was your grandmother who never knew,' Gran tells him. 'When I did not go home as soon as your father expected, he came, thinking either you or I was ill.'

'Which you were,' Maude affirms.

'Sick in mind and at heart,' Gran says. 'Certainly I was that and more, so when I knew I was expecting a child of the—' She intercepts a questioning look from my father. 'Oh! I was sure, there was no doubt.'

We are all seated around the table now, though I have no recollection of sitting down. Gran startles me when she puts her hand on my arm. 'I'm sorry you have to hear this, but I wouldn't want your father to have to tell you in the future, and he might have needed to one day.'

I want to ask why, why, why? But know it is best just to listen as she goes on.

'At home, the story was gradually given out that I was not well, I was staying with my mother. In fact, your father paid for Maude and I to go to the south coast until such time as the child was born. It was to be adopted . . .'

'But when the time came, Jessie nearly died, and so did the child.'

'It was a difficult birth. I was anaesthetized at the last, and I think he was damaged then, poor boy.'

'So, in the end, we couldn't part with him, poor little mite. We brought him back to my mother, and she adopted him. Let everyone think just what they liked – and they did. They thought he was mine,' Maude scoffed. 'But I didn't care, I'd never been disposed towards marriage – seen too much of it.'

'My God,' Pa breathes. 'So, this child – this man, if he is still alive – is both my brother and my uncle?'

I had heard stories of children growing up thinking that their mother was their sister, but this situation held an added nastiness – not just a girl in trouble, but my great grandfather had raped his son's wife, my gran, who is sitting here with us telling the story.

'When I finally came home, almost a year later, your grandfather and my unsuspecting mother-in-law had moved away into a smallholding in the next village, leaving the farm to us. We rebuilt our lives, we loved each other, always had, but he never forgave his father. Alexander Bennett never came to either of the farms again, though my mother-in-law did, and was always lamenting that we never had another child.'

I wonder at the ironic tragedy of life, of lives. The portrait of Alexander Bennett would not languish much longer in the hall of our home. I plan to burn it.

'Last year my mother died,' Maude said.

I am not sure why Maude should suddenly interpose this remark.

'Oh dear.' My response sounds inadequate as I try to understand the traumas these older women have been through together.

There is a noise outside, we hear the back door open and a man's step coming along the short passage.

'Hello,' Mr Benjamin says, beaming at us all seated around the table. 'Shall I make some tea?'

It hits the two of us at the same moment. I hear my father say, 'My God,' softly under his breath and I understand why the attics of the farmhouse were emptied to furnish Mr Benjamin's cottage; I understand the significance of Miss Seaton's remark about her mother dying; I understand what Gran meant about passing on the responsibility. I understand they want to ensure his future.

I also see the likeness. He is like my father in height, in colouring, though not in physique – farm work has not developed his shoulders, and whatever happened at his birth has stripped the light of normal intellect from his eyes.

In this moment of physical stillness, all kinds of readjustments are silently made. This man is – I struggle between the split generations a moment, then decide – this man is my uncle.

My father spreads his hands wide on the table, full span, as if taking as much support as he can to raise himself, and when he does, it is slowly, as if from some long hard labour.

He goes over to the still-smiling Mr Benjamin, puts out a hand, which the other man takes and shakes with innocent joyful happiness.

'No, you come and sit down, old chap. We're going to have a brandy.'

Twenty-Four

B y the time Colleen's daughter is born the following April, Mr Benjamin has become part of our lives. His very unawareness of his relationship to us, and the impossibility of ever explaining it to him, makes for a feeling of obligation on our side, which is repaid time and time over by his intuitiveness. He is often able to distract us from our darkest moods of sorrow and loss.

He can imitate bird calls to a nicety, trill the notes of the song thrush, and has real blackbirds answering and questioning the song of an intruder on their territory. Mr Benjamin – and we still call him this, it just seems right – gives some light in our lives.

We do become sure of one thing. He is a son of the land in spirit if not in physique, for he loves all the animals, watches and understands their pleasure or their distress. He would have made a fine companion for my father, a better pupil than I ever was.

I sometimes catch Noel regarding him intently when he helps with the horses. He learns so quickly to handle a horse, buckling each strap the old man indicates, talking to the animal more as if it were brother than beast; looking as if he is in heaven when Noel lets him ride to and from the fields. Once Noel looked from my father to Mr Benjamin and said, 'Lot alike those two, except in the head department.'

The other saviour my father has is Grev, for of all outside the family he is the one who rouses Pa to a state of interest in the farms. Together they plan replanting the periphery of the new

270

path through Red Pool Spinney. Grev not only walks our land with him but consults him about the estate. He says that his sisters were both well-endowed to the extent that the estate has little margin of capital. I wonder if this is true, but I am pleased he comes, pleased he takes such an interest in us both. He diverts me for the time he is there, a bit like Mr Benjamin, but I still feel anchored in the past – more than anchored, I feel fettered to some huge burden I daily drag around with me.

I am continually wrestling with thoughts of man's infidelity, and worse: my great grandfather; my own father, then there's George and Colleen having to get married – and Ian – that feels still like the last and ultimate betrayal.

What was the saying? Better to have loved and lost than never to have loved at all. Was it better? I wonder. I think I would rather have been like Miss Seaton, having seen and feared the bad side, so never yearning for any part of such feelings.

Perhaps it is thoughts like this that make me take out the locket with its two strands of hair and pack it into a small box and then an envelope. I address it to Ian care of his father, and mark it *To await addressee's return.* The moment I drop it into the letterbox I regret it. I remember the feelings I had as I cut off his hair, the excitement, the closeness – the love I felt for him. Now I have nothing but a schoolboy's penknife.

I am walking away from the postbox when the estate jeep draws up alongside me.

'Just the lassie I was looking for,' Grev hails, leaning across to open the door. 'Jump in.'

'I'm not your lassie, nor anyone else's,' I mutter, then ask, 'Why, where are you going?'

'Wherever m'lass . . . m'*lady* wants. Come on, get in. I want to talk to you.'

'I'm going to see Colleen.'

'Can be arranged.'

'I can walk, thanks. It's not far.'

'It's quicker by car. I have an errand at the blacksmith's, then

I could pick you up. We could go for a spin, a drink at a pub. It's a nice evening.'

'No thanks.' I walk away, overwhelmed by regrets for the pendant languishing at the bottom of the pillar box.

At Noel's cottage I find not just Noel and George and Colleen, but Mr Benjamin sitting nursing the baby. He's everywhere, I find myself thinking, and there are nappies everywhere too: airing on a rack over the range, in a bucket by the sink, a folded pile on the table. The clutter is similar to that in the Rawlins' cottage when all the children were small, only worse. The baby's bath time has obviously only just finished and the small bath is on a stool, a clothes horse stands draped with a blanket to keep off draughts and there is a pile of baby clothes on the corner of the table. All is chaos, contented chaos. Mr Benjamin is clearly overwhelmed with the honour of holding the baby. He encircles it with his arms as if he is holding the Christ child.

I judge him to be the real fool he is, he has nothing to look forward to, nothing he can achieve for himself, he relies unwittingly on goodwill. I look from him to Colleen and George, this cramped cottage, all the inconveniences.

'You alright, love?' Colleen asks. 'You look a bit peaky.'

Not so peaky that I cannot see that love and contentment beam from all their faces, and I cannot bear it.

'She's grown.' I divert all attention to her baby.

'Not in two days,' Colleen says. 'It's only two days since you saw her.'

'I tell you, she's grown. Her face has uncrunkled more and everything.' I lean over and touch the tiny fingers, which stretch out. I put my finger in the palm and the fingers close over me.

Mr Benjamin nods and smiles. 'Clever,' he says.

'Very clever,' I agree, and prise free of the exquisite grasp. I know I must make some excuse, must leave or I shall upset this gathering with an outburst of tears, or worse, anger.

I make an excuse which sounds valid, another trip to the stables, but as Colleen ushers me out, she sees Greville driving away from the blacksmith's shop. 'Oh, look! You can get a lift.' She raises her hand and arm, waves, then points to me.

'Thanks,' I say briefly and run up the street to the jeep, climb in and slam the door.

Grev turns to speak, then turns away and drives. I am not sure where we are going, neither do I care. I sit staring straight ahead, battling with futile anger and bitterness at all my losses, all the things I'll never have again.

After some time, he pulls off the road into a side lane. We bump some distance along this until we come to open pasture overlooking a river. I know we must be in the east of the county, for the hills are larger, rolling, with more areas of woodland on their slopes, and the water is more river than brook. He sits quite still for a moment, then he gets out. 'I'll go for a walk along the bank.' He points to his right. 'That way.'

I sit still and watch him go, tormented still by the sound of that small box landing in the postbox, by the urgent wish that I had not done such a thing. Now there is a penknife and some faint initials on a gate – not much for what I had thought to be the love of my lifetime. What a fool.

Noel's cottage bursting at the seams with love and contentment, with Mr Benjamin holding baby Katie, had not helped. I find the grace to admit it must be an ordeal at times: the bedroom arrangements, a baby waking through the night; the tiny kitchen; Noel seeing his beloved Dawdie's things put aside, as they must be, to make room. Not easy.

Grev reaches the river without looking back, and turns to the right just as he said. He has given me time and room to recover, plus the security of knowing just where he'll be if I need him.

A sudden gust of wind raises a small cloud of yellow pollen from long hazel catkins on the hedge nearby; on the riverbank below, willows are already sheened green with leaf and to the left there are bluebells, a splash of blue under silver birches. Grev has chosen a pretty place. My mother would have loved this – another spring.

Always be Bess, won't you. Her voice speaks in my mind.

The Bess she brought up would not be bitter about her best friend's happiness, nor send back gifts so tenderly given. *Things happen and we must move on.*

It's not easy to be me anymore. I have so many regrets and so much love with no one to give it to. Why aren't you here to tell me what I should *do*?

What she had told me to do was to go to Cornwall, but there was no point now, no point, particularly now I had sent back the locket for Ian to discover when, if ever, he came back to England. It seemed unlikely he would, not for years and years anyway.

'Things happen and we must move on.' I repeat her words aloud. They give rise to a sigh so heavy, so weary, it seems to come from the bottom of my soul. The choice is be bitter, stagnant, or move on. I still have my father, and that would have been enough at one time. Then there are my horses, the farms, Greville – poor Grev – he deserves better than the treatment I have just meted out to him. I must try harder. It sounds like a condemnation from a school report, but I climb out of the jeep and walk towards the river.

I meet him coming slowly back from some distance along the bank. He has his hands pushed deep into his pockets but shoulders still square. Training, I suppose. I remember straightening my shoulders against the lavatory wall at school. When he sees me, he pulls his hands out like a boy caught slouching. I remember how punctilious he was in obeying his grandmother's requests as a boy.

'Sorry,' I say when I am near enough. 'I was just being rude and selfish.'

'Never.' He shakes his head. 'Come on, I want to talk to you.'

We drive to the next village and swing into a pub yard.

'The sisters are coming at the weekend,' he says once we are seated with our drinks in a tiny back snug behind the bar.

'I'll remember to keep a low profile,' is my reaction.

'Ah! So, the dreaded sisterhood have had a few potshots at you, have they?'

'Once or twice,' I admit. 'And they certainly didn't like you teaching me to drive around the estate.'

'They're just bullies. I'm convinced they have projects, the get-Greville week, or the batter-Bess day. When I was young my sisters used to gang up on me. Between the two of them I had no chance. They have vicious tongues when they collaborate, as I know to my cost. I don't suppose growing up has banished that capacity.'

'It hasn't,' I answer.

'Let's hope they never gang up on either of their husbands. Poor devils.'

'Greville!' I laugh in spite of myself.

'Which one do you think they'll gang up on first?' he asks.

'No, I'm not taking part in this.'

'It'll be the vicar, the Very Reverend Wallace. You'll see. Poor chap – poor being the operative word.'

'Really!' I say, then stop, guilty of succumbing to his gossip. 'You're just trying to distract me.'

He holds up his hands in innocence. 'Only with the truth.'

'Tommie could manage over the weekend. We've nothing on and with the weather this mild the horses can stay out. I needn't come to the Hall . . .'

'No, no, that won't do at all. You'll come to dinner on Saturday, that's what I wanted to ask you.'

'Not sure they'll appreciate my presence. They rather see me as a kind of stable hand.'

'Did you think I hadn't noticed?' he says. 'I want you as my guest to put things straight in their minds. Dinner Saturday. You're expected. I'll get Harding to pick you up, then I'll drive you home.'

That I am expected by Lady Philipps is entirely clear, for she actually walks from the estate office to open the front door for me herself.

'Come on, my dear, I'm a laggard today. Come upstairs and talk to me while I change.'

'Am I too early? I'm sorry.' I follow her up the stairs thinking this is rather strange, for there is no sign of an approaching dinner party. Downstairs is certainly silent, upstairs there are voices. It sounds like Anthea and Daphne calling to each other from adjoining rooms, laughing.

'My granddaughters,' Lady Philipps confirms. 'Come on, m'dear, this way. I've moved rooms recently, taken a corner of the house, made quite a cosy suite.' She goes ahead, opens the door on to an east-facing room which has a view of the side lawns of the house and of the flaring remains of a sunset. 'My bedroom faces the same way. Come through.' She leads the way. I see there is a black dress and a matching cardigan laid out on the bed. She crosses the bedroom at a diagonal and opens the door to a sitting room.

'There, what more could an old dear want?' she exclaims.

I look round and realize it reflects much of her life. Photographs, a frame full of military memorabilia, badges, flashes, what looks like an Indian fretwork ivory-inlaid table; a display of framed cross-stitch work, samplers, landscapes; a large bookcase full of well-used volumes; a desk cluttered with what are obviously estate maps and the inevitable lists of work in progress, mostly in my handwriting. Easy chairs, a very comfortable-looking sofa. The choice of carpet and drapes in greens and blues makes it a woman's room, but a woman who for most of her life has had a man's role to fill. There is no pretence here, no show, these rooms are like Clara Philipps herself, honest and straightforward.

'It's perfect for you.'

'That's what I can't make Daphne and Anthea understand.' She wags a finger. 'For me! This is how I want things, not tarted up to some fashion or other. Rubbish and clutter is, I understand, their verdict.'

I go to the window at the far side of the room. 'So, this must face to the west. We're on the other side of the house.'

'That's right, get the morning sun in here. Look, I found some old albums for you to look at.' She indicates a chair and passes over another such album as resides in the bottom of my own grandmother's cupboard. 'Jessie and I go back a long way, as you will see, and have few secrets from each other.' She lowers the volume into my lap, adding with a smile. 'I'll go and change.'

'I soon discover pictures of the two as schoolgirls in loosely sashed dresses, wearing their thick locks of hair long, with wide dangling ribbons. They are holding hands in most of the younger pictures. Later, as young women, they stand side by side, shoulders touching, dresses not quite fitted, but very slinky. Then come wedding photographs. I study Lord Philipps and catch a resemblance to Greville about the mouth and chin.

Then I am startled to find a photograph of Lady Philipps with Gran and Miss Seaton, the background unfamiliar, but at the seaside; a cold day, for they all have big coats on, hats, scarves, gloves. It is obviously the kind of snap one of those promenade photographers takes as you walk by. They walk in a line: Miss Seaton, Lady Philipps, Gran. Gran's coat is full, voluminous; the other two wear more fitted garments. Could this be when the two women went to the coast before Mr Benjamin was born? Had Clara gone to see her friend? If so . . .

'That was taken on the pier.' I am startled to find Lady Philipps standing by me, near enough to see what I am studying. She has changed and retidied her hair, and stoops to retrieve the book from me, which she holds open at the same page. 'Your father should take him in, let him live at the farm. We all have skeletons in our family cupboards. It must be nice to have the opportunity to do something for one innocent victim.'

With that, she closes the book. 'And that's the last word I shall ever say on the subject.'

I follow her down to dinner feeling rather stupefied. Greville is in the dining room. He hands me a sherry as we walk in and pecks me on the cheek. 'Hi!' he says. 'Been shown Gran's quarters?'

I nod. Had he known what she intended, or had he guessed from my arrival down the stairs? There is more noise from that direction and Daphne and Anthea enter, talking still, but then stand as if completely aghast by what they find in the dining room, or what they don't find.

'Where is everyone?' Daphne asks.

'This is it,' Lady Philipps says. 'A small family party.'

The way both girls turn their eyes on me is almost comic.

'Family?' Anthea inquires.

'Oh! I think we've known Bess long enough for her to be considered—'

'Almost family.' Grev fills the gap, and, taking my elbow, 'Come on,' he says, 'I'm hungry, had a long day. You know the Armitage cottage? The one with the roof problems . . .'

He takes me through, sits me between himself and his grandmother and talks shop.

For a time the sisters are quiet, and I also realize that Lady Philipps is enjoying the situation entirely when she comments, 'What a pleasant change to have a man dominating the conversation for once.'

'More unusual still, as I've four to deal with,' Grev says. 'Doesn't seem like home at all. I'm so used to being henpecked.'

I wonder just how much truth there is in his remark. Lady Philipps has always made her presence felt wherever she is. The girls undoubtedly take after her in this respect – as well as in their looks.

'So, Bess, you work for him. Do *you* henpeck him?' Anthea demands.

'Bess helps in the office some afternoons,' Grev corrects.

'Well, whatever – whether she receives wages or in kind, that's how I'd put it.'

'Yes, so would I,' I answer. 'But I hope I am never guilty of being disrespectful. I admire the way Grev comes up with ideas for the estate, within the budget left to him.' On the instant, I realize I have offended both sisters. I've managed to be too familiar and comment on the estate budget all in one sentence.

'Well!' Anthea throws down her napkin. 'If this is the total company for the evening, you'll excuse me.'

'No,' her grandmother says. 'We won't.'

For a moment the situation is balanced between outright revolt and capitulation.

'I hope this evening may give you a better understanding of the situation here. Greville is in charge of this estate, and this is his house. You will always be welcome here – this is your childhood home, and we wish to see you here – but you will show your brother and his guests the same courtesy we give to your husbands. I will no longer tolerate the childish sniping you indulge in whenever you come to see *the Hon.*'

'Now you will excuse me. I shall retire to the rooms you have done your best to ridicule to all and sundry. What you should remember is that my friends in the county and in the Hunt are longer-standing than yours. They tell me of your nonsense. Goodnight. Goodnight, Bess, I shall see you on Monday, no doubt. It's one of your afternoons in the office, isn't it?'

When she has gone there is silence until Grev says, 'Consider yourselves told off, girls.'

'Oh, piss off!'

'Charming! Hope the bishop doesn't know you use such language.'

'Did you and your stablegirl plan all this?'

'You will not be welcome in my house if you do not mend your ways, but no, actually it was Grandmother's work entirely. I thought it was going to be the usual bash when you two are here, all your friends, the usual fatted calf, red-carpet treatment. One, or both of you, must have really got up Gran's nose last time you were here.'

His words seem to hit home, for they exchange quick guilty glances. The new suite of rooms perhaps. Daphne turns to the drinks tray as Grev and I walk out on to the terrace.

'Take me home, Grev, will you?'

'I really didn't know you were to be the only guest.'

'I do believe you. I think your grandmother had one or two messages to deliver this evening.'

279

'Really?' he asks, but I shake my head. I need to think about all this.

'Will they come again?' I ask as we drive.

'The sisterhood?' He laughs. 'Don't worry, they will not be abashed for long. Tomorrow morning you won't know anything has been said. Anthea likes her free hunting here too much. Her chap's not got a bean, she only married him so she wasn't left on the shelf on her own. She's dipping into her dowry like mad to furnish their rectory.'

'And Daphne?'

'Daphne . . .' he considers. 'I believe Daphne is rather small beer in the hierarchy in Norfolk. There's aristocracy in the family. When she comes home, she's treated, and acts, like royalty; gives her ego the required boost before she goes back.'

'Think so?'

'Yep. We all need our egos underlined with red ink from time to time, make them seem important.'

'Even Daphne?' I still feel doubt, but we're at the farm. 'Come in and have a coffee.'

'Gosh! We never got to coffee, did we?'

'Back already?' Pa rouses himself from sleep before the aga.

'We're going to have coffee. Want some?'

'And a brandy then.' Receiving a nod from Greville, he goes off to fetch the tray. 'Warmer in here,' he adds, pouring two good measures and a smaller one for me.

We lift the settle round so all of us are cushioned and comfortable.

'Nothing's happened to bring you home early?' he asks, studying us as we sit opposite.

'We've had one of my grandmother's moments of truth,' Grev says, grinning over the rim of his brandy balloon.

'Oh!' Pa grunts with appreciative knowledge of such events. 'Painful?'

'For the sisters,' Grev confirms. 'A little embarrassing for Bess seeing the Philipps family red in tooth and claw.'

I shake my head, too pleasantly soporific to answer, maybe

it's the brandy or the warmth, but I feel really relaxed. Pa gives a grunt of laughter and we all sit staring at the red embers in the open aga.

It feels as if we have all reached some kind of base, some kind of camp, where we sit replenishing our energies for a new journey. There is a kind of sad contentment around us. We are silent, locked in our own thoughts for a long time. Pa gets up once and refills our glasses, but no one speaks.

I wonder if it is the beginning of acceptance. *The tears will stop sometime.* Colleen's mother had gathered me into her arms and said that, but even as I think this, I feel tears threatening. Perhaps the anger stops first, the senseless anger that bursts out in stupid attacks on barn doors, or gates. I look across at Pa, who smiles and nods at the two of us sprawled on the settle.

'Yes.' Grev rouses himself. 'I should go and let you good people get to bed.'

I see him out.

'Thanks for coming,' he says and leans over before he gets into his car, then kisses my cheek.

'Thanks for having me,' I say formally, but on impulse kiss him quickly again. It brushes his lips as he lowers himself into the car. He pauses between standing and sitting, then murmurs, 'Sleep well, Bess Bennett.'

Twenty-Five

I come to realize it is from this evening that Greville and I
begin to be seen as regular companions. We are asked to
tennis parties, expected at neighbouring hunts, point-to-points,
dinners; and people often enquire as to the whereabouts of the
one from the other. I had not realized my father was also aware,
or reading anything into this closer companionship, until the
following spring.

I plan to get him back on to his horse. He has not ridden since
we lost Ma. His horse, like Ma's, has been at the Hall. In the
middle of one Monday morning I arrive back at the farm riding
Glenda and leading his horse. The clatter of a couple of horses
arriving in the yard has several people coming to see what's
going on. George and Noel pop out like little weather men from
different doors in the yard, and Pa comes more slowly from the
direction of the orchard.

'What's this?' he asks.

'Thought you might like to go and have a look at your new
herdsman, and I'd like to see how Colleen is settling in.'

'She'd like that,' George endorses, 'she was in a rare old flap
when I left her – moving, and new neighbours, all over one
weekend.'

'We could give the horses a treat over their old haunts, they'd
like that too,' I say beguilingly. 'Then ride up to Paget's farm.'

I am anxious to see how Colleen is coping with her first day,
her first full day, managing alone with Katie and settling into
one half of the newly completed division of the old Paget
farmhouse. Pa had wondered at breakfast how his new herds-

man and his wife were settling into the other half. To arrive casually on horseback with his daughter, who wants to see her best friend, is, I know, a good way to arrive without seeming officious.

'Well, yes, I suppose everything's alright here,' Pa enquires of Noel, who grins at me, recognizing the ploy.

'Fine, boss.' He does not quite add, *Off you go*, but his nod implies it.

'Hmm, not sure I can still get on a horse unaided,' he says and, taking the reins from me, leads his hunter to two old millstones that have been used as a mounting block for generations. From these he swings into the saddle with ease and receives a round of applause, started by George, but in which we all rather thoughtlessly join. His horse bridles, swings round before he has his second stirrup, but he is immediately balanced and takes control.

'Not lost your touch,' Noel calls.

'Just as well,' he says reprovingly, but he is enjoying the feel of a horse under him again, everyone can see. 'Alright, Bess. Off we go.'

I lead back down the lane to the bridleway. We can trot and canter here, and if we want, gallop, but I shall leave that to Pa.

'It's a pity we're nearly at the end of the season,' I call. 'Only this week left. Would you turn out?'

'No, I think not. A lot of people I've not seen for a while, maybe better if I wait until the autumn now – but I will.'

'Wonderful, wonderful,' I breathe to the wind and thrill to the feel of being out with him again, of talking freely, amicably. It adds to the feeling of being reconnected with life again – a different life, but living.

We draw up together near our galloping field, but he shakes his head. 'Enough for one day. Let's go and see how our new tenants are doing.'

We ride side by side now, companionably, the horses steaming a little and our faces glowing. Riding, like walking, loosens tongues. When bodies are busy, it seems to me, the brain relaxes, feels free to be open and candid, and we talk of many things.

'You are seeing a lot of young Philipps these days,' he comments.

'Grev. He's kind, makes me laugh.'

'That's as good a recommendation as any.'

'He's been very good to us both, hasn't he? Well, Lady Philipps too, of course.'

'You could do worse than Greville Philipps,' he says, and taps his heels into his horse's flanks to go ahead to open the next gate. I watch him as he leans over to release the latch, reins his horse backwards to open the gate wide, ushering me through.

Marriage had been on everyone's mind the evening before, when there had been a dinner party of twenty-two at the Hall. The red carpet treatment to say au revoir to the sisters, who were once more returning to their wifely duties after a week at home.

The discussion over coffee had been about a titled couple who were being spectacularly divorced in a London court, with all kinds of seedy details of covert observations, hotel bookings in false names. It had been headlined across the front pages of the more lurid Sunday papers. Anthea, conscious of her role in the Church, perhaps, had issued what sounded like a personal challenge to her brother, demanding if he found himself in a marriage that was failing, would he resort to divorce?

'No,' Greville had answered firmly. 'If I ever undertook marriage, it would be a lifelong commitment. My wife would be my first consideration in all things – for ever.'

His ardour had silenced the company. Anthea had looked nonplussed.

'Lucky for some girl, then,' Daphne had said, and pushed past me to leave the circle and the conversation.

I do know that, should Grev ask me to be more than a friend, I *could* certainly do worse. I know without Pa telling me. Telling me just sets up a resistance, really. Perhaps all I would have to fear would be Grev's devotion. Would I ever be able to live up to such lifelong dedication, to being first in all things to him?

For the rest of the way, I ponder Grev, the odd contrasts in his make-up: his propriety and yet his wicked sense of humour, a quality remarkably lacking in his sisters. He often clowns and mimics, but if there is real trouble, no one could be more concerned, more genuinely upset. I find his refusal to have dogs at the Hall difficult to understand. I know he lost a pet tragically when he was a boy, but it was so long ago. After a time, most people feel the need to fill the gap. Pa has always said three or even four dogs come into and share most country people's lives.

He raises a hand as we come in sight of the old Paget farm, and I appreciate just how much work and money has gone into the old house. It has been reroofed and tastefully made into two dwellings, the former back and front doors now serving the two separate homes, with a new side door made for each family.

'And have you been to the spinney recently?' Pa asks. 'The ground cover has totally hidden the scars the machines made around the path and the new trees are all alive, in bud.'

'What about old Paget's pantry?' I ask.

'There's still a smaller pond and a few waterbirds,' he says with a laugh, and I know he's remembering Daniel Paget toting his shotgun behind two small black ragamuffins. I push the memory of the boy away, but not before my loss to a lady with a rose garden in Malaya inflicts a stab of pain.

Like a Victorian picture of married bliss and motherhood, Colleen appears framed in the threshold of her new home, Katie on her hip. She waves as we ride nearer, but my father allows his horse to slow to a mere amble.

'It's all for you, Bess,' he says. 'Whatever I do with the land is for you, and yours, whoever you marry.'

He makes it sound like something he has been wanting to say for a long time, but, I wonder, why now? Perhaps seeing Colleen? I am at a loss for words, but it does free me from the idea that he has an exclusive preference for Greville. Then he clears his throat and I wait for a condition, a reservation.

'But do you know what I would like? To think that the Bennett name will still be linked to all this, to all we've done here. We've been good farmers, tended the land well. I want to ask you to keep Bennett as part of your name, whoever you marry. You could make it double-barrelled in true county style. Bennett-Smith, Bennett-Jones, that kind of thing.'

'You must have prayed for sons.' I remember my childhood regrets that I had not been a boy for him.

'It wasn't to be. And –' he turns to look at me – 'I wouldn't have changed you for the world.'

I keep my eyes fixed on Colleen as we ride slowly nearer, but I feel I've been awarded a medal, crowned by approval from my father. It is something I have strived for all my life.

'After that, how could I refuse?' I say, and reassure him that Bennett will always be part of my name, though I add, 'Not that anyone has asked me to marry them yet.'

'Oh, they will!' he says with mock resignation. 'They will, never fear.'

Colleen walks out to meet us now. 'You'll be my first guests,' she calls. 'I've unpacked most of the crockery.'

'I'll have a word with Mason and his wife first,' he says, leaving me to tether the horses, and with a half bow to Colleen. 'Back in a moment, young mistress of the house.'

'What a transformation,' I say as I enter a kitchen bright with yellow gingham curtains and tablecloth, the walls whitened, the slab floor bright with woven rugs. A tiny vase of wild violets stands in the middle of the windowsill. I wonder if George went out early and picked them for his wife and their new home.

'A lot of the things were wedding presents that have just been stored away until now. Oh, Bess! I am so happy to have a home of my own.'

'I suppose Noel is a bit relieved. You were pretty cramped.'

'Especially as we've another on the way,' she says, looking coy.

I gasp in surprise. 'Aren't you supposed to wait until you move into a new house? You know, new house, new baby.'

'I know, we didn't exactly plan it.' She shakes her head, tuts but looks radiant. 'Or at least not quite so soon.'

'Motherhood suits you.' I feel so tender towards this woman. 'Tell you what, *you*'ve looked much better these last few weeks, and today better still.'

'I'm not thinking *all* the time of what I've lost, or not so much anyway, and you know I don't *just* mean Ma.'

'I know,' she said. 'I know. It seems worse somehow when it's wilful. I mean, people can't help dying.' She breaks off, dives for my arm and pulls me to her, Katie on one hip, me on the other side. 'I didn't mean to upset you.'

'I know that,' I say, and take Katie from her. 'Wow, you're getting a heavy girl. What's your mummy feeding you on? I know, butter and cream, cakes and buns, pies and sausages.' I jig her at each word and she giggles. The more I jig, the more she giggles, until we both think I'd better stop, she laughs so uproariously, head thrown back, cheeks red as cherries. 'Well, no guessing who she takes after. You, Katie, are a giggler like your mum.'

'And you really are something like your old self,' Colleen says. 'What's happened?'

'I suddenly feel on something like my old terms with *my* dad,' I tell her.

'Your pa?'

I nod.

'I'm so glad,' she says, then looks over to the small wood-burning aga and cries, 'Look, my kettle's boiling already.'

'Gosh! You've really cracked this housekeeping lark.'

'Oh! Your Auntie Bess is a tease,' she tells the giggling Katie, knuckling gently into her daughter's tummy.

From this day, it seems we all settle into a new pattern: Colleen within ten minutes walk, Pa freer now he has two of his main workers living nearby. It's decided our horses are to go back to the farm after the final week's hunting, so we can hack out together.

Before the last hunt we have two days of heavy spring showers, enough to make the grass soft, slippery in parts, the gateways and jumps muddy and the ditches run, but everyone turns out to make the most of the day. I feel part of my job is to advise the young where to follow and where not, to avoid the jumps with big ditches on the far side, as these can have your pony slipping back and cause a nasty fall.

I advise, and do the opposite myself. Near the end of the afternoon, an hour or so after taking my second horse, which today is Glenda, I take a spectacular tumble. One minute Glenda and I are sailing high over the hedge, then I hear a hoof catch a protruding branch on the far side and the flight becomes a nosedive. Her head and neck seem to form a circle and my horse is going the wrong way, backwards, and upside down into the ditch. I fly on forwards, all breath knocked out of me as I thud into the ground. I can't get my breath as I perform a heavy glissade face down. I feel grass and mud in my mouth. It occurs to me that I must be making a real deep rut in the field as I slip from consciousness.

There seem to be an awful lot of people around me when I come round, a lot of bustle and talking, distant shouting. I remember the same distant echoey voices as I came round from having a tooth out. I have no idea of time and expect to be in hospital, not lying on my back looking up at a clear spring sky, still with all the paraphernalia of hunting and hunting folk around me. Someone says I should not have been turned over and I can hear someone shouting about an ambulance. Then, as air returns to my lungs in short painful inhalations, I try to say I'm alright, only to be immediately shushed.

Then I hear Greville's voice, a stir in the circle, and he is kneeling by my side. 'Bess?' he enquires. 'I think you should lie still.'

I lift a hand to wipe mud and grass from my lips, then turn my head away and spit heartily to rid my mouth of some of the grit.

'I'm alright,' I tell him, and try to sit up to see if I am. He puts an arm under my shoulders as I persist. He looks paler than I've ever seen him before. I wonder where his horse is, if perhaps he has fallen, but his clothes are only mud-spattered, unlike the thorough plastering of every part I can see of myself.

'I am alright,' I reassure him again and pull myself up to a sitting position, but my ribs hurt, ache with the effort of drawing air back into them. 'Oh, Glenda!' I have a vivid picture of her neck curved at a bad angle back under her. 'Is she alright?' I question urgently. He nods and leans back a little so I can see her. One of the hunt servants is holding her head firmly while she whinnies and drums her hooves uneasily. She is always upset if someone falls off her back. 'I must tell her I'm alright.'

'Let's find out if you are first,' he says and orders, 'Can you all stand away, please. Let's have some air.' The crowd of hunt supporters, who largely follow on foot and bicycle, drop back to his order. Slowly, because really I am not sure what I have done to myself, I pull up my knees.

'I'll hold firm while you try to pull yourself up. If I start hauling you about I might do worse harm. You'll know if it hurts too much to carry on.' He pauses to nod his face very close to mine to emphasize the point. 'And you will stop, won't you?'

'I will.' I nod my promise. He holds out his arms and I pull myself up. 'Just winded, I think. Let me walk a bit.' With his arm around my waist, I hobble over to Glenda.

'It's alright, old girl, it wasn't your fault. We're both fine. Good girl!' She shakes her head and snickers at me and is calmed. I hear one of the watchers say, 'Well, would you believe it?'

'Horse sense,' her companion says.

'Want to look at the hedge,' I tell Grev, who does not question, just helps, as I walk stiffly away from the roadway and the onlookers to where I fell. A piece of the layered hedge has been broken and has sprung out. The thick branch makes a real hazard for an unsighted horse coming from the far side. 'I'll get it seen to,' Grev says. 'And now, how is it?'

I stretch straighter. 'I'll be fine,' I tell him. 'I can ride back, if you'll give me a leg-up.'

'Just one moment,' he says. 'Turn to face me.' He lifts a finger to my forehead. 'There's just a bit here.'

I feel him push a finger across my brow.

'What is it?' I ask. 'Am I bleeding?'

'No, there was a clean bit.'

Only Harding sees us return to the Hall after we have left the horses at the stables in Tommie's charge. 'Come on,' Grev tells me. 'You can have a bath and I'll find you something of Anthea's to wear, she's more your size than Daphne. There's masses of stuff in their old rooms.'

'You could put a horse blanket on your car seat and drive me home.'

'No, get cleaned up here. There's no one around to worry you. Gran won't be back for ages. I'll rustle up some coffee and sandwiches.'

I luxuriate in one of the extra-long baths the Hall possesses, so long it's impossible for me to touch both ends, however much I stretch out. I lie in the hot soapy water long enough to feel the stiffness of the fall ease, but I'm surprised to see bruises already coming out on my thighs, and my toes! I slip into one of the white towelling robes on the door and wonder if Grev has found me anything to wear.

He is coming along the landing with clothes over his arm. 'Found something!' He extends the arm. 'A sweater and slacks.'

'They'll do fine,' I say, then extend my foot. 'Look at my toes, they must have got all bruised and bashed inside my boots. They're black already.' I look up to find it is not my foot he is looking at but my face, me, all of me.

'Bess.' He comes forward, dropping the clothes as he comes. 'I've' – he takes me into his arms – 'been wanting to do this for ages.' He holds me a moment longer then pulls back so he can see my face. 'Don't look so startled. I love you, you must know.'

I shake my head and open my mouth to speak, then close it as he stoops to kiss me. My lips feel rigid for a moment, then soften and tremble under his.

'Bess, marry me.'

I think I just swallow before he speaks again.

'Either go and put a lot of clothes on, or marry me.'

I push my arms up and around this very pleasing young man's shoulders and think, *Bennett-Philipps*, Pa *will* be pleased. I could do worse.

'Yes,' I say.

He does not answer. Well, he does not speak, but his hands slip inside the loose robe, his fingers cold over my still-glowing flesh. I feel I stand on some boundary, some border between girl and woman and to resist now would seem churlish and a tease, which I am not.

Twenty-Six

W atching the young couple rushing off to London to buy an engagement ring, Edgar is reminded of the day his daughter slid down from her horse at a City Show years ago. He had felt alerted then by the feel of a young woman's body, not a girl's, sliding through his hands. He remembers he had been so shocked he had nearly let go. Now he looks and calculates there is a new blossoming.

Bess turns and waves. 'See you tomorrow. Take care. Will you be alright on your own?'

'I'm quite a big boy,' he calls back, but, as the sports car moves off, his daughter's chiffon scarf flying almost like a cliché out of the side window, he has never felt so alone. Perhaps striving and hoping for things has kept him going, now seeing them coming to fruition is leaving him with ample time to lapse, to stagnate.

Going indoors, followed by Brac, who watches him intently to see what he intends, he ponders the story Bess told him that morning. He had been amazed to learn that Clara Philipps had been party to his mother's secret right from the beginning. Women in all their infinite variety never fail to amaze him. He had certainly viewed Maude Seaton with vastly more respect and patience since he had known the truth about Mr Benjamin and the woman's own family background.

He had always respected Lady Philipps, and now more so, for he had not judged her capable of keeping a secret for so many years. He had always judged her to have a wise head, but a still tongue had not seemed her style. He is told she is planning for the new circumstances in her life, moving on. Certainly she is not in danger of stagnating. She has already announced that she will have a kind of modern dower house built on the edge of the estate and move out of the Hall as soon as it is ready. Grev and Bess have insisted there is no need, the house is large enough, but she insists, saying she wouldn't have wanted her mother-in-law, or in her case grandmother-in-law on the premises when she was a bride. She plans to take Harding and his wife there with her as housekeepers, and has arranged for the sale of her grandmother's jewellery to raise the money.

He wonders if he has any chance of emulating Clara's practicality and lack of sentiment, as he wanders upstairs and sits at Fay's dressing table looking at himself in three lonely angles. He reaches forward and lays his hands on Fay's brush and hand mirror, telling her that while *he* feels enervated, Bess is doing a fair job of being decisive. She has resisted the pressure to have friends of the Philippses as her bridesmaids, or the Philipps sisters as matrons of honour. She has fixed a date in early October so that Colleen will have the birth of her second baby well over and can be matron of honour, with little Katie as her bridesmaid. 'That's not going down too well with Daphne and Anthea,' he says aloud. 'Though they have inflicted the Rev. Wallace on the couple to officiate.'

He thought about the coming ceremony at the City Cathedral. The last time he had been there was for Fay. He had asked Bess about this, but she had said something about the cathedral being big enough to hold all kinds of emotion, but he feels it is as much to do with Alexander Bennett's overbearing granite cross in the parish churchyard. He has seen how she walks and angles herself not to have it in her view when she visits her mother's grave or walks in and out of the parish church. She would see it as a symbol of all that is wicked.

He picks up the brush and mirror, holds them as Fay held them hundreds, perhaps thousands, of times. To understand Bess, he thinks, is to understand himself, and perhaps one day his daughter would know enough of life to fully understand her father.

'You know if we'd been gifted with sons and more daughters, Bess would always have been closest to my heart.'

Tears flood his eyes but do not fall as he imagines Fay agreeing, *She walked in your shadow as a child.*

'Now I feel I'm beginning to walk in hers.' He lets the brush and mirror fall back, straightens them into their places. 'Why aren't you here, Fay?'

'You alright, Mr Bennett?' Stella asks when she arrives at twelve o'clock, but Stella is not one to wait for answers. 'Everyone is saying what wonderful news about Miss Bess, good match for both of them. You'll have a lot on your mind, I expect, all the arrangements. Ah! And it's sad Mrs Bennett is not here.'

He takes the soup she makes, eats the sandwiches she makes and listens to instructions about a casserole in the aga for later, and leaves her to the cleaning. He hovers near the car. He'd had no intention of going to the village, but now he nods Brac in and drives to his mother's.

The gates to the yard are open, so he parks inside, goes in and through the house, finding both his mother and Miss Seaton sound asleep in their armchairs. He coughs several times, moves a chair about, and finally lifts the little brass bell from the table near his mother and tinkles it. Neither stirs. Bess had said she felt they were beginning to find Mr Benjamin's loving but constant attentions a little overwhelming, and that they might appreciate seeing him rather less often than two or three times each day. It had been an aspect of the situation he had not thought about.

He sits down to wait, wondering what his own reactions would be to having the continual presence of his half-brother, half-uncle, at the farm. It would partly rectify a wrong.

'Have you been here long?'

He looks up to find his mother's steady gaze on him.

'No, no. You were both so sound asleep.'

Maude now rouses. 'Oh, dear! I must have closed my eyes for a second.'

'Or three,' Edgar says, and they all smile, more relaxed in

each other's company since understanding has laid criticism low.

There comes the noise of water running, then of crockery being moved in the kitchen.

A low exclamation of dismay escapes Maude. 'He's back already.' Then she consults the mantle clock. 'Well, no, not already. We've been asleep for two hours and more. He'll be making tea.'

'You've something on your mind.' He finds his mother watching him closely as they listen to Maude and Mr Benjamin talking, but before more could be said Mr Benjamin comes in carrying a tray of teacups with milk, sugar and a home-made sponge cake.

'Hello, old chap,' Edgar greets him, shaking hands as Mr Benjamin comes beaming over to him. Edgar's handshake is long and thoughtful, and he feels a tug at his heartstrings. This simple man is his blood relation.

'So, at least some of the wedding arrangements are now definitely settled,' his mother states after waiting to see if Edgar was going to make a different lead.

'Strange isn't it,' Maude says. 'I always thought Bess would finish up with that Sinclair boy. They seemed very fond of each other, right up to the day they went away. Then, after that, there was the day he met her from school before he went abroad with the army. Funny nothing came of all that.' She sighs and sips her tea. 'No harm in telling now. I saw them kissing the day that woman threw her husband's things out into the street.

Neither answers, but Edgar remembers something else about the day at the City Show when he realized his girl was becoming a desirable young woman. He remembered wanting to hit young Sinclair on the nose, remembered feeling the threat of him stealing his daughter's affection, in a way he had not feared from Greville Philipps.

It was a blessing the Sinclairs had gone, and Bess had got over the childhood infatuation. He turns the conversation back to the wedding. 'I want Bess to have a supper and dance here at her home after the formal luncheon in town – a do for the locals, like our harvest suppers, only larger, more lavish. We've got the big barn and perhaps we could have a marquee. I wondered if you would all come up, say tomorrow afternoon. I'll get Stella to make us a tea and we could all have a look round and you could give me your advice about it all.

'I'd love to,' his mother says.

'I mean Maude and Mr Benjamin too.'

'Ben will love that,' his mother confirms. 'He loves the farm.'

'Does he?' Edgar asks, though he knows very well he does.

He was not quite clear why he wanted the three to come to the farm until he saw them all there – then he knew. He was assessing how Ben would fit in if he lived at the farm, what his own reactions would be. He even watches his dog, gauging her reactions. Brac has never had any doubts, she treats Mr Benjamin as one of the family, sits and leans against his knee as readily as she comes to Edgar's.

He had not meant to broach the subject so soon but, finding himself alone with his mother as they assess the big barn, he finds himself making the suggestion.

She pushes out a hand to the barn wall, grips a timber.

'I'm sorry, mother, I shouldn't have said anything.'

'No, Edgar, this would –' she pauses as if it is difficult to find the words – 'ease my sense of guilt, set him where he should be.'

'Guilt?' Edgar is astonished. 'You've no cause.'

'I left him behind when I should have brought him home. I . . .' she looks up with sudden honest resolve. 'I hated that child before he was born, hated the idea of him every moment *before* he was born.'

He thinks of the long months of a woman's pregnancy, a woman exiled, *shut away privily*. 'That's not surprising,' he says.

'Perhaps not, but, ever since, I have felt it was my fault he was not better blessed, that hating him so much damaged him in some way.'

Edgar goes to put his arms around her, pat her shoulder. 'I think not.'

'Poor Mr Benjamin,' she says, her hand running restlessly up and down his jacket lapel.

'You did your best for him, the best at that time. Now we can do a little more.'

'You're sure about this, Edgar?' He sees her now as the mother caring for her other son. 'I don't want him ever being let down again.'

'All my instincts say it's right. He fits here at the farm, you can see.'

'Perhaps we will see what he says after the wedding, then. Let's not complicate matters until then.'

'It's quite strange. Now the idea's been put to me, I think I'm really looking forward to it.'

'Maybe you've found a new child to look after.'

'And you don't mind not seeing so much of him?'

'Maude and I are getting old, weary in the afternoons,' she says with a grimace about his visit the day before. 'And he'll come to see us often enough, I'm sure of that. He has the best of all natures. Don't ever let it be spoilt, or spoil him. Care for him, Edgar.'

'I will, Ma,' he promises.

He is a proud man as he walks up the long aisle of the cathedral with his daughter on his arm. He knows Bess is right, this place is big enough to contain all emotion. Now decked for a wedding, it can hold the clouds of bright hats and flowers and buttonholes as majestically as if it were created for nothing else.

He smiles and holds out a hand for bonnie little Katie as she comes up behind Bess with her mother. Katie, in long yellow dress, holds a ball of yellow rosebuds. Colleen, in a darker gold, takes Bess's bouquet of white roses and white lilies as they prepare for the service to begin. He sees the little nod of reassurance Colleen gives to his daughter. He's reminded of the times he has seen Colleen clinging to Bess as the cows ambled by, and is overtaken by the thought that, just as they played together in the meadows, now they are playing in the fields of life. It threatens to overcome his composure. He lifts his chin sharply and pushes such melodramatic metaphors away.

He feels the matron of honour and her bridesmaid make a small country cameo among the city splendour of the rest of the wedding, the two sides of his daughter's life perhaps, and none the worse for that.

But as the photographs are taken outside the cathedral, and the crowds show their approval, it is these two, besides his spectacularly beautiful daughter and her handsome husband, that have the onlookers clapping. His mother and Clara Philipps insist on having a photograph taken with Colleen and Bess – *the special friendship group*, Clara calls it. Her granddaughters do not look impressed.

The formal reception and luncheon is at the City Hotel, and these arrangements have been overseen by Fay's family. It is splendid, everything either the well-connected Tophams or the landed Philippses could desire. This is followed by Edgar's own idea for an evening party and dance at the farm, like the harvest suppers, but much grander in decoration and style, with a marquee and a live band. He has arranged coaches for those who wish to be transported to the farm and back.

He notices that while the Philipps girls and their husbands do not show enthusiasm for this, they come even so.

Shortly after the party has regathered at the farm, Bess and Greville reappear in going-away clothes. Greville's sports car was supposed to have been hidden until this moment, but when it is driven round to the front door for their departure, it is well bedecked with ribbons, streamers and tin cans, and the whole inside liberally strewn with pink paper rose petals.

The laughing, exhilarated crowd raise a cheer as they see the car. He sees Bess placing her bouquet carefully on the back seat. Nothing has been said but a vice clamps his heart – she will be taking it to her mother's grave. The village churchyard will be the married couple's first port of call.

He is very conscious of all he has given away to this man – his daughter, his beautiful, dignified, clever girl. Greville Philipps had better treat her right. At that moment he does have the impulse to give this young man a good shake to make sure he remembers.

At the last moment, with Grev in the car and the engine roaring to life, Bess runs back to him, kisses him. 'Thanks for everything,' she breathes, then, pulling at both his hands, she brings him to where his mother and Maude stand. 'Look after him, Gran,' she says, kisses both women, much to Maude Seaton's confused red-faced delight, and is gone in a rattle of tin cans, more cheering and more confetti. Grev honks his car horn until they are far down the lane and long out of sight.

With the couple away, they all turn back, Edgar to ensure his guests have a really good time – and his guests to do just that. Edgar feels he will remember this wedding party as the time the gentry behaved like village folk and the village folk looked on and wondered – for a time. Once the dancing begins, the locals forget the differences and put on their best display of village-hall virtuosity, while some of the sportsmen, game for anything, show some of the more staid villagers how to good-time.

Colleen stops for the first dance then retires with her young family. Katie, quite exhausted, refuses to be parted from her ball of rosebuds. Mr and Mrs Rawlins, May and Mavis stay on until the first coach comes for those ready to leave. No one troubles to enquire about Roy Rawlins these days. He has gone his own way for so long.

When the last coach goes and the band and caterers are all packed and away, Edgar finally manages to persuade his mother and Maude he really does not need them to stay the few hours until morning, when George and his herdsman will arrive back for the milking. Noel drives them home in the trap.

Relieved to be alone, Edgar walks through the deserted barn and marquee, the atmosphere redolent with cigar and cigarette smoke, lingering yeasty bar smells – even the air feels dusty and unsettled, as if still stirred to the rhythm of dancers. He craves to fill his lungs with unused, unexhausted air and walks on through the orchard, where his feet catch wasp-eaten shells of fallen apples. He walks on through the first meadow, stopping in the middle, expanding his arms backwards, breathing deeply of the dew-laden pre-dawn morning.

'So, that's it,' he whispers, and for a moment does not feel alone.

Three weeks later with Bess back from a honeymoon in the Highlands of Scotland, Mr Ben, with his mother and Maude, is invited to the farm and the idea that he might like to live there is gently introduced.

'Now Bess is married to Greville, she will live at the Hall,' his mother says.

'Yes.' Mr Benjamin nods approval.

'So, Edgar will be all alone here at the farm.'

All alone takes the smile from the man's face.

'So, I wondered' – Edgar takes up the proposal – 'if you would like to come and live here with me?'

'Live here?'

'Sleep here, have your own room here, for always.' Edgar feels an unexpected moment of panic in case he should refuse.

'Sleep?' He looks at his mother, who nods, and he goes on, 'At this farm with the animals, and feed the chickens, look at the sheep . . .' He pauses then stabs a finger towards Edgar. 'Help Noel.'

'With the horses, yes,' Edgar confirms, wishing he could control the threat of tears. 'This would be your home.'

'My home?' Mr Benjamin says the words with wonder, nodding away as if he would never stop.

'Yes, old chap. You've come home.'

Twenty-Seven

T hough I have no one to compare my husband with, I come
to feel, to know, that he is a wonderful lover. He seems to
know about erotic parts of my body I had no knowledge of. A
lightest touch of his finger behind an ear alerts my senses like an
electric shock. 'Where did you learn such scrumptious delica-
cies?' I ask him and he says, 'In the prostitutes' dens of Soho
when I was in the army,' and I don't know if he is joking or not.

When I press him, he says, 'Well, lassie, if you must know, it
was in the arms of a sex-starved master's wife at boarding
school.' And I still don't know if this is the truth, or whether he
is just an instinctive man who can find out what pleasures his
wife. I *think* it is this.

One late evening in the close aftermath of love, I lie thinking
of all he gives, and in that unguarded moment, I think of
something I miss quite a lot.

'What a pity you won't have a dog. All that wonderful
caressing you could give it.' I imagine his fingers behind the
beast's ear.

He rises from our bed, as if jerked out by a rope. 'Don't ever
say that. Don't remind me of dogs and caring, and losing.'

'I'm sorry, I wasn't thinking.' I go to join him, looking down
over the moonlit lawns, and although he slips an arm around
me, my remark has driven his mind elsewhere. I wonder just
what happened to make him so inflexible, so upset.

'I can't bear it, you know – losing things, losing people.'

He turns me to him and holds me tight. I move in against
him. He is aroused again. His hands hold both passion and

tremor, but before I submerge in this love-making I wonder if he does not love me too much, too many eggs in one basket.

We share everything; the estate, life, county events, Pa's plans. Together we share the excitement of buying Mr Benjamin a horse; together we ignore the odd snide, leading comments about *a cuckoo in the nest*, or *birds coming home to roost*, when people note the physical similarities between Pa and Mr Ben – and these are particularly striking when they are both riding. Grev, who was taken into the secret before our marriage, just says,'Hold firm. Speculation is one thing, knowledge quite another.' Noel, who is supposed to know nothing, says, 'Strangers will just think they're brothers.' It is left at that.

We go to the theatre, and to the cinema quite often, and when Laurie Lee's book *Cider with Rosie* is published, we read it out loud to each other. *Contentment with a dash of zest*, Grev calls this novel about country life and love. We often read things aloud to each other.

I live a wonderful life and in our second year of marriage we holiday in Switzerland, learning to ski, revelling in the atmosphere of Hotel Bergère, St Moritz, the air, the snow, the scenery.

The following April, our son is born: Richard Greville Bennett-Philipps, heir and beloved of both families. We call him Dickie to the chagrin of Grev's old nurse, who is reinstated at the Hall. Dickie is a contented baby and life is very good.

It is in the morning of the last day of August when Pa telephones with the news that he has heard via Noel that Roy Rawlins has been killed in a motorcycle accident. We tell each other we are not surprised. The talk for years has been that he would either kill himself or someone else. Apparently he has done both. Even so, this does not alter the fact that the family will be grieving. I take Grev's car and go to Paget's farm, only to find that Colleen is out, no doubt with her mother, so I drive there.

Mrs Rawlins opens the door to me. 'I'm so sorry,' I say, giving her a hug, patting her back. Everyone is there except Mr

Rawlins, who is away working and, although he has been told the bad news, is still travelling home. Colleen is upstairs.

'I've asked her to look in our Roy's chest to see if there's anything about what he would wish done. I don't expect so, but he kept that old tin chest locked and his keys were brought back by the police . . .' She stops in the middle of this statement and shakes her head. 'He was a bad lad at times but he was ours.'

'Of course he was, and you must remember the good times, all of you must.' I exchange wry smiles with Colleen's sisters, who, still in their green factory overalls, are amusing Katie and her little brother, threading buttons from a tin. Katie and William do not call and race to fall on me as they do when I visit them at home. They sense something is very wrong and look at me uncertainly over their strings of buttons.

Just at this moment Colleen comes downstairs. I turn to say how sorry I am about Roy, to give her a long hug, but her expression makes me just stand and stare at her. She looks like one who has just seen a ghost, or confronted the Devil. She holds a bundle of papers – envelopes – in both hands.

'Oh, Bess!' she begins, then crumples into a chair. 'What has he done?'

'What is it?' Her mother bustles forward, anxious for her eldest daughter. 'What have you found?'

'Letters,' she says.

'Letters?' Beginning at the base of my spine, my whole body goes icy cold, as if I already know what she is going to tell me.

'In Roy's chest?' her mother asks. 'What are they?'

She holds them up and Mrs Rawlins takes them, looks at the top one, then fingers through, looking at odd envelopes here and there right through to the bottom of the bundle. Then she half extends her hands towards me. 'They're written to you, at our address.'

My heart first hammers then labours to go on beating. I feel as if I have been stricken by some crippling blow and shall never recover. I must have extended my hands, for I find I am holding the letters, a heavy, thick bundle, too much to span with one hand.

I see that they have all been torn open, opened and read by Roy Rawlins. The top envelope has a clear round postmark: *London 2.15 pm 30 September 1953*, two days after Ian and I went to the Abbey Park; when he gave me the locket and we put pieces of our hair into either side; when I stood between his knees hacking off his blond hair, making a near-bald patch; when we ate fish and chips. In this letter would be the address for me to write to while he was being shipped out to the Far East.

My knees now give way and I sit at the table, the pile slipping into a small avalanche between the children's outdoor clothes, a bowl of potatoes and all the coloured buttons.

'They never came through our letterbox, I swear,' Colleen vows.

'No, I'm sure. Our Roy was never up when the postman came. So, how could he get your . . .' Mrs Rawlins begins, then trails off, and I look at her sharply, for she knows. Suddenly, as she asks the question, I see she knows the answer.

'My God,' she breathes, and slips down on to a chair facing me across the table. 'But why?'

'Just sheer spite,' Colleen says through tight lips.

'But how? How?' I insist. I feel I am tottering on the edge of some yawning gap in my life.

'How?' Mrs Rawlins repeats. 'How? Because his friends were as wicked as he was. All along he's been bosom friends with a lad, a man, who used to work for the Post Office. He was postman here in the village when' – she nods towards the letters – 'when these would have come.'

'You mean he took them out of the mail?'

'Oh, yes!' Colleen confirms. 'He and our Roy would think it was good fun. Getting one back on my high-faluting friends. "See you're still pals with the high-faluting Bennetts," he'd say, then snigger and tap the side of his nose. I see why now.'

'Bess, what are you going to do?'

'What can I do?' I ask. Heartsick is how I feel, then anger takes over. 'Is this man still delivering mail?' I demand. 'He must be stopped, prosecuted.'

304

There is another stillness in the kitchen. 'He was on the back of the motorbike. They were both killed.'

I remember driving, remember the letters slewed on the seat beside me. I remember arriving at the farmhouse, empty at that time of the morning, and taking the letters with me, through the kitchen and up the stairs, only recollecting that I no longer live there when I open my bedroom door and see the bookless bedside table, the litter-free dressing table.

I kneel by my single bed and take up the first envelope. I pull out the letter with the army post office address on the top, two folded sheets. My hands are trembling too much to hold the letter. I put it flat on the bed, my hands framing the paper.

October 1st 1953

My Darling Bess,

Did not have time to write yesterday, it was all go – injections, collecting tropical kit, stencilling our names and numbers on kitbags not wanted on voyage.

We've been ordered about all day (well, ever since we were called up really), so now I am ordering you to remember you promised to pay me in letters for the locket – I hope you are wearing it for me.

So, my darling, I am off to the far side of the world, but nothing will ever be as exciting and wonderful to me as the moment I held you while you cut a bit out of my scalp. Later I found you had drawn blood! Don't worry, I'll live – honest. I'd have braved much more to earn your dark curl, which I keep next to my heart.

Write soon, my darling. Must rush to get this into the post before they find some new chore.

You are always in my heart. All my love always.

Yours,

Ian.

Write soon.

There followed kisses.

Write soon. I feel the words come as if on a long moaning wind, words from the ghost of a lover still yearning. Write soon.

Then a different voice, a memory of Roy Rawlins saying he would get even with me. *I'll get you*, he had said, and I give him a nod, hope it's a satisfaction to him, and wonder about divine retribution.

I touch the remaining pile. Roy has fingered and read them all. For all these years he has known the bewilderment, the agonies, all the misunderstanding these letters must contain. I wonder at the twisted satisfaction he must have found in keeping them from me, and in watching his sister's dismay when nothing arrived for her high-faluting Bennett friend. Perhaps he even made odd enquiries about why Colleen was always looking for the postman. I could imagine he would have done that. Never having had a girlfriend himself, he would have taken pleasure in spoiling my life, disappointment so often leads to spite. I scan the pile, there must be over thirty. 'Oh, Ian!' I yearn. 'Ian!'

I read this first letter again, but cannot bring myself to open another – not yet – not now. There is a lot of coming to terms before I can read more. I am hurt now; I expect to be tormented by the later letters.

All those years wasted, all my decisions coloured by a betrayal that in fact had never happened. Ian must have felt just as betrayed, just as deserted – and I had administered a final insult, I had sent that locket, with the beautiful chasing of lilies – and its broken chain – back to his father, back to *'await addressee's return'*. My heart pounds and I exclaim aloud. I remember Mr Sinclair's words: *You ask after Ian, which surprised me. He did mention some time ago that he had not heard from you and, to be honest, I think this had some bearing on his decision to sign on for a second term in the army.*

'What's this?' a voice asks behind me, and I turn to find my father in the doorway. 'I thought I heard someone upstairs. What's happened?'

'I . . .'

'Why are you here? Where's Greville? Has something happened?'

I can see his distress growing, but though I stand and shake my head and say everyone's fine, he obviously knows I am not. He comes to the bed and I cast a hand in the direction of the letters, but it takes me a long time to make sense enough for him to understand.

'So, they are all from Ian Sinclair – written to you at Colleen's address.' He pauses, his glance at me sharp. 'Just after he went into the army, or before that, when he first left the village?'

I do not reply; too late to feel guilt at the deceit.

He bends closer and can see some of the dates on the Post-Office stamps. He murmurs an answer to his own question.

'Always knew Roy Rawlins and that postman were up to no good, too big an age gap for normal friendship,' he says darkly. 'What are you going to do with these?'

'The letters? I've only read one.' I begin to replace the letter, tuck in the roughly torn edges of the envelope.

'Perhaps it would be as well to leave matters like that.'

'What do you mean?'

'I mean, you should leave them unread.'

I shake my head at him. 'I couldn't.'

'What good is it going to do now? It's over, past, gone; you've moved on, married with a son.'

The strange thing is, I don't feel moved on, I feel more as if this discovery has reconnected me, drawn me backwards.

'The best thing to do is leave them here for me to burn.'

'No!' I exclaim. 'No, I couldn't do that.' I pick them up, bundle them in my arms. I am not giving them up now, possibly not ever.

'So, where are you thinking of taking them?' he asks. 'Not back to the Hall?'

'Of course. I live there, and these are my letters.'

He shakes his head at me. 'You'll be doing wrong,' he judges. 'Very wrong.'

All the bridges we have rebuilt since my marriage seem in danger of collapse as we face each other. 'Then I'll take the consequences,' I say. 'But these are my letters.'

'I hope there are no consequences. I hope you're discreet enough to ensure there are none,' he says, turns and leaves. I am the child again, devastated because she's given the wrong answer, failed. I listen to him go downstairs and out of the house.

In the kitchen I find a small string bag, put the letters in it and plan to go back to the Hall stables. I have two stable lads now as well as Tommie, but at least twice in a normal day I am there to answer any queries, to check all is going as I like it.

I drive in that direction but keep going, past the stable entrance. I have no idea where I *am* going, just aware I am not ready to encounter anyone. Then I see the great triangle of trees in the hollow of the three hills, its summer canopy of birch, ash and hazel in full splendour. Red Pool Spinney. This feels the right place.

I park, think of walking to the pool, taking the letters. I sit and wonder again at the number of them. His confidence in my love had perhaps even outlasted mine. Had there been just three or four, or even ten or eleven, I believe I might have read them then and there, but the thought of the questions, the misunderstanding, the loss of hope, lies on me like a terrible weight. I feel it would have been better if Ian and I had drowned as children, never known those fleeting tentative days of love.

Perhaps I should not read them at all. What good *will* it do? Pa is probably right, there could be consequences, but even as I contemplate wild and stupid ways of disposing of the letters, I know I am never going to part with them. I am going to take them with me and hide them until I have read and reread them, until I have absorbed every last trauma and emotion, until it is played out like grief over a period of mourning – and truly it feels like a piercing, new bereavement.

When I get home I can hear Grev outside with Nanny Lewis and Dickie. It sounds like a lively game of horses. From the back of the stable block I glimpse Greville on all fours below the terrace, nanny holding Dickie on his back as he scrambles and bucks. It's top favourite game at the moment.

I walk away, straight to the house, take the string bag to the office, where I have a desk devoted to the stable activities. I pull open the bottom drawer and push the bag under a miscellaneous selection of old and new carbon paper.

Then I go outside.

'Hello. Where have you been?' Grev asks. 'You've missed the Oaks and the Grand National.'

'This child will never sleep,' nanny says, her own face flushed with the activities.

Dickie holds his arms up to me and I pick him up and bury my face in his tummy. My son takes the action as a new game, screws his fists into my hair and squeals. I have to be disentangled.

In the days that follow I only wish I could disentangle my emotions from the letters. I still have not read them, still they haunt me. I know I do have to fetch them out and read them before I can completely lay the ghost of *might have been*. I know I have to do this soon, for Grev has asked me several times if I am well: 'You're very pale. Let's go to the sea for a bit, take Dickie and nanny, leave them on a beach and go and make love in the sand dunes.'

'In a little,' I say. 'Let's see the City Horse Show over first.'

'Perhaps you're overworking. You are looking peaky.'

'No, I'm fine, honestly, but the seaside's a good idea.'

In the afternoon, when Grev goes off about estate business, I take the string bag of letters to the rooms Lady Philipps used before she moved to the new dower house. These are officially closed up, the furniture sheeted. I shall not be disturbed here.

I procrastinate, pace about, but go at last to her table near the window, open the curtains and pull off the dust sheet. The letters are more or less still in date order. I sort and spread them in rows, the one I have read top left, down to the thirty-third, bottom right. Then I get up and leave them. I go back only in the evening, when Grev has gone to keep an appointment with a tenant. Dickie is asleep and nanny's in the room next to him, knitting and listening to a play on the wireless.

Almost as if I am torturing myself deliberately, I open that first letter again, spread the pages flat on its envelope. Only then do I take up the second, the address is the same Army post office, but on top Ian as written:

The High Seas

My Darling Bess,

I really do mean high seas. Now I know why the Bay of Biscay has a name for bad weather. I have not been as seasick as most. Bets are being laid on how many go to meals. The lowest has been three out of a complement of over a thousand.

I understand we take on mail at Gibraltar, so I can't wait. The officers try to find us all things to keep us occupied – mind, at the moment most are glad to just lie on their bunks and wish we were at home, or at least on some other bit of terra firma. I wouldn't mind not being at home if only *you* were *here*, or say in Gib waiting for the boat. Oh happy thought! But your letters will be.

All for now. We're expecting a lifeboat drill and we have to get all the queasy up to muster. That's going to be fun. Also short letter because, as you can see from the writing, it's a bit like being a dice shaken up in a cup.

Love, love, love,

Ian.

The next letter is headed Gibraltar, but now the words and phrases mirror his disappointment.

So, no post for me, or at least not the letter I was hoping for. Dad wrote, he seems OK. Not sure where our next landfall is, some say before we enter the Suez Canal, the other end of the Med! Can I wait until then to hear? Suppose I haven't much choice. Know something must have happened to keep your letters from me. Has the village post office burned down?

Not something – *someone*. Even now I ache to explain. Again I put the letter aside, walk to the far side of the room, and view the other thirty letters I have so far not even taken from their envelopes. I wonder what I am resurrecting. I resolve to look at just one more. This time I take one from the middle.

I keep thinking that I must be writing to the wrong address. Then I find myself wondering if you, or Colleen, or her address, really exist. I seriously wonder whether I can have dreamt all that happened between us, our promises, then I panic and wonder if something has happened to you? But you see, my father has been having a local newspaper sent down to Cornwall so he can give me any news. He tells me your name is in the newspaper as winning events at horse shows, so I know you are alright. Bess, whatever has happened in *your* life, know that mine and my feelings about you are the same. Body, soul, spirit, I want you. I love you with all my heart.

The signature is just *Ian*.

My hand hovers over the last letter, but I feel I owe it to him to do this properly. I must make my way there fairly, must go back to the fourth letter and, over the days and the weeks, read my way through his sufferings.

As the weeks do go by, his torment – *Please just tell me where I stand* – must show in my face, for one evening towards the end of August, Grev delivers an ultimatum that if I do not go to see the doctor, he will send for him.

'I thought we were to go away,' I protest. 'That's what I was looking forward to, going to the sea.'

'Fine, if you feel up to it.' He seizes my hand as I try to walk away and, keeping hold of it, takes me out through the doors of the sitting room to the terrace, down the steps to the garden. 'What is it, Bess?'

I shake my head.

'I'm not a fool; something has happened.' He takes two rapid strides so he is ahead, facing me, bringing me to a halt. 'It's nothing like your mother, is it?'

I shake my head fiercely, ashamed he should be worrying about something like that. 'No, of course not. I would go to the doctor if it was anything physical.' I realize immediately I have given myself away, brush past him and walk on over the close-mown lawns towards the more natural environment around the lake. I would run if I thought it would end this conversation.

'So, it's a worry,' he states, as if he intends to track it down, dissect it – as if he might cure it. 'So, tell me what you are worrying about. The stables? Your father? For goodness' sake, Bess. I can't bear to see you so distressed.'

'Distressed?'

'It's the only word I can think of that describes how you are. It's been going on for weeks and weeks. Nanny says you're distracted.'

'Nanny?'

'Yes, and with Dickie.'

Distressed and disturbed, even with my own baby! I feel trapped, embattled, by what I realize is true. I had thought that concealing the letters was all I had to do. 'I'm sorry,' I say, but know it is not enough. 'I'm being stupid. It's nothing, Grev, nothing. I'll be fine in a while.'

'So, you've some trouble you are not willing to share with me.' His voice is very quiet.

'It really is something you can't help with.'

'Not if you shut me out.'

'No one, *no one*, can help.'

I step away from him, throw up my arms in that instinctive gesture of wishing to be left alone.

'Please just leave it, Grev. Please, just for now. I may tell you later.' I know this is unlikely and add, 'Sometime.' He does not follow as I walk towards the lake. I know I have wounded his feelings dreadfully, and I know there does have to be a resolution, an ending to this reliving of the past, but I have difficulty dragging my thoughts away from the sentences and the sentiments. I know them by heart.

> I want to remind you of all we promised to each other, but feel this may not be fair if you have met someone else. I just have to tell you that I cannot bear to come home and find you engaged or married to someone else.

Two letters later:

> So, I have decided to sign on here and hope to serve out my time overseas. I have made contact with an elderly English matriarch who owns part of a tea plantation. She wants a rose garden designed for her home in Kuala Lumpur . . .

An elderly English matriarch. So much for my Chinese beauty in the *Straits Times Magazine*, so much for Roy Rawlins and his talk of finding a Chinese beauty – and all the time he had known the truth. For years I had been the butt of his twisted sense of humour.

I reach the lake, then immediately turn back towards the house. I can enter by the side door and be unseen. This was one of the reasons the rooms were chosen by Lady Philipps, because she could come and go without disturbing the rest of the household.

I have been back with the letters some half an hour when I

hear a noise behind me. I turn to find Grev there, his hand on the main light switch.

'No!' I exclaim. 'Don't put the light on.'

'What is this?' he asks, and he sounds apprehensive, almost fearful.

'It's . . . I've been sitting in this half-light, it will hurt my eyes.'

'Why,' he asks, 'have you been sitting here, in rooms that have been shut up, the furniture sheeted down? I think you do have to tell me what this is all about.'

He does not switch on the light, but comes to stand next to me, overlooking the table.

'Bess,' he whispers. 'What *is* all this?'

After a few moments silence I answer, knowing that I do owe it to Grev to tell him everything. 'I think we had better have the light on after all,' I say.

So, soon all is revealed, the story told. He sits on the arm of a sheeted armchair and listens, only two or three times asking a question.

'But the worst thing I have done,' I say as the monologue ends, 'is to send the locket he gave me back to his father to await his return. It will be like a final insult.'

'So, this boy was your first love?' Greville's voice sounds even.

'A boyhood crush . . .'

'And the girl, what about her?'

'The girl? Me? Yes, a childhood passion,' I admit and laugh as I relate the story of the golden day in the harvest field, the first time I saw Ian, and of the pear he presented to me.

Lost in the reverie, I am startled as Grev suddenly takes my hand.

'You were a long way away then,' he says.

'Yes.' I sink down on my knees next to where he is now sitting in the shrouded armchair. 'We don't realize how golden our own childhood is until it is too late.'

'What did Hardy say? "Childlike, I danced in a dream;

Blessings emblazoned that day; Everything glowed with a gleam—" '

' "Yet we were looking away!" ' I finish the quotation.

'It went a little beyond childhood, I think,' he says.

'The last time I saw Ian was the day I left school, the day he was recalled from leave to go abroad. A long time ago.'

'And the time since not regretted?'

His words are so mildly spoken that for a few seconds I do not comprehend that they are a question.

'You and Dickie? Never for a moment. You have been – you are – wonderful, everything I could ask for in a husband and father. Grev, I'm so sorry about—' I throw a gesture towards the table. It's just that it was such a shock. I spent so long as a girl wondering what had happened to Ian, why he hadn't written, and all the time, he had.'

'We've been a bit bedevilled by Sinclairs, haven't we?' He gets up and we both stand looking at the letters. 'I suggest you tie them all with a ribbon and put them away in a drawer.'

I just stand shaking my head, not at the idea, but at the whole game of love and life.

'Well, you do what feels right for you,' he adds. 'I think I need a drink.'

Two days later, I have made a pile of the first eleven letters. I have joined Dickie and nanny more often for fun and games and tried not to show that in my heart nothing has been resolved. If it is possible to love both the man I have lost and the man I have, then I do.

One evening when we sit on the terrace after dinner, I realize that what I do wish above all else is that Ian should know what has happened. I ache for him to know that I did not let him down.

'So, where have we got to?' Grev suddenly asks.

I sense a change, an impatience, in his voice and manner.

There is no point in pretending I don't know what he is talking about. 'I just wish he could know that his letters never arrived.'

'Why?' The question is abrupt and, when I do not answer, he adds, 'What difference will it make now?'

'None, of course. It's just that he does not know the truth.'

'I wonder if you know the truth,' he asks.

'What do you mean?'

'I mean, the truth about your own feelings,' he says. 'Or mine.'

'You must admit it's an awful thing to have found out . . .'

'Your life could have been different,' he puts in.

'Well, yes, it could have, of course it could have.' If he wants to speak plainly, so be it. 'Perhaps what I need to do to put matters right is contact Ian's father, let him know the truth.' I am pacing up and down now, thinking out this solution. 'I could ask him to let Ian know and I could also ask him to return the parcel with the locket, if he would do that.' I turn back to Grev as the idea grows. 'I could tell him to open the packet so he knows it is as I say, then return it. Then Ian wouldn't receive what would seem like a final insult, the last slap in the face, when he is – he was – so constant for so long.'

'Constant for so long.' He pecks out the words, then adds, 'So it seems everything does not always come to those who wait.'

I cannot believe these words are a coincidence, Ian used the very same phrase. 'You've been reading the letters.'

'Yes,' he admits. 'One should always assess the enemy.'

'For goodness' sake, Grev – the enemy! You can't feel threatened by letters written before we were married. We have a son, we're secure, established – for life, Grev.'

'Just so, Bess, but that doesn't seem to have made you able to stop raging about what might have been.'

'Raging!'

'Inside your head.'

'Thinking – yes, thinking – not raging, Grev. I have not stormed, or raged, or even shed a tear.'

'Not that I have seen, no.' He suddenly gets to his feet.

'I married *you*, remember.'

'Yes, I remember.'

'Bess, do you know what I think you should do?' His voice has lost its edge now. 'I think you should go to see Ian's father, tell him what has happened, ask him to give you the parcel you sent. Then I think you should come home, put the locket with the letters in a nice scented casket and let us get on with our lives.'

Twenty-Eight

A week later I say goodbye to Grev before he leaves for business meetings in Leicester. It is almost a formal farewell. We kiss briefly and confirm the facts of my planned two-day stay, with two days to drive there, and two days back – just under a week.

I plan to overnight somewhere near Taunton, intending to set off around ten on the Friday morning, when I feel the traffic should be light, but Dickie delays me. Usually just a happy placid baby, content whether he is with nanny, or me, or his daddy, this morning he refuses to be parted from me, fretting first, then screaming, until even our patient nanny says she feels he either needs the doctor or a smack.

'Could he be teething?' I ask.

'He could sense you're going away,' she tells me.

'Do you think so?' I ask, but secretly wonder if she is right – animals sense things, why not people, certainly, why not your own baby?

'Don't worry, I'll soon be back,' I croon to him, but there is no way I will leave him while he is like this.

It is mid-afternoon when finally he falls asleep. Nanny and I make the judgment that he is neither hot nor feverish, and that I should go before he wakes again.

'Such a paddy,' nanny whispers as we paw over the pram.

The late start means I am immediately behind the early week-enders with their caravans. Once the roads narrow there is little chance of passing them, and if I do there is always another ahead. I just hope they are all heading for somewhere like Weston-super-Mare and will soon leave the route south-west.

By the time I reach the far side of Bristol, I am exhausted, find a small bed and breakfast with a parking lot at the side, and sleep soundly, more soundly than I have of late, for I suddenly have the overwhelming feeling of freedom. The people around me are strangers, no one is concerned with my doings or my comings and goings. I can, for the first time in years, really be me, Bess.

The second day, I creep behind trains of caravans, spurt between them and am overtaken by night and fog just before I reach Bodmin Moor. It is ten o'clock Sunday morning before I drive into St Ives.

If I had thought the roads narrow before, now there seems barely room for even my small MG on these steep cobbled streets. I crawl down to the harbour wall. I ask my way and have to retrace the tortuous drive up to the top of that precipitous hollow, crammed to the brim with cottages and terraces of houses, which from the top look as if they have been built one on top of the other.

Soon I find the street I am looking for. These houses stand clear of the jumbled town and look straight out to the sea's horizon. I decide to park and walk. It has taken me an extra day to arrive here, but I think it would be good to find a hotel near the sea after I've seen Ken Sinclair.

The last time I saw him was the day his wife threw his belongings into the street. Mr and Mrs Rawlins had taken him home and George had so carefully repacked his belongings. The last news I had of him was his own letter to say he was happy and living with a lady artist. I had presumed he meant a painter, but as I count the house numbers the woman who is adorning the step of the house I want looks more gipsy than artist. She is sitting on a hard-backed chair in the doorway, her face turned up to the sun, basking and delighting in the warmth. She has a scarf around her neck hung with tiny brass coins. Her skirt is black, with red embroidery, her blouse low-slung from the point of each shoulder.

319

I walk past, slightly averting my eyes as I recheck the house numbers, but as I return and my shadow passes over her again, she opens her eyes and smiles. I warm to her immediately. Then, behind her in the room itself, and at an easel, I recognize Ken Sinclair.

He does not immediately recognize me, and my hesitant approach does not help. I see that the woman realizes that I must think her a gipsy. She laughs and pulls the scarf from her shoulders. 'I'm modelling,' she says.

'I've come to speak to Mr Sinclair.' I smile but am unsure of my reception, and realize that while his face and manner exude happiness, his facial scars are still the first thing any stranger must notice. 'Bess Bennett-Philipps, or just Bess Bennett when we last met.'

For a moment the smile disappears, then good manners take over. 'My dear girl, how nice to see you. Come in, come in. This is my wife, Barbara.'

I turn to meet the woman's nod. So, they are married. I feel delighted for him.

'Hello,' she says. 'I'm pleased to meet you. I know I've heard the name.'

'Yes,' Ken Sinclair says with rather heavy confirmation. 'You've just arrived at the end of my lesson. Barbara is teaching me the art of oils. Well, she's trying to.'

'He'll be good,' she confirms. 'He has the eye, only needs the techniques. Come through, my dear. Tea?'

I dutifully admire the canvas, though it seems to me it is as yet hardly begun. Over tea – in a pleasant room with its french doors open wide to the view, the sound and smell of the sea – I tell the reason for my visit.

Mr Sinclair shakes his head. 'It shows you should trust your own instincts about a person. I always felt you and Ian would make a go of it. But unfortunately, my dear, you are too late to retrieve the pendant. Ian came home from the Far East three weeks ago, and I am afraid I gave the package to him then.'

Barbara had listened with a growing air of dismay and anger.

320

'What a terrible thing for anyone to have done. I have heard of mothers who have kept letters from sons or daughters, thinking they know best, but I've never heard anything as wicked as this. Why, it's damaged both your lives.'

'What are you going to do, m'dear?' Ken Sinclair asks.

'Well, I think you should go and see Ian. He's only half an hour from here. He deserves to know the truth,' Barbara says.

'That is what I thought,' I answer, though my throat feels tight at the thought of Ian only thirty minutes away. 'I would like the chance to explain.'

'The road's straight along the coast and Ken could draw you a map of the village, show you exactly how to reach the cottage. It's right on the cliffs. Ken inherited it from his aunt, and kept it in case Ian wanted it when he came home. Fortunately the tenant he had in it left only a month ago, so Ian's moved in, for now anyway.'

'There is one thing, Bess, you can always rely on – being well informed whenever you visit Barbara Sinclair.'

Barbara tuts and aims a cushion at him, but does not throw it. Instead she turns to me. 'So, you are married with a son?' she says and I nod. No need to say anything; I see both understanding and sympathy in her eyes. I think Ken Sinclair has at last the right wife, and I wish him continued joy; he has suffered enough.

I am soon on my way again, refusing to stop for anything to eat, though I am really famished, and I think Barbara knows this, for she thrusts two apples into my hand. 'Eat as you drive.'

The coast road is high and beautiful. I journey past tiny villages with romantic names – Zennor, Treen, Morvah – that nestle below on slopes and cliffs down to the sea. It seems an idyllic landscape, with farms on the rolling green slopes and away to the left, inland, the moors and craggy outcrops of rock.

I need to find Ian and the cottage before evening, then I will need to find somewhere to stay. Reaching St Just, I notice a largish hotel-cum-public-house and, turning towards Cape Cornwall, there are houses with vacancy signs, so this should not be a problem. Tomorrow I shall begin the drive back to the Hall.

After all that has contrived to keep us apart, I cannot believe I am about to see Ian again, and a great cautious part of me feels I should be very clear what I intend to do after this meeting.

As Mr Sinclair instructed, I turn left towards an ancient burial mound, park my car between several others whose occupants are in their cars or standing about watching the sunset, which is spectacular. I do no more than glance at the great theatrical orange ball dipping down into the sea. The rays gild the rough stony track and I remember Ian's description of this place when he first saw it: *the cottage is actually on a cliff path, halfway between sea and sky, with spectacular views – bet it's awe-inspiring when the sea's rough . . .*

I find the whole situation awe-inspiring as I round a bend, and a cottage, its back lodged in the cliff itself, comes into my view. This must be the place. I feel I have come upon it too quickly. I think of the letters I have brought with me, layered in the bottom of my case. I need to pause, think how to begin. Then, heart pounding, giving myself no time to retreat, I rush to the door, knock, louder than I had intended. If I had planned to knock and run, like a village child playing a prank, I would not have escaped, for it opens almost immediately.

I feel struck dumb, though my mind says yes. Yes, this is the place, and this is the man.

Ian Sinclair seems taller, his face is certainly leaner, cheekbones more pronounced; not tanned so much as old colonialists I have known. He is looking stern, the intrusive knocking unwelcome, his chin jutted out as if to take a blow. His hair is its summer white-blond – and I cannot bear it. I make some kind of noise and half turn away. I should not have come. I should have let my father burn the letters unread. Colleen should never have brought them out of her brother's box.

322

'Bess?' The voice is full of question and disbelief. 'It *is* Bess.'

The world is becoming very faint, his voice remote. I am surely not going to faint. I put out a hand to the door frame and find it held. I am drawn inside the cottage and lowered into an armchair. Once he is sure I am safely settled, he moves across the hearth to sit opposite. 'Be still a moment or two,' he says.

'I'm sorry, it was a shock seeing you after all this time.'

'A bigger one for me, I assure you, Bess Bennett-Philipps.'

'Yes.' I agree with all the judgments he is making. 'But there is something you should know.'

I stare fixedly at the worn rug, so the sight of him does not impede this telling. He does not interrupt. He absorbs every word, is so still it feels as if he is absent, recreating every moment of writing those letters, mailing them from across the world, reliving that past we were not allowed to share. In this telling I lose myself, for now I can truly share the hours, days, weeks, months – years – of waiting and hoping. When I am finished, we are both newly appalled by the crime and by our loss.

I hear him sigh – long, despairingly – as from the bottom of his heart.

I add my own final regret. 'I wish with all my heart I had not returned the locket. When I saw the letters, I wanted it back so badly. I felt as if I had delivered a final insult.

'If he were not dead, I could kill him,' he mutters. He sits forward, elbows on knees, hands gripped tight. He startles me when he looks up and demands, 'But why? Why? What had we ever done to Roy Rawlins?'

I remember a ridiculous thing. 'I once kicked his bucket,' I say, then can't believe I've uttered such an absurdity. Our burst of laughter teeters me over into tears and I cover my face with my hands, trying to hide them and wipe them away.

'Why didn't you kick him?' he asks from very close, and I find he is kneeling by me.

'Why didn't I just. Oh, Ian! I just needed you to know the truth.'

'We've wasted all those years.' Very tentatively he takes my hands. 'So, you've read all my letters now.'

'Many, many times. Each time, they tore my heart.' I press my hands, my palms, together very tight inside his hands.

'It was the same for me every time I read about you in the *Leicester Advertiser*. Dad posted it to me regularly when I opted to stay out East. I'd scour the columns, then, when I found you mentioned, it was such agony, but I couldn't give up looking.'

I look down at our hands. 'A lot has happened since we said goodbye.'

He turns my hands between his, first one way, and then the other, as if he is wringing his hands with mine inside them. 'A lot has happened, but a lot has stayed the same. I have thought and dreamt about you often enough.'

'I only married when I was quite sure you were never going to return. I convinced myself the lady you were designing the rose garden for was young and beautiful and this was the reason you were never going to return.'

'When I read of your wedding and the birth of your child, I thought that was the end.'

'Yes,' I agree, and we pause but neither of us moves to untwine our hands. 'I have a son. We call him Dickie, he's . . .' I was going to say he is a good baby, then I remember his tantrums before I left, and wonder if he is still fretting.

'Your father will be pleased, linking your names – an heir for both families.'

'Yes. You would remember Greville, of course. He's been wonderful to me, Pa – and Ma before she died – so caring in every way.'

He does not answer but as he kneels before me he opens his hands so mine lie freely in his palms, free to be lifted clear, but I cannot.

'Oh! My dear, darling, Bess, what will we do?'

'What can we do?' I ask, but I don't want him to answer. If neither of us speaks or moves, what harm are we doing? We've been cheated of so much, what harm does this do?

'Look, I only know you can't just go. Have you eaten?' he asks. 'I was about to have – well, I'm not sure whether you'd call it tea or supper – but we can sit and nibble while we talk some more. I have some beer.'

'Please.'

'We've had some strange meals together,' he says as he finds another plate and motions me to the chair opposite him. He cuts crust from a new loaf, passes cheese, lettuce and tomatoes and levers the crown caps from two bottles of milk stout. 'Ice cream, then fish and chips, do you remember?'

I watch his swift efficiency, remember the way he used to shop at the local Co-op, quite unashamed of being seen with a shopping basket, as all boys – and many girls – were then. He learned to fend for himself a long time ago. We eat, each of us familiarizing ourselves with the man and woman, who used to be boy and girl together. What at first are quick glances become steady gazes, scrutiny.

'Your hair's still just as wavy and black,' he says.

'And yours is just as bleached by the sun.'

'Do you remember Miss White and that awful whistle she used to toot for us to march into junior school?'

'Do you remember the brook and Red Pool Spinney?' I tell him about the new path and the properly husbanded woodland.

'It doesn't sound so much fun,' he says.

'Nothing has been such . . . since . . .' I begin, then shake my head.

'Another bog you are falling into,' he says gently, then extends a hand across the table.

When he had released my hands before, leaving me free to move mine from his, I had not done so. This is one step further, this is a step I should not take. It feels like the first step on a new journey as I watch my hand go to meet his. He takes it and covers it with his other hand. 'So,' he says. 'You know my feelings have not changed. I love you as much as ever I did.'

'But we must be different people now.'

'I don't feel very different.' He holds on to my hand. 'Do you? Honestly?'

'Perhaps it's not so much feelings that matter now.'

'Duty, you mean,' he says.

'And vows, marriage vows.' I am beginning to regret that prayer book and how I checked the words of the vows when my father strayed with this man's mother.

'They would have been the vows we made to each other if we had not been cheated.'

'That's true.' And it's as if I hear Noel's voice mocking me. Circumstances alter cases, is that what you think? I get up quickly, glance at the window like some trapped creature. 'It's getting dark, I should go, I've done what I set out to do. We can't alter the past.' I stoop to pick up my handbag and move towards the door.

He stands up suddenly, his face sombre, deeply hurt. 'One moment,' he says, and goes to the sideboard. From the top drawer he takes out a package. I recognize it immediately. He puts it into my hand.

'I bought it for you. It was always yours.'

We are very close and I look up into his face to thank him, to say something about treasuring it for the rest of my life, but when I am close to him, I merely sway towards him.

'Bess,' he whispers, and stoops to kiss me on the lips. I try not to kiss him back but it is impossible, I love this man, I always have and always will. I am lost to the meaning of right or wrong.

We kiss for a long time, then continue in short sweet sips, in between which he tells me he will never be able to let me go again. He would sooner die than lose me again. I feel I have not begun to live until this moment, nothing in the world is as important as this overwhelming passion I feel for Ian. It was always meant to be.

'Come upstairs,' he whispers into my hair and leads me by the hand.

*   *   *

I had thought Greville a good lover, and so he is, but with Greville, I realize, the giving has all been on his part. I had been a kind of onlooker drawn and persuaded into the game.

With Ian, the sensuality does not have to be stimulated or coaxed. He gently unbuttons my blouse and I want to hasten him on, to do it for him. This love is a mutual giving and pleasuring.

'I can't lose you again,' he tells me when I stand naked.

'My love,' I later cry out to him.

Then I lie by him and cry inside for him, for my baby, for myself and perhaps most for Greville. Great-hearted, well-meaning, second-best Greville. I sense no good will come of this, could imagine the overwhelming condemnation if it was ever found out, and even as I lie by the man I truly love above all others, I know I have to return to Greville. It is only after we have made love a second time and we have both slept a little, that I wake to realize the morning is coming and that I promised to telephone Greville the evening before.

I creep from the bed and go downstairs. I think that it would be possible for me to slip away now without the drama of explanations or the trauma of parting, but I fill the kettle and make tea. Then I hear the floor creak above and know Ian is awake. In seconds he is downstairs wrapped in a check wool dressing gown.

He comes quickly and seizes me in his arms. 'I had a terrible moment of panic when you were not there.'

'I remembered I promised to ring Grev last night, he'll be worried. There's a phone box near the shops, I think.'

He nods. 'Wait until I'm dressed and I'll come with you. We can walk, then I'll buy some fresh bread – and the butcher here makes wonderful sausages. We'll have a real appetite for breakfast by the time we get back, not that I haven't now.'

We smile our secrets, but I have to be cruel.

'I have to go back, you know.'

'Your baby, I know. But we do have to go on seeing each other.' The certainty in his voice matches that in mine.

'I don't want to hurt my husband either; he doesn't deserve it.'

'But then, neither did we,' Ian persists. 'I'll come to Leicester, we could meet.'

'But where?' I really mean it is not possible.

'In the milk bar near your old school. Four o'clock, two weeks from today.'

This immediate pinning down of a place and time strands all my good intentions. 'You can't recapture the past,' I tell him.

'I can have a jolly good try.' He encloses me in his arms and I try to resist, but he whispers in my ear, 'A man must make love to feel love, and a woman must feel love to make love, and you can't tell me you don't feel love.'

It is much later than I intend when we reach the telephone box. Ian stands outside with a great fresh loaf and sausages in his shopping bag. I watch him as I ask the exchange for the number and then put in the required number of shillings.

'Greville? It's me.'

His voice is anxious.

'I know, I'm sorry. I forgot until I was settled for the night.'

'So, have you seen Ian Sinclair?' he asks.

'I went to his father's first in St Ives. He's married now to a really nice woman. I am really pleased for him.'

'Good, and . . .'

'I'm seeing Ian today,' I say and fight to keep my voice level as, at that moment, Ian turns towards the telephone box and smiles. 'Then I shall start back tomorrow.'

'Tomorrow. So, you won't be home until the day after that?'

'No. Everything's alright, isn't it? No problems with Dickie or at the stables, or anything?'

'No, there's nothing wrong this end.' There is a pause, then he adds, 'You took the letters with you.'

'Yes. I'm not sure why I did really. Proof who I was, perhaps.'

'Do you think Ian Sinclair may not recognize you?' he asks as

Ian takes a step nearer and peers at me through the small thick panes.

'I don't think there's any fear of that.'

'No, neither do I,' he says, then I hear the dialling tone cut in.

Twenty-Nine

T wo weeks. I can think of little other than the way I will plan my trip into town. It makes for a restless, uneasy state of mind. When I am at the stables, I want to be with my baby, when I'm with Dickie I am overwhelmed by my love for the child – when I'm with Greville I feel like a scarlet woman. The next moment I am again devising a list of *essential* things I *must* go to town to buy. I silently rehearse the words, the lies, I shall have to tell Grev and nanny.

By the end of the first week, what *is* due is a visit home. Pa has rung twice but each time Greville has answered and I have not rung back. Then the weekend looms and I wonder if it will be easier to see him for the first time after Church, when the congregation linger outside to gossip before dispersing for substantial Sunday lunches. I go to the farm on Friday afternoon, deciding I can put it off no longer.

I find him overseeing the movement of sheep from one pasture to another. 'So, you saw him?' he asks immediately.

'I saw him and explained, yes.'

'Did you tell Greville?'

'Of course.'

'It takes you a week to come and tell me *of course*.'

'It's all you, or anyone else, needs to know. Where's Mr Benjamin?'

He stares at me hard and I return his look without flinching. Like father, like daughter, I think, for he must have planned *his* assignations, thought out how he would deceive.

'Mr Benjamin is at the house,' he says at last, then demands,

'So, has it helped matters to go? Is Greville happy with what you have told him?'

'You had better ask him.'

'Perhaps I will,' he says.

'Be careful where you meddle, Pa,' I tell him with an authority I did not know I had, an authority perhaps born of fear and necessity once one is set on a dishonest path.

'And you, my girl, be careful what you do.'

He turns away from me momentarily, goes across to close the gate as Brac finishes the work and comes panting back to lie near him.

'Are you going up to see Colleen? She's been asking after you all week.'

'I'll likely see her on Sunday after morning service. It's taken a day or two to go through the stable work that has piled up, and nanny wanted a couple of days off, so I've been busy.'

'Dickie alright?'

'Of course. Come over Sunday for lunch, bring Mr Benjamin. I'll ask Gran and Maude.'

'Greville seemed stressed when I saw him yesterday.'

I want to say for goodness' sake drop the subject, instead I explain, 'He's busy – a tractor broke an axle, and a tenant causing a nuisance to a neighbour, you know the kind of thing.'

'I know that kind of thing, yes.'

I'd like to say he probably knows all about the other kind of thing too, but I dare not. I just know I am not convincing him that all is as it should be. *Takes one to know one* would be old Noel's verdict – takes one fornicator to know another. My old damnation of Pa, my references to the holy book, do seem like the proverbial chickens come home to roost.

We walk back towards the house in silence. I wonder if Ian gets his sensuality from his mother. Clearly my father had been unable to resist her. I wonder if I am like my father and this is why he now doubts me. I glance at him at the same moment as he looks at me. Colour rushes to my face and he stops walking.

'Bess, whatever happened between the two of you in Corn-

331

wall, for God's sake let that be the end of it.' He strides on, only pausing to call back, 'I'll see you Sunday.' I walk back to my car without entering the house.

'So, we're having a family dinner,' Greville says. 'Good. I'll ask Gran up, shall I?'

'Of course,' I answer. Jessie and Clara always have something to talk about; they'll cover any awkward silences.

They do, for a time, but when I carry Dickie away for his afternoon sleep, Clara follows.

'Are you alright m'dear?' she asks.

I nod.

'I don't want you to tell me anything, but Greville is more upset than he is allowing you to know. Don't hurt him, Bess. I am never sure he can take being hurt.'

Nanny comes to take Dickie from me, but I elect to carry him to the nursery, very aware that Lady Philipps is standing watching me go upstairs.

That evening, when all our visitors have gone, the Hall seems larger and emptier than usual and the gulf between the two of us wider. I feel he is waiting for some move on my part, some greater confirmation that all is well.

'Bess Bennett,' he muses quietly.

The use of my maiden name alarms me.

'Have you come back to me?' he asks.

'Yes, Grev, I'm back.' And in that moment I know I have to stop Ian coming to Leicester. There will be no liaison, no further deception. I cannot keep up a pretence of normality, I have to make it so.

'I'm back, Greville.' I go to him and put my hand on his shoulder as he sits so hunched and still. 'Truly back – for good. It was upsetting and it has taken me a day or two to come to terms.' I move to crouch in front of him.

'With what you have lost?' he asks.

'Perhaps more filling the gaps, the years. It felt important we should both know that we had not broken our sacred vows to write.' I laugh as if those vows had been mere childish promises, while plagued by thoughts that I have broken my promises to my husband: *and keeping thee only until him as long as ye both shall live*. But I have reached a point where confession would be self-indulgent. What I have to do is make reparation, rebuild Grev's trust and happiness.

'Did he give you back the locket?'

This question does catch me off-guard and I find myself on my feet at the window.

'Yes, he did.' I force my voice to be calm and my legs to move back towards him. 'He gave me the locket, so that was put right, then we expressed our anger with Roy Rawlins, even though the man is dead.'

'That was important, was it? A release of anger.'

'He said it was a bit like grieving,' I reply. 'Part of the process.'

'Ian said it was like grieving,' he repeats, adding, 'Grieving for what you thought was lost.'

'Grieving for something that is over – and Ian and I *are* over,' I emphasize as I resolve to write to Ian tomorrow morning. I can do this safely from the estate office and later in the morning I'll pop away from the stables to post it. It will be like a bereavement, a secret loss, an overwhelming sadness I must hide, but there will be some consolations – I shall be able to look my father in the eye again.

I make the letter brief and to the point, post it with the knowledge that it is the right thing to do and promise myself, and Grev, that there will be no period of martyrdom. I can also go and see Colleen and tell her about finding Ian, not what it will cost me to remove Ian permanently from my life, though she may guess. We have always been so instinctive about each other's true feelings.

I hurry to the stables, needing to be drawn into the normal routine, but when I arrive there is an emergency of the kind I always dread. One of the older horses is in real distress. Tommie believes it has twisted its gut and may have to be put down. I ring the vet and the owner to come. In the meantime we struggle to keep the beast on its feet, but it is obviously in agony. The vet confirms Tommie's diagnosis, the animal is put down, and arrangements for the carcase to be collected made.

That evening Grev asks, 'Busy day?' I tell him of the trauma. He immediately mutters something I do not hear and leaves the room. I hear him searching for something in the study, then the library, and go to ask, but he waves me away. 'I'll find it,' he says. It is some three-quarters of an hour later that he comes back carrying a small silver bell, which he hands to me. 'My father and my grandfather used to ring this bell whenever one of their horses died or had to be put down.'

'Where did you find it?'

'At Gran's. She'd taken it with her to the new dower house. You'll ring it,' he prompts, 'for the horse today.'

'But it wasn't one of our own, and it's gone now . . .'

'I'd like you to ring it. I'll go with you to the stables.'

'It's almost dark, Greville.'

'Do it for me,' he says and we walk over to the stable block and I stand in the middle of the yard and ring the bell. It has a clear sweet tone and I can appreciate that to solemnly toll it for a long-beloved horse would be a fitting gesture; it would be for the passing of a friend, but this feels bizarre. I ring it three times, which seems the appropriate number to me, if there is anything appropriate about this at all.

I try to make conversation as we return but he seems totally preoccupied.

'You talked of us going to the sea earlier in the year. Is it too late now, do you think? I'd like to go, have a break, just the two of us – or the two of us plus nanny and Dickie. Sea air is good at any time of year.'

'I think it is too late,' he says.

Later, when he comes to bed, he says goodnight and turns away from me. When I wake the next morning he has already gone. He has not had breakfast. Later, at lunch time, when he does not appear, I begin to ask questions. Then I walk over to the new dower house to see if he is with his grandmother. Mrs Harding is there but her husband has driven Lady Philipps to visit friends on the other side of the county. Mrs Harding has not seen Mr Greville. 'Lots of places he could be, ma'am. Wouldn't know where to advise. Is there a message if I see him?'

'Just say I was wondering where he was, but it's nothing urgent.'

'He came last night, of course, for the bell, and a rare job we had finding it.' She looks at me strangely and I wonder if she thinks I requested the bell.

I walk back by the garages and discover to my surprise that none of the vehicles are missing, so, wherever he has gone, he has walked. So, he has not gone far, I judge. I go to the nursery and casually ask after him from nanny, but she shakes her head. 'I thought he seemed very down when he came to say goodnight to baby last night.' Her voice holds that note of censure which means things are not to her liking but it is not her place to say so.

At dusk the telephone rings. I run to it. 'Grev?' I enquire.

There is an awkward pause, a cough, and a rather disgruntled elderly female voice asks, 'Is Mr Philipps there, please?'

'Not at the moment,' I reply. 'Can I help? Mrs Philipps speaking.'

'Mr Philipps had an appointment with Mr Joshua Hincks this afternoon but did not keep his appointment.'

'Oh! I'm sorry. I'll get him to ring tomorrow, shall I?'

'If you would, please. Mr Hincks kept a half hour free for him.'

I want to say something really rude, like *Gee whiz, big deal*, but think better of it. Mr Hincks is the senior member of the law firm the Philippses use.

Now I am more disturbed. I try to put his strange behaviour about the horse's death down to his hatred of losing any animal, but I know he had hardly ever seen the horse in question except at a distance, certainly would not know it from the several others pastured together.

335

Then I begin to wonder if he has had an accident somewhere, perhaps even somewhere quite nearby, and is lying helpless, unconscious. I leave the house and begin a search of the outbuildings, the garages. Then, finding Tommie still there, I enlist his help. ' 'Tis funny, I've not seen him at all today, come to think, and that's unusual.'

I go back to the Hall expecting to see lights in our rooms, the curtains open and Grev roaming about between estate office, library, sitting room, as he always does before dinner – restless, usually wanting to talk over the day's events as we eat and before he settles to a newspaper or a novel.

There are no lights except in the nursery and the kitchen. I delay dinner and, after much hesitation, ring my father. 'I'll come over,' he says immediately and rings off. He comes with George, Mason, his herdsman, and Brac. 'I thought we might need people to help look. Pity you haven't got a dog, that would have led us to him if he's had any kind of accident.'

The mention of a dog makes my blood flow like ice. *Don't ever remind me of dogs and caring and losing.* Grev's words echo and deafen me to all else. *I can't bear it, you know, losing things, losing people.* It ties up so closely with his distress about the horse.

'So, have you rung everyone you can think of, looked in the stables and sheds?' Pa is brisk, efficient; orders me to fetch one of Grev's coats. 'Have you been round the lake and up into the birch wood beyond? Harding, you know the men. Will you round them up and go through all the sheds and stables again, thoroughly? There are no cars, or other vehicles gone? No bicycles, or horses? Bess?'

I come to with a start. 'No, no.' I have just remembered that Grev once offered to jump into the lake if it would help.

We search all night, the police are called in to help. Everyone now has been contacted – the likely, the unlikely – and people drive over to help with the search. Everywhere there are lanterns and torches panning across areas looked over several times already.

Lady Philipps comes up to the Hall as soon as she arrives back from her trip. 'I blame myself,' she says. 'I should have come back with him when he came for the horse bell. He said you'd had one put down?'

I nod. 'But I doubt he had even seen it except at a distance, and it was all dealt with and away hours before.'

'He was upset then, and it did remind me of some of the depressions he had as a boy, though I thought the army had cured him.'

'Depressions?'

'Just a failure to cope for a time when things went wrong.'

'Like when he lost his dog?'

'That was the worst time.' She stops and puts a hand over her mouth. For the first time since I have known her, I see real consternation in her eyes.

'How did that dog die?' I ask, and while her alarm grows I become coldly certain.

'It became entangled in a discarded fishing line on the bank, and, we think, struggled to free itself and fell into the lake and drowned.'

'Grev's fishing line.'

'Yes, he always blamed himself.'

'We should tell the police,' I say.

'Yes, I'll go, I know the superintendent. She walks purposefully over to a small group of men standing in the light from the terrace, in the same place I had stood and seen my father forcing Mrs Sinclair away from the Hall. I begin to walk down towards the lake, but it is firmly suggested that 'the ladies should stay near the house, just in case there is a telephone call.'

So we stand in the near darkness overlooking the lake. 'Look for a small rowing boat.' I hear the order being repeated, echoing down over the grounds. The lights of the searchers gradually seem to come together and encircle the water, their beams stippling the ripples.

The superintendent comes to the house and telephones for the underwater search team. They come with inflatable boats, and for hours we see the lights go from the boats into and under the water. It all has a mesmeric effect. We cannot take our eyes from the operation. We stand so still our legs are slow to respond when we do try to move. Soon the boats seem to be in the centre of the lake. They must by now have covered the whole area and found nothing.

'I'm going to walk down there,' I decide.

'I'll come with you,' Clara says.

I think we both feel there is reason to hope that our surmises have been wrong, but even as we walk nearer, there is a difference in the manner and attitude of the vague black figures we can see outlined against the arc lights on the boat. They are more still, more focused over one of their number being helped out of the water. We both go forward much quicker.

'Result, sir,' one of the men calls from the boat to the shore. We find ourselves next to the superintendent. 'You should have stayed at the house, ladies,' he tells us. 'I'll be with you shortly.'

Neither of us moves as he goes to meet one of the boats, which is pulling back to the shore. One of the frogmen is outlined in the boat's own light as he porters his air tanks and face mask ashore. The superintendent takes his arm and walks him away from us. We can just make out the murmur of the man making his report.

'I'd like you to come back up to the house with me,' the superintendent says to us, then to a constable he says as an aside, 'Get Policewoman Williams to the house.'

I want to demand to be told, but we are escorted, a hand kindly under our elbows, helping us back up the slope of lawn. The lights are put on and, as the superintendent begins to tell us what they have found, the policewoman pours brandies from the sideboard.

'My men have found the boat and there is someone in it. We cannot raise the body immediately without destroying evidence, and I am afraid I cannot allow that to happen. I will have to bring in lifting equipment, so we must wait until daylight.'

'Is it my grandson?' Clara asks.

'We're not sure, but I'd be foolish to give you false hopes. I understand that the boat was seen in the boathouse yesterday by one of the gardeners, and your grandson is missing. I don't think there is much doubt, m'lady. I am very sorry.' He bends over me and puts his hand on my shoulder. 'And for you and your son, Mrs Philipps. I'll leave Williams with you, and my men will stand watch in the grounds. Please don't hesitate to ask, if there is anything we can do.'

There are yet more consultations outside and my father walks up from the lawn into the room. I had forgotten he was there.

'He is entangled in fishing gut, which is apparently wrapped round and round his body, hands, feet and the seats of the boat.'

The world around goes suddenly very dark. I come to myself in bed, a strange bed. I turn my head to see Clara Philipps slumped in an armchair by the bed with the thin cold grey light of morning outlining the window.

Thirty

I am not sure how I get through the days, and the nights are desolate. I am plagued alternately by guilt and anger, but when I might expect it to be just the opposite, Clara Philipps becomes my stalwart companion. She moves temporarily back into the Hall, using the suite of rooms she previously prepared for herself, and the two of us manage our grief as best we can. Harding comes too, to help with the constant callers. The messages of sympathy are quietly and carefully worded as Greville's funeral is delayed for a post-mortem. The coroner makes a dispensation releasing the body for burial, but there has to be an inquest.

The funeral is a quiet family affair, and just as Anthea's husband had assisted at our wedding service, he now officiates at my husband's funeral service. Greville's sisters are devastated, curiously diminished by their brother's suicide. I recall Greville saying how they loved their visits to the Hall for the hunting, how they too needed their egos underlining from time to time. I tell them they must make their usual visits, and they appear overwhelmingly grateful, and stress the importance of Dickie as a comfort to me, and to the Philipps estate. 'At least we have an heir.'

It is the first moment that I feel I do have a right to be at the Hall. Greville's will has left everything to me after provision for his grandmother, with the Hall in trust for his firstborn son. He had signed the will shortly after our wedding.

There is a stigma to a death like this, and I feel everyone is

340

very circumspect in their dealing with me, except my father. He is at the funeral but leaves immediately afterwards and has not been to the Hall since. That he blames me is obvious – to me – although there arc so very many visitors, letters and cards to deal with that Clara does not remark on it.

I do not see Colleen on her own until she comes to the Hall some days after the funeral. She is clearly both agitated and distressed, looks around the room as if she is trapped. I suggest we go for a stroll.

'Sometimes it is easier to talk when you walk,' I say, for she clearly has something on her mind.

Once outside, and out of hearing of anyone, she throws her arms around me, weeps copiously, blaming her brother for Greville's death, for everything. 'If he had not kept back those letters, you would never have been here.' She throws out a hand at the Hall. I shake my head, but she will not be contradicted. 'I know, I know, so don't try to dissuade me. It is all our Roy's fault, or my fault for having such a brother. Perhaps it's my fault most of all because our Roy was always jealous of you and the way we were friends.'

'Your fault? You can't think that?'

'I shouldn't have presumed to be your friend.'

'Oh, Colleen! I haven't much left; only you and Dickie, and . . .' I shake my head. 'Not even my father. He blames me, you know.'

'I do know, and I've told him he's wrong, but he won't listen.'

'I feel I have lost everything.' We walk on and I tell her all about finding Ian, but that I had decided I would never see him again. She weeps, but I cannot weep. I feel arid and tired, like a terrible desert where nothing will ever live again.

'If it were not for Dickie,' I begin, but she looks at me with such alarm I do not continue. 'You will keep coming?' I feel desperate she should not forsake me. 'Bring the children. Come soon. Dickie would like that.'

*   *   *

341

The inquest is held some three weeks after the funeral. It is quite a formal affair, with the coroner reading the facts of the case, statements from the police and others. Clara and I hold hands as we begin to fully appreciate the planning that had been done by Greville. He had taken the boat to the middle of the lake; there, the police surmise, he must have partly swamped it, before tying his body and his legs to the boat seats with reels of fishing line. He then capsized the boat and was so entangled he would have had no chance of escape once the boat went over.

A verdict of death by drowning while the balance of the mind was disturbed is recorded. We are mortified to find Greville again the subject of newspaper headlines.

Just before Christmas I walk to the stables and Tommie raises his forefinger and says, 'Someone to see you, boss. In the tack room. He's been coming for days, waiting for you to turn up. I told him you don't come so often, but he wouldn't listen.'

I frown. Who on earth would do a thing like that? The tack room is the only outhouse that boasts a stove, and by it, in an ancient armchair thrown out from the kitchen, is Noel.

'Come on, m'lass.' He holds out a hand for me. 'I've been waiting on you.' He gives his words an upward note of pretended exasperation. I pull a stool up next to him and he holds my hand.

'So,' he says. 'How are things going?'

I shake my head. 'They're not, are they. They'll never go again, I don't think.'

'You listen, m'lass. Life goes on, and it'll be willy-nilly unless you take hold of it.' He gives my hand a gentle shake and for the first time I feel tears spring to my eyes. This wise old man, who all my life has come out with his adages and maxims, does it again, makes the tears fall with his simple honest assessment. 'Take the reins, get a grip,' he tells me.

'It sounds like you're giving me a riding lesson.'

'Takes a bit of balance to keep life under control,' he says. 'A bit of balance, a bit of pressure from the knees, an occasional dig of the heels and you can be off again.'

'Noel.' I lean on his jacket, which is about in the same state as the armchair. 'I do love you.'

'Aye, lass, and I've loved you like you were my own ever since you first staggered around that farmyard.'

I lean and let the tears run on and on. 'I sometimes wish you didn't have to grow up at all,' I sob.

'Well,' he says very gently. 'You always were a contrary little bugger. A chip off the old block.' He pauses, then says with an intensity I haven't often heard in his voice, 'You should go and see him, he won't come to you.'

'I'm not sure he wants to see me,' I say in no more than a whisper.

'He may not know he does, but he does.' The old man's voice is full of certainty. 'He does.'

'He blames me.'

'Blaming's always easier than forgiving, and understanding takes a bit more effort than both, I reckon.'

The tears exhaust me, but that night I sleep properly for a few hours. I wake resolved to take Noel's advice, and I ache to see my father. Even if he rejects me, I know I must go.

Mr Benjamin is in the milking shed when I arrive, helping to swill out and generally clean down the parlour after the morning milking.

'Wondered where you were,' he said, nodding happily to me. 'Said to Edgar, where are you?'

'That was nice, Mr Benjamin, nice to be missed.' This man has more good instincts than half a dozen so-called normal people. 'Where is my father?' I ask.

He grins and points behind me. Pa stands unsmiling in the kitchen garden. I know what he will be doing, cutting some of the berried holly to decorate the church for Christmas. This will be at Maude Seaton's insistence, she is one of the main helpers with this task. Christmas is not something I have thought about.

He begins work again, throwing the heavily berried branches on to a clean sack.

'I blame you,' he says.

'I know you do, but you're wrong. I didn't intend to upset Greville – ever.'

'Ah! But did he know that?' He savages an extra-thick branch, twists and turns the secateurs around it before it separates from the bush.

'I told him.' And as he turns to look at me I nod. 'I did tell him.'

'You don't look very well,' he adds.

I shrug. I know the tears have left my eyes looking sunken and black-ringed.

'So we've both lost our partners in life,' he says.

'Yes,' I say, but I do not to know whether I mean Greville or Ian.

'Know how each other feel, then.' He layers more holly on the pile.

'It would be a comfort to me if you would come and let Dickie get to know his maternal grandfather. He hasn't too many close relations. I think it is important he knows you.'

He stops work and stares hard at me. I return the look, thinking our histories are not unalike. We betrayed our legal partners, and then as if by some divine punishment we have both lost them.

'Your mother always said we were too much alike,' he begins. 'Too much alike, too able to see each other's wiles, perhaps, to rub along easily together.'

'Or perhaps caring too much for each other, so that every word of criticism cut to the bone,' I say.

'Is that how it was?' he asks, his hands falling heavily to his sides. 'Is that how it was?'

'It's how it still is, Pa,' I tell him. 'I do care too much. Every critical glance of yours cuts me, and if we're so alike, then you should understand all I have lost and given up. My first love was Ian Sinclair; I was cheated out of that. I found him again, and I gave him up, though I knew in my heart of hearts this was the man I loved in a way I never loved, or would love, another. Then I lost the man I had decided I should spend the rest of my life with.'

'Yes,' Edgar says and remembers wanting to punch young Sinclair on the nose. Now he knows why. Sinclair had been the most threat to him, Sinclair had been the man who had claimed his daughter's heart.

'I was thinking,' he said. 'I might get young Dickie a farm for Christmas. I went into that shop in Leicester, Robotham's. You can buy all the farm animals, churns, tractors, everything. What d'you think?'

'I think he would be lucky to have such a grandpa.'

He holds out his arms and I am the child again, approved of, forgiven, understood, I hope. From behind us we hear Mr Benjamin laughing and clapping. 'And an uncle,' I add, 'with the nicest nature in the world.'

In the months that follow I look back and see that it was Noel, who began my push up from the bottom of the pit of despair, then the regular visits of Colleen with the children and then my father who were my saviours.

Dickie adores the days that Colleen brings the children over, and nanny says it is good for him to have other children to play with.

One day the following spring, we take the three children for a picnic near the brook where we played as children. Nanny is making daisy chains as the children collect the flowers.

'Come on.' Colleen takes my hand and draws me away.

I wave to nanny and the two of us walk away. 'It's May the first today,' she begins.

'May day, yes. Why?'

'I promised to tell you something on this day. Well, I promised *not* to tell you something *until* this day.'

'What's this about? Not another baby?'

'Well, there is that, yes,' she says.

'You're expecting again!'

She nods. 'We always intended to have three. It has the family feel about it, three.'

I give her a great hug of congratulation. 'So, you won't mind if it is a boy or a girl this time. Does your mother know?'

'Not yet, you're the first I've told.'

I wonder if I might try to knit something for the coming baby. It is not a skill I am much practised in, but nanny could guide me.

'But I have something else to tell you.'

'Oh! Look, our stepping-stones. Come on, let's see if we can still do it without stopping.'

'Aren't we too old for such larks?'

'Never!'

'That sounds more like your old self,' she says as I start to cross. 'Which is what Ian is waiting to hear.'

I try to turn to look back at her and slip into the water. 'What did you say?'

'I said it is what Ian is waiting to hear, that you are more yourself.'

I wade back to her side of the brook. 'Is this what . . .'

'What I promised not to tell you until today.'

'But, I don't understand.'

'Ian read of Greville's death and wrote to me at Paget's Farm. You must have told him I lived there. He said he had had a letter from you, but he wanted you to know, when you were over the first shock of losing Greville, that he would still be around. In fact, he said I was to write to him and let him know whether he was to meet you at the milk bar, you just have to say when. He's waiting for you, Bess.'

Two weeks from that day I drive into town, park near St Catherine's and walk down to the milk bar. Ian is sitting with his back to the door. I walk to his table and sit down opposite him, slide one hand across the table. He takes hold of my wrist, like one laying hands on a lifeline, before he looks up.

'Thank God,' he says.